Bringing Light to Twilight

Perspectives on a Pop Culture Phenomenon

Edited by
Giselle Liza Anatol

BRINGING LIGHT TO *TWILIGHT*
Copyright © Giselle Liza Anatol, 2011.

All rights reserved.

First published in 2011 by
PALGRAVE MACMILLAN®
in the United States—a division of St. Martin's Press LLC,
175 Fifth Avenue, New York, NY 10010.

Where this book is distributed in the UK, Europe and the rest of the world,
this is by Palgrave Macmillan, a division of Macmillan Publishers Limited,
registered in England, company number 785998, of Houndmills,
Basingstoke, Hampshire RG21 6XS.

Palgrave Macmillan is the global academic imprint of the above companies
and has companies and representatives throughout the world.

Palgrave® and Macmillan® are registered trademarks in the United States,
the United Kingdom, Europe and other countries.

ISBN: 978–0–230–11067–0

Library of Congress Cataloging-in-Publication Data

Bringing Light to Twilight : Perspectives on a Pop Culture Phenomenon /
Edited by Giselle Liza Anatol.
   p. cm.
ISBN 978–0–230–11067–0 (hardback)
   1. Meyer, Stephenie, 1973– Twilight saga series. 2. Young adult fiction,
American—History and criticism. 3. Vampires in literature. I. Anatol, Giselle
Liza, 1970– , editor compilation. II. Kramar, Margaret. Wolf in the woods.
III. Meyer, Stephenie, 1973– Twilight saga series. Commentary on (work):

PS3613.E979Z63 2011
813'.6—dc22   2010043537

A catalogue record of the book is available from the British Library.

Design by Newgen Imaging Systems (P) Ltd., Chennai, India.

First edition: June 2011

10 9 8 7 6 5 4 3 2 1

Printed in the United States of America.

INGING LIGHT TO *TWILIGHT*

CONTENTS

Part III   Class, Race, and Green Space

Acknowledgments

There are many, many people to whom I owe thanks for helping me to complete this work, but I would like to express particular gratitude to the following: Lee Norton, for initially approaching me and having faith in the importance of this project, and all the people at Palgrave who helped in the final steps in the process; the contributors, for their insightful writing, but especially for their patience as I hit technological snags along the way; Kristen Lillvis, for her meticulous, intuitive, and speedy indexing work; the members of KUKC—Kim Warren, Ann Rowland, Nicole Hodges-Persley, and Tamara Falicov—who again provided invaluable feedback and emotional resources; the participants of the *Twilight* discussion group at UMKC, who helped me to see some of my own blindspots; Rachel Ewing, who allowed me a few extra days of quiet time in front of the screen; Dee Hurt, for her endless patience and quiet strength; Mylisha and Miles Hurt, who kindly waited as I read "one more paragraph" or wrote "one more sentence" before tending to their needs. And an extraspecial thank you to Miles for taking a bite for the team.

INTRODUCTION

GISELLE LIZA ANATOL

In a society that moves as fast as ours, where every week a new "blockbuster" must
be enthroned at the box office, or where idols are fabricated by consensus every new
television season, the promise of something everlasting, something truly eternal,
holds a special allure.

— Guillermo del Toro and Chuck Hogan[1]

[E]very age "discovers" what in a work of art relates most to its own needs and
desires, even if the artist himself was not consciously aware of all he created.

— Lester Friedman[2]

OF THE MYRIAD BOOKS, television programs, and films about vampires that have
flooded US culture at the start of the twenty-first century, the most commercially
successful to date is the *Twilight* series by Stephenie Meyer. Between the publication
of the first novel, *Twilight* (2005), and June 2010, when the spin-off novel *The Short
Second Life of Bree Tanner* was released, the four-volume saga had sold more than 100
million copies.[3] The initial installment was the best-selling book of 2008; the fourth
and final narrative, *Breaking Dawn,* sold 1.3 million copies on the first day alone. The
popularity of *Twilight, New Moon, Eclipse,* and *Breaking Dawn* led US teens to vote
Meyer into one of the top two spots of the American Library Association's "Teens'
Top Ten" contest for four years in a row: in 2006, J.K. Rowling still reigned supreme,
and *Harry Potter and the Half-Blood Prince* was placed first, with *Twilight* ranking second[4]; in 2007, approximately 6,000 teenagers across the country selected *New Moon*
as their favorite book of the year; and in 2008, over 8,000 voters named *Eclipse* as
number one. Astoundingly, J.K. Rowling's *Harry Potter and the Deathly Hallows* came
in second place; an ABC news story remarked on how *Eclipse* had struck the seemingly invincible Rowling from her "perch atop bestseller lists. Not bad for someone
who, a few short years ago, never would have dreamed of being a writer."[5]

The *Twilight* novels have been translated into thirty-seven languages, and their
popularity earned Meyer the title of *USA Today*'s 2008 "Author of the Year," as well as
numerous comparisons to J.K. Rowling. *Twilight* might very well be the most significant children's literature series since the *Harry Potter* novels: as of September 2010, the
four novels had spent 162 weeks on the *New York Times* best-selling [children's series]
list, accompanied by P.C. Cast and Kristin Cast's *House of Night* vampire novels,

which occupied a place on the list for 106 weeks—largely, one might argue, due to the influence of Meyer's work. And in 2009, more than half a million *Twilight*-related items were sold on eBay, second only to New York Yankees paraphernalia, popular especially in light of the team's World Series win.[6] Therefore, when I was offered the opportunity to gather a diverse group of writers to delve into the *Twilight* books, I jumped at the chance.

Bringing Light to Twilight: Perspectives on a Pop Culture Phenomenon makes no claims for justifying the aesthetic quality, widespread acclaim, or adult readership of Meyer's fiction; rather, its primary goal is to take a rigorous analytical view of the books—one that can be appreciated by those inside *and* outside the academy. The contributors and I hope that although most (but not all) of these chapters have been produced within university settings, they will inspire conversations across a variety of audiences—teenagers and senior citizens, Mormons and Buddhists, college professors and junior high school students, stay-at-home moms and Marxist theorists. The *Twilight* series needs interrogation: it should not be rejected as simply pulp, pop culture, or the latest fad; neither should it be glorified as inviolable, sacred object. Whether Meyer's books serve as time-passers, a vehicle for escapism, literacy training, exercise for the imagination or rational thinking, conditioners of social norms, models for dealing with problems, a means for improving a cranky or despondent mood, and/or a cultural artifact, they can affect and sway their readers, and this volume uncovers some of the ways this process is accomplished.

When the chapters for this collection were originally compiled, only one other critical exploration of Meyer's novels was readily available: *Twilight and Philosophy: Vampires, Vegetarians, and the Pursuit of Immortality,* edited by Rebecca Housel and J. Jeremy Wisnewski (2009). Since that time, however, many other works have come to light. *Twilight and History,* by Nancy Reagin, provides young adult readers with historical contexts for various characters in the series. Approaching the novels from a religious standpoint, both *The Twilight Phenomenon: Forbidden Fruit or Thirst-Quenching Fantasy?* by Kurt and Olivia Bruner and *Touched by a Vampire: Discovering the Hidden Messages in the Twilight Saga* by Beth Felker Jones target older readers—particularly the parents of *Twilight* teens. *Bitten by Twilight: Youth Culture, Media, & the Vampire Franchise,* edited by Melissa Click, Jennifer Stevens Aubrey, and Elizabeth Behm-Morawitz, focuses on the cultural, social, and economic aspects of the series. We anticipate that *Bringing Light to Twilight* will enter into scholarly conversation with these texts as well.

"BATTY FOR BEAUTIFUL VAMPIRES"[7]

At the end of the first decade of the twenty-first century, there are few adults in the English-speaking world who have been untouched by the most recent surge of vampire narratives. The term "First Wave" might be used to describe some of the earliest fare—British popular literature of the nineteenth century (although the British by no means invented the genre)—writing such as John Polidori's short story "The Vampyre" (1819), James Malcolm Rymer's penny-dreadful *Varney the Vampire* (1845–1847), Joseph Sheridan LeFanu's *Carmilla* (1872), Mary Elizabeth Braddon's frequently anthologized "Good Lady Ducayne" (1896), and Bram Stoker's

Dracula (1897). The 1970s brought about a resuscitation of vampire stories—a sort of "Second Wave"—following the publication of Anne Rice's now-classic *Interview with a Vampire* (1976). An Amazon.com editorial review of Rice's novel asserts that with her innovative narrative, "Rice refreshed the archetypal vampire myth for a late-20th-century audience."[8] Likewise, a 1977 stage production of the 1927 play *Dracula*—itself a recovery of Stoker's novel—earned Tony Awards for Best Revival and for Edward Gorey's costume design; Frank Langella, who was nominated for the Tony in the Best Leading Actor category, went on to reprise his role in the popular 1979 horror film. The blaxploitation movie *Blacula* (1972)*,* starring William Marshall, and the independent film *Ganja and Hess* (1973) both brought vampire narratives to predominantly black audiences and critiqued the "whites only" view of vampires that accompanied earlier narratives. One can see tide-like circularity in these visions and revisions—different plot elements, characters, aspects of "folk" culture rush in and are carried out with each sweep of the current.

Writers like Rice, Poppy Brite, Suzy McKee Charnas, Brian Lumley, Christopher Moore, and Chelsea Quinn Yarbro have long had an impressive fan base, but relative newcomers such as Octavia Butler (*Fledgling*), Melissa de la Cruz (the *Blue Bloods* series), Tananarive Due (the *Living Blood* books), and Charlaine Harris (the Sookie Stackhouse novels) are part of the Third Wave swell that seems incapable of satiating an ardent—and growing—readership. Buffy the Vampire Slayer has found company among Anita Blake, Vampire Hunter, and Damali Richards from L.A. Banks' Vampire Huntress legends. On primetime and in syndicated US television, vampire-plot episodes have appeared on *The X-Files, CSI, Crossing Jordan,* and Disney Channel's *The Wizards of Waverly Place.* While series with vampire protagonists such as *Blade, Forever Knight, Moonlight,* and the BBC's *Being Human* have not been able to garner and sustain the viewership of shows like *Buffy* and *Angel,* the fact is they are continually being pitched and produced. *The Vampire Diaries* has a strong teen and young adult following, earning several 2010 People's Choice Award nominations, and the success of the first season of HBO's *True Blood* rivaled that of more "realistic" programs such as *The Sopranos* and *Sex in the City.*[9] In film production, a proliferation of vampire movies has blanketed world markets: for example, *Daybreakers* (2009) in the United States, *Thirst* (2009) in South Korea, and the Swedish sleeper hit *Let the Right One In* (2008).[10]

In children's literature, where at one time vampires would have been taboo—too brutal and frightening for youthful imaginations—one can find illustrated readers such as *Bunnicula,* Joann Sfar's graphic novella *The Little Vampire,* Angela Sommer-Bodenburg's *Little Vampire* series, Adele Griffin's *Vampire Island* books, Sienna Mercer's *My Sister the Vampire* series, the more macabre Cirque du Freak novels by Darren Shan, or *Vampirates: Demons of the Ocean* by Justin Somper, and so-called comprehensive guides such as Amy Gray's *How to Be a Vampire: A Fangs-On Guide for the Newly Undead* and Lisa Trutkoff Trumbauer's *A Practical Guide to Vampires.* For the young adult (YA) reader, P.C. Cast and her daughter, Kristin, co-author the *House of Night* books, which take place in a vampire finishing school; somewhat similar in setting are Richelle Mead's *Vampire Academy* series and Rachel Caine's Morganville Vampires narratives.[11] M.T. Anderson's *Thirsty* features a confused teenage vampire; and strikingly, in this age of alluring, seductive vampires, Neil Gaiman's

The Graveyard Book, winner of the 2008 Newbery Award for most distinguished contribution to American children's literature, features Silas, the somewhat paternal and never explicitly named vampire figure who protects and provides for protagonist Nobody Owens. Vampires may be corpsely cold, but they are definitely "hot" in the current market. But this is just one reason for dedicating an entire collection of essays to *Twilight.*

WHY ENGAGE IN THIS PROJECT?

I have seen many adults scratch their heads, mystified by Meyer's spectacular popularity. Words like "insipid," "vapid," "shallow," and "sexist," often pop up. One of my former children's literature students commented, "[Meyer]'s writing is about as deep as a puddle." She—along with many others who rallied around her—found the *Twilight* books to be deficient in both style and depth when compared to the *Harry Potter* series. It should be noted, however, that like J.K. Rowling and other fantasy favorites C.S. Lewis and J.R.R. Tolkien, Stephenie Meyer incites powerful loyalties: "[t]he critic who has the temerity to question the pleasure given to children by [her] series is very likely to be met with incredulity"—if not hostility.[12]

To further explain my interest in this *Twilight* project, I turn to commentary by children's literature scholar Jack Zipes. Although stated in response to the Harry Potter phenomenon, he aptly describes the dangers of an uncritical—and by this, I mean un-analytical—view of children's literary series. Zipes posits that the "phenomenal" aspect of the reception of certain books often obscures the criteria "for anyone who wants to take literature for young people seriously." He continues: "The ordinary becomes extraordinary, and we are so taken by the phenomenon that we admire, worship, and idolize it without grasping fully why we regard it with so much reverence and awe."[13]

As I argued was the case for Rowling's books in my collections *Reading Harry Potter: Critical Essays* (2003) and *Reading Harry Potter Again: New Critical Essays* (2009), it is *exactly* because the *Twilight* saga has become so incredibly popular that it is intellectually and socially significant. Regardless of what nonenthusiasts think of the aesthetic value or substance of the books, because they are consumed so voraciously they should be taken quite seriously. As British children's literature scholar Peter Hunt argues, the writers read by the most children are those who must be examined most carefully: it is these authors "whose attitudes and politics are most likely to be stamped (through subconscious osmosis) into the national consciousness."[14] Through young adulthood, children are impressionable, and can be emotionally and intellectually prone to automatically accepting the ideological constructs underlying all texts, from illustrated storybooks to chemistry textbooks to television commercials. Michael Benton provides a strong example when citing a study of 115 eighth and eleventh grade students' responses to magazine advertisements and short fiction: researchers found that the student-readers were predisposed to obscuring the lines between fiction and reality when speaking about the magazine images; they were also unlikely to respond critically to any of the texts.[15] And thus, while most teen readers would probably be able to distinguish the fantastical elements of Meyer's novels as fiction, I wonder about their understanding of the social interactions that occur in Bella's world, where the protagonist is so readily embraced by her in-laws and gets to live happily ever after. Adults involved in young people's lives must not necessarily look for behaviors that readers will mimic with precision; very few, except for the very young, will engage in this type of conduct. Rather, a key part of interpreting literature is uncovering the emotional responses that readers have to the characters and situations—people, places, and events that present a particular ethos as irresistibly appealing, repugnant and revolting, or somewhere in between. Teenagers will not necessarily read the *Twilight* novels and literally confuse their own world of homework and bad-hair days with Meyer's imaginary world of vampires and werewolves, but they very well might begin to imagine *themselves* in different ways, with young women in particular identifying more with marriage than college, with risking one's life for one's first love, with serving as a passive shield rather than an active sword.[16]

Only by reading and re-reading and analyzing a story that presents its world in sometimes confusing ways can we strive to see our own world more clearly. Thus, the contributors examine not only what the saga explicitly states, but also what the narratives imply, what they disguise, and what they assume. The chapters that follow do not seek to destroy the world of fantasy; instead, they strive to loosen up the restrictive boundaries between pleasure and intellectual pursuit, and allow enjoyment at the same time as a critical engagement with the texts.

THE CHAPTERS

The chapters in Part One of *Bringing Light to Twilight* were selected around the theme of "Literary Contexts: Past and Present." The contributors explore intertwining traditions and intertextual references—whether those be to previously published works, like Perrault's fairy tales or gothic novels, or to more recently published writings that use *Twilight* as a source text. The description provided by contributors Kristina Deffenbacher and Mikayla Zagoria-Moffet serves us especially well: pulling from the theories of Julia Kristeva, they posit all instances of intertextuality as a type of vampirism, drawing life from and simultaneously transforming other narratives.

Chapter 1, "The Wolf in the Woods," exposes parallels between the first novel in Meyer's series and early versions of the Little Red Riding Hood folktale. In doing so, contributor Margaret Kramar explores how *Twilight* perpetuates many conventional fairy tales' insistence on women's sexual chastity and submission to masculine authority. Indeed, Isabella Swan's life reads very much like a Cinderella story: Bella is rescued from the apparent drudgery of cooking and cleaning—and school—to embark on a whirlwind romance and marriage to Prince Charming, her very own knight with shining fangs.

The *Twilight* saga also clearly falls heir to a long line of commonly read vampire literature: before Meyer, before Anne Rice, before Bram Stoker, one could find vampire lore in the works of Heinrich Ossenfelder, Johann Wolfgang von Goethe, Lord Byron, and John Keats, among others.[17] Meyer's saga follows in the tradition of the mid-eighteenth-century gothic novel, which intermingled features from the classic horror story and the chivalrous romance. Meyer also overtly embraces the Byronic hero of the Romantic tradition—the misunderstood character who experiences alienation because he pursues his individual ideals rather than the social and cultural norms of his time. This description fits Edward to a "T."

Much print has already been dedicated to Meyer's blatant allusions to the "classics" of British writing: *Twilight* plots, themes, character names, dialogue, and epigraphs invoke Shakespeare's *Romeo and Juliet*, Jane Austen's *Pride and Prejudice*, and Emily Brontë's *Wuthering Heights*.[18] In chapter 2, "Textual Vampirism in the *Twilight* Saga: Drawing Feminist Life from *Jane Eyre* and Teen Fantasy Fiction," Deffenbacher and Zagoria-Moffet describe how Charlotte Brontë's *Jane Eyre* functions as another critical piece. Rather than reading Meyer's Bella and the fiercely independent Jane oppositionally, they argue that Meyer, like Brontë, attempts to confront the tensions between women's sexual vulnerability and desire. Chapter 3, "Serial Experiments in Popular Culture" by Carole Veldman-Genz, brings us closer to the present day in her textual comparison: she juxtaposes the *Twilight* saga with Laurell Hamilton's popular *Anita Blake, Vampire Hunter* series, the first novel of which was published in 1993. Like Deffenbacher and Zagoria-Moffet, Veldman-Genz attempts to understand current incarnations of the women's empowerment movement—particularly third-wave feminism—through *Twilight*.

The next chapter—Kim Allen Gleed's "*Twilight,* Translated"—studies Meyer's original novel next to Luc Rigoureau's French version, and provides insights as to what happens to both text and audience in the process of translation. Gleed contends that the practice not only increases readership, but also reveals much about the culture for which the narrative has been adapted. Chapter 5, "Variations, Subversions and Endless Love: Fan Fiction and the *Twilight* Saga," tackles another practice, and another culture—that of fan fiction (writing by fans that revisions favorite texts)—which takes place on the Internet. Maria Lindgren Leavenworth alleges that by continually extending and/or repeating the romantic core story, fanfic writers transform themselves from seemingly passive readers to active readers and writers. Chapter 6, "True Blood Waits: The Romance of Law and Literature," also explores notions of "romance"—a figurative affair between law and literature. Lawyer Meredith Wallis intuits that the true love story of the saga is not, as might be first assumed, between Bella and Edward, but instead the narrative's fascination with jurisprudence.

Children's literature has long been read as subversive, whether because texts allow children to collude with the authors and each other against the adult world, or because they allow readers a form of escape. And yet, Peter Hunt wonders how subversive these narratives can really be: "It could be argued that they share with much popular culture the disruptive surface that disguises a profound conservatism."[19] Many of the chapters included in *Bringing Light to Twilight* interrogate the ways that Stephenie Meyer supports conventional ideology in her series, especially when it comes to gender. Rather than simply alleging that the author presents a sexist narrative with a distressingly passive heroine, however, the writers of the chapters in Part Two pursue the issue from a complex array of perspectives. Tammy Dietz, who was raised Mormon, uses her personal history in chapter 7, "Wake Up, Bella!" to critique the gender ideals she finds represented in Meyer's books, which she attributes to the author's religious faith. In chapter 8, Rhonda Nicol argues that although Bella Swan is often viewed in stark contrast to the "feminist darling" of Buffy the Vampire Slayer, it is more productive to consider the two characters as contemporaneous pop culture artifacts that reveal much about the current state of feminism. Chapter 9, "'One is Not Born a Vampire, But Becomes One,'" examines representations of motherhood in the *Twilight* series. Merinne Whitton asserts that the saga depicts mothering as the epitome of women's fulfillment; in the end, the narratives posit that mothering is what women are for.

Chapters 10 and 11, as well as Chapter 12 from Part Three, turn more explicitly to investigations of Edward Cullen. Tracy Bealer's "Of Monsters and Men" contends that, by focusing exclusively on Bella as a submissive female figure, critics fail to see the ways that Edward challenges normative gender roles. In "The *Other* Edward," Joseph Sommers and Amy Hume provide a distinct counter argument to Kathryn Kane's piece on the heteronormative imperative in the *Twilight* series.[20] They explore how Edward's refusal to penetrate Bella—in both the vampiric and the literal, sexual sense—configures him as an "ideal" boyfriend, but also "queer." Michael Goebel's chapter, "'Embraced' by Consumption: *Twilight* and the Modern Construction of Gender," demonstrates how Meyer supports capitalist cultures' conceptions of masculinity and femininity as rooted in the attainment of wealth. Goebel remains unshocked by the success of the *Twilight* books and other vampire narratives of the past few decades: "it is not surprising that American culture, driven by material consumption, gravitates towards a figure like the vampire."

Goebel's chapter provides the transition to the third section of the collection—chapters on "Class, Race, and Green Space." In chapter 13, we move from Goebel's literary analysis of class in the novels to an examination of commodities and class in the mainstream culture influenced by Meyer's books and films. In "Fashion Sucks...Blood?" Angie Chau reflects on the disparity between the fictional characters' attitudes about fashion and ways that "vampire fashion" is manipulated by marketers and popular media. Chapters 14 and 15 address issues of race: in "Trailing in Jonathan Harker's Shadow," Joo Ok Kim and I maintain that, very much like Bram Stoker's character in *Dracula*, Bella functions in *Twilight* as a kind of ethnographer: she occupies a position of power inaccessible to both Edward and Jacob, who figure as racialized "others" in her observations of the werewolf and vampire cultures. In "The Great American Love Affair: Indians in the *Twilight* Saga," Brianna Burke uses Meyer's novels and the film adaptations to lay bare how stereotypes of First Nations people are perpetuated. And Tara K. Parmiter employs an ecocritical approach in chapter 16, "Green is the New Black: Ecophobia and the Gothic Landscape in the *Twilight* Series." She argues that by challenging notions of gothic settings as dark, dismal, and frightening, Meyer subtly encourages readers to embrace the outdoors and resist the "uneasiness with nonhuman nature" typical of many twenty-first century subjects.[21]

As scholars such as Karín Lesnik-Oberstein and Maria Nikolajeva have claimed, one cannot develop theories that posit a singular, nonindividualized "real" or "normal" reader. A "Twi-hard" of thirty-five, for example, might not be able to see Meyer's vampires as potential symbols of human relationships with the divine, while a nineteen-year-old philosophy major might.[22] Another reader might not be able to perceive some of Edward's attitudes toward Bella as dangerous, whereas the teen survivor of domestic abuse might readily intuit this idea from the narratives. One participant in a discussion group I attended identified Bella as "frustrating" in her lack of self-confidence and her obsession with Edward's perfection; another saw her as a realistic portrait of a "boy-crazy" high school student; yet another found her sexuality "empowering."[23] A reader's analysis will be affected by numerous factors, including age, the era she grows up in, nationality, culture, racial or ethnic background, education, life experiences, gender, position in the sibling lineup, and socioeconomic class. Because of this, what any reader—but particularly young readers—will take from the *Twilight* books is impossible to pinpoint or to project. A more valuable approach, I believe, is considering what topics some of them might question—either as they read, a few weeks down the road, or years into the future—or areas in which they could be challenged.

This book therefore does not lay claim to any "correct" answers that can fit the experiences of every member of every community. Most of the issues raised in the project have many defensible positions; we simply present them as topics to think about and explore. All literary works contain "gaps" that allow individual readers to make individual inferences, link ideas, build metaphors, and conceptualize characters in certain ways. By interpreting a text, filling in the gaps, and creating meaning from the words on the page, the reader "makes choices.... [and thus no] reader"—neither child nor adult—"can ever exhaust the full potential of any text."[24]

The contributors to this volume are quite varied in nationality and background—they currently reside in the United States, England, Sweden, and Germany.[25] While most are literary scholars, the professions of creative writing and law are also represented. Similarly, readers of this collection could also be quite varied: students interested in investigating the field of children's literature, writers of young adult texts, librarians, teachers, sociologists, stay-at-home parents, those who want to know more about the books that have captivated the attention of the young people in their lives, nonspecialists in English who are interested in delving deeper into the meanings of *Twilight* and its sequels, or are simply curious about what a few academics have to say about the series. Even though all of these readers will have different backgrounds, purposes, and understandings of what Meyer's books do (or aim to do), we anticipate that *Bringing Light to Twilight* will inspire continued thought and discussion.

NOTES

1. Guillermo del Toro and Chuck Hogan, "Why Vampires Never Die," *The New York Times, Op-Ed Column.* July 31, 2009. http://www.nytimes.com/2009/07/31/opinion/31deltoro.html?_r=1&emc=etal&pagewanted...[Accessed 13 August 2009]
2. Lester D. Friedman. "The Edge of Knowledge: Jews as Monsters/Jews as Victims." *MELUS* 11.3 (Autumn 1984): 49–62.
3. When writers refer to the *Twilight* saga throughout this collection of essays, they are not including the *Bree Tanner* novella—an offshoot of *Eclipse,* Meyer's third novel in the series—unless specifically noted.
4. Over 5,000 teens voted on-line.
5. Eric Horng (August 19, 2007). http://abcnews.go.com/WN/Story?id=3499052&page=1. Accessed September 19, 2009. More than 11,000 teenagers participated in the 2009 contest, putting John Green's *Paper Towns* in the top spot and Meyer's *Breaking Dawn* in second place. Book titles are nominated by members of teen book groups in fifteen school and public libraries around the United States. The winners are announced during Teen Read Week in October.

6. "Twi-hards" bought 523,429 items, while 551,230 Yankees-related purchases were made. "EBay Tells Us What Was Hot in '09," *The Kansas City Star.* Pop Culture section (December 10, 2009): 25.

7. Ibid.

8. http://www.amazon.com/Interview-Vampire-Anne-Rice/dp/0345337662. Accessed January 14, 2010.

9. *True Blood,* based on *The Southern Vampire Mysteries* by Charlaine Harris, has captured television audiences with 3.7 million viewers watching the second season premiere in June 2009 (the largest number of HBO viewers since the series finale of *The Sopranos*). The show earned numerous award nominations and a Golden Globe Award for its first season. *The Vampire Diaries* premiered in September 2009.

10. The Dracula story has been woven into scripts about topics as wide ranging as the abduction of American Indian children who were then placed in government boarding schools. Thomas L. Carmody's *The Only Good Indian* (2009), directed by Kevin Willmott, features Henry McCoy, a white sheriff who conceives of Native people as inferior savages. In terrorizing them with the threat of vicious beatings he is monster; by aiding in the draining away their traditional ways of life via relocations, religious conversions, and education, he is a vampire. His nightmares about past brutalities also transform him into a figure of the Living Dead.

11. Many thanks to Sabine Planka for providing with these additional titles: *Look for Me By Moonlight* by Mary Downing Hahn, *The Silver Kiss* by Annette Curtis Klause, and *Companions of the Night* by Vivian VandeVelde. The works of Amelia Atwater-Rhodes should also be mentioned here.

12. Peter Hunt, *Children's Literature,* 201. As prominent children's literature scholar Jack Zipes has argued, the success of serialized literature—from *Harlequin Romances* to the *Harry Potter* series—is about literature transformed into product. Zipes asserts that series are not designed to stimulate *readers'* intellectual processes but rather to stimulate *customers* to buy—and keep on buying—merchandise: books, games, trinkets, CDs, DVDs, and clothing. This would definitely appear to be in effect with *Twilight*; merchandise from Edward shower curtains to fast-food children's meals has blitzed the market. An Amazon.com mass email sent on Monday, October 5, 2009 announced a "Twilight Saga: New Moon" [Movie] Premiere Prize List including a hardcover boxed set of the series, a copy of *New Moon: The Official Illustrated Movie Companion,* the two-disk special edition DVD of the *Twilight* film, a Barbie Bella doll and a Barbie Edward doll, the soundtrack to the *Twilight* film, a *New Moon* board game, a *Twilight* hat, scarf, and glove set, and a lion and lamb keyring. In the Spring 2010 edition of *Signals*—a fundraising catalog for Public Television—one could order personalized "Surrender [fill in the name]" T-shirts with an emblem of the Wicked Witch of the West. Strikingly, the names supplied in the sample photograph are Edward and Jacob. The following page featured a personalized baseball T-shirt with the name "Cullen" printed on the back of the sample (25, 26).

13. Zipes, *Sticks and Stones,* 171 and 173, respectively.

14. Hunt, *Children's Literature*, 36.

15. Michael Benton, "Readers, Texts, Contexts: Reader-Response Criticism," *Understanding Children's Literature: Key Essays from the International Companion Encyclopedia of Children's Literature.* Ed. Peter Hunt (New York: Routledge, 1999), 81–99.

16. On the one hand, adolescent and young adult readers can feel a sense of triumph when observing how much responsibility Bella—and by extension, they themselves—must and can bear. Meyer's novels allow young people to identify with a character who triumphs even though she, like them, thinks herself powerless. In their daily lives,

children and teens typically lack of control of many things that adults can take for granted; young adults often feel small in influence, if not in size. And thus Bella—despite her clumsiness and seeming ordinariness—provides a positive role model: she learns that she possesses and she develops a unique talent through the course of the series (she can shield her thoughts from the telepathic vampires and shield her friends and family from physical harm); she is also able to choose her own path in life, going against her parents' desires and social norms when she marries her true love rather than going to college or dating a "normal" boy, and defying Edward's desires when she decides to keep her baby and succeeds in being transformed into a vampire.

According to others, however, Edward's extra century of life experience makes his relationship with Bella prominently imbalanced and akin to statutory rape; his sneaking into her bedroom to gaze at her sleeping, disabling her truck engine, and other "protective" actions resonate with stalking behavior. Further, Bella's obsession with a lover who warns her of his danger to her safety suggests her ultimate lack of power and control. "[F]ear should never be an aphrodisiac [...] It distresses me to see that in any form, whether or not it's supernatural.[...] It's the idea that [...] however much in danger you feel, love has to conquer." Kathleen Megan, "Fear As an Aphrodisiac: Some Scholars Find Disturbing Elements in 'Twilight' Books. Romantic, or Dangerous?" *The Hartford Courant.* Courant.com (November 18, 2009): 1, 1–3. Accessed January 14, 2010. http://articles.courant.com/2009-11-18/news/09111712259486_1_young-girls-dangerous-twilight-books/

17. Authors, respectively, of "Der Vampyre" (1748); "Die Braut von Korinth" ["The Bride of Corinth"] (1797); "The Giaour" (1813); and "Lamia" (1819). Stoker's *Dracula* was first published in 1897; Rudyard Kipling's "The Vampire" was published in the same year. Rice's Vampire Chronicles began in 1976 with *Interview with the Vampire.*

18. The epigraph to *Eclipse* references Robert Frost's "Fire and Ice," setting up the continuing conflict between the werewolves (fire) and vampires (ice), as well as Bella Swan's personal conflict, deciding between Jacob Black (fire) and Edward Cullen (ice). Bella's very name, which translates as "beautiful Swan," appears to be a direct reference to Hans Christian Andersen's nineteenth-century fairy tale, "The Ugly Duckling." There are numerous other allusions that could be explored, although there is not the time or space to do so here: the epigraph from Book One of *Breaking Dawn* is drawn from a poem by Edna St. Vincent Millay; the epigraph from Book Two comes from *A Midsummer Night's Dream*; Orson Scott Card's *Empire* provides the source of the epigraph to Book Three; etc.

19. Peter Hunt, ed., Introduction, *Understanding Children's Literature: Key Essays from the International Companion Encyclopedia of Children's Literature* (New York: Routledge, 1999), 5.

20. Kathryn Kane, "A Very Queer Refusal: The Chilling Effect of the Cullens' Heteronormative Embrace," *Bitten by Twilight: Youth Culture, Media, and the Vampire Franchise,* eds. Melissa A. Click, Jennifer Stevens Aubrey and Elizabeth Behm-Morawitz (New York: Peter Lang, 2010): 103-118.

21. These chapters, of course, might be arranged in a variety of ways. My essay with Kim, for example, could easily have been placed in Part I; Veldman-Genz's piece fits in Part II as well as Part I.

22. See, for examples, essays in *Twilight and Philosophy: Vampires, Vegetarians, and the Pursuit of Immortality,* eds. Rebecca Housel and J. Jeremy Wisnewski (Hoboken, NJ: John Wiley & Sons, 2009).

23. *Twilight* Discussion Group, led by Brenda Bethman, Director of the Women's Center, and Lindsay Quinn, a graduate student in Women's, Gender, and Sexuality Studies. February 2010, University of Missouri-Kansas City.

24. Bernice E. Cullinan, in collaboration with Mary K. Karrer and Arlene M. Pillar, *Literature and the Child* (New York: Harcourt Brace Jovanovich, 1981), 7.

25. When soliciting abstracts for the project, I received proposals from scholars around the world. The United States, Canada, Great Britain, Sweden, France, Italy, Germany, Australia, and New Zealand were among the countries represented.

PART I

LITERARY CONTEXTS: PAST AND PRESENT

THE WOLF IN THE WOODS: REPRESENTATIONS OF "LITTLE RED RIDING HOOD" IN *TWILIGHT*

MARGARET KRAMAR

ALTHOUGH IT MASQUERADES AS A TEENAGE GIRL'S OBSESSION with a brooding and mysterious vampire, lurking beneath the veneer of Stephenie Meyer's *Twilight* is the ageless dialectic of the helpless female devoured by the predatory male. Whether as Bella she succumbs to the charming Edward Cullen or as Little Red Riding Hood to the rapacious wolf, the result is the same: by corporally consuming her through rape or marriage, the voracious male destroys her.

That similar basic story structures, motifs, myths, and legends reoccur in numerous cultures separated geographically and historically is a cornerstone of the theories of Swiss psychologist Carl Gustav Jung (1875–1961), who espoused that all humans share a collective unconscious and therefore through their stories and symbols, and especially dreams, reenact similar archetypes, which he defined as "mental forms whose presence cannot be explained by anything in the individual's own life and which seem to be aboriginal, innate, and inherited shapes of the human mind." Jung further stated that "elements often occur in a dream that are not individual and that cannot be derived from the dreamer's personal experience."[1] And indeed, Stephenie Meyer disclosed in an interview that the novel *Twilight* began for her as a dream of a young woman being embraced by a young male vampire in a meadow.[2]

Although the little Red Riding Hood motif is very pervasive in popular American culture, it is impossible to measure or quantify the influence it may have had on Meyer's artistic process, unless she were to directly reference it. Nevertheless, *Twilight* resonates with the imagery and motifs of the French "Little Red Riding Hood" tale written by Charles Perrault in 1697 and the German Jacob and Wilhelm Grimm "Little Red Cap" version of 1812. In both tales, a little girl wearing either a red hood or cap is accosted by a deceitful wolf on her way through the woods to her grandmother's house. The wolf, having devoured the grandmother, dons her bed-clothes and frightens the girl with his big ears, hands, and teeth before devouring her. In the Grimm version, a passing hunter slits the wolf's belly open, liberating both the girl and her grandmother. In the Perrault version, the two are not as fortunate: the tale ends after the wolf gobbles up Little Red Riding Hood so both she and her grandmother remain entombed in his bowels.

Even though Bella is seventeen at the beginning of the novel and Little Red Cap's age is not specified, both are young, virginal, innocent maidens journeying toward womanhood. While each must learn to define herself in relation to the world outside her childhood home, one of Bella's specific developmental tasks is to define herself in relation to men.[3] *Twilight* is an explication of the choices she makes, and how she is impacted by those choices.

The novel opens with Bella's mother driving her to the airport. Unlike Little Red Riding Hood, who has her mother's blessings, Bella departs over her mother's pro-testations. In any case, both heroines leave their maternal homes and venture away from maternal sustenance to hammer out their own identities in eerie, threatening landscapes.

Little Red Riding Hood is a pampered child. In the Perrault version, her mother "doted on her," and her grandmother was "even fonder."[4] Little Red Cap's protective mother reminds her to get an early start, not stray from the path, say good morning to her grandmother, and not peek in all the corners before she sets off on her jour-ney. Bella, however, is alone in the universe, more of a caretaker to her mother than her mother is to her. Before she gets on the plane, Bella panics as she stares at her mother's "wide, childlike eyes," asking herself, "How could I leave my loving, erratic, hare-brained mother to fend for herself?" because it is Bella who has been paying the bills, and putting gas in the car and food in the refrigerator. Bella later confesses her emotional isolation from her mother, who although closer to her than "anyone else on the planet, was never in harmony with me, never exactly on the same page."[5] She has moved to Forks because she sensed her mother's preference for traveling with her new husband rather than mothering her.

The transparency of the contrasting parental styles afforded the maiden of the folktale and the teenager of the novel may come more clearly into focus when cur-rent issues such as a high divorce rate, latchkey supervision, or the lack thereof, and working mothers absent from the home are superimposed. From the vantage point of her sterile world, is it any wonder that Bella will greedily grasp any warmth offered to her, even if from a potentially destructive source? Even though Bella goes to live with her father, he is no better at parenting her or providing emotional sustenance than her mother. Since her parents' divorce when she was a baby, Bella has only seen Charlie for a few weeks during the summer. Because Charlie is a man of few words who is absent during the day at his police job, Bella dreads an extended car ride with him because "neither of us was what anyone would call verbose, and I didn't know what there was to say regardless."[6] Further, in her father's house, it is Bella who moth-ers Charlie by cooking for him and doing his laundry.

The Cullen sibling clan, apart from their vampire issues, is also characterized as being emotionally frozen out. They sit by themselves in a corner of the cafeteria, nei-ther talking nor eating. Bella describes them as being "chalky pale, the palest of all the students living in this sunless town. Paler than me, the albino."[7] The Cullen children, all adopted, come from somewhere in frigid Alaska, and are also known as "the cold ones" to their Quileute enemies.

Edward Cullen is also strongly characterized as possessing an acute sense of smell. He leans rigidly away from Bella when she is seated next to him in biology class, "averting his face like he smelled something bad,"[8] because, as he later explains to her, "every person smells different"[9] and comes in different flavors. In this way, Edward Cullen is clearly the wolf. Further, his eyes are alternately described throughout the novel as being coal black and a deep golden, honey color. He repeatedly warns Bella that he is dangerous, that it is better that they not be friends, and that he is the world's best predator. At the end of the novel, he growls, with his lips pulled back to expose perfect teeth. Although Meyer casts Edward as a vampire and ascribes certain portions of vampire lore to him, the imagery that surrounds him is often lupine.

While the Quileutes are the literal wolves in the series, Edward is able to comfortably coexist as both vampire and werewolf because in mythic legend the vampire and the werewolf are inexorably intertwined. In the *The Vampire Book: The Encyclopedia of the Undead* (1994), J. Gordon Melton states that werewolves and vampires have been reported as existing side by side in the mythologies of many cultures, and that in the southern Balkan countries the term *vrykolakas* has referred to not only werewolves, but also the ritual wearing of wolf pelts among Slavic tribes, and the vampire.[10] Werewolves and vampires are synonymous in that both are capable of transforming themselves through supernatural means into beasts that prey on the blood and flesh of humans. According to H. Sidky in *Witchcraft, Lycanthropy, Drugs and Disease* (1997), sixteenth-century demonologists believed that werewolves—actually witches who shifted shape into wolves in order to commit atrocities—acquired "fleetness of foot; bodily strength, ravenous ferocity; the lust of howling; the faculty of breaking into places, and of silent movement; and other such animal characteristics, which are far beyond human strength or ability."[11] Likewise, Edward displays the supernatural abilities of defying gravity and seemingly transcending time and space as he makes his unexplained appearances, flying like a jet through the forest.

Notable in establishing the conflation between wolf and werewolf is that Little Red Riding Hood encounters a werewolf in the older oral folktale upon which the fairy tale is based, "The Story of the Grandmother."[12] In this story, a little girl is charged with carrying a hot loaf and bottle of milk to her grandmother. At the crossroads "she met the *bzou.*" In a footnote, the narrator states: "I asked the storyteller: 'What is a *bzou*?' He replied: 'It's like the *brou,* or *garou* [werewolf; the modern French form is *loup-garou*]; but in this story I have never heard anything said except *bzou.*'"[13] Further, fairy tale scholar Jack Zipes in *The Trials and Tribulations of Little Red Riding Hood* credits Marianne Rumpf with establishing that the original villain in French folklore from which "Little Red Riding Hood" is derived was "probably a werewolf, and that it was Perrault who transformed him into a simple, but ferocious, wolf."[14]

Little Red Riding Hood can be interpreted as a part of a matriarchy. She travels from one maternal residence to another on the feminine errand of delivering food. However, neither the mother nor the grandmother are able to protect the child from the evil, external world the wolf represents. In order to accomplish her mission, she must journey through the woods, that liminal zone harboring unrepressed desires and longings, and possibly danger. In folklore and mythology, ventures into the woods often signify an initiation, a journey in search of self, or the beginning of the transformation of the heroine. Dante opens his classic and celebrated epic *The Divine Comedy* by stating, "Midway upon the journey of our life I found that I was in a dusky wood; For the right path, whence I had strayed, was lost."[15]

Bella leaves her mother in sunny, dry Phoenix to come to the forests of the Olympic Peninsula of northwest Washington State to live with her father in the tiny town of Forks under a "near-constant cover of clouds" in "gloomy, omnipresent shade" in a forested landscape.[16] She is literally at a fork in the road as she commences her new life, and the misty surroundings that block the clear light of day and reason signify that hers is not a mere physical journey, but that of the soul. At this crossroads, the traditional meeting place of witches and sorcerers, where the little girl of "The Story of Grandmother" encounters the *bzou*, Bella will encounter her own imaginary demons, as well as those suppressed fears, attitudes, and desires she projects onto the external world.

For both Bella and Little Red Riding Hood, their forays into the woods signify uncertainty, confusion, and literally and psychically straying from the path. In the Perrault tale, Little Red Riding Hood is a "little village girl"[17] who traverses the forest wilderness toward her grandmother in another village. In the Grimm tale, Little Red Cap apparently lives in a village with her mother and must abandon her civilized surroundings to visit her grandmother who lives in the forest "half an hour from the village."[18] Correspondingly, when Bella sets off from her father's house, throwing on her raincoat and a pair of boots before entering the "ever-encroaching" forest, she confesses: "My sense of direction was hopeless; I could get lost in much less helpful surroundings."[19]

During her first foray into the forest, Bella, frightened and alone, feels dwarfed by the strange and menacing vegetation that surrounds her in the gray mist: "The ferns stood higher than my head, now that I was seated, and I knew someone could walk by on the path, three feet away, and not see me."[20] The visual effect is that of a cinematic close shot in that the reader senses that at any moment a menacing predator could intrude upon Bella. The Red Riding Hoods, guileless and innocent, have no fear of the sinister wolf who accosts them in the forest, but the reader, viewing the scenario from a more sophisticated perspective, senses their impending doom. Yet this simple but ferocious creature who accosts Little Red Riding Hood in the woods possesses some anthropomorphic qualities that belie his bestial estate. He is able to speak, and his conversations with her reveal craftiness, a deception only possible through the ability to reason. He is a strange supernatural mutation of beast and man, and as such, according to Bishop Olaus Magnus in 1658, "may change his human form, into the form of a wolf entirely, going into some private cellar or secret wood" lest broad daylight reveal his diabolic metamorphosis.[21]

Grimm's wolf considers Little Red Cap to be a "juicy morsel" who will taste even better than the old woman, whereas Perrault's wolf "would have very much liked to eat her" upon their first meeting, but is constrained by some woodcutters who are in the forest. Although few modern people confront predation by wild animals, that the wolf posed a serious threat to Little Red Riding Hood's physical existence would have been intuited by the audiences of the original tales. According to Sidky, populations of the common European wolf (*Canis lupus*) rebounded during the fifteenth and sixteenth centuries after the Black Death of the fourteenth century decimated human numbers, reversing deforestation. Consequently in France, where onslaughts of wolves preyed on cattle and occasionally attacked humans, numerous people were burned as werewolves.[22]

Similarly, in asking Edward if he is like a bear, and he replies he is more like a lion, Bella becomes aware that Edward is a predator who poses a very real physical danger. Moreover, a spurned boyfriend observes of Edward, "He looks at you like...like you're something to eat,"[23] an accurate assessment considering that Edward occasionally absents himself for several days to hunt animals to lessen the temptation of dining on humans. Bella chokes back her hysteria, but a small giggle escapes. On the surface, she is amused because Mike has zeroed onto the truth without knowing that Edward is a vampire, but more tragically, Bella, overwhelmingly infatuated with Edward by this point in the narrative, retains her sanity by constructing a complex system of lies and subterfuges. Not only does she keep her father and friends at bay with evasive, little white lies as to her whereabouts, but she is internally wrestling with the possibility of a liaison with a man who could kill her. Bella and other readers are bombarded with the strains of mistreated females wailing numerous variations of "stand by your man" every day, so no chord of dissonance is struck when Meyer adds her name to the chorus. Not so apparent, of course, after the musicians pack up and the stage lights have dimmed, are the grizzly, decidedly unglamorous consequences of blind submission to toxic love. The teenaged Bella knows that she should not be talking to a wolf, unlike the more childlike Perrault and Grimm heroines who do not fear the wolf due to their innocence.

However menacing the wolf may seem, in the fairy tales, he also evokes the buffoon because he looks so silly in grandmother's clothes and is ultimately outsmarted by the huntsman in the Grimm version. In this trickster aspect, he is brother to the French Reynard the Fox, who also strives yet often fails, and other tricksters who populate myths and legends. In "Ancient Myths and Modern Man," Joseph L. Henderson describes four evolutionary cycles in the hero myth, the first being the trickster cycle, which corresponds to the "earliest and least developed period of life. Trickster is a figure whose physical appetites dominate his behavior; he has the mentality of an infant. Lacking any purpose beyond the gratification of his primary needs, he is cruel, cynical and unfeeling."[24] In that many fairy tales explicate initiation rites and delineate the obstacles an adolescent must overcome before he individuates into a successful adult, often by marrying and assuming adult responsibilities, there obviously can be no successful union between the puerile Little Red Riding Hood and the groveling, self-absorbed wolf.

Edward is not portrayed as selfish and unfeeling—a repeated motif is the self-restraint he exerts to resist consuming Bella in *Twilight*—but nevertheless, he is incapable of compromise. Bella realizes that union with him must be on his terms, and transforms her own personality and lifestyle to blend in with him and his family.

Although Little Red Riding Hood's age is unspecified, the patriarchal wolf is clearly portrayed as older than she is. In the Perrault version, the girl meets "old Father Wolf" in the woods, and the Grimm huntsman addresses the wolf as "you old sinner." His checkered past and more extensive life experiences bestow the wolf with dominance over the innocent, naïve child. The ages of the characters in *Twilight* provide a striking parallel: Bella is seventeen, and although Edward is ostensibly seventeen as well in this bodily incorporation, as a vampire he is ageless. Born in Chicago in 1901 and changed into a vampire in 1918 when, at seventeen, he was dying of influenza, he knows the music of the 1950s, 1960s, 1970s, and 1980s, and much more. In a patriarchal culture where father knows best and girls marry men old enough to be their fathers, Bella is at a definite disadvantage because her limited worldview of seventeen years is myopic and his spans the centuries.[25]

Akin to Little Red Riding Hood, Bella at seventeen is inexperienced in the ways of men. Upon learning that Rebecca, a slightly older friend, is married, Bella is stunned and amazed. When Edward brushes her cheekbone with his hand, it is arguably the first time she has been touched romantically by a man. Although she finds Edward fascinating and tantalizing, their relationship is tenuous, hedged by uncertainty. She can't even be certain of his physical presence in that she exclaims, "It was hard to believe that someone so beautiful could be real. I was afraid that he might disappear in a sudden puff of smoke, and I would wake up."[26]

However, even though the heroines perceive that the wolf may be a predatory older figure, they are tantalized by the mystery surrounding him. Bella spurns the romantic attentions of Mike, a significantly baby-faced blonde boy who helps her find her next class on the first day of school. Likewise, she dismisses Eric, a boy with typical teenage skin problems, classifying him as overly helpful and a chess club type. These merely mortal boys, who might support her in a mutually beneficial relationship, are presented as too predictable, too pedestrian, and too young. Instead, she prefers the elusive Edward, initially noncommittal and mercurial, who has a dark aspect that is potentially dangerous. There is just something irresistible about the tough, bad antihero, and some fatal flaw lurking inside certain women like Bella that makes them want to walk on the wild side.

In the conventional fairy tales, the crafty wolf induces the girl to stray from the path by distracting her with the wild abandon of the beauty of nature, knowing that the delay will guarantee that he reaches grandmother's house first. Perrault's Little Red Riding Hood gathers nuts, runs after butterflies, and makes nosegays from wildflowers. The Grimms' wolf entices Little Red Cap to notice how "the woods were full of beautiful flowers," the sun's rays were dancing through the trees, and the birds were singing. Although some scholars assert that the teeming fertility of nature represents Little Red Cap's detour from the straight path into idleness or sensuousness, the French folklorist P. Saintyves (1870–1935) perceived the ritual of the May Queen through both folktales. May Day festivities included young maidens picking flowers and making crowns out of them. Further, the woods during the first days of May are not only bursting forth with new life, but said to be haunted by "*mauvais esprits et les bêtes redoutables.*"[27] These "evil spirits and fearsome beasts" like to play tricks on travelers, particularly female voyagers, as they pass through their haunted domain. Likewise, during the twelve nights following Walpurgis (May 1), sorcerers such as Nordic Fenrir the Wolf become bolder because these are the last days of their winter reign, which Saintyves used to explain the presence of the trickster wolf in the fairy tales.

Aside from T.S. Eliot's statement that "April is the cruellest month,"[28] the juxta-position between the promising gaiety of spring and evil marauders playing tricks on unsuspecting females seems unlikely, yet the same binary appears in *Twilight*. In the scene of their first kiss, Edward, the devouring vampire, and Bella discover a sunlit meadow that teems with color and life, in stark contrast to the gloomy skies that usually shroud them. Unexpectedly Bella steps into a pool of yellow light, "filled with wildflowers—violet, yellow and soft white," hears a bubbling stream nearby, and walks slowly though the soft grass and "warm, gilded air."[29] The sensuousness and fertility reminiscent of May that surrounds Little Red Riding Hood also envelopes Bella.

Certainly for the duration of *Twilight*, there is no sexual relationship between Bella and Edward. Although they keep his presence in her bedroom secret from her father, chaste Bella and Edward sleep through their first night together without physical pas-sion. Over lasagna she learns that Edward has been spying on her almost every night, and prowling in her bedroom and listening to her talk in her sleep. He is also like the wolf waiting in the grandmother's bed for the girl to arrive: once upstairs in her room, Bella calls for Edward through the open window, but he startles her by calling from behind: "He lay, smiling hugely, across my bed, his hands behind his head, his feet dangling off the end, the picture of ease."[30] He is the very picture of the cunning, rapacious wolf who relaxes knowing that he will soon taste victory. When Edward reaches out, it is with long arms that pick her up as though she were a toddler. She is no match for his vampiric strength, just like the big arms, big ears, big eyes, and big teeth underscore the physical superiority of the wolf over the defenseless girl before he gobbles her up. In this reading, the danger she faces as she drifts to sleep in his cool arms is not about sexual consummation, but that he will literally consume her.

Considering the numerous descriptions of Edward's flesh being pale and cool as stone, he may be likened to a corpse. As someone who does not need food and never sleeps, he is divorced from the daily demands of the physical body. In that Bella worships Edward as this marble monument frozen in time, this "perfect statue, carved in some unknown stone, smooth like marble, glittering like crystal,"[31] it may be argued that she subliminally lusts for the tranquility of the grave. Through her self-destructive attraction to Edward, she manifests a death wish because the descrip-tive imagery of *Twilight* alludes to the vampiric state as timeless, an assured eternity of Elysian Fields where the stress and pain of daily living will intrude no more. For Little Red Riding Hood and her grandmother, existence within the wolf's belly terminates corporal existence, but because the duration is also dark, peaceful, and quiet, it may be argued that the tragic dimension of their abrupt demise in Perrault's version, fur-ther eclipsed by the didactic moral that ends the tale, is softened.

But even though Edward looms as a danger to Bella throughout *Twilight* and ulti-mately destroys her later in the series because she becomes a vampire, on at least three occasions in *Twilight* he functions as her savior. By casting Edward in this role, Meyer engages the fairy tale motif of the prince who rescues the downtrodden Cinderella or dormant Sleeping Beauty. As a dark blue van is skidding toward her in an icy parking lot, Edward Cullen miraculously appears to shield Bella from the collision. He does so in this scene with two large and long hands, analogous to the anatomically asym-metrical body parts of the wolf who lies in bed awaiting Little Red Riding Hood.

Bella, largely rendered as a weak and defenseless female (she also faints at the sight of blood in biology class), gets "scooped [. . .] up in his arms, as easily as if I weighed ten pounds instead of a hundred and ten."[32] This trope of being whisked away by protective masculine arms, so universal in popular culture, which some women carry to the extreme of abdication of their own will, choices, and life goals in exchange for lifelong subservience to the male, is extolled as an honored role for women. Precipitating the third rescue is Bella's walk in deserted urban streets as night falls: she encounters a group of threatening hoodlums. Because she has abandoned her friends and strayed from the path, these predatory men become the wolves. Arguably, her rape or murder by the hoodlums is preferable to an eternal vampiric existence, but nonetheless Edward's car materializes out of thin air, he orders her to get in, and they speed away. So whether the male aspect manifests as predator or savior of the heroine, the underlying premise is that the female, powerless to direct her own life, either willingly submits to him or lacks sufficient strength to resist.

In the Grimm tale of Little Red Cap, a strong, able-bodied huntsman rescues both the grandmother and the girl from the belly of the wolf. Therefore the girl, mother, and grandmother—three generations of women lacking a male presence—are helpless when it becomes necessary to protect and defend themselves. Instead they rely on the circumstantial synchronicity of a male huntsman who "happened to be passing by the house."[33] In an unexpected parallel with the fairy tales, Bella is nearly killed by another vampire because he threatens to hurt her mother. The older females in the matrilineal line, either the grandmother easily dispensed by the wolf or the mother who sends her daughter out into the woods, or Bella's hare-brained mother, unwittingly endanger the heroine. Zipes attributes the appearance of the huntsman/savior, an addition absent from both the Perrault and oral tales, to an 1800 verse drama by Ludwig Tieck, in which the gamekeeper or hunter ("*Jäger*") does not save Little Red Riding Hood, but does manage to kill the wolf. The German word *Jäger* was associated with the police, so thus according to Zipes: "Salvation comes only in the form of a male patriarch who patrols the woods and controls the unruly forces of nature— both inner and outer."[34]

Unlike Rapunzel, Sleeping Beauty, or Cinderella, who evolve into maturity by marrying their princes at the end of the tale,[35] Little Red Riding Hood is repulsed by the hairy wolf with all his phallic protuberances. The wolf is leering and menacing, with lust glinting in his eyes. Even if she were not revolted by his appearance and wanted to form a partnership with him, she fails miserably. His dominance overpowers her and he literally consumes her. Perrault's Little Red Riding Hood "becomes one" with the wolf when she is inside his body, but at the expense of her own life.

Grimms' "Little Red Cap" ends with two alternate encounters with two different wolves. In the first incident, the girl and the grandmother fill the wolf's body with large stones so he dies when he attempts to run away, and in the second, another wolf drowns in a big stone trough by lusting after sausages. So Little Red Cap and the grandmother ultimately triumph, but not without the huntsman's intervention. So what has Little Red Riding Hood learned in the Grimm version? She has learned to avoid the sexual entanglements of wolves, and retreats back into prepubescent innocence that may again be compromised if she strays from the path. The matriarchal harmony is restored and Little Red Cap will continue bringing cakes from her mother to nourish her grandmother indefinitely. Little Red Cap fails to evolve into a woman by marrying either the wolf or the huntsman; she remains frozen as a good girl. Regressing back into the uroboric mother environment is her salvation; dealing with the sensual male with no paternal huntsman to save her will be her downfall. Too immature to cope with a male, Little Red Cap is titillated by the sensual flowers in the forest, but is devoured by the ultimate sensual pleasure, a sexually mature male.

Edward serves as a perfect "wolf" in that, though sexually desirous and desiring, he is not permitted to consummate the sexual act in *Twilight*. Although he claims he cannot read Bella's mind, he always says the right things at the right time. His romantic timing is exquisite. He is perfect, an eloquent soap opera actor who never botches his lines. A real male is still too threatening for Bella. On the precipice of romantic love, the girl prefers an ephemeral being onto whom she can project her magical fantasies. Edward never belches. He never throws his dirty socks on the floor. In this aspect, *Twilight* perfectly dovetails the genre of the fantasy-based bodice-ripper romance.

In *Reading the Romance: Women, Patriarchy, and Popular Literature* (1984), Janice Radway provides a cultural analysis of the literary romance genre, insisting that not only are the romances analogous in plot to the standard fairy tale, but also serve the same purposes for her female readers. She states that her readers, cognizant of the genre, not only "willingly admit that romances are fairy tales or fantasies,"[36] but also adhere to the formalism of demanding that the romances fit into a narrowly defined structural mold: "These same women exhibit fairly rigid expectations about what is permissible in a romantic tale and express disappointment and outrage when those conventions are violated."[37] One of the expectations is the "gradual removal of emotional barriers between two people who recognize their connection early in the story" and another is an ideal heroine who is "differentiated from her more ordinary counterparts in other romance novels by unusual intelligence or by an extraordinarily fiery disposition."[38] Although Bella hides her histrionic emotional state under a compliant exterior, her extraordinary intelligence manifests as participation in an advanced academic placement program in Phoenix and a school essay about whether "Shakespeare's treatment of the female character is misogynistic."[39]

The heroines described by Radway are also characterized by "childlike innocence and inexperience," and, similarly to Bella, are seventeen to twenty years old and "completely unaware that they are capable of passionate sexual urges."[40] Further, Radway states that the ideal romance "begins with its heroine's removal from a familiar, comfortable realm usually associated with her childhood and family,"[41] and that the dark, romantic hero is "always characterized by spectacular masculinity" in that "almost everything about him is hard, angular, and dark."[42] Finally, recognizing that the romance "leaves unchallenged the male right to the public spheres of work, politics, and power," Radway asserts in her conclusion that "the romance avoids questioning the institutionalized basis of patriarchal control over women even as it serves as a locus of protest against some of its emotional consequences."[43] That the current of patriarchy flows through the French and German fairy tales, the modern romance genre and Stephenie Meyer's *Twilight* is no surprise, but what is disturbing is the somnolence that smothers resistance to formulaic gendered behaviors and recognition of inherent inequities.

That the *Twilight* series is a runaway best seller and praised lavishly by fans indicates that Stephenie Meyer has located a vein leading to the hearts and minds of numerous girls and women who are part of the current culture.[44] Amidst this acclaim, comparatively few dissenting voices have articulated that the basic theme of the female's complete submission to the male tramples the concepts feminism has encouraged such as independence and self-actualization.

In her seminal study of adolescent girls, *Reviving Ophelia* (1994), therapist Mary Pipher laments that "something dramatic happens to girls in early adolescence," noting that their IQ, math, and science scores plummet, they lose their resiliency and optimism and become less curious and inclined to take risks. She also notes that "fairy tales capture the essence of this phenomenon," noting that the feminine hero-ines are "rescued by princes and are transformed into passive and docile creatures."[45] What is it about the current cultural milieu that causes females, especially adoles-cents approaching sexual maturity, to give everything away in the name of love? Does the biological mandate to reproduce and subsequently be in relationship to a male, reinforced by cultural, social, political, and economic norms, ultimately override any other ambitions that nourish self-determination or independence? "The Story of Grandmother," the oral tale upon which Perrault's "Little Red Riding Hood" is based, offers an alternative to feminine self-annihilation: a spunky young girl who escapes from the wolf through her own wits. In *Little Red Riding Hood Uncloaked* (2002), Catherine Orenstein argues that "The Story of Grandmother" proves an exception to the mythology dictum that the hero who sets out on a wisdom journey must always be male. The *bzou*, which might be a nefarious male figure, attempts to thwart the girl, but she escapes and instead attains independence.

In "The Story of Grandmother," when the "little girl"[46] encounters the werewolf, he asks whether she is taking the Needles Road or the Pins Road. Orenstein notes that in choosing a path of pins or needles, the girl embarks on a female initia-tion rite, in that such tools symbolize feminine coming-of-age rituals around the world, and especially in France, where "sending a young girl to apprentice with the seamstress for a year or so was, according to one scholar, a bit like sending her to finishing school."[47] And in grandmother's house, although the werewolf manages to kill the grandmother and get the girl undressed in bed beside him, once the girl realizes that the grandmother is hairy, has long nails, big shoulders, big ears, and a big mouth, she cleverly states that she needs to go outside to relieve herself. The *bzou* ties a woolen thread to her foot and lets her go, but once outdoors, she successfully escapes.[48]

This female success is eliminated by Charles Perrault, who first penned "Le petit chaperon rouge" in 1697 for the French court of the Sun King, Louis XIV. The court was similar to a sort of "Vegas at Versailles," where wealthy nobles gamboled while peasants starved.[49] In this era, the fairy tale was told primarily among adults, and filtered through to the court from the ladies' salons, the "elegant drawing-room gatherings that were the feminine heart of seventeenth century Parisian intellectual life." As a member of the French Academy, "the old boys club that met in the Louvre, which had been established earlier in the century to debate the most important intel-lectual matters of the day," Perrault was privy to the controversy about gender and the feminist assertions emanating from the salons, such as the right to marry or remain single, to refuse to have children, and to look after their own affairs. Thus, his fairy tales "express these struggles."[50]

Perrault clearly did not champion the aspirations of the educated aristocratic feminists. Instead, he introduced the red cap, which is absent from "The Story of Grandmother." As Orenstein delineates, "Little Red Riding Hood" is a cautionary tale about the dangers of female promiscuity. The little hood or *chaperon*, which doubles to indicate a matron who protects girls from untrustworthy young men, is red, "the color of harlots, scandal and blood, symbolizing her sin and foreshadowing her fate."[51] The visceral color of red pulses through written versions of the fairy tale beginning with Perrault: the red color of the hood, the red blood of the grandmother that the girl drinks in the oral tale, and the red color of meaty flesh being ripped and consumed. Red is the central marrow of a woman's initiation into menstruation, the rupturing of the hymen and childbirth. Bella, strikingly pale in appearance, cannot successfully manage the red life forces pulsing through her body: she faints at the sight of blood. Her blood scent is what draws Edward to her, yet her liaison with Edward increasingly exposes her to physical injury. Toward the end of *Twilight*, Bella is attacked by another vampire, James, who breaks her leg, rips her scalp with glass, and ignites her with pain. When she regains consciousness, her beloved Edward is at her side. By straying from the path in order to associate with vampires, she has been mangled, battered, and broken with her flesh ripped apart. Her version of red is not Cupid's valentine, but blood from severed vessels.

In a parallel to Bella's choices of suitors in *Twilight*, Perrault inserts a moral in verse at the end of his tale, which was generally edited out of later editions:

> I say Wolf, for all wolves
> Are not of the same sort;
> There is one kind with an amenable disposition
> Neither noisy, nor hateful, nor angry,
> But tame, obliging and gentle,
> Following the young maids
> In the streets, even into their homes.
> Alas! Who does not know that these gentle wolves
> Are of all such creatures the most dangerous![52]

So even Perrault recognized that the nerd—the boring and dependable Mike or Eric—is not nearly as threatening as the charming, smooth-talking Edward. Yet in Perrault as in *Twilight*, the scripts are interchangeable: the male is the predator and the female is the prey. The male cannot control his animal lust and the female is powerless to resist him. The male successfully satisfies his needs at the expense of a female who has no agency, sense of direction or agenda dictated by her own aspirations.

By the early nineteenth century when the Grimms interpret the tale, the red hood remains and a powerful male, the savior huntsman, who is external to both the matriarchal familial line and the intrigue contrived between the girl and the wolf, arrives like a *deus ex machina* to save the day by delivering the girl and her grandmother from the darkness of the wolf's belly to the reasoned light of day. He takes a scissors and cuts open the wolf's belly, performing a miraculous cesarean birth in which, "after he made a couple of cuts, he saw the little red cap shining forth."[53] He appropriates from these women the essential feminine function of giving birth. They can't even manage their own bodies without the help of a man. In the social milieu of the Grimms, patriarchy was firmly entrenched.

In *The Great Cat Massacre* (1984), Princeton historian Robert Darnton argues that folktales are "historical documents,"[54] and Catherine Orenstein likewise notes that fairy tales catalog not only "broad elements of human experience but also the particular details of each day and age."[55] What is fascinating about Perrault's French cake and little pot of butter, which in the German version becomes a bottle of wine, is that the storyteller made choices, and these details, hardly trivial or insignificant, provide a snapshot, a holographic image, a predigital recording of a culture otherwise lost in a time when such technologies did not exist. Darnton argues, "Other people are other. They do not think the way we do," and admonishes his readers that "we constantly need to be shaken out of a false sense of familiarity with the past, to be administered doses of culture shock."[56] Under the mantle of otherness, both despair and promise reside: despair in that the obscure or seemingly insignificant artifact in the folktale will never be unearthed or translated correctly, and promise in that significant information about our lifestyles will be transmitted to future generations through our art. The portraits of teenagers that Meyer creates in *Twilight*—their jargon, daily activities, dress, and cultural mind-set—obviously mirror the operative fundamentals of modern culture, and these gendered attitudes and behaviors have not changed substantially since the seventeenth century. Yet even though these variables are presently assigned to fixed positions, time will alter the kaleidoscopic arrangement so that new relationships and patterns may emerge. "The Story of Grandmother" is a treasure gleaned from the past because it breaks the mold of the passive female who abdicates her selfhood in service to the male.

Unfortunately, modern teenagers, who conceptualize their present situation as "forever," and for whom a month is an eternity, may not be able to extricate themselves from Bella's mind-set or question her underlying assumptions analytically. This is regrettable because *Twilight* poses a dilemma regarding which of the two protagonists poses the biggest threat: Edward, the bloodthirsty vampire, or Bella, a prisoner of her own constrictive choices.

However, even though she is locked down by her adolescent passions and subservient frame of reference, Bella does have choices. She has always had choices. Her challenge is to shatter the formulas carved in stone by patriarchal attitudes and improvise some new fairy tales of her own.

NOTES

1. Carl G. Jung, *Man and his Symbols* (New York: Laurel-Dell, 1969), 56–57.
2. Meyer specifically stated, "In my dream, the basics of which would become the meadow scene in chapter 13, I can see a young woman in the embrace of a very handsome young man, in a beautiful meadow surrounded by forest, and somehow I know that he is a vampire." She became so intrigued with the characters that "I just wrote and let whatever happened happen." "Interview with Stephenie Meyer," *Journal of Adolescent & Adult Literacy* 49 (2006): 630–32. http://www.jstor.org/stable/40017638 (accessed May 2, 2010).

3. Whether Little Red Riding Hood has yet entered adolescence is subject to extensive debate, especially among psychoanalytical theorists. For example, in *The Forgotten Language: An Introduction to the Understanding of Dreams, Fairy Tales and Myths* (New York, 1951), 235–41, Erich Fromm asserts that the red cap is a symbol of menstruation, but historian Robert Darnton in *The Great Cat Massacre and Other Episodes in French Cultural History* (New York, 1984) lampoons this theory, stating that Fromm relied on details that "did not exist in the versions known to peasants in the seventeenth and eighteenth centuries" (11).

4. Charles Perrault, "Little Red Riding Hood" in *Little Red Riding Hood: A Casebook*, ed. Alan Dundes (Madison: University of Wisconsin Press, 1989), 3–6.

5. Stephenie Meyer, *Twilight* (New York: Megan Tingley Books, 2005), 4 and 10.

6. Ibid., 5.

7. Ibid., 18.

8. Ibid., 23.

9. Ibid., 267.

10. J. Gordon Melton, *The Vampire Book: The Encyclopedia of the Undead* (Detroit: Gale Research, 1994), 676–77.

11. H. Sidky, *Witchcraft, Lycanthropy, Drugs, and Disease: An Anthropological Study of the European Witch-Hunts,* vol 70, American University Series XI (New York: Peter Lang, 1997), 216–17.

12. Paul Delarue (1889–1956), a French folklorist, in *The Borzoi Book of French Folk Tales* presents a manuscript of "The Story of the Grandmother" from the collection of A. Millien which was told by Louis and Francois Briffault, at Montigny-aux-Amognes, Nievre, about 1885.

13. Paul Delarue, "The Story of Grandmother" in *Little Red Riding Hood: A Casebook*, ed. Alan Dundes (Madison: University of Wisconsin Press, 1989), 15.

14. Jack Zipes, *The Trials & Tribulations of Little Red Riding Hood*, 2nd ed. (New York: Routledge, 1993), 19.

15. Dante Alighierei, *The Divine Comedy: The Inferno, Purgatorio and Paradiso*, trans. Lawrence Grant White (New York: Pantheon, 1948), 1.

16. Meyer, 3.

17. Perrault, 4.

18. Jacob and Wilhelm Grimm, "Little Red Cap [*Rotkappchen*]" in *Little Red Riding Hood: A Casebook*, ed. Alan Dundes (Madison: University of Wisconsin Press, 1989), 9.

19. Meyer, 136.

20. Ibid., 137.

21. Sidky, 216–17.

22. In England, where the wolves were extirpated through organized hunting and massive deforestation by the sixteenth century, reports of werewolves were nearly nonexistent. Sidky, 220–22. Zipes concurs that in France, more than any other European country, there was a "virtual epidemic" of men accused of being werewolves, akin to women prosecuted as witches. He attributes to Marianne Rumpf the correlation between the prevalence of oral nineteenth-and-twentieth century Little Red Riding Hood tales and regions having a high number of werewolf trials during the fifteenth through seventeenth centuries. Zipes, 19–20.

23. Meyer, 221.

24. Joseph L. Henderson, "Ancient Myths and Modern Man" in *Man and His Symbols*, ed. Carl G. Jung (New York: Laurel-Dell, 1969), 104.

25. Although it is currently in vogue for older women to pair with younger men, an apparent spin-off from the self-affirmations of feminism, traditionally marriage between a

younger, childlike bride and an older man has been viewed as natural and logical, and not the reverse, even though demographers note that it would be preferable for women to marry men at least several years younger to mitigate lengthy widowhoods. A mature woman possessing desire was formerly the object of scorn and disgust, especially one who designed to "rob the cradle." Recall that the psychic deterioration of Blanche in Tennessee Williams' drama *A Streetcar Named Desire* was partly attributable to her predilection for seducing younger men.

26. Meyer, 87.
27. P. Saintyes, *Les Contes de Perrault,* (Paris: Librarie Critique, 1923), 221.
28. T. S. Eliot, *The Waste Land* (San Diego: Harcourt-Harvest), 1997), 3.
29. Meyer, 259.
30. Ibid., 297.
31. Ibid., 260.
32. Ibid., 97.
33. Grimm, 11.
34. Zipes, 36.
35. Joyce Thomas in *Inside the Wolf's Belly* (Sheffield, England: Sheffield AP, 1989) points out that in the fairy tale, marital union has symbolic significance that transcends the contemporary concept of marriage as "dead end" or limiting if it is the only role available for women: "As s/he has attained the greatest of material and societal rewards, so does s/he attain the greatest of human, emotional and sexual rewards through that union...Logos and Eros are balanced, are fused; Yang and Yin are again contained within the cosmic round" (39). Thomas further blames "stereotype perpetuated by our culture" for reprinting "Snow White" but deleting "The Robber Bridegroom" in which a courageous heroine assumes an assertive role (38).
36. Janice A. Radway, *Reading the Romance: Women, Patriarchy, and Popular Literature* (Chapel Hill, North Carolina University Press, 1984), 109.
37. Ibid., 63.
38. Ibid., 123.
39. Meyer, 143.
40. Radway, 126.
41. Ibid., 134.
42. Ibid., 128.
43. Ibid., 217.
44. According to a book review by Shambrala Norris, *The Twilight Saga* has become "one of the most well-known teen vampire romance series in the world" and *Twilight* is a "breathtaking beginning to a wonderful series." Shambrala Norris. "Twilight by Stephenie Meyer—Book Review," (July 14, 2010). http://romancefiction.suite101. com/article.cfm/twilight-by-stephenie-meyer-book (accessed August 21, 2010). More nuanced is Caitlin Flanagan, who confesses in an *Atlantic Monthly* article that "I hate Y.A. (young adult) novels; they bore me," but continues that "*Twilight* is fantastic...It's also the first book that seemed at long last to rekindle something of the girl-reader in me," and "stirred something in me so long forgotten that I felt embarrassed by it," which she later identifies as "what sex and longing really mean to a young girl." Caitlin Flanagan, "What Girls Want," *The Atlantic Monthly* (December, 2008): http://www. theatlantic.com/magazine/archive/2008/12/what-girls-want/7161/ (accessed August 21, 2010). Flanagan has zeroed into the marrow of *Twilight*: it recreates those breathless days when infatuation is the center of an adolescent girl's universe, and what he said, or how he looked at her, goes on for page after page. The tragedy is that some

women never move beyond an adolescent ideation of what constitutes "true love," and live diminished lives as a result.

45. Mary Pipher, *Reviving Ophelia: Saving the Selves of Adolescent Girls* (New York: Putnam, 1994), 19–20.

46. There is no mention of a red hood or cap, indicating that Perrault introduced this element to his version of the story. This change is noteworthy because as Jack Zipes states, much of the scholarship surrounding the fairy tale is centered on the significance of the red cap: "As we know, numerous modern studies have focused on the red cap in Perrault's tale as a symbol either of the sun or puberty. Neither viewpoint is correct. Perrault used the word *chaperon,* which was a small, stylish cap . . ." Jack Zipes, " 'Little Red Riding Hood' as Male Creation and Projection" in *Little Red Riding Hood: A Casebook,* ed. Alan Dundes (Madison: University of Wisconsin Press, 1989), 122. Delarue also comments that the numerous oral tales ascribe various clothing articles to the heroine, such as a white bonnet, green garter, white coat or red shoes, from which "one discerns the error of those who have wished to find a symbolic sense in our tale, taking their departure from the name of the heroine with a red headdress in whom they perceive the dawn, the queen of May with her crown, and so on" (18).

47. Catherine Orenstein, *Little Red Riding Hood Uncloaked: Sex, Morality, and the Evolution of a Fairy Tale* (New York: Basic-Perseus, 2002), 81.

48. Delarue, 15–16.

49. Orenstein, 23.

50. Ibid., 31–32.

51. Ibid., 36–37.

52. Perrault, 6.

53. Grimm, 11.

54. Robert Darnton, *The Great Cat Massacre and other Episodes in French Cultural History* (New York: Basic, 1984), 13.

55. Orenstein, 12.

56. Darnton, 4.

CHAPTER 2

TEXTUAL VAMPIRISM IN THE *TWILIGHT* SAGA: DRAWING FEMINIST LIFE FROM *JANE EYRE* AND TEEN FANTASY FICTION

KRISTINA DEFFENBACHER AND MIKAYLA ZAGORIA-MOFFET

THE PUBLISHING INDUSTRY HAS BEEN QUICK TO CAPITALIZE on the *Twilight* saga's extensive references to *Wuthering Heights, Pride and Prejudice*, and *Romeo and Juliet*; Harper Collins reprinted all three texts with covers that echo those of the *Twilight* books and carry an endorsement from "Bella & Edward."[1] Sales of *Wuthering Heights* increased dramatically when it was marketed alongside *Eclipse*, and the success of the *Twilight* books and films have inspired new productions of *Wuthering Heights* and *Jane Eyre*,[2] the *Twilight* saga's unnamed but central intertext. Because the *Twilight* saga has given new life to texts that sustain its own romantic plot, vampirism is a useful metaphor for understanding its intertextual relationships—particularly its incorporation and revision of *Jane Eyre*. Indeed all intertextuality, as defined by Julia Kristeva, can be read as a form of vampirism, as "any text is the absorption and transformation of another."[3]

The *Twilight* saga draws more from *Jane Eyre* than the precedent and pedigree of its epic romance: the series incorporates the bookends of the female *bildungsroman*, or novel of development, as Charlotte Brontë scripted it. Bella Swan, who, like Jane Eyre, narrates (much of) her own tale, initially describes herself in Janian terms, as a plain young woman who is set apart from others,[4] and "who, for all her swansdown potential, has no great expectations," as critic Sandra Gilbert describes young Jane.[5] In the final book of the saga, Bella, like Jane at the conclusion of *Jane Eyre*, finds her place in the world through her relationship with a Byronic Edward (Cullen for

Bella, Rochester for Jane), and in each narrative, some supernatural intervention sets heroine and hero on more equal footing.

A crucial difference—especially in a series about vampires—is that Bella does not fight to keep self and soul together along the way, as Gilbert and Susan Gubar describe Jane Eyre's journey.[6] Meyer's repeated invocation of *Jane Eyre* as intertext suggests a developmental arc where there is none, and thus helps to reconcile what is only a physical makeover (albeit a radical one) with a resolution that combines the rewards of Jane's struggles and the achievements of the contemporary, questing fantasy heroine. Bella Swan is no Jane Eyre, nor is she a Buffy Summers; yet she is, in the end, both. Midway through the final book of the *Twilight* saga, Bella morphs from helpless prey to fiercely capable warrior, a female role that is central to other subcategories of teen fantasy fiction, texts that tend to incorporate more fully the feminist drive and developmental arc of Brontë's novel.[7] By intertextually drawing feminist life from the paradigmatic heroine and plot of *Jane Eyre*, Meyer prepares readers for the conversion of a character who at first embodies "feminine" passivity and a central story that is strictly neogothic romance until that point when heroine and narrative confront the problem of women's sexual vulnerability and resolve—however mythically—tensions between female subjectivity and heterosexual desire in ways that reflect both third-wave feminist ambitions and twenty-first-century popular discourses about gender.

Thus in its vampiric relationship with *Jane Eyre*, the *Twilight* saga both feeds upon and transforms Brontë's female *bildungsroman* and gothic romance, itself "a paradigmatic example of how a woman writer responds to and revises traditional plots for women."[8] Critics, fans, and Meyer herself have noted extensive connections between the *Twilight* novels and *Jane Eyre*, and have generally defined the relationship between these narratives in terms of one-to-one correspondences.[9] Commentators who have examined this intertextual relationship tend to characterize those aspects of the *Twilight* saga that do not correspond to the "original" text as failures of Meyer and/or her heroine (when commentators differentiate between them); Bella and her narrative are then seen as only weak or incomplete copies of Jane Eyre and the novel that bears her name. In Abigail Myers' analysis, for instance, Bella comes up short in comparisons with Jane; Myers therefore cannot find Bella a "feminist hero."[10] By invoking a static reading of *Jane Eyre* as a standard against which to measure the *Twilight* saga, such responses deny the fluidity and complexity of intertextual relationships, which multiply rather than foreclose interpretive possibilities. Reading the *Twilight* saga in dynamic relation to its intertexts, however, especially *Jane Eyre* and twenty-first-century teen fantasy fiction, demonstrates ways in which Bella Swan is both far less and far more than Jane Eyre.

"SHALL WE CALL YOU JANE?"[11]

Numerous *Twilight* fan sites identify *Jane Eyre* as a primary source of inspiration for the books, and many readers have noted that, as Meyer herself puts it, "there are elements of Edward in Edward Rochester and elements of Bella in Jane."[12] Comparative analyses of the *Twilight* saga and *Jane Eyre*, such as Myers' "Edward Cullen and Bella Swan: Byronic and Feminist Heroes...Or Not," tend to focus on parallels and differences between the Edwards and between the heroines, again situating Brontë's characters as the immutable originals. Critical and online discussions of the texts have been particularly concerned with the extent to which Edward Cullen is, like Edward Rochester, a Byronic hero, and with the appropriateness of Bella's choices in comparison to Jane's, given the Edwards's status as "dangerous lovers."[13] Such readings tend to condemn Bella for choosing to stay with her Edward at the risk of her life and perhaps soul rather than choosing to leave him, as Jane leaves Rochester when the revelation of his living wife and his plea for Jane to stay with him as his mistress put her soul in danger.[14] Jane's choice has been critically understood in the context of the warning provided by the story of Bertha, Rochester's captive first wife and Jane's dark, "Vampyre" double[15]; Bella's choices similarly need to be understood in relation to the narratives of her doubles in the *Twilight* saga, particularly those of vampires Rosalie Hale and Alice Cullen. Together, Rosalie's and Alice's stories, like Bertha's in *Jane Eyre*, speak of women's vulnerability and confinement, but also of a vengeful, self-protective strength and acuity.

Rosalie Hale functions as a double for Bella Swan, both as character and storyteller. In *Eclipse*, Rosalie initially frames the narrative of her human past as a fairy tale: as a beautiful young woman, she desires the romance and domestic bliss that a poorer friend finds through marriage, along with the rise in class fortune that completes the Cinderella story. Believing she has found her "prince" in a son of the local, bank-owning "royalty," Rosalie is unprepared for the dark side of the patriarchal romance: women's vulnerability to male sexual violence and control. Rosalie's tale of her sexual assault by her drunken fiancé and his friends is the story of what could have been Bella's tragic end. In *Twilight*, Bella wanders off in Port Angeles and finds herself cornered by a group of men, all drunk and calling toward her. They surround her, but Edward's sudden presence and rescue saves her from repeating that part of Rosalie's story. Meyer suggests that as a human woman, Bella has no control of the situation and must rely on a man to defend her from these other men; as a vampire, Bella's experience could parallel the conclusion of Rosalie's story exactly, overriding victimization with the ability to exact revenge, without physical or social limits to restrict her. As Rosalie's and Bella's bodies transform, so do their narratives, from patriarchal fairy tales to stories of women's self-reliance and equalizing strength.

Alice's story of transformation also parallels Bella's, in a more direct and sinister way. James, in his hunt of Bella, corners her and to extend the moment, informs her of the "one and only time my prey escaped me."[16] James's information regards Alice, who was institutionalized and confined as a human girl, presumably because of the visionary power she had even before she was a vampire. Meyer links the experiences of Alice and Bella through James's fear of Edward transforming Bella—as someone did for Alice—before he can finish his hunt and kill her. Like Rosalie, Alice was unable to protect herself and had to rely on someone else to change her. And, once a vampire, Alice possesses the ability to defend herself and those she cares about; she simultaneously throws aside her mortality and her weakness as a victim. Even her mate, Jasper, tells Bella that there is no need to worry about her, as Alice is more than capable of taking care of herself, and even bests Jasper himself in hand-to-hand combat.[17]

Rosalie's sexual assault and Alice's forced confinement serve to contrast their previous, human existences with their vampiric "lives." Once the two women have gone through the change, their ability to protect or avenge themselves increases exponentially. Both victims become much more than their oppressors could ever imagine—stronger, more vicious, and capable of handling themselves in a world that previously did not afford either one that opportunity. Most significantly, Alice's and Rosalie's narratives show what could have, and almost, happened to Bella—a common thread linking mortal female existence. Vampirism grants Rosalie, Alice, and later Bella the ability to throw off traditional, normative gender expectations and overcome repeated instances of women's victimization, creating a complicated dialogue between overarching narratives of modern, Western female traumatic experience and the fantasy of a future devoid of these stories.

In her book *No Turning Back: The History of Feminism and the Future of Women*, Estelle Freedman suggests that "...learning to live with rape rests upon the historical construction of irrepressible male violence that women can ignite. The impact of this legacy is twofold. First, fear remains a part of women's daily consciousness."[18] Correspondingly, in Rosalie's case, fear of her trauma is mitigated by her potential to physically punish the men who abused her, but it does not stay her memory of the incident. Meyer's portrayal of this scene leaves little to the imagination; despite Rosalie's apparent success, beauty, and current happiness, she tells Bella that she recalls every single thing about her experience clearly, and then adds, "I thought of nothing else. And so I remember this, when so many pleasant memories have faded away completely."[19] Although Rosalie appears to no longer fear the men, as she murders them shortly after the assault occurs, the memory of her trauma remains fresh in her mind, signaling the lasting ordeal of her rape.[20]

For Bella and for the *Twilight* saga's readers, Rosalie's story is a haunting reminder of mortal women's vulnerability in patriarchy, as Bertha is for Jane in *Jane Eyre*. Bertha's murmurs and eerie laughter from her prison room in Thornfield Hall's upper story echo Jane's own expressions of anger at women's social limitations, forced dependency, and confinement.[21] Jane's vampiric double enacts Jane's rage over the oppression she has suffered under patriarchy, as represented by her male cousin's unchecked taunts and violence against her at the start of the narrative, by her schoolmaster's unmerciful and abusive treatment of the girls in his care, and by Rochester's manipulation and control of women, including his household employee, Jane.[22] Bertha bites and attempts to drain the blood from her brother, who is complicit in her confinement, and sets a fire that maims Rochester and destroys the ancestral mansion that represents his power. As vampires, Rosalie and Alice are able to avenge and protect themselves against what *should* anger Bella: male violence and control, the threat of which the mortal Bella lives under and the experience of which she repeatedly endures. Yet for much of the *Twilight* saga, Bella seems to resemble the passive, impossibly forgiving Helen Burns more than the fiery Jane Eyre; in *Twilight*, Bella begs her rescuer, Edward, not to avenge her near-gang-rape or her expected murder at the hands of James, and what little resistance or resentment she shows in response to Edward's controlling behavior is largely passive and easily dispelled. Like Jane, Bella suffers as a result of her lover's domineering behaviors, which reinforce and exacerbate the inequality between them. It is Bella's responses, especially as they seem to differ from Jane's, that cause contemporary feminists such concern about the *Twilight* saga and its popularity, especially among girls and young women.

There is certainly cause for concern in Bella's tolerance of actions that can be characterized as stalking, manipulation, and abuse, and in the potential for young, female readers to accept and even desire such behavior in a male partner.[23] But as Naomi Zack persuasively argues, this risk can only increase if feminists refuse "to engage those mass views and ideals" behind the phenomenal popularity of the *Twilight* books and films, and "to analyze what is important and pleasurable about them to those who hold them."[24] One way to understand the pleasure and even empowerment that many young, female readers find in the *Twilight* saga is through analysis of its intertextual relationship with *Jane Eyre*, a text that has sustained popularity with the same young, female demographic *and* is of great consequence to feminist critics.[25] Because many of Edward Cullen's most disturbing behaviors resemble those of Edward Rochester, because Bella's responses parallel many of Jane's own (as distinguished from the actions of her dark double), and because so many feminist readers have articulated how they nonetheless read *Jane Eyre* as a pleasurable and empowering novel, analyzing Edward and Bella's relationship in the invoked context of Rochester and Jane's romance can help to clarify—without justifying or apologizing for—some of the most controversial aspects of the *Twilight* saga's textual and cultural dynamics.

In both *Jane Eyre* and the *Twilight* saga, after each Edward—Rochester and Cullen, respectively—declares his love for the heroine, she chooses to stay with him and engage in a courtship that poses significant risks to her body and soul and that continues an established pattern of manipulation and control. From the beginning, each Edward is unpredictably surly and brooding; in true Byronic fashion, he gives the heroine warnings of the danger that he poses to her and states cryptically that he is breaking all the rules in drawing her to him.[26] Each Edward manipulates the heroine's feelings for him through these mixed messages and by alternately ignoring and focusing intensely on her. Edward Rochester's manipulation of Jane's feelings is more overt, if no less coercive: he forces her to witness and encourages her belief in his performed courtship of another woman, up to—and well into—his proposal to Jane. And, most significantly, Rochester does not tell Jane about Bertha before his proposal, and thereby attempts to draw Jane into a false marriage and a position, as his mistress, outside of society and the system of belief so central to her being.

Bella fully understands the mortal peril of accepting and returning a vampire's declaration of love; although Jane does not know all of the risks she takes in accepting Rochester's proposal, she knowingly places herself in danger by staying, unprotected, in her employer's home after he has made his desire for her clear. When she and Rochester come in from the garden at midnight, kissing, Jane immediately comprehends the grave look that Mrs. Fairfax, the head housekeeper, gives her. And while Jane believes the housekeeper has misconstrued their relationship, she takes to heart Mrs. Fairfax's warning to "keep Mr. Rochester at a distance: distrust yourself as well as him. Gentlemen in his station are not accustomed to marry their governesses."[27] Jane is, in effect, gambling with her life, just as Bella more literally bets her life on Edward's self-restraint, knowing that he can kill her if he loses control in a moment of passion.[28] If Rochester does not contain his desire for Jane, if she cannot "keep him from the edge of the gulf" by maintaining a distance between them until their marriage, her story will likely become the far more common one, that of the seduced and abandoned servant.[29] Indeed, when the impediment of an existing marriage is revealed and Rochester asks Jane to go away with him anyway, it is her certainty that this would be her end—that she would eventually be deserted and despised by him as were his mistresses before her—that gives her the strength to refuse him.[30] Her refusal prompts a ferocity in Rochester that he barely restrains: after warning Jane that if she won't hear reason, he will "try violence," he speaks in a voice that turns her "stone cold with terror—for this was the pant of a lion rising," and he declares that she is "a mere reed" that he can bend, uproot, and crush.[31] There are clear echoes in the scene in *Twilight* in which Edward Cullen uproots trees to demonstrate the strength that would make it impossible for Bella to fight him off, and then describes his love for her as a lion's for a lamb.[32] What stays Rochester's hand is his conviction that rending Jane's "brittle frame" will not get him what he wants: her indomitable "spirit," with its "will and energy."[33]

The greatest danger that their respective Edwards pose to the heroines of *Jane Eyre* and the *Twilight* saga is to their spirits, to their independence and will; a key difference between the heroines is that Bella seems ready to sacrifice hers in a way that Jane, ultimately, is not. However, the difference between them is not as great as it might first appear. Brontë makes it clear that without the timely revelation of Rochester's existing wife, Jane would have entered a (false) marriage based on inequality and some submission of her independent spirit to the will of her despotic idol. Before the wedding, Rochester desires to put a diamond chain around Jane's neck and dress her in finery that she resists, declaring that she would then no longer be Jane Eyre.[34] She accepts only two sober dresses, yet he gives her a smile "such as a sultan might, in a blissful and fond moment, bestow on a slave his gold and gems had enriched."[35] The independence that Jane asserts in refusing most of his gifts is understood to be a temporary gesture; Rochester playfully warns Jane, " 'it is your time now, little tyrant, but it will be mine presently: and when once I have seized you, to have and to hold, I'll just—figuratively speaking—attach you to a chain like this' (touching his watch-guard)."[36]

Like Jane, Bella is made anxious by the inequality between her and her beloved Edward, and by the gifts that reinforce that inequality: in *Twilight* she asserts that "a man and a woman have to be somewhat equal," and in *New Moon* she tells Edward that she does not want him to spend money on her, as that throws them more "out of balance."[37] Edward Cullen's despotism manifests itself differently than does Rochester's, in part because while Jane is essentially alone in the world as an orphan ("that is the best of it," Rochester says),[38] Bella is part of the world and connected to her mother and father, as well as to both friends and enemies whom Edward fears will take her away from him. Edward's jealousy as well as his protectiveness drive his controlling behaviors: he enters Bella's bedroom and watches her without her knowledge or consent, he withholds information from her, and he attempts to determine whom she sees and where she goes, going so far as to kidnap her for her "protection."[39] In this behavior, Edward resembles another Victorian Byronic figure: Heathcliff from Emily Brontë's *Wuthering Heights*, a character that Edward himself describes as "ghastly" and "malignant."[40] In *Eclipse*, Jacob Black gives a more contemporary diagnosis of such behavior and Bella's endurance of it: "You know, I saw this story on the news last week about controlling, abusive relationships"—and there

Bella cuts him off.[41] It is important, though, that the narrating Bella gives Jacob's judgment space within her narrative, and that she resists her beloved's more controlling behaviors even as she chooses to stay with him, as does Jane up to the revelation of an insurmountable impediment to her marriage to Rochester.

Bella primarily resists Edward by defying his attempts to keep her from spending time with her best friend, Jacob. The extreme measures to which Edward drives her—she has to elude him and escape from his agent, Alice—seem to make him recognize the extremity of his own behavior. Edward admits that he has been in the wrong and promises to trust Bella's judgment from that point forward.[42] As Leah McClimans and J. Jeremy Wisnewski assert, while "structures of dominance are not thrown off in one day or by one decision," Edward "continues to increasingly trust Bella's decisions" thereafter; "he gets better."[43] The increasing trust and emerging equality between them after Edward's realization counter Abigail Myers' reading that,

> The key difference between Edward Rochester and Edward Cullen is that Rochester learns his lesson. Because Jane has the ovaries to show him that she won't put up with his crap—and backs up her statements with a predawn escape that confounds him and breaks his heart—Edward Rochester truly understands how selfish and short-sighted he is.[44]

While Bella's repeated escapes to Jacob and to the reservation where she feels "free" are not as strong a declaration of independence as is Jane's leaving Rochester to fend for herself in the world, both actions lead to the Byronic Edwards recognizing their selfishness and amending their ways.

This is not to deny the significant differences between Jane Eyre and Bella Swan. Jane chooses to head into the world alone to protect her self and soul; Bella chooses to stay with Edward and seems to have little self or soul apart from him. Yet in the context of her respective narrative, each heroine's choices ultimately lead to both self-realization and a loving relationship that is more egalitarian than any (mortal) alternatives. Jane takes to heart the warnings provided by Bertha and by Rochester's mistresses; her decision to leave Rochester is a decision to not repeat their stories. Bella's choice is not just to stay with Edward, but also to become a vampire, despite his opposition to that alternative. In opting for vampirism—or the Cullens's "vegetarian" version of it—Bella is choosing a way of being in a relationship and in the world that will keep her from repeating Rosalie's and Alice's human experiences of victimization.

Bella makes a "life" choice that is more empowering than the alternatives represented by the mortal women in her life, including her childlike, dependent mother, Rene, and the domesticated, vulnerable "wolf girl," Emily.[45] Bella describes her mother's eyes as "wide" and "childlike," and in a moment of panic before leaving Rene to go and live with her father, Bella reasons, "Of course, [her mother] had Phil now, so the bills would probably get paid, there would be food in the refrigerator, gas in her car, and someone to call when she got lost, but still…"[46] Rene, clearly unable to handle any situation without support from another, is left in the capable hands of a man; Bella, while still human, is at times in a position of relatively childlike weakness and is dependent on her much stronger male protector.

While feminist critics have objected to this characterization of Bella and her roles as housekeeper and cook for her father,[47] her representation of traditional femininity pales in comparison to the depiction of Emily, who will never have an opportunity to challenge or rise above normative gender expectations. Although the relationship between Emily and the werewolf Sam—one in which traditional gender roles are upheld and celebrated—is read by Bella and others as sweet and romantic, the dark side of this way of life is legible on Emily's face, which is covered in claw-mark scars that Sam gave her in a fit of uncontrollable rage. Emily will always be vulnerable in her relationship with Sam since she lacks the potential to develop into a being with powers equal to her imprinted mate's—an option Bella has. Furthermore, Bella's assertion of her right to choose is underscored by her expressed concern for the toddler Claire, on whom the pack member Quil has "imprinted": "Doesn't Claire get a choice here?"[48]

Of course, Rene's and Emily's roles and relationships are not the only human options available to Bella. But in a patriarchal society and rape culture, there is no position that a woman can choose that is free from gender oppression and physical vulnerability, as the stories of Alice's and Rosalie's human lives further illustrate for Bella and for the *Twilight* saga's readers. Vampirism offers Bella an opportunity that her alternatives cannot afford her. As Bonnie Mann notes, "…we discover that Bella wants to be a vampire, not only to avoid out-aging Edward and live with him in immortal bliss, but because in the vampire world, all bets are off when it comes to gender."[49] For example, while Rosalie's beauty and her vanity are still her most noted characteristics, as a vampire she is also the best mechanic in the Cullen family, and she is responsible for having saved Emmett—a brawny and tough icon of traditional Western masculinity—from the bear that she found mauling him.[50] Alice Cullen also blurs conventional gender roles: she is graceful and fashion-obsessed, yet she also constantly tells others what they must do and, given her visionary powers, she is usually obeyed. Most importantly, in Rosalie and Emmett's and Alice and Jasper's romantic relationships, neither partner is dominant. For Bella, vampirism with the Cullens represents a liberating alternative to the oppressive dependency and scarring vulnerability represented by the human stories of Alice and Rene, and Rosalie and Emily.

After settling into her vampiric "life," Bella declares, "I had found my true place in the world, the place I fit, the place I shined."[51] Similarly, after the transformations that enable Jane to reunite with Rochester on more equal terms at the end of *Jane Eyre*, she describes their relationship as having "brought to life and light my whole nature."[52] Both heroines' choices—together with some timely supernatural intervention—lead to their realization of full selfhood and romantic love. These "both/and" resolutions require a revision of gender roles and a redistribution of physical power, through "divine justice" in *Jane Eyre*, and through vampiric transformation in the *Twilight* saga. At the conclusion of Brontë's novel, a newly financially independent Jane returns to a blinded and crippled Rochester who has been "humbled" by his "Maker"; he is wearing Jane's pearls, and he is dependent on her now superior physical abilities.[53] In *Breaking Dawn*, Bella takes to vampirism in command of herself and with physical strength greater than that of the strongest vampire she knows.[54] Each relationship is then characterized as a marriage of equals: Jane declares, "I am my husband's life as fully as he is mine,"[55] and after her transformation, Bella describes herself and Edward as "*together*—both active participants now. Finally equals."[56] Both heroines describe themselves as liberated from "restraint"; Jane is "at perfect ease" and Bella has "no fear—especially not that."[57] Jane and Bella no longer fear male aggression or control, at least while secure in their respective fairy-tale houses, set deep in lush woods.

Both heroines realize "a marriage of true minds" in a fantastic space: Jane and Rochester unite as equals in the Shakespearean "Green World" of Ferndean, removed from corrupt social expectations and influences;[58] Bella joins Edward in a parallel, supernatural world where human rules and threats are void. In *Jane Eyre* and in the *Twilight* saga, an implicit critique of gender norms can be found in the fact that it takes both supernatural intervention and the possibility of a space apart from human society for the heroine to achieve and reconcile full selfhood and romantic love. That the resolutions of both texts also require bodily transformation—Rochester's impairment and Bella's empowerment via her vampiric metamorphosis—reveals the enduring significance of women's physical and sexual vulnerability and fear, an issue central to many contemporary young women's negotiations of independent self-hood, romantic love, and heterosexual desire. Indeed, critic Laura Miller attributes contemporary fantasy fiction's enormous popularity with female readers to its being "peculiarly suited to wrestling with the quandaries of early twenty-first-century womanhood," particularly the fear of "surrendering control over your destiny[...] should you fall under the spell of a particularly irresistible suitor."[59]

The contemporary fiction that Miller describes is, like *Jane Eyre*, a cross of fairy-tale and coming-of-age narrative;[60] while the *Twilight* saga uses fantasy to address some of the same quandaries of early womanhood as do these intertexts, it does so without a coming-of-age journey. But if the physical method of her transformation renders Bella something less than a Jane Eyre, it also makes her into something more. Bella's story does not end when she and Edward take possession of the fairy-tale cottage in the woods, as Jane's narrative does; similarly, her transformation into a vampire ultimately does not *remove* Bella from the world she has known, but rather also positions her in another, more dangerous social order, from which she cannot escape. By becoming a vampire, Bella gains abilities she lacked as a human and realizes a desire that she voices throughout the course of the saga: the ability to defend herself, her family, and other loved ones. At the end of *Breaking Dawn*, Bella defends an entire community against the corrupt patriarchs of their social order, a resolution that connects the *Twilight* saga to teen fantasy texts that focus on warrior heroines, such as Amelia Atwater-Rhodes' *Demon in My View* and Kristin Cashore's *Graceling*. These heroines' journeys bring them to self-actualization and the ability—or at least the possibility—of reconciling romance and strong self-identity. Simply put, Bella's story elides the quest and the internal struggle with self-realization, but gives her all of the benefits attained by the heroines within this subgenre that more fully incorporates both.

Bella's decisive actions in the epic battle at the end of *Breaking Dawn* invoke the fierce, aggressive strength that these warrior heroines demonstrate throughout the course of their respective journeys and novels. Characters such as Atwater-Rhodes' Jessica or Cashore's Katsa work tirelessly (if not always self-consciously) to find their place in other worlds. Each of these heroines transforms herself as she moves from an environment of ridicule or abuse to one of self-empowerment, awareness, and the ability to overcome any enemy. While Bella's physical transformation allows her this last element of a warrior-heroine's journey, her sense of self does not develop over time; rather, it is consistently rooted in her love and devotion for Edward and her desire to become a vampire, if only to become the defender she envisions. In this manner, Bella's characterization is read by many fans of the saga as actualized from the beginning—she knows what she wants, pursues that goal in spite of obstacles, and does not have a crisis of conscience along the way. Her ability in the end to maintain a loving, sexual relationship *and* act as a self-reliant, fearless agent, to be a devoted mother *and* community defender, endows Bella with a heroism desired by many young readers and feminists alike. Reading the *Twilight* saga in relation to its intertexts prompts a crucial conversation to be had between these groups, about what it is in our shared social reality that makes such "both/and" identities and resolutions the stuff of fantasy for so many.

NOTES

1. Adam Dawtrey, "Twilight gives new Brontë films wings," *Guardian.co.uk* (December 2, 2009), Web. Accessed April 12, 2010. np. The covers can be seen on the Harper Collins website, http://browseinside.harpercollins.com/index.aspx?isbn13=9780061962257.
2. Dawtrey.
3. Julia Kristeva, *Desire in Language: A Semiotic Approach to Literature and Art*, Thomas Gora, Alice Jardine and Leon S. Roudiez, trans., Leon S. Roudiez, ed. (New York: Columbia University Press, 1980), 66.
4. Stephenie Meyer, *Twilight* (New York: Little Brown and Company, 2005), 10.
5. Sandra M. Gilbert, "Plain Jane's Progress," *Signs* 2.4 (1977), 783.
6. Sandra M. Gilbert and Susan Gubar, "A Dialogue of Self and Soul: Plain Jane's Progress," in Patricia Ingham, ed., *The Brontës* (London: Pearson Education, 2003), 46–69.
7. The genre of teen fantasy fiction, with its wide array of heroine characterization, plot development, and representations of coming-of-age, can at this point be viewed as divisible into subgenres or subcategories. These subgenres are suggested by the patterns of these textual elements; for example, a novel featuring a fiercer, more warrior-like heroine from the beginning, such as Frewin Jones's *Warrior Princess* or Tamora Pierce's *Trickster's Choice* and *Trickster's Queen*, falls into a different theoretical subcategory than does the *Twilight* saga because of Bella's initial damsel-in-distress characterization as well as differences in the overall arc of the stories, in interactions with romantic interests, etc.
8. Tamar Heller, "*Jane Eyre*, Bertha, and the Female Gothic," in Diane Long Hoeveler and Beth Lau, eds., *Approaches to Teaching Charlotte Brontë's* Jane Eyre (New York: The Modern Language Association of America, 1993), 49.
9. See, for example, Karen Valby, "Stephenie Meyer: 12 of My 'Twilight' Inspirations," *EW.com: Entertainment Weekly* (September 29, 2009), Web. Accessed February 10, 2010. np.
10. Abigail E. Myers, "Edward Cullen and Bella Swan: Byronic and Feminist Heroes . . . Or Not," in Rebecca Housel and J. Jeremy Wisnewski, eds., *Twilight and Philosophy: Vampires, Vegetarians, and the Pursuit of Immortality* (Hoboken, NJ: John Wiley & Sons, 2009), 158–9.
11. Edward to Bella. Meyer, *Twilight*, 173.

12. Valby.
13. Deborah Lutz traces the development of the "dangerous lover" archetype from Regency dandy to Victorian Gothic villain/hero such as Rochester to the Byronic heroes of contemporary mass-market Gothic romances in *The Dangerous Lover: Gothic Villains, Byronism, and the Nineteenth-Century Seduction Narrative* (Columbus, OH: Ohio State University Press, 2006).
14. See, for example, Myers, 159–60.
15. Charlotte Brontë, *Jane Eyre, Norton Critical Edition*, 3rd ed. (New York: W. W. Norton & Company, 2001), 242. Jane describes Bertha as having "red eyes" and appearing like "the foul German spectre—the Vampyre"; Gilbert argues that Bertha functions as Jane's "dark double" (Gilbert, 796).
16. Meyer, *Twilight*, 447.
17. Stephenie Meyer, *Eclipse* (New York: Little Brown and Company, 2007), 395–6.
18. Estelle Freedman, *No Turning Back: The History of Feminism and the Future of Women* (New York: Ballantine Books, 2002), 282.
19. Meyer, *Eclipse*, 158.
20. Ibid, 163.
21. Gilbert, 788.
22. Ibid, 796.
23. Rebecca Housel, "The 'Real Danger': Fact Vs. Fiction for the Girl Audience," in Rebecca Housel and J. Jeremy Wisnewski, eds., *Twilight and Philosophy: Vampires, Vegetarians, and the Pursuit of Immortality* (Hoboken, NJ: John Wiley & Sons, 2009), 177–90.
24. Naomi Zack, "Bella Swan and Sarah Palin: All the Old Myths are *Not* True," in Rebecca Housel and J. Jeremy Wisnewski, eds., *Twilight and Philosophy: Vampires, Vegetarians, and the Pursuit of Immortality* (Hoboken, NJ: John Wiley & Sons, 2009), 128.
25. Rainer Emig asserts that the need to assess "the intertextual impact of a text like *Jane Eyre* is made evident by its well-known, publicly acknowledged, and even empirically confirmed status as one of the most important British novels of all times," especially for adolescent girls. See "Blasting Jane: *Jane Eyre* as an Intertext of Sarah Kane's *Blasted*," in Margarete Rubik and Elke Mettinger-Schartmann, eds., *A Breath of Fresh Eyre: Intertextual and Intermedial Reworkings of* Jane Eyre, (Amsterdam: Rodopi, 2007), 391–404.
26. Myers, 150–1; Brontë, 116.
27. Brontë, 226.
28. Bonnie Mann reads this gender reversal in Edward and Bella's relationship as part of a "feminist subtext" in the *Twilight* saga: "The most surprising thing about Bella's romance with Edward is not that Edward has to resist the urge to perforate her pulsing jugular vein, but that he, not she, puts the breaks on their erotic encounters. Knowing that any loss of control spells death for his beloved, Edward's restraint allows Bella to be the one consumed by desire." "Vampire Love: The Second Sex Negotiates the Twenty-First Century," in Rebecca Housel and J. Jeremy Wisnewski, eds., *Twilight and Philosophy: Vampires, Vegetarians, and the Pursuit of Immortality* (Hoboken, NJ: John Wiley & Sons, 2009), 140.
29. Brontë, 233.
30. Ibid, 266.
31. Ibid, 258 and 271.
32. Meyer, *Twilight*, 261–74.
33. Brontë, 271.
34. Ibid, 220–1.

35. Ibid, 229.
36. Ibid, 231.
37. Meyer, *Twilight*, 473–4; Stephenie Meyer, *New Moon* (New York: Little Brown and Company, 2006), 13.
38. Brontë, 218.
39. Meyer, *Twilight*, 318.
40. Meyer, *Eclipse*, 28.
41. Ibid, 223–4.
42. Ibid, 190.
43. Leah McClimans and J. Jeremy Wisnewski, "Undead Patriarchy and the Possibility of Love," in Rebecca Housel and J. Jeremy Wisnewski, eds., *Twilight and Philosophy: Vampires, Vegetarians, and the Pursuit of Immortality* (Hoboken, NJ: John Wiley & Sons, 2009), 171.
44. Myers, 159.
45. Bella refers to Emily as "the wolf girl" when they first meet in *New Moon*.
46. Meyer, *Twilight*, 4.
47. See, for example, Mann, 132–3.
48. Meyer, *Eclipse*, 176.
49. Mann, 141.
50. Meyer, *Eclipse*, 166.
51. Stephenie Meyer, *Breaking Dawn* (New York: Little Brown and Company, 2008), 524.
52. Brontë, 372.
53. Ibid, 379–80.
54. Meyer, *Breaking Dawn*, 520–21.
55. Brontë, 384.
56. Meyer, *Breaking Dawn*, 482.
57. Brontë, 372, and *Breaking Dawn*, 482.
58. The "Green World" is a literary concept defined by critic Northrop Frye in *The Anatomy of Criticism* (Princeton, NJ: Princeton University Press, 1957), 182–4. Frye asserts that in this space of transformation and discovery, typically in a forest, the demands of the real world are left behind and conflicts are resolved, enabling personal growth and a commitment to life and marriage.
59. Laura Miller examines gender dynamics in paranormal fiction, including novels by Laurell K. Hamilton, Patricia Briggs, and Charlaine Harris, in "Buffy fans: read this. The spirit of the vampire slayer lives on in the kickass young heroines of urban fantasy fiction," *Salon.com* (23 June 2009), Web. Accessed February 10, 2010. np.
60. Ibid.

Chapter 3

Serial Experiments in Popular Culture: The Resignification of Gothic Symbology in *Anita Blake Vampire Hunter* and the *Twilight* Series

Carole Veldman-Genz

Intrinsically polysemous in nature, the Gothic, throughout its many cultural incarnations, has remained one of those chameleon ideas, which, to all intents and purposes, must always be explained in order to acquire meaning. Gothic speaks to us through the ages in voices that are inherently evanescent, yet scriptable; it exceeds the laws of one single generic code and instead warrants easy absorption into a multitude of historical genres. "There is no point," then, as Victor Sage and Allan Lloyd Smith point out, "in thinking of the Gothic as 'pure'; it is an apparent genre-badge, which, the moment it is worn by a text, becomes an imperceptible catalyst, a transforming agent for other codes."[1] For the purpose of this chapter, I am keen to put forward an understanding of the Gothic as liminal discourse—that is, a discourse motivated by barriers, boundaries, and limitations. This conception is, of course, not entirely novel. Fred Botting has famously evaluated the Gothic in terms of its "fascination with transgression and the anxiety over cultural limits and boundaries."[2] Put simply, Gothic depends on the existence of boundaries, distinguishing the natural from the unnatural world, the Self from the Other; Gothic fear, in its turn, depends on the breach of boundaries or the threat of such a violation. The Gothic play of entrapment—being denied points of access and exit—and of excess—pushing beyond the limits of what we know and are—signifies a powerful discourse of ambivalence that resonates among a multitude of genres and media. This piece investigates intersections between the Gothic and several conspicuously successful pop culture series of the 1990s and the 2000s, particularly Laurell K. Hamilton's *Anita Blake Vampire Hunter* series (1993–) and Stephenie Meyer's *Twilight* saga (2005–2008). Generally speaking, I argue that these intersections forge links between contemporary social agendas, feminisms, and popular culture. I am particularly interested in the ways the texts overlap with understandings of postfeminism and third wave feminism,[3] and, more specifically, how they point to the contradictions and conflicts in current thought on sexuality, gender, and corporeality. The approach taken here is a character-based comparison of the series' neo-Gothic heroines and heroes, identifying key representations and generic affiliations and exploring how these relate to feminist debate and social concerns of the late twentieth and early twenty-first centuries. In brief, I will demonstrate that the narratives' distinctly Gothic imagery and characterizations enable the rallying of diverse sociopolitical and generic discourses, turning neo-Gothic heroes and heroines into loci of prolific, yet never straightforward, dialogue and negotiation.

In the last fifteen years, the diffusion of Gothic symbology across popular culture has given rise to many series of Gothic-inspired fads: hit TV shows like *Buffy, the Vampire Slayer*, and its spin-off *Angel*; the teenage vampire horror series *The Vampire Diaries* and HBO's *True Blood* (based on Charlaine Harris's *Sookie Stackhouse* novels); and literary developments such as Laurell K. Hamilton's best-selling adult fiction series *Anita Blake Vampire Hunter* and, more recently, Stephenie Meyer's phenomenally successful *Twilight* series (ostensibly for young adults). These popular texts swarm with established Gothic markers—vampires, werewolves, zombies, witches, and ghosts—while straddling different genres with ease. They blend Gothic tags with contributions from fantasy, hard-boiled detective fiction, romance, erotica, and young adult fiction. This technique of genre-blending presents us with an interesting set of questions: What happens to Gothic markers once they coalesce with young adult fiction, the action genre, or erotica? Do such encounters with the generic Other facilitate the articulation of other liminal discourses, such as third wave feminism or postfeminism? To what extent do these often contradictory experiments of mainstream culture dare us to go beyond the barriers of characterization and plot? And, finally, to what degree might these points of exit actually neutralize the pungency of the Gothic bite? I address these questions in the following two sections, first examining serial representations of neo-Gothic heroines, then moving on to investigate their male counterparts.

GOING BEYOND: THE MONSTROUS NEO-GOTHIC HEROINE

In this part, I discuss the *Anita Blake Vampire Hunter* series and the four-book *Twilight* series, as well as considering Joss Whedon's *Buffy, the Vampire Slayer* (1997–2003) and Charlaine Harris's *Sookie Stackhouse* (2001–). I focus on these series not because of the homogeneity of their plots and representations, but because they constitute a diverse and often conflicting mix of images and cultural gestures. This, of course, does not mean that there is no common ground between the narratives. All four, for one, feed on the same neo-Gothic imagery and, hence, there are many inescapable similarities—especially between vampire slayer Buffy Summers and vampire executioner Anita Blake. Both are a far cry from the Radcliffean heroine of sensibilities; that is, the stereotypically victimized and impressionable young maiden prevalent in Ann Radcliffe's late eighteenth-century female Gothic, a figure best known for her almost pathological immersion in all things fearful, her physiological sensibility, and her perpetual persecution by sinister Gothic villains. Although Anita's, Buffy's, and Sookie's femininity is equally pronounced as that of the classic Gothic heroine—all are short, pretty, and petite—it is deceptive according to mainstream standards in that it is not to be mistaken for passivity or weakness. "I'm no one's victim," tough-as-nails vampire hunter Anita Blake explains; "I'm a girl; get over it. I'm petite and I clean up well; get over that, too."[4] In Harris's *Sookie Stackhouse* series, a feisty Sookie displays similar self-assurance in her own empowerment; she may be a "sweet little éclair on the outside" but is a "pit bull on the inside."[5]

The arms-wielding super-girls Anita and Buffy for one fend for themselves in their ever more supernatural worlds, powered by an activist militancy and equipped with their flippant assertiveness and their own supernatural powers. In as much as these action heroines are visions of strong and independent women, their originating logic has an agenda that is clearly informed by feminism on some level.[6] In this vein of thought, Elyce Rae Helford argues that "we would not have female action-adventure heroes without a feminist [. . .] consciousness."[7] Television critics and feminist scholars alike have heralded Buffy as a "feminist activist,"[8] whose "spectacular agency—her (literally) fantastic facility for kicking ass—has come to function as feminist comfort food."[9] The same comments could be applied to US Marshal Anita Blake, who is a "bigger motherfucker" than any of the supernatural thugs she hunts down.[10] Hamilton positions Anita as a distinctly active and empowered heroine whose life choices and character development defy and reverse gender stereotypes. In Anita's words, "I'm not a prize to be won. I'm not the princess that needs rescuing from the dragon. I'm the prince and I kill my own monsters."[11] While their cultural politics are irrefutably laden with contradictions indicative of the many crosscurrents within contemporary feminist thought, *Anita Blake* and *Buffy* rescript the tale of women's victimization and vulnerability that has traditionally been inscribed on the Gothic female body. They replace it with stories of an empowered physicality, although this empowerment is often internally divisive and problematic and, as a consequence, has much in common with what Carol Siegel calls "third wave concepts of identity—such as the combination of toughness and femininity, self-assertion and voluptuous yielding."[12]

Third wave feminist, postfeminist, and popular feminist discourses have undoubtedly all left their varied marks on the series under discussion.[13] The figure of the action heroine, which dominates the plots of two of the four series, is a salient case in point, tying Gothic characterization to wider feminist contexts. To me, feminist interventions in *Anita Blake* and *Buffy* are acutely apparent in the texts' eschewal of gender categories, in particular the way their neo-Gothic heroines' gender exceeds the binary laws of the masculine/feminine logic. Battling on the "boundary between feminist transgression and patriarchal containment," these action heroines display "feminine" bodies along with typically "masculine" assertiveness.[14] The gender dynamics of the female action adventure are as much driven by the heroines' agency-informed empowerment than their potentially objectifying hyperfemininity. Their hybrid, hot-rather-than-hard bodies suggest the various ways in which the "shero" must be read as a cultural product with shifting and contradictorily invoked significations.[15] In other words, the female action hero imbues a nexus of converging, yet conflicting identifications; just as the differently prefixed feminisms that make up its configurations (post/popular/third wave etc.) lack fixed signifiers with an easily identifiable and demarcatable body of ideas. The action-adventure heroine is thus indicative of the many rifts existing between third wave and postfeminism, as well as their overlaps and continuities.[16]

Let me briefly put the above considerations into a wider sociocultural context. The cultural agendas at stake in *Anita Blake* and *Buffy* cushion any activist impulses on their heroines' part within an aesthetics of commodification—since Anita's and Buffy's sexy bodies remain subject to overt objectification—and a depoliticized language of neoliberal individualism. Much has been said about neoliberalism as a means of what Foucault terms "governmentality" (i.e., the policies through which citizens are being governed). I understand neoliberalism here as the construction of individuals through self-regulatory discourses based on choice and self-government, rather than political/economic obligation. This stance privileges the personal over the political and connects with notions of agency and empowerment, so as to produce the "injunction to render one's life knowable and meaningful through a narrative of free choice and autonomy—however constrained one might actually be."[17] With its ambivalent logic of obscured meanings, Gothic provides a particularly fitting back-drop for twenty-first-century feminisms' muddled politics of contradictions. In fact, to me, it seems entirely plausible that the liminality of Gothic should encourage the avowal of other "frontier discourses," such as third wave feminism or postfeminism. As Patricia Mann argues, these frontier discourses "bring us to the edge of what we know, and encourage[s] us to go beyond."[18] The series' heroines—Anita, Buffy, Sookie, and *Twilight*'s Bella Swan—all *go beyond*. They overstep the Gothic barrier that distinguishes natural humanity from supernatural monstrosity; however, they do so engaging different cultural discourses and with divergent generic outcomes.

Anita, Buffy, and Sookie have always trodden a fine line around this barrier: they have always been Other in their supernatural powers. Sookie Stackhouse, for example, has been created "straddling [the] wall" between human and supernatural.[19] Like Edward Cullen, Sookie is telepathic—part of her attraction to vampire Bill Compton is that she can*not* penetrate his mind. While Bill categorizes her powers as a "gift"[20] at the start of *Dead Until Dark* (2001), she is identified as "Crazy Sookie" by a bar patron,[21] an embarrassment to her father,[22] and someone who "just didn't fit into her [mother's] world."[23] In each of the series mentioned, the category "human" is ever more contested as their heroines increasingly immerse themselves in their supernatural worlds. Consequently, the ambiguity of their roles becomes more pronounced as the series progress. In the season 6 episode "Bargaining" (6101),[24] Buffy, not unlike a vampire, is resurrected. Drinking a vampire's blood turns Sookie into an "enhanced human"; it makes her feel "very strong, very alert, very quick-witted, and oddly enough [...] very pretty."[25] Anita, on the other hand, self-admittedly turns monstrous. In the *Vampire Hunter* series' ninth installment, *Obsidian Butterfly* (2000), she confesses, "I couldn't let the monsters win, not even if it meant becoming one of them."[26] Over the course of the by now nineteen-novel long *Vampire Hunter* series, Anita's hypersexualized body grows into a central site of assembly for all things supernatural, up to the point where it is almost impossible for her to "play human anymore."[27] Here, the female body becomes *über*-Gothic in that it hosts ever new supernatural abilities: Anita is a born necromancer with the power to raise and control the undead; a human servant to St. Louis's master vampire Jean-Claude; a member of a supernatural triumvirate together with Jean-Claude and werewolf king Richard Zeeman; a *panwere*, that is, a carrier of five types of lycanthropy virus; and a succubus feeding on the sexually charged *ardeur*, the intense supernatural craving for sexual energy and metaphysical powers that drives her from one sexual conquest to the next. Evading categorization, Anita's ever-growing supernatural portfolio carries immense interpretive potential; it challenges the fixity of human nature and instead draws attention to the fragility of human norms and the performative, contingent, relational character of identity. At the contested intersections of feminism and popular culture, there could not be a more suggestive discursive site, a more evocative embodiment of the conflicting convergences of modern-day feminisms and Gothic border-crossings than Anita Blake's made-up, internally divisive body.

But what of our fourth heroine, *Twilight*'s Bella Swan? Teenager Bella is certainly no action-adventure heroine, and intentionally so. *Twilight*'s author Stephenie Meyer once told a journalist that, "There are so many girls out there who do not know kung fu, and if a guy jumps in the alley they're not going to turn around with a round-house kick."[28] Where Anita and Buffy embody superhuman strength and assertiveness, Bella, at least in the first three installments, is distinctly human, and therefore weak; where Buffy and Anita are extraordinary, Bella is common and essentially featureless, "a vacant, flexible skin into which the reader can insert herself."[29] While the ass-kicking super-girls play up to readers' fantasies of empowerment (manufactured or otherwise), Bella's ordinariness constitutes her relatability. Meyer describes her character's appeal as follows: "I didn't realize the books would appeal to people so broadly. I think some of it's because Bella is an everygirl. She's not a hero, and she doesn't know the difference between Prada and whatever else is out there."[30] In its resolute dismissal of brand consciousness and female heroism, Meyer's phrasing makes clear that the *Twilight* series should be read against postfeminist fare such as *Sex and the City*, in which consumerism and lifestyle choices delineate individual achievements, as well as against female action adventures with their diverse feminist trappings. Here, then, is a purposefully distinct cultural script at play. No Manhattan singleton, desperate housewife, or hyperfeminized action heroine, Bella is an every-girl with no real distinguishing traits, apart, perhaps, from her crippling clumsiness. Not one for boosting her own morale, Bella describes herself variously as a "coward," an "idiot," and "extremely insignificant."[31] Her proneness to accidents places her in a constant line of danger and, since she cannot fend for herself, she is in desperate need of a protector. Enter teenage heartthrob and vampire Edward Cullen. If Bella were not already convinced of her own vulnerability, Edward does his best to reinforce that notion. "I'm not quite that delicate," she says, to which Edward replies, "Aren't you?"[32] He later reasserts: "[Y]ou are so soft, so fragile [...] You don't realize how incredibly *breakable* you are," and again reinforces the idea of her defenselessness when he states: "[K]eeping you safe is beginning to feel like a full-time occupation that requires my constant presence."[33]

Edward's rhetoric echoes the victim mythology of traditional female Gothic. Bella's portrayal in the series' first three installments *Twilight* (2005), *New Moon* (2006), and *Eclipse* (2007) recalls the professional victims of novels such as Ann Radcliffe's *The Mysteries of Udolpho* (1794) much more than the ass-kicking action heroines we saw earlier. In the series' final installment, *Breaking Dawn* (2008), Bella's best friend werewolf Jacob provides a fitting description of her anachronistic femininity: "[T]he girl was a classic martyr. She'd totally been born in the wrong century."[34] It is in these respects that the *Twilight* novels react against the complexities of post-feminist empowerment and third wave erotic liberalism. In its retrograde embrace of Bella as hapless "damsel in distress," the series refers to traditional narratives of female victimization and passivity[35]; it calls to mind what Diane Long Hoeveler terms the "professional femininities" of old Gothic and harks back to unambiguous gendered dynamics inspired (at least partly) by neoconservatism.[36] In line with their young adult marketing, Meyer's books advocate comfortingly traditionalist values of monogamy, chastity, and marriage. Bella and Edward's interspecies romance remains unconsummated until they enter wedded bliss in *Breaking Dawn*. For the duration of three books, Bella, along with the predominantly female readership, is skillfully kept in a state of prolonged sexual anticipation; the love scenes between her and Edward are highly suggestive and erotically charged, turning the reading experience into a taunting thrill, which should strike a note with adolescent readers whose potentially limited sexual experiences might not extend beyond those figured. As Glennis Byron observes, "these books exploit their appeal to the teenage audience with a combination of titillation and denial long familiar to those in the consumer society of the big tease."[37]

Meyer's espousal of sexual restraint and impulse control must, of course, be read in the context of her well-publicized upbringing in the Church of Jesus Christ of Latter-day Saints (LDS) and is, unwittingly or not, instilled with politically and religiously ripe overtones. Her treatment of teenage sexuality speaks of and to current subcurrents in the US cultural climate, silently referencing in-vogue Christian abstinence movements such as the Silver Ring Thing.[38] With this in mind, the words "Be safe"—Edward's constant advice to the perpetually accident-prone Bella—take on a different meaning.[39] Mormon housewife and mother of three, Meyer is clear about her position: "I grew up in a community where it was not the exception to be a good girl. It was sort of expected. And all of my friends were good girls too, and my boyfriends were good boys. Everybody was pretty nice. And that affects how I write my characters."[40]

Only marriage legitimizes Bella and Edward's engagement in sexual activity; yet, it does not remove the intrinsic dangers of interspecies intercourse. The couple's first sexual encounters during their honeymoon on Isle Esme leave Bella covered in bruises and result in an immediate and troubled pregnancy during which her semi-vampiric love child threatens to consume her from the inside out. However much Bella insists that she enjoys her first sexual ventures, the evident implication at this stage must be that sex can be harmful and inevitably destructive.[41] Regardless of Bella's life-threatening condition during her accelerated pregnancy, *Breaking Dawn* espouses a manifestly pro-life message, attested by Bella's rejection of abortion and willingness to self-sacrifice. Conforming to Meyer's LDS background—the church's official website calls abortion a "war on the defenseless and the voiceless. It is a war on the unborn"[42]—Bella's refusal to abort is couched in religious terms. She firmly believes that "this is all going somewhere good, hard to see as it is now. I guess you could call it *faith*."[43]

Sex only becomes entirely safe for Bella once she crosses the Gothic barrier dividing human insipidity from the excess of vampiric perfection. Bland and ordinary, humanity is always found wanting in the *Twilight* series. Bella's victimhood is tied inextricably to her human status and stands in stark contrast to the near-indestructible flawlessness of her werewolf and vampire friends. Only as a vampire does Bella find distinction; only then does she turn into a super-girl, protecting (as in *Breaking Dawn*) her new vampire family from the avenging coven of the Volturi. "It was like I had been born to be a vampire," she explains. "I had found my true place in the world, the place I fit, the place I shined."[44] Bella's rite of passage from human to vampire is a transition from ordinariness to extraordinariness and, in this, clearly suggestive of Meyer's idealization of vampirism as a higher state of being. The Cullen family members are angelic rather than demonic. Bella's vampiric conversion is accordingly not the traditional fall from grace, as in classic vampire lore, but an ascent to a near-paradisiacal condition—befitting rather than challenging Christian beliefs of the afterlife. At the same time, Bella's transmutation also invites interpretation derived from feminist dialectics, in particular Naomi Wolf's designations of "victim feminism" and "power feminism."[45] The transformation from victim to super-girl can thus be interpreted as a switch of feminist allegiances, transcending the realm of victim feminism—characterized by a woman's sexual purity and "identity of powerlessness"[46]—to emerge with power feminism's attributes, "unapologetically sexual" and "self-assertive."[47] Once the conversion is complete, gone are the mortal threats that came with sexual engagement or Edward's self-flagellating recriminations for putting Bella's human life on the line. Vampire Bella can "really appreciate [Edward] now," as there is "[n]o caution, no restraint. No fear—especially not that. We could love *together*—both active participants now. Finally equals."[48]

With the species switch over and done with, one can assume that Bella and Edward's future love life will be blissful and trouble-free—after all, *Breaking Dawn*'s last chapter is reassuringly entitled "The Happily Ever After."[49] Nonetheless, it is fair to say that Meyer's engagement with sex and teenage sexuality is by no means unproblematic, candid, or impartial. Sex, for one, can never be afforded direct representation in Meyer's series; it remains purely suggestive and distinctly off-screen at all times; nor is it freed from the heterosexual reproductive imperative preached by most Western religions, as the newlyweds, against all odds, fulfill their duty to "be fruitful and multiply." *Twilight*'s overall conservative sexual dynamics—promoting consecutive stages of restraint, marriage, and reproduction—deviate from the more tolerant treatment of sexual activity in Harris's *Sookie Stackhouse*. A "poster girl for interspecies tolerance," Sookie is strictly monogamous, yet takes great pleasure in exploring her own sexuality, first with vampire Bill and then weretiger Quinn and vampire Eric.[50] Once deflowered, Sookie can only marvel at the sexual gratification she experiences with vampire Bill, as sex "with him [is] absolutely great. I had never dreamed it would be that wonderful."[51] Meyer's shying away from the subject of sex, however, clashes most markedly with the libertine and unfettered erotic expression advocated in Laurell K. Hamilton's *Anita Blake.*

Hamilton describes her series as "overtly sexual [...] sometimes violently sexy," her writer's motto being "If it can bleed me, eat me, or fuck me, I want to write about it."[52] Heroine Anita Blake must act on her own desires and feed her *ardeur* to avert serious repercussions. More than sexual gratification is at stake as human servant Anita has inherited her master Jean-Claude's need to feed through sex and love. If she does not "feed" regularly, she, along with all her supernatural dependants, will die. Each novel puts Anita in a situation that requires sex with one or more of her mostly supernatural lovers to keep her charges and herself safe. Early in the series, Anita might still dream of white picket fences and wedded bliss; her progression through the books, however, suggests that only "by overcoming her fear of her own desires she can emerge a true heroine, powerful enough to right wrongs done to the weak and shield the vulnerable from exploitation."[53] Anita simultaneously changes from someone who in Book 1, *Guilty Pleasures,* quips, "I don't date vampires; I kill them,"[54] to someone who recognizes the common blend of light and dark in all creatures—humans *and* supernaturals. As she explains in the series' sixteenth install-ment, *Blood Noir* (2008), "Sometimes it's not the light in a person that you fall in love with, but the dark."[55]

Driven from conquest to conquest, Anita is as much sexual predator as victim of her supernaturally enhanced sex drive, a "female Casanova" collecting boyfriends, lovers, and one-night stands in her stride.[56] Her ever-growing harem includes, among others, master vampire Jean-Claude, werewolf king Richard, wereleopards Micah and Nathaniel, werelion Haven, and werewolf stripper Jason. Some of her lovers are bisexual (although, interestingly, Anita rarely crosses that particular barrier herself), most of them have supernatural abilities and all of them enjoy Anita's need for recre-ational self-gratification. Haven, for instance, praises Anita's sexual prowess, stating that sex "is not your hobby, Anita, it's your passion. You like sex, really like sex, more than any woman I've ever been with."[57] There are insistent analogies here to classic vampire fare such as Bram Stoker's *Dracula* (1897). Hamilton's is a gender-reversed retelling of the tale of the omnisexual vamp seducing a parade of lovers. Yet in this case, the seductions are not necessarily those into exploitative relationships, as in traditional vampire stories; instead, men trade stereotypically masculine aggrandize-ment for feminine ego effacement. The "Brides of Anita"—a wordplay on the 1960 British Hammer horror movie *The Brides of Dracula*—have no major say in how this heroine lives her life: Anita "date[s] like a guy"[58] and needs "men who [are] okay with being the power behind the throne, not the ass on it."[59] Hamilton's books run the gamut of marginalized sex acts. Anita freely experiments with unorthodox sexual practices and erotic constellations, telling us, for example, that "bondage and submis-sion worked just dandy for me."[60] Not to be restricted to the normalcy of monogamy, her domestic arrangement of choice in *Blood Noir* is a ménage à trois. To put her preference in her own words: "there was just something about being pressed between two men [...] that simply did it for me."[61]

Lovers of such semipornographic fare will find their share in Hamilton's explicit novels. The series offers an increasingly elaborate proliferation of erotic structures and sexual identities. In *Anita Blake*, Gothic border-crossings go hand in hand with the articulation of the boundary-pushing discourse of female erotica. In contrast to the *Twilight* saga, intercourse is divorced from reproductive essentialism. As Anita states in *Bullet* (2010), "I'm a US Marshal, a legal vampire executioner, and I raise the dead for a living. None of these jobs would work with a baby."[62] In Hamilton's series, sex becomes a "reflexive project of self-definition."[63] The construction of an active and self-expressive female sexuality articulates a "sexual subjectification" that takes all pleasure—even marginalized or conflicting pleasure—seriously.[64] While the artistic value of this exertion is rightly questionable, the ramifications for cultural politics and current feminist thought should not be underestimated. To my mind, Hamilton's books offer particularly fertile ground for feminist investigation as the erotic discourse at stake requires its female subject to be fully constituted. Anita does not dread the monstrous Other but beds him with a gusto and bodily awareness that speak of contemporary conceptualizations of women's sexuality and to third wave feminist ideas of erotic liberalism and self-government.[65] Hers is a typically third wave feminist "quest for sexual satisfaction" in which "no sex toy" shall be left "unturned and no sexual avenue unexplored."[66] Not "a girl-girl" but "just a woman," Anita does not have "an agenda beyond the pleasure."[67] Her "girl culture" remains distinctly untainted by the micropolitics of postfeminist advancement, in which women "married for money and politics and potential alimony."[68] The series' emphatic prioritization of female sexual pleasure thus resonates with the third wave feminist ethic of acceptance, which foregrounds "pleasure over the *politics* of pleasure."[69] Put into a wider cultural context, the books' unabashed eroticism aligns with the Western cultural phenomenon of sexualization that has been widely diagnosed as the mainstreaming of pornography, pornification, or porno chic.[70] In this respect, *Anita Blake* takes its rightful place amongst the "*pornosphere*," promoting a "democratization of desire" and the "emergence of a more diverse and pluralistic sexual culture than has traditionally been accommodated within patriarchal capitalism."[71] Or put more simply in Anita's words, "I pushed the jealousy away. It wasn't who we were. There was enough love, enough sex, enough for everyone. When there's enough, you don't have to be jealous of anyone."[72]

"I DON'T *WANT* TO BE A MONSTER"[73]: THE HEROIC NEO-GOTHIC MONSTER

As we have seen in the previous section, Anita and Bella, and other pop culture icons like Buffy and Sookie, all go beyond. And they never do more so than when they invite the monsters into their beds. Whereas the character development of the neo-Gothic heroines typically progresses from "human" to "monstrous," their monstrous male counterparts inversely cross over into the "human" category. Traditionally, Gothic boundaries have been asserted through the discourse of monstrosity and their breach is presumed to evoke Gothic horror. In the series discussed here, however, absolute distinctions and impermeable demarcations between "human" and "monster" are increasingly eroded. Categorical boundaries prove invariably leaky rather than immutable. Their integrity is consistently flouted as the categories "human" and "monster" are persistently interwoven. Boundaries are, thus, breached from all sides. This results in storyworlds where the limitations of humanity and monstrosity are ever more malleable; it produces generic encodings that are lacking in the Gothic horror induced by boundary violations; and it elicits characterizations that proliferate in hybrids: heroines whose human exclusivity is diminished by their assembly of monstrous attributes and heroes whose monstrosity becomes ever more acceptable, if not desirable.

The serial plots on offer deal in more and more immersive worlds; that is, worlds in which monstrosity is, albeit reluctantly, embraced and shared by all. In *Anita Blake's* gritty setting of St. Louis, for instance, one only has to "scratch them deep enough" to find out that "vampires [are] just people."[74] Here, species boundaries are irreversibly blurred as the monstrous and monstrosity are written into the codes of the mainstream—making this a locale of Urban Fantasy, rather than Gothic. Ruled by the same set of laws as the heroine, Hamilton's supernaturals blend with humanity enough to function as recognized members of society; enough to interact with humans on a social and economic level; enough to pay taxes. These monsters are "legal citizens [...] They have the right to be loved just like everyone else."[75] The same is true of the United States represented in the *Sookie Stackhouse* novels: vampires have "c[o]me out of the coffin" and are "the newest [...] legally recognized" minority group.[76] Although they are ostracized by most of the human community, Sookie is thrilled when one enters the local bar in which she waitresses to purchase a bottle of synthetic blood. Pleading for a differentiated approach to the newly legalized supernaturals, she believes that vampires "are just as different among themselves as humans are."[77] Vampire Bill seems a safe enough romantic option for her as he displays distinctly ordinary habits and craves reassuringly human comforts: he shops at Dillard's, wants to "live mainstream," yearns for a "home," and seems as "normal as the guy next door."[78] In the *Twilight* saga and *Buffy*, the conventionalization and tolerance toward the monstrous might not be quite as expansive; yet, here too, the monsters deserve to be loved. In all of these series, the traditional Gothic threat of male predation is diffused to such a degree that the monster—the vampires and werewolves populating these plots—becomes a feasible, if not entirely domesticated, romantic lead. Gothic markers converge in the way that the monster often becomes indistinguishable from the hero of old Gothic. And while the vampire's bite has conventionally been read as forced sexual intercourse, the exchange of bodily fluids between *these* heroes and heroines (haematological and other) is entirely consensual. No bloodsucking fiends of old Gothic, Sookie's devoted admirer Bill, Buffy's vampire lovers Angel and Spike, Bella's high-school sweetheart Edward and Anita's boyfriend Jean-Claude are in line with the troubled outsiders that Anne Rice's *Vampire Chronicles* (1976–2002) have made so popular. They are examples of what Jules Zanger calls the "new" vampire, ruled by complex emotions, endowed with a sense of morality and capable of evoking sympathy.[79]

The series' vampiric lovers are worthy of compassion, capable of feeling "human" emotions such as love and, importantly, they ooze sex appeal. Part tortured souls, part male pinups, these monsters are clearly constituted as objects of desire and the heroines' sexual attraction to them is entirely expected. Here, the monstrous male body is sexualized in the same ways that the female body has been objectified for centuries. This is particularly apparent in Hamilton's explicit novels. Flaunting their sexualized allure, most of Anita's supernatural lovers (who, intriguingly, all seem to work or have worked as strippers) are "walking wet dream[s]."[80] Much of the series' textual and visual vocabulary relies on the representational praxes of erotica; these remain, however, mainly reserved for the depiction of masculine sexiness. The following description of master vampire Jean-Claude is typical: "Jean-Claude all black curls and that beautiful face. [...] he was all male no matter how pretty he looked. It helped that he was naked on top of the sheets. Nude, there was no mistaking him for anything but oh so male."[81] Hamilton's portrayal of the monstrous male body implies an active and sexualizing female gaze that opens up positions of female authority and sets up female desire as fully endorsed and legitimized. Predictably, Meyer's young adult series is a lot tamer as far as the overt sexualization of its vampire lover is concerned; yet, Bella's desiring gaze is just as active and authoritative as Anita's. In her eyes, Edward has "the most beautiful soul, more beautiful than his brilliant mind or his incomparable face or his glorious body."[82]

Bella's descriptions of Edward throughout the four books reverberate with a groupie-alike adoration similar to that voiced by millions of teenage readers or the hordes of screaming young girls at the *Twilight* movie premieres.[83] The perfect teenager fantasy, Edward Cullen is clearly not the stuff of Gothic nightmares, but "more angel than man."[84] Bella spends the better part of every novel groveling before his magnificence: "How well I knew that I wasn't good enough for him" is a typical musing on her part.[85] Meyer's characterization of Edward diverges from the traditional image of the vampire as callous seducer and replaces it with the infinitely more docile figure of the high-school sweetheart. In this, it is symptomatic of the ways in which the series moves away from the Gothic and toward a more domesticated and "safer" generic alternative. In *Breaking Dawn*, Bella provides an apt account of this generic conversion: "Edward had always thought that he belonged to the world of horror stories. Of course, I'd known he was dead wrong. It was obvious that he belonged *here*. In a fairy tale."[86] Call it fairy tale or call it romance, Meyer's series, in essence and most particulars, resurrects the age-old boy-meets-girl scenario. Despite their outward Gothic trappings, the four books replay the classically romantic quest for love, which is delayed by a series of obstacles that the lovers' desire must overcome. As Laura Miller puts it, "Some imaginary worlds multiply, spinning themselves out into ever more elaborate constructs. *Twilight* retracts; it finds its voluptuousness in the hypnotic reduction of its attention to a single point: the experience of being loved by Edward."[87]

Stephenie Meyer sanitizes the vampire genre to such a degree that her monsters become idealized Others.[88] The Cullens are generic crossovers who set out to "conquer the boundaries of a destiny that none of us wanted. To try to retain whatever essential humanity we can."[89] This recovery mission has let them beyond the generic boundaries of the Gothic, beyond subhuman monstrosity, even beyond humanity. *Twilight*'s supernaturals are a cut above humans. Myth busters in their own right, they safely walk into sunlight (despite their giveaway, reflective skin); they do not sleep in coffins (in fact, they do not sleep at all); and, unlike the lone outsiders of traditional vampire tales, they are bound by strong and functional family bonds. Their beauty, strength, and morality—after all, the benevolent, baseball-playing Cullens are "vegetarian" vampires—place them in the league of superheroes. Their abstinence from human blood is a striking evocation of the rational mind ruling over instinctual drives. In keeping with her religious background, Meyer tells us that such superhuman self-discipline and moderation will elevate its practitioners to angelic heights, turning Gothic monsters into romantic heroes.

CONCLUSION

I have argued that the *Twilight* saga, the *Anita Blake Vampire Hunter* novels, and numerous other popular vampire series displace Gothic boundaries distinguishing the natural from the unnatural, the human from the monster. They do so by relocating Gothic monstrosity at the heart of their characterizations and by absorbing the monster into the laws of their imaginary worlds. The monstrous becomes a shared quality, an integral part of their heroes' and heroines' makeup. The world-building strategies in these narratives create textual hybrids that draw on a multitude of generic and cultural discourses. It would be a mistake to underestimate too quickly the reinvigorating potential of these practices or to collapse the complexities embedded in their cultural/feminist politics—even when such points of exit might actually engender the disablement of Gothic markers.

NOTES

1. Victor Sage and Allan Lloyd Smith, *Modern Gothic: A Reader* (Manchester: Manchester University Press, 1997. Print), 2.
2. Fred Botting, *Gothic* (London: Routledge, 2005. Print), 1.
3. As ever with emerging theories and practices, third wave feminism is a contested and shifting signifier. I am particularly interested in the definition Leslie Heywood and Jennifer Drake provide in *Third Wave Agenda*: "Third wave feminists often take cultural production and sexual politics as key sites of struggle, seeking to use desire and pleasure as well as anger to fuel struggles for justice" (4). See, Leslie Heywood and Jennifer Drake, eds., *Third Wave Agenda: Being Feminist, Doing Feminism* (Minneapolis: University of Minnesota Press, 1997. Print).
4. Laurell K. Hamilton, *Skin Trade: An Anita Blake, Vampire Hunter Novel* (London: Headline Publishing, 2009. Print), 187 and 13.
5. Charlaine Harris, *Living Dead in Dallas* (New York: Ace Books, 2002. Print), 18.
6. There are a fair number of critics discussing the postfeminist, third wave feminist or popular feminist cultural politics embedded in *Buffy* and the *Anita Blake* series. See for example: Carol Siegel, "Female Heterosexual Sadism: The Final Feminist Taboo in *Buffy, The Vampire Slayer* and the *Anita Blake Vampire Hunter* Series," *Third Wave Feminism and Television Jane Puts it in a Box*. Ed. Merri Lisa Johnson (London: I.B. Tauris & Co, 2007. Print), 56–90; Claire Knowles, "Sensibility Gone Mad: Or, Drusilla, Buffy and the (D)evolution of the Heroine of Sensibility," *Postfeminist Gothic Critical Interventions in Contemporary Culture*. Eds. Benjamin A. Brabon and Stéphanie Genz (Basingstoke: Palgrave MacMillan, 2007. Print), 140–153; Patricia Pender, "'Kicking Ass is Comfort Food' Buffy as Third Wave Feminist Icon," *Third Wave Feminism: A Critical Exploration*. Eds. Stacy Gillis, Gillian Howie, and Rebecca Munford (New York: Palgrave MacMillan, 2007. Print), 224–236.
7. Elyce Rae Helford, "Postfeminism and the Female Action-Adventure Hero: Positioning Tank Girl," *Future Females, the Next Generation: New Voices and Velocities in Feminist*

Science Fiction. Eds. Marleen S. Barr and Lanham Boulder (New York: Oxford: Rowman & Littlefield, 2000. Print), 293.

8. Irene Karras, "The Third Wave's Final Girl: Buffy the Vampire Slayer," *Thirdspace* 1.2. (2002). Web. http://www.thirdspace.ca/articles/karras.htm. Accessed May 30, 2010. np.

9. Pender, 227.

10. Laurell K. Hamilton, *Flirt: An Anita Blake, Vampire Hunter Novel* (London: Headline Publishing, 2010. Print), 149.

11. Laurell K. Hamilton, *Bullet An Anita Blake, Vampire Hunter Novel* (London: Headline, 2010. Print), 176.

12. Siegel, 58.

13. In "'Kicking Ass Is Comfort Food' Buffy as Third Wave Feminist Icon," Patricia Pender discusses *Buffy* as a "quintessentially third wave cultural production" (234); Carol Siegel discusses the *Anita Blake* series "as a sort of slash response to Buffy that takes popular feminism further into the areas of unrestricted female sexual expression that the third wave has begun to explore" (67). See, Patricia Pender, "'Kicking Ass is Comfort Food' Buffy as Third Wave Feminist Icon," *Third Wave Feminism: A Critical Exploration.* Eds. Stacy Gillis, Gillian Howie, and Rebecca Munford (New York: Palgrave MacMillan, 2007. Print); Carol Siegel, "Female Heterosexual Sadism: The Final Feminist Taboo in *Buffy, The Vampire Slayer* and the *Anita Blake Vampire Hunter* Series," *Third Wave Feminism and Television Jane Puts it in a Box.* Ed. Merri Lisa Johnson (London: I.B. Tauris & Co, 2007. Print).

14. Stéphanie Genz, *Postfemininities in Popular Culture* (Basingstoke: Palgrave MacMillan, 2009. Print), 159.

15. Sidney Eve Matrix, "Badgirls, Cyberchicks, and Postfeminists in US Pop Culture," Web. http://www.tc.umn.edu/~mstri001/wost3306/Description.htm. Accessed June 12, 2006. np.

16. Sarah Banet-Weiser insists that postfeminism is a "different political dynamic than third wave feminism" (206), while for Yvonne Tasker and Diane Negra, the "popular idiom" of postfeminism is set in contrast to the "more scholarly category" and "self-identification" of third wave feminism (19). In contrast, Stacy Gillis, Gillian Howie, and Rebecca Munford insist that "definitions of and assumptions about both third-wave and post-feminism often overlap in a variety of ways, highlighting a number of similarities and continuities" (xxvii). For a review of this critical debate, see also, Stéphanie Genz and Benjamin A. Brabon, *Postfeminism Cultural Texts and Theories* (Edinburgh: Edinburgh UP, 2009. Print), 156–62. See, Sarah Banet-Weiser, "What's Your Flava? Race and Postfeminism in Media Culture," *Interrogating Postfeminism: Gender and the Politics of Popular Culture.* Eds. Yvonne Tasker and Diane Negra (London: Duke University Press, 2007. Print), 201–226; Yvonne Tasker and Diane Negra, introduction to *Interrogating Postfeminism: Gender and the Politics of Popular Culture.* Eds. Yvonne Tasker and Diane Negra (London: Duke University Press, 2007. Print), 1–25; Gillis Stacy, Howie Gillian, and Munford Rebecca, introduction to *Third Wave Feminism A Critical Exploration Expanded Second Edition.* Eds. Stacy Gillis, Gillian Howie, and Rebecca Munford (Basingstoke, Hampshire: Palgrave MacMillan, 2007. Print), xxi–xxxiv.

17. Rosalind Gill, *Gender and the Media* (Cambridge: Polity Press, 2007. Print), 260.

18. Patricia S. Mann, *Micro-Politics: Agency in a Postfeminist Era* (Minneapolis: University of Minnesota Press, 1994. Print), 208.

19. Charlaine Harris, *Dead Until Dark* (London: Gollancz, 2009 (2001). Print), 296.

20. Harris, *Dead Until Dark*, 59.

21. Harris, *Dead Until Dark*, 49.

22. Harris, *Dead Until Dark*, 58.

23. Ibid.

24. The episode numbering system indicates season and overall episode number. Thus, 6101 means sixth season, episode 101.

25. Harris, *Dead Until Dark*, 236; 221. Sookie discovers further supernatural traits as the series progresses as she is not only telepathic but also part fairy.

26. Laurell K. Hamilton, *Obsidian Butterfly* (New York: Ace Books, 2000. Print), 251.

27. Hamilton, *Skin Trade*, 185.

28. Meyer quoted in Radish. See Christina Radish, "Twilight's Author and Director Talk About Bringing The Film To Life," *MEDIA BLVD Magazine* (Sept. 17, 2008), Web. http://www.mediablvd.com/magazine/the_news/celebrity/twilight%27s_author_and_director_talk_about_bringing_the_film_to_life_200809171287.html. Accessed November 4, 2009. np.

29. Laura Miller, "Touched by a Vampire Preteen girls—and their grown-up moms—are sinking their teeth into Stephenie Meyer's gothic "Twilight" books by the millions. Move over, J.K. Rowling," Web. http://www.salon.com/books/review/2008/07/30/Twilight/index.html. Accessed February 12, 2009. np.

30. Meyer quoted in Kirschling. See, Gregory Kirschling, "Stephenie Meyer's 'Twilight' Zone," Web. http://www.ew.com/ew/article/0,,20049578,00.html. Accessed December 23, 2009. 1.

31. Stephenie Meyer, *Twilight* (London: Atom, 2005 (2009). Print), 35; 38; 285.

32. Meyer, *Twilight*, 173.

33. Meyer, *Twilight*, 271; 185.

34. Stephenie Meyer, *Breaking Dawn* (London: Atom, 2008. Print), 187.

35. Meyer, *Twilight*, 46.

36. Diane Long Hoeveler, *Gothic Feminism: the Professionalisation of Gender from Charlotte Smith to the Brontës* (Liverpool: Liverpool University Press, 1998. Print), xiii.

37. Glennis Byron, " 'As one dead': Romeo and Juliet in the 'Twilight' Zone," *Gothic Shakespeares*. Eds. John Drakakis and Dale Townshend (New York: Routledge, 2008. Print), 176.

38. The Silver Ring Thing is a para-church youth ministry that promotes the message of abstinence until marriage. The movement is directed at teenagers and has gained a growing following in the US. See http://www.silverringthing.com/.

39. Byron, 181.

40. Meyer quoted in Kirschling, 1.

41. There are distinct similarities between the treatments of teenage sexuality in the *Twilight* saga and *Buffy*. For Buffy, sex leads to nothing but trouble. She cannot engage in sexual activity without self-disgust or regret. Her list of lovers includes the notably named vampires Angel and Spike, the mortal demon fighter Riley, and the college student Parker, with whom she experiences a humiliating one-night stand. When she loses her virginity to Angel in the Season 2 episode "Surprise" (2025), her vampiric lover, by the terms of a gypsy curse, reverts to being a soulless monster. As Rhonda Wilcox says, "a young woman's worst fear is realized when, after they sleep together, her partner's behavior is monstrous" (112). See: Rhonda Wilcox, *Why Buffy Matters: The Art of Buffy the Vampire Slayer* (London: I.B. Tauris & Co, 2005. Print), 112.

42. See, https://www.itsaboutlove.org/ial/ct/eng/site/pregnant/what-are-my-options/abortion/the-lds-perspective/.

43. Meyer, *Breaking Dawn*, 190.

44. Meyer, *Breaking Dawn,* 524.

45. In *Fire with Fire*, Naomi Wolf distinguishes two different feminist traditions: power feminism and victim feminism. While victim feminism is "severe, morally superior and self-denying," power feminism is "free-thinking, pleasure-loving and self-assertive" (180). Victim feminism casts women as "sexually pure" and describes the ways in which women seek "power through an identity of powerlessness. This feminism takes our reflexes of powerlessness and transposes them into a mirror-image set of 'feminist' conventions" (147). In opposition, power feminism sees women as "sexual, individual, no better or worse than their male counterparts" (xvii). In its entirety, Wolf's argument is too divisive and complex to provide an all-explanatory interpretative framework; in fact, her emphasis on the political dimension of consumerism and her contention that "good pleasures make good politics" cannot be reconciled with Meyer's series (149). See, Naomi Wolf, *Fire with Fire: The New Female Power and How It Will Change the 21st Century* (London: Vintage, 1994. Print).
46. Wolf, 147.
47. Wolf, 149; 147.
48. Meyer, *Breaking Dawn*, 482.
49. Meyer, *Breaking Dawn*, 742.
50. Charlaine Harris, *Definitely Dead* (New York: Ace Books, 2006. Print), 128.
51. Harris, *Dead Until Dark*, 181.
52. Hamilton, *Flirt*, 163; 171.
53. Siegel, 85.
54. Laurell K. Hamilton, *Guilty Pleasures. Anita Blake, Vampire Hunter* (New York: Berkley Books, 1993. Print), 355.
55. Laurell K. Hamilton, *Blood Noir An Anita Blake, Vampire Hunter Novel* (London: Orbit, 2008. Print), 296.
56. Hamilton, *Flirt*, 3.
57. Hamilton, *Bullet*, 175.
58. Ibid.
59. Hamilton, *Flirt*, 152; 126.
60. Hamilton, *Blood Noir*, 17.
61. Hamilton, *Blood Noir*, 19.
62. Hamilton, *Bullet*, 372.
63. Simon Hardy, "Feminist Iconoclasm and the Problem of Eroticism," *Sexualities* 3 (1) (2000): 77–96. Hardy, 87.
64. Rosalind Gill, "From Sexual Objectification to Sexual Subjectification: The Resexualisation of Women's Bodies in the Media," *Feminist Media Studies* 3.1 (2003): 100–106. Gill, 2003, 100.
65. The pleasure-orientated, sex-radical attitudes of third wavers are discussed for example in Astrid Henry's "Taking Feminism to Bed: The Third Wave Does the Sex Wars". See, Astrid Henry, *Not My Mother's Sister: Generational Conflict and Third-Wave Feminism* (Bloomington: Indiana University Press, 2004. Print), 88–114.
66. Debbie Stoller, "Sex and the Thinking Girl," *The BUST Guide to the New Girl Order*. Eds. Marcelle Karp and Debbie Stoller (London: Penguin, 1999. Print), 84.
67. Hamilton, *Blood Noir*, 153; 139.
68. Hamilton, *Blood Noir*, 153.
69. Melanie Waters, "Sexing It Up? Women, Pornography and Third Wave Feminism," *Third Wave Feminism A Critical Exploration* (expanded second edition). Eds. Stacy Gillis, Gillian Howie, and Rebecca Munford (Basingstoke, Hampshire: Palgrave MacMillan, 2007. Print), 258.

70. For discussions of pornography and porno chic, see McNair, 1996 and McNair, 2002; on pornification, see Paul, 2005. As I have discussed elsewhere, the cultural phenomenon of sexualization materializes in the woman-friendly erotica produced by British publishing house Black Lace and romantica e-publisher Ellora's Cave. Blending *ars erotica* and romance, romantica combines a romance-driven plot with plentiful and graphic sexual scenes, sexually explicit language, and erotic constellations that may go beyond coupledom. Both publishing houses describe their venture in semifeminist terms. The Ellora's Cave website proclaims that the premise of romantica is that "women's sexual experiences are legitimate, positive, and beautiful." The Black Lace website similarly prides itself, announcing, "We never underestimate female sexuality." See, http://www.ellorascave.com/whatisromantica.asp; http://www.blacklace-books.co.uk; Carole Genz,"The More the Merrier: Transformations of the Love Triangle across the Romance," *New Approaches to Popular Romance Fiction*, Eds. Eric Selinger and Sarah Frantz (Jefferson, NC: McFarland, forthcoming); P. Paul, *Pornified: How Pornography is Damaging Our Lives, Our Relationships, and Our Families* (New York: Owl Books, 2005. Print); Brian McNair, *Mediated Sex: Pornography and the Postmodern Culture* (London: Arnold, 1996. Print); Brian McNair, *Striptease Culture: Sex, Media and the Democratisation of Desire* (London: Routledge, 2002. Print).
71. McNair, *Striptease Culture*, 11; 12.
72. Hamilton, *Bullet*, 318.
73. Meyer, *Twilight*, 163.
74. Hamilton, *Bullet*, 341.
75. Hamilton, *Skin Trade*, 84.
76. Harris, *Dead Until Dark*, 1.
77. Harris, *Dead Until Dark*, 152.
78. Harris, *Dead Until Dark*, 52; 120; 106; 66.
79. Jules Zanger, "Metaphor into Metonymy: The Vampire Next Door," *Blood Read: The Vampire as Metaphor in Contemporary Culture*. Eds. Joan Gordon and Veronica Hollinger (Philadelphia: University of Pennsylvania Press, 1997. Print), 19.
80. Hamilton, *Blood Noir*, 274.
81. Hamilton, *Skin Trade*, 31.
82. Meyer, *Breaking Dawn*, 24.
83. Glennis Byron provides telling examples of the adoring reader comments in discussion forums on the *Twilight* phenomenon: "omg omg omg i loooooooooooove Edward"; "so sad how guys arent realy like that . . . i love Edward!!!!!!"; "OMG i abslouty LOVE edward cullen! Im OBBSESSED w/that book & new moon!"; "holy crap lve that book i wanna marry edward!!! Lol he is my love.." (quoted in Byron, 168). See, Glennis Byron, "'As one dead': *Romeo and Juliet* in the 'Twilight' Zone," *Gothic Shakespeares*. Eds. John Drakakis and Dale Townshend (New York: Routledge, 2008. Print), 167–85.
84. Meyer, *Breaking Dawn*, 23.
85. Miller, para.10.
86. Meyer, *Breaking Dawn*, 479.
87. Miller, para. 10.
88. Of course, this statement mainly refers to the Cullens, as Meyer's world-building offers a differentiated approach to vampires and allows for both good and bad vampires.
89. Meyer, *Twilight*, 268.

CHAPTER 4

TWILIGHT, TRANSLATED

KIM ALLEN GLEED

TRANSLATION, BROADLY DEFINED, is the act of transforming the appearance of
something. Certainly, when screenwriter Melissa Rosenberg and director Catherine
Hardwicke adapted Stephenie Meyer's best-selling novel to create the film version of
Twilight, a type of translation occurred, namely, the transformation of the novel from
one medium to another. As a result, many fans who read *Twilight* before seeing the
movie had mixed reactions because the film "translation" of the novel did not match
their interpretation. If we expand the term to its very broadest definition, translation
is also the act of interpreting anything. Every single reading of *Twilight*, taking this
broadest of definitions, therefore becomes a translation, with every reader becoming
a "translator" of the story as she or he interprets Meyer's work and creates the scenes
and images in the mind's eye. We might even go so far as to say that *Twilight* itself is
a translation, since Stephenie Meyer has explained on several occasions that the idea
for the novel came to her in a dream that she "translated" into characters and plotlines
in the light of day.

More narrowly defined, which is how we normally understand the term, translation is the act of "rendering from one language into another."[1] This definition allows
for the linguistic element of translation, but does not necessarily encompass all of
the cultural and artistic choices required when working with a text. In the same way
that *Twilight*'s screenwriter and director were forced to make potentially unpopular
decisions so that the novel would fit into a new medium, translators of the work into
different languages also need to make difficult choices so that the novel will be both
linguistically and culturally acceptable and appropriate. When Meyer's first volume
in the saga was published in English in October 2005, it was simultaneously published in other languages, thanks to the stir it had caused in the publishing world.
As Jennifer Brown notes in her article "*Twilight* in Translation," thirteen publishers
bought the translation rights to the novel even before the Bologna Children's Book
Fair where the book was previewed to sellers, more than six months before *Twilight*
was published.[2] For the majority of international, non-English-speaking readers, the
foreign language translation of *Twilight* is the only version of the novel they will ever

know. However, studying a translation side-by-side with the original can teach bilingual readers a great deal, not only about how a translator has interpreted and adapted the novel for a new audience, but also about the spaces between the languages and cultures and how translation attempts to bridge that gap. In this chapter, we will look closely at the differences between the English and French versions of Stephenie Meyer's novel, not for the purpose of critiquing the translator or declaring the translation to be "good" or "bad," "faithful" or "unfaithful" (fans have already done more than their fair share of that), but to learn what happens both to a text and to a reader as a result of the process of translation. Translation obviously allows for the expansion of an audience of a text, but it also expands the text itself, giving the text a type of afterlife. Translation also results in subtle but significant changes to suit the tastes and expectations of the target audience. Translation can reveal a great deal, not only about the text itself but also about the culture for which it has been adapted. In the case of Luc Rigoureau's translation of Meyer's novel, we can intuit that French readers desire characters who are more forceful than their American counterparts. Uncovering differences such as these can lead to a greater understanding of French culture on the part of US readers.

Before moving into the specifics of the French translation, we shall first look at some of the other foreign language translations of *Twilight* that have been published. Over thirty translations of *Twilight* have appeared so far, including French, German, Spanish, Polish, Italian, Mandarin Chinese (traditional and simplified), Korean, Japanese, Russian, Portuguese, and Danish, just to name a few. Some translations, French for example, use the cover from the original, but others develop a cover illustration that would appeal more to their target culture audience. The Japanese cover features a manga-like design, while the German cover features a photo of a young woman (presumably Bella) with a long, pale neck. The Dutch version of the novel uses the US cover, but with a twist—there is a heart-shaped bite taken out of the apple.[3]

Another significant difference for some of the translations of the first installment is that several break Meyer's nearly 500 pages into two or more volumes to suit their readers' tastes. Japan has released two versions of their translation, one which stays close to the original novel, and a three-volume graphic novel. As for English-to-English translations, *Twilight* was adapted for a British-English edition, and the first installment of the English-language graphic novel version with illustrations by Young Kim was published in March 2010.

In general, many of the foreign-language translators chose to literally translate the word "twilight" for their titles, but others take a different approach. The French title, about which we will speak more momentarily, is "*Fascination*," literally, fascination, while the German translator plays a bit with language and image, using the title "*Bis zum Morgengrauen*," translated back into English as "until dawn." The cover art, however, features an additional, shadowy "s" on the end of the word "*bis*," making it "*biss*," or bite, thus emphasizing the vampire/horror element of the saga. The Finnish title, "*Houkutus*," or "temptation/seduction," hints at the nature of Bella and Edward's relationship and the power they have over each other.

As stated earlier, the purpose of this study is not to nitpick and point out passages in which the translator got it "wrong." Fansites do more than enough of that, and one of the main French sites developed and maintained by *Twilight* fans has a discussion board titled "*Luc tu [ne] sais pas traduire*"/Luc, you don't know how to translate," which is dedicated to pointing out perceived (as well as a few actual minor) flaws in Rigoureau's translations. (It would be appropriate at this point to note that Luc Rigoureau has been awarded the Prix Chronos for translation work, and spent years working in publishing before becoming a translator. In addition to the *Twilight* saga, he has also translated over eighty other titles, mainly in the young adult category.) It usually tends to be those self-identified "semifluent" individuals who are all-too-ready and willing to disparage a translation of a work they love, typically because the translation does not precisely match the one they may have done in their heads while reading. Bilingual readers (and readers who know just enough of a foreign language to proclaim themselves semifluent) are the ones who enjoy the type of carping and fussing over word choice, which is not necessarily productive or revelatory about the process of translation. To the uninformed, translation might seem like a simple linguistic puzzle to be solved or a mathematical equation in which a word in one language precisely equals one in another. But it is obviously much more than that. Translation requires not only a native fluency in the language into which one trans-lates (the target language) and as near-native fluency as possible in the language from which one translates (the source language), but also a very sensitive understanding of both the source and target culture. From there, a series of difficult decisions must be made: How do I adapt this work to make it acceptable and appropriate for the target audience? What will a reader expect from a novel of this type? What do I need to change in order to "localize" this text and help it to fit the target culture? Should I leave all the foreign elements in place and add footnotes so that my target readers will understand those elements? Or, do I localize some elements and leave others? What is the best approach to translating this text? Clearly, this is not only a linguistic exercise, but a complex task that requires a great deal of cultural understanding and insight.

Now that we have a better sense of how we will be using translation to discuss the novel, we can move into the specifics of the French version, looking at the instances where there is a marked difference between the source and the target. The space between the two versions offers the reader an opportunity to think critically about both the process of translation (including the elements of language and culture that allow or prevent translation) as well as the novel itself and how we interpret it. As mentioned above, *Twilight* was translated into French by Luc Rigoureau and was published at the same time as the English counterpart. The most striking differ-ence at first sight between the English and the French is the title. Rigoureau chose *Fascination* (literally, "fascination") for the French volume, and continues with this theme for the rest of the saga, translating *New Moon* as *Tentation* ("temptation"), *Eclipse* as *Hésitation* ("hesitation"), and, finally, *Breaking Dawn* as *Révélation* ("revela-tion"). Instead of taking Meyer's theme of basic celestial phenomena for titles of her books and translating those titles into French, Rigoureau opts for stages in the devel-opment of a relationship, following the course and progress of Bella and Edward's romance. Bilingual readers critique him on this, citing the fact that "twilight" can be expressed in French, and that the most obvious choice for the title would have been *Crépuscule* (the Spanish and Portuguese translations went this route, both using *Crepúsculo*). However, the word *crépuscule* in French does not have the same connotation it does in English, as both a time of the day but also a stage in a person's life. Certainly the word has multiple layers of meaning in the novel. Twilight, the time between sunset and dusk, is the safest and easiest time for Edward Cullen, but he shares with Bella that it is also the "saddest" because it marks the closing of the day, another end in an endless procession of days for an immortal.[4] In the final pages of the novel, as Edward and Bella discuss her becoming a vampire, Edward uses the term "twilight" to refer to both the last moments of the day as well as the so-called twilight years of a person's life. He asks Bella if she is truly ready to become a vampire, ready "for this to be the twilight of your life, though your life has barely started."[5] *Twilight*, sequentially the first of the four celestial phenomena Meyer uses in her titles, is thus the starting point of a series and representative of what is happening in the volume. Rigoureau's choice of *Fascination* for the title of the translation, though controversial because it does not capture the symbolism of "twilight," fits the overarching theme of the novel (the utter fascination that Bella and Edward feel for each other) and also provides the first emotion in the sequence of emotions felt by our protagonists over the course of the saga.

Other differences in the French translation are more subtle, but are also the result of careful planning and difficult decision-making on the part of the translator. Some of the features of the English *Twilight* are difficult to maintain in the French. For instance, early on in the book, we see Charlie Swan, Bella's father, affectionately calling her "Bells." Although this is what we first hear him call Bella, Charlie uses this nickname fairly infrequently and mainly in situations when he is feeling especially loving toward his daughter. He is a man of few words and is uncomfortable showing great emotion, so his use of "Bells" helps to reveal the depth of his love when other forms of expression fail him. The nickname is a term of great endearment for him. In French, however, Charlie only ever uses "Bella," which works naturally in French while "Bells" does not transfer well. It is interesting, though, that the translator did not use "Belle" for Charlie's pet-name for Bella in French. It would have worked in a similar way as the English, revealing the softer side of Charlie and highlighting the special nature of this father–daughter relationship. Rigoureau does not change *any* of the character names to make them francophone, however. Edward remains the same and does not become "*Édouard*," for example. As a translator Rigoureau does not localize the text in any way, meaning the distinguishing features of the setting remain the same, from the now-famous small town of Forks, Washington, to the specifics of the US high school system and overall cultural aspects. For those elements that would be unexpected or foreign to his French audience, such as metal detectors in schools, people under eighteen driving, and the American holiday Thanksgiving, Rigoureau provides explanations in brief footnotes.

Another striking difference between the English source text and the French target text has to do with linguistic register. In English, there is no distinction between a formal and informal "you"; however, there is in French. While most contemporary French teenagers would immediately use the informal *tu* form (the second person singular), Edward, having been born in 1901, would very likely have a different sense of propriety, especially when he first meets Bella, who notices that his mode of expression sounds a bit old-fashioned. We do not get a sense of this in the French translation, however, as Edward's language is as informal and casual as the other characters in the book from the moment we first hear him speak. In French, Edward says: "*Tu dois être Bella Swan,*" a literal translation of "You must be Bella Swan," but one which uses the informal *tu.*[6] Edward's outdated speech does not come through here, but it would have if the translator had used the formal *vous* form: "*Vous devez être Bella Swan.*" Perhaps Rigoureau wanted to make Edward seem like a believable teenager, or was picking up on Edward having told Bella that the Cullens try to fit in, justifying the change in linguistic register. Whatever the reason, the tone does not match—Edward is formal and courteous in English, but informal and relaxed in French. Another example of this comes in the same conversation between Edward and Bella in biology class, when Edward asks "It's too bad about the snow, isn't it?" which Rigoureau translates "*Dommage, pour la neige, hein?*" The French here is more casual, primarily due to the use of *hein,* which is similar to "eh?" in English. To keep the same polite, formal register in French, Rigoureau could have used "*n'est-ce pas*" in place of "*hein.*" Certainly Edward, as his relationship with Bella progresses, would shift to the *tu* form when speaking with her, but it seems unlikely, given his age, that he would have begun using it right from the start.

Indeed, not all the characters in *Fascination* use the informal *tu* instead of the polite, formal *vous.* Carlisle Cullen, when he meets Bella in the hospital, uses the *vous* form in addressing her, and Edward uses *vous* when speaking with Mr. Banner and Charlie. Therefore, the shift in Edward's linguistic register points to two possible deliberate decisions on the part of the translator. As stated above, Rigoureau may have been trying to make Edward fit in with his teen contemporaries (who only use *vous* when addressing particular, nonfamilial adults), or he may have been making Edward acceptable for his contemporary French audience who would have recognized the strangeness of a teenager's using formal speech with another teen. The flaw in this second line of reasoning is that English-language readers would have likely noticed (as Bella does) that Edward's speech is a bit outdated and overly polite. Changing the linguistic register changes Edward, and makes Bella's recognition of the way Edward speaks "with unfamiliar cadences and phrases that better fit the style of a turn-of-the-century novel than that of a twenty-first-century classroom" seem bizarre.[7]

Another element of the novel is also highlighted in the translation, namely Edward's supernatural good looks. In the English, Meyer is no stranger to superlatives when describing Edward Cullen's physical features, and Rigoureau takes her lead but goes one step further, elevating him to the status of a Greek god. We first see this in Edward's exchange with Mrs. Cope, the school receptionist. He is trying to get his class schedule changed when Bella enters the room. Edward notices her presence (he is assaulted by her scent), turns to glare at her, and then "He turned back to the receptionist."[8] In French, after Edward looks at Bella, she narrates: "L' Apollon s'adressa de nouveau à la secrétaire," which, translated back, gives us "The Apollo turned back to the receptionist/secretary."[9] In English there is no mention of Edward's looks in this scene, but Rigoureau (perhaps unnecessarily) reinforces this element for the French readers. In English, Bella describes Edward as having a "heavenly face,"[10] and this is translated as "*visage d'Apollon*" in French,[11] equating his handsomeness with that of the Greek god Apollo, whom the French understand as the god of music, song, and poetry (as we do in the United States), but also one who was devastatingly beautiful yet unlucky in love. This reference and the connection made with Edward stress not only our protagonist's good looks, but also reinforce the precarious nature of his relationship with Bella. Later in the novel, when Bella confesses to her father that she is dating Edward, she tries to explain to him which of the Cullens he is, thinking to herself "The beautiful one, the godlike one." In French, she muses: "*L'Adonis, le dieu vivant.*"[12] Again, Rigoureau opts for naming specifically which god Edward embodies, choosing Adonis over Apollo here to reinforce his good looks and desirability. The translator's choice is interesting because the chance that these two Greek gods would resonate symbolically with a French audience (particularly a young adult one) are about the same as their English-speaking counterparts. Naming the gods specifically as Rigoureau does adds little to the text, but it does change Bella slightly, making her perhaps more bookish in French than her English-speaking counterpart.

Edward in the French translation seems slightly more brooding and more dangerous, and Bella seems more aware of the risky situation in which she has placed herself. In the scene where Edward and Bella are having their first lunch together in the cafeteria, he shares with her that he has given up trying to avoid her. His intentionally vague explanation for this unexpected turn of events confuses Bella, who asks:

> " 'So, in plain English, are we friends now?'
> 'Friends . . . ,' he mused, dubious.
> 'Or not,' I muttered."

In French, the exchange is translated as follows:

> "*–Alors, en bon anglais, ça signifie que nous sommes de nouveau amis?*
> *–Amis . . . rêvassa-t-il, dubitative.*
> *–Ou ennemis, marmottai-je.*"[13]

Bella's retort in French is much more specific than the one she offers in English, emphasizing the opposite and contrary nature of their relationship (they can be either "friends" or "enemies"). But there is another element of the translation that warrants examination. The "plain English" in the source text is rendered "*bon anglais*" in French [literally, "good English"] despite the fact that they are obviously speaking French and there are several ways to express the idea of speaking clearly without keeping the reference to the English language. This is another example of the translator's choice not to localize the text, not to transfer the setting to France, and make it obvious that our novel takes place in the United States.

Later in the same scene, Edward tries to convince Bella that she is better off staying away from him, telling her that he may not be the "superhero," but the "bad guy" instead. Bella responds with "You're dangerous?" in English, making a guess in the form of a question to which she instinctively knows the answer. In the French, she seems more certain, saying "*Tu es dangereux . . .*" without a question mark, and the fact that Bella guesses at this is not present in the French.[14] The French-language Bella is slightly more self-assured than her English-language counterpart and simultaneously more fully aware of the threat facing her.

The scene in which Bella and Edward are in the nurse's office after she faints in biology class offers another chance to compare the English and French counterparts.

Edward advises Bella to leave the office when Lee Stephens, who has passed out at the sight of his own blood (not someone else's as Bella had done), arrives. She does so, and Edward is surprised, saying "You actually listened to me." In French, he is more dominant, telling Bella "*Tu m'as obéi, pour une fois*"—literally, "You obeyed me, for once."[15] She tells him that it was not his command but rather her own senses that guided her: she states that she could smell Lee's blood, to which Edward responds, "People can't smell blood." The reader knows the implication behind Edward's assertion and can almost hear the emphasis on the word "people" (as opposed to vampires, of course). Rigoureau translates this phrase: "*Pour la plupart des gens, le sang n'a pas d'odeur*," which, if we translate back to English, reads "For most people, blood has no smell."[16] The emphasis of the sentence shifts in translation, with "people" as the subject in English to "*sang*/blood" as the subject in French. This is characteristic of Rigoureau's emphasis on the vampire theme, which is still being foreshadowed at this point in the novel. We know Edward is not "normal," but we are not certain exactly what he is yet. Meyer's emphasis on "people" alerts us that he is not a person, while Rigoureau's placing the importance on "*sang*/blood" gives us an even more obvious clue. That scene, however, is not the first one in which Rigoureau puts the French reader on alert by hinting at vampirism. In the English edition, when Bella learns about the Cullens from Jessica, she recounts that "the youngest, one of the Cullens, looked up and met my gaze." In the French version, we find "*le plus jeune entre eux, un des Cullen, plongea les yeux dans les miens*," meaning he looked deeply into her eyes, but the verb used in this expression, *plonger*, is also the one which would be used to describe sinking one's teeth into something, thus foreshadowing and emphasizing the vampire motif.[17]

As stated above, Edward comes across as much more brooding and even menacing in the French than he does in the English, emphasizing (and perhaps even sensationalizing) his vampire nature. When he and Bella are driving home from Port Angeles and she reveals that she knows the truth about him, she goes on to share that it does not matter to her what he is. He is furious with this, and when she says it's too late for her to change how she feels, he snaps, "Never say that." In French, he is angry and rude, telling her "*Tais-toi!*" which translates as "be quiet" or "shut up" and is nowhere near as polite or pleading as the English.[18] Later, when discussing their upcoming outing together, Edward urges Bella to tell Charlie of their plans, and when she asks him why, he offers: "To give me some small incentive to bring you back." In French, Edward is more ominous, and this sentence is rendered: "*Histoire de me donner une bonne raison de te ramener vivante!*", which translates back to English as "To give me a good reason to bring you back alive."[19] Certainly the "alive" is understood in the English version, but our courteous, genteel vampire does not utter aloud the implied threat.

Edward is more intimidating in French not only with Bella, but also with his sister Alice. As Bella escapes with Alice and Jasper to Arizona while the rest of the family deals with James and Victoria at the end of the novel, Edward cautions Alice to "keep your opinions to yourself." Later, when Alice and Bella are alone, Bella inquires about the process of becoming a vampire. Alice is caught off-guard and struggles with her decision, telling Bella "Edward doesn't want me to tell you that."[20] In French, Edward seems to have more power and influence over his sister, who says "*Edward m'a interdit de te reveler,"* which translates back into English as "Edward has forbidden me from telling you."[21] Edward's not wanting Alice to tell and forbidding Alice from telling are quite different, and point to Rigoureau's consistent choice to make Edward more dangerous, dark, and brooding than he is in the original.

Edward, however, is not the only character who experiences a shift in personality when translated into French. Bella also changes slightly, as stated earlier, becoming more confident and self-assured in French than she is in English. She is still as clumsy as ever, but when speaking with Edward, she has an edge that is not anywhere near as pronounced in the original. When she is telling Jessica about her impromptu date with Edward in Port Angeles, she knows he will be listening, and purposely makes comments for his benefit. She tells Jessica that Edward "drives like a maniac," and then thinks, "I hoped he heard that." In French, she seems more certain that he will overhear, thinking, *"Tiens, prends ça, Edward!"*, essentially telling Edward to "take that!"[22] Later, when Edward informs Bella that he is not the only male attracted to her, she mumbles "I don't believe it." Her French response is more accusatory, *"Tu mens,"* or "you lie."[23] In the same scene, Bella becomes annoyed at Edward's suggestion that she could not handle herself alone in Seattle, narrating, "I was miffed." In French, the focus shifts from the emotion Bella feels to what she thinks about Edward, and she exclaims, *"Le goujat!,"* inwardly calling Edward a boor or a lout.[24] Bella is never this harsh with Edward in English, even at the beginning of the novel when she cannot understand why he reacts to her so negatively in their first biology class. When he "spies" on her in gym class after she piques his curiosity, she is temporarily annoyed with him, telling him, "You're unbelievable." Bella's reaction in the French version is stronger and angrier, evidenced in her *"Je te déteste!,"* or "I hate/detest/loathe you!"[25] In both versions, she recovers quickly and forgives him, but the force behind her words in French is uncharacteristic of our American protagonist, even if said partially in jest.

Another example of Bella's French counterpart being slightly more forceful than her English-language equivalent is seen when Edward and Charlie meet formally for the first time, before the ill-fated baseball game in the clearing. Charlie invites Edward to have a seat and Bella grimaces at the impending conversation. Rigoureau, in addition to making Charlie more brusque (he says *"Assieds-toi,"* or "Sit down" instead of "Have a seat, Edward"), also adds to Bella's reaction.[26] In French, instead of simply grimacing, Bella thinks: *"Nom d'un chien! On n'allait quand meme pas y passer la soirée!"*, which loosely translates back to English as "Shoot! We're going to be stuck here all night!"[27] Interestingly enough, *nom d'un chien* is a very old-fashioned and rather mild expression of frustration, which would better fit Edward than Bella. These examples stand out among other more subtle ones to create an overall effect of Bella having more confidence and "attitude" in French than she does in English.

Some other areas where the translation differs from the English text provide some insight into the interpretation and approach of the translator and offer the foreign language reader a slightly different understanding of the novel. *Twilight* is difficult to categorize: officially marketed as young adult fiction, the saga has defied that category. It seems clear that although many see the novels as romance, the French translator made a clear attempt to highlight the horror aspect as well, as discussed above in regards to the emphasis of the vampiric element. Even the romance holds eerie resonances. Returning to the scene in which Edward and Bella first speak with each other, she asks him how he knew her name. He tells her assuredly that everybody knows her name, and that "The whole town's been waiting for you to arrive." The French underscores this, and Edward shares, "*Tu étais attendue comme le messie, tu sais,*" or, "You've been as anticipated as the Messiah, you know."[28] Rigoureau's word choice seems to predict the eventual relationship between these two individuals, and how they save each other both literally and figuratively—almost supernaturally. One final example in which the French expands upon the English and reinforces the theme of danger is in the first-kiss scene. Edward tenderly cautions Bella to "Be very still," and we hear her think in response: "as if I wasn't already frozen." In French, after Edward speaks, Bella thinks: "*Pas de danger! J'étais pétrifiée,*" or "No danger! I was petrified."[29] Rigoureau's use of the word *pétrifiée* here has the perfect double entendre: petrified means both terribly frightened as well as frozen in place, and certainly Bella experiences these two simultaneously.

Translation, regardless of how "faithful" or how well-adapted to a target audience and culture, will always be regarded as a version of the original, a mirror-image that reflects back while at the same time revealing differences. The differences between *Twilight* and the French *Fascination* seem quite subtle, but are significant enough to create a shift in a reader's overall impression of the novel and its characters. The pioneering translation theorist Eugene Nida suggests, "all types of translation involve 1) loss of information, 2) addition of information, and/or 3) skewing of information."[30] It seems surprising, then, not to mention praiseworthy, that nothing has vanished in the space between the English and French versions. Certainly there are additions and places in which things seem slightly askew, but nothing has been lost in the process. The French Bella and Edward are more assertive versions of their English-language ("original") counterparts, and this could point to French literary preferences and expectations, the translator's understanding and interpretation of the original, or, most likely, a bit of both. A good translation is a sort of echo of the original: there may be some mild distortion, but what bounces back is utterly recognizable. By this definition, *Fascination* is a good translation, providing the novel with a new audience of readers, and a second life for our protagonists.

NOTES

1. Merriam-Webster Dictionary.
2. Jennifer Brown, "*Twilight* in Translation," *Publishers Weekly*, October 31, 2005. Web. http://www.publishersweekly.com/article/CA6278874.html
3. Stephenie Meyer has a link to some of these covers on her website, www.stepheniemeyer.com, but a simple Amazon.com search for "*Twilight*" and the foreign language will also work.
4. Stephenie Meyer, *Twilight* (New York: Little, Brown, 2005. Print), 233.
5. *Twilight,* 497.
6. Stephenie Meyer. *Fascination.* Trans. Luc Rigoureau (Paris: Hachette, 2005. Print), 55.
7. *Twilight,* 138.
8. *Twilight,* 27.
9. *Fascination,* 39.

10. *Twilight*, 107.
11. *Fascination*, 122.
12. *Twilight*, 357; *Fascination*, 379.
13. *Twilight*, 88; *Fascination*, 102.
14. *Twilight*, 93; *Fascination*, 107.
15. *Twilight*, 100; *Fascination*, 115.
16. Ibid.
17. *Twilight*, 22; *Fascination*, 33.
18. *Twilight*, 190; *Fascination*, 208.
19. *Twilight*, 214; *Fascination*, 234.
20. *Twilight*, 389; *Fascination*, 413.
21. *Fascination*, 439.
22. *Twilight*, 202; *Fascination*, 221.
23. *Twilight*, 210; *Fascination*, 230.
24. *Twilight*, 213; *Fascination*, 233.
25. *Twilight*, 222; *Fascination*, 243.
26. *Fascination*, 381; *Twilight*, 358.
27. *Fascination*, 381.
28. *Twilight*, 44; *Fascination*, 56.
29. *Twilight*, 275; *Fascination*, 298.
30. Eugene Nida, *Language Structure and Translation* (Stanford, CA: Stanford University Press, 1975. Print), 27.

CHAPTER 5

VARIATIONS, SUBVERSIONS, AND ENDLESS LOVE: FAN FICTION AND THE *TWILIGHT* SAGA

MARIA LINDGREN LEAVENWORTH

TEXTS THAT RESONATE WITH AN AUDIENCE often give way to retellings and reworkings, the purposes of which may vary from being highly critical of the source text to illustrating a desire to never allow the original story to end. The popularity of Stephenie Meyer's novels can be measured in terms of sold copies, but also in terms of the amount of fan activities connected to the narratives. Fan fiction, or fanfic, is one expression of contemporary fan involvement with previous texts; the term today describes mainly Internet-published stories. The *Twilight* saga has resulted in an unusually large number of fan fictions; on the largest collective site, FanFiction. net, there are more than 175,000 stories to date.[1] Plotlines, characters, and narrative details from Meyer's novels are, using established fanfic vernacular, referred to as canon, and fanfic authors enter into an intertextual dialogue with this canon as they create alternative stories, developments, and/or perspectives. The varied fan-created products (fan fiction, fan films, and fan art) and the different approaches to the canon suggest that readers are both active and critical.

My analyses focus on five fan fictions published on the website *Twilighted*[2] that illustrate different tendencies in Meyer's fan base, or fandom. The selection is by no means comprehensive, and the results of my investigation cannot be used to assess the fandom, nor the 6,000-plus texts on this particular site. What my examination demonstrates, however, is that certain elements in Meyer's canon, such as the restricted, first-person perspective, the emphasis on chastity, and the de-fangedness of the vampires, are resisted as fanfic authors present alternative constructions of both agency and sexuality and subvert elements connected to character development as well as to the themes of (blood)lust and sexual abstinence.

The close ties between a fanfic and its canon(s) entail both repetition and reinterpretation, yet fan fiction is seldom included in contemporary theoretical discussions about adaptations and other forms of highly intertextual narratives. Linda Hutcheon, for example, concludes that fan fiction falls outside the scope of her definition of adaptation, simply because fanfic represents "never wanting a story to end" rather than "wanting to retell the same story over and over."[3] In other words, the exclusion is a result of variations on canon elements that entail differences rather than similarities. Considering, however, the transformations that always take place in an adaptation, and the sometimes minute alterations between canon and fanfic, I would argue that fan fiction can and should be considered in more general adaptation discussions. Theories concerning remediation (the study of how texts move from one medium to another without necessarily losing their original characteristics) similarly profit from incorporating the fanfic form, and analyses bring valuable insight into how contemporary readers position themselves in relation to canons of different kinds.

If adaptation and even intertextuality are perceived as too narrow to encompass the changes and alterations that take place within a fan fiction, a more usable term, Abigail Derecho suggests, is "*archontic.*"[4] She employs the Derridean notion of the open archive to define a relationship between texts, different from traditional notions of intertextuality that posit all texts as mosaics without necessarily acknowledging sources of inspiration and influence. Fan fictions are openly announced as variations on the canon and fanfic authors commonly express their indebtedness to canon authors and relinquish all claims to having "invented" characters and/or plots.[5] Further, the archive, according to Derecho, "is not identical to the text but is a virtual construct surrounding the text, including it and all texts relating to it";[6] that is, each fanfic becomes part of the archive to which subsequent authors relate.[7] Archontic texts are not endlessly telling the same story, but expand the archive by varying the associations to elements within it. Therefore, while all texts examined here offer deviations from the *Twilight* canon, some contain elements that, simultaneously, are infinitely repeated. I argue, therefore, that fan fictions need to be read with an eye to both what they subvert or vary *and* what they endlessly recycle.

CROSSOVERS: NARRATIVE GAPS, LOGICAL GAPS, AND DIRTY DANCING

To read, write, and analyze fan fiction necessitates a fairly comprehensive knowledge of the canon and the elements in it. It is also important that the canon "allows" fanfic treatments of themes, characterizations, and plot developments. Sheenagh Pugh argues that

> [f]anfic happens in the gaps between canon, the unexplored or insufficiently explored territory. For that to happen, the gaps must be left, and the territory must exist—i.e. the canon writers must not spell too much out, but there must be somewhere to start from and something to build on.[8]

The *Twilight* canon contains a number of narrative gaps, utilized by fanfic authors to various ends. The restricted narrative perspective in Meyer's canon (first-person novels mainly narrated from Bella's perspective) creates one such gap. Thoughts belonging to other characters have to be verbalized to become known to the reader and events may remain puzzling, due to Bella's limited insight. Many fanfic authors seize the opportunity to present events from other characters' perspectives, thereby adding to the archive's representations of emotional responses and thoughts.

5by5creations'[9] nine-chapter fanfic *Soul Searching* and her one-chapter sequel *Vanquish* represent Edward's and Alice's perspectives, respectively, and enable an alternative understanding of these characters' emotions and motivations.[10] These fan fictions are categorized as "crossovers" as they combine narrative details from the *Twilight* canon with plot elements from other texts—in this case, Joss Whedon's TV series *Buffy the Vampire Slayer* and *Angel*.[11] Played out in the canon gap created by Edward leaving Bella in *New Moon*, *Soul Searching* outlines Edward's reasons for his choice and his decision to track down and kill Victoria to further ensure Bella's safety. Edward's path takes him to Los Angeles, and to a meeting with another vampire: Angel. All events in 5by5creations' two fanfics are played out during the time Bella is grieving Edward's absence (a time period which in the canon is indicated only by chapter titles signaling the passing of months), thus enabling the author to stay true to the canon. Both stylistically and in terms of plot, the fan fictions illustrate a clever mix between the introspective romance of Meyer's text world and remediated versions of the fast-paced action of an *Angel* or *Buffy* episode.

The choice to cross two vampire worlds might seem obvious, but also results in logical gaps the author textually works to close. Giles and Wesley, the two vampire-knowledgeable Watchers from *Buffy* and *Angel*, for example, have no inkling that "good" vampires such as the Cullens exist. When questioned by Wesley, Edward thinks "I was clearly other to this man who had seen so much in his lifetime."[12] Conversely, Edward has never dreamed of a world in which vampires do not have to strive to hide themselves. Some of the logical gaps produced by this collision of worlds cause 5by5creations greater problems than others. Why, for example, have the Cullens, like other vampires and demons, not been drawn to the Hellmouth? Angel says: "I am very surprised that none of your kind has ended up here" and Giles is reported as being "very disturbed that an entire subset of demons could be missing from the historical record."[13]

The difficulties that Angel and the Watchers have with categorizing Edward serve to situate him, and by extension the Cullens, in a larger literary context. Whereas the eighteenth- and nineteenth-century literary vampire often represented the Other and the frightening consequences of lost willpower and control (over both life and sexuality), the trope today also signifies attractive alternatives to human existence. Milly Williamson states that "[t]he 'new' vampire has ties of family and friendship, which locate it problematically in the realm of the emotions. This is a humanized terrain, which is more ambiguous in its depiction of good and evil."[14] Meyer's vampires, "communal rather than solitary,"[15] represent an ideal contemporary family, despite its vaguely incestuous configuration.[16] Their emotions and existential doubts are no longer Other and they are also both figuratively and literally de-fanged, posing little of the traditional vampire's threat to humans. In a conversation with Angel in *Soul*

Searching, Edward sums up this existence: "We don't see ourselves as part of the supernatural really. [...] We are a part of the, forgive me for sounding cliché, but part of the circle of life. The balance."[17]

Not so the vampires featured in the Whedonverse and 5by5creations' crossover fanfic, where they (mostly) are monsters to be feared and slayed. Although Angel is a "good" vampire as well, the differences between him and Edward are initially pronounced, to the extent that each character is unable to identify the other as a vampire. When Angel briefly transforms, "his eyes changed to a bright yellow and fangs descended," Edward thinks that he is "everything human vampire mythology called for,"[18] drawing attention to his own human-sembling nature. However, Edward is unusually powerful: he is impervious to the stake, can control his bloodlust, and merely glitters in the sun, which makes both Angel and Buffy compare him, in stylistically Whedon deadpan, to "a disco ball."[19] The physical strength and speed Edward possesses in the canon are used in the fanfic to more brutal ends. For example, he partakes in the slaying of a vampire, complete with the conventional stake to the heart; "a cloud of dust explod[ing] from where it had been."[20] This and other violent fights depicted in the story link Edward to more threatening and dangerous past and contemporary vampires, a connection that is exacerbated by the slight mocking of the sparkling, well-behaved vampire of Meyer's canon.

One central issue in Meyer's novels is the debate about whether or not vampires have souls, particularly as the potential lack of such is the main reason why Edward hesitates to transform Bella. Edward's musings on this subject in *Soul Searching* are paralleled by Angel's double existence. As the evil, soulless Angelus, he does not have to assume responsibility for the sins he has committed, whereas in his ensouled state he struggles with remorse following his monstrous actions. The contrast between the moral and amoral vampire embodied by Angel significantly affects Edward's soul searching and he begins to feel convinced that "[m]aybe the soul was more a product of choice than an inherent quality. You could choose to have a conscience or to ignore it."[21] The active choices the Cullens make in the canon are all influenced by this line of reasoning, and constitute a strong intertextual link to Edward's expressed concerns here. His crumbling beliefs in the absence of his own soul also make him question his need to protect Bella from a vampire existence. 5by5creations suggests that the seeds of his eventual decision to turn Bella are sown here, in the meeting with Angel and Buffy, an addition to the *Twilight* archive made possible by the shift in narrative perspective.

Vampire milieus are not the only ones utilized in crossover fanfic, and a less obvious route is taken in *Love Man*, coauthored by starshinedown and pogurl, which combines the *Twilight* saga with Emile Ardolino's film *Dirty Dancing*.[22] The fanfic illustrates a complete removal of vampiric and supernatural elements by transferring Meyer's characters to the film's 1960s setting and having the roles of Johnny Castle and Frances "Baby" Houseman textually "played" by Edward and Bella. By crossing these textual universes, the fanfic authors accomplish two things. Firstly, they rewrite the end of *Dirty Dancing* to show "what...our two lovers [did] after that last dance at Kellermans," as the authors write in the summary preceding the fanfic. That is, their rewrite makes the sexual tension of the last film scene find its outlet. Secondly, by balancing the connections with and expansions of the visual text with strong intertextual links to Meyer's canon, the authors encourage the reader of the fanfic to envision Bella and Edward rather than Baby and Johnny, and, importantly, envison them as making love, which is never explicitly shown in Meyer's canon. The absence of a detailed love scene in the *Twilight* saga is in this way amended and *Love Man*, like countless other fan fictions, adds its own particular version of it to the archive.

The stress on canon characters' sexuality and the physical expressions of their desires suggest the impatience with which many fanfic authors regard Meyer's stress on abstinence before marriage. The crossover combining the chaste romance of the *Twilight* saga with the considerably more erotically charged *Dirty Dancing* enables these fanfic authors to create a "natural" focus on sexuality, but they still adhere faithfully to both canons and utilize similarities between characters to build up a believable setting for the ensuing love scene.

Both canons initially depict an unequal relationship between the central characters. In Ardolino's film, the insecure and homely Baby is pitted against the considerably more experienced and attractive Johnny, and, although considerably chaster than Johnny, Meyer's Edward also attracts significant attention from women. Furthermore, both male characters are portrayed as having abilities the female characters lack: in Edward's case, superhuman speed, mindreading, and vampiric strength; in Johnny's, exceptional skills on the dance floor. These imbalances result in a sense of disbelief, in both Baby and Bella, when Johnny and Edward profess to being attracted to them. In *New Moon*, Bella characterizes Edward's interest in her as "unfathomable," and even in *Breaking Dawn* she "trie[s] to comprehend...the surreal fact that this amazing person" is devoted to her.[23] Lines like these are echoed in *Love Man*, as when Bella expresses surprise at Edward's desire for her with the statement: "How could she have attracted someone so amazing?" In contrast to Meyer's canon, however, this is a rhetorical question rather than a sign of a continued sense of low self-esteem. The change in tone has the effect of portraying the character as considerably more assertive and rather aligned with Baby who, in Ardolino's film, exhibits a growing self-confidence and sexual curiosity.

Although Bella is not depicted as sexually passive in Meyer's novel (she is, after all, the one who takes initiatives to physical closeness) Edward's self-restraint, figured in terms of control over his bloodlust, results in the couple's chastity. That is, Edward controls Bella's desires, as well as her survival. Some critics have applauded the depiction of young adult love and the deferred sexual union in the canon. Caitlin Flanagan, for example, argues that "Bella's fervent hope...that Edward will ravage her, and that they will be joined forever" resonates with young readers, particularly young women, and that his restraint proves a much needed alternative to the pressures exacted on contemporary girls for being responsible for abstinence.[24] Other critics are less pleased. Feminist scholar Christine Seifert labels the first three novels in the canon "abstinence porn" and argues that the violent consummation of the love affair in *Breaking Dawn* represents anything but an equalization of the relationship. "If the abstinence message in the previous books was ever supposed to be empowering, this scene...undoes everything," she argues.[25] After the couple's marriage in the fourth novel, and with Bella still human, the reader witnesses her bruised body and torn pillows in the aftermath of the first sexual encounter. Bella then hides her bruises and tries to anticipate Edward's frustration and anger. The protagonist's power in the relationship is further diminished as her agency in the sexual relationship is described in terms of her "badgering [Edward] about the sex thing."[26] Seifert maintains that Bella's lack of control after marriage mirrors and even exacerbates her powerlessness.

> Bella is not in control of her body, as abstinence proponents would argue; she is absolutely dependent on Edward's ability to protect her life, her virginity, and her humanity. [...] When it comes to a woman's virtue, sex, identity, or her existence itself, it's all in the man's hands. To be the object of desire, in abstinence porn is not really so far from being the object of desire in actual porn.[27]

These canon characterizations are not automatically questioned in fanfic, but many authors choose to portray sexual encounters between the characters with emphasis on the psychological and physical fit between the characters. *Love Man* exemplifies this tendency through descriptions such as "Edward inside of her just felt *right*." The unequal power positions they have started from also give way to a more equal relationship, through a role reversal, as Edward is represented as "bashful and nervous" and Bella as more assertive. She is not afraid of verbalizing her desires, is described as "bold" and "empowered" and exhibits no fear of rejection. At the end of the fanfic, after detailed descriptions of the mutual seduction, the characters profess that nothing compares to what they have just experienced. Despite his fairly extensive experience in this story, modeled as it is on Johnny Castle's previous love life, Edward says: "I didn't know it could be, it *would* be like this," which indicates the centrality of love and reciprocity to lovemaking. While the graphically described sex might qualify the fanfic text as porn, the objectification of the female body and the associated lack of power in Meyer's "abstinence porn" is supplanted with a sense of both characters remaining in control of decisions concerning their bodies.

The absence of vampiric elements in *Love Man* means that the canon's reason for abstinence—Edward's superhuman strength and the danger of him hurting Bella—is no longer an issue. Other fanfic authors employ different strategies, but with the same end result: the depicted lovemaking destabilizes one of the founding principles in Meyer's canon. Many stories put great emphasis on the kind of equality that is foregrounded in *Love Man*, where both characters initiate sex. In this way, fanfic authors subvert not only the canon's theme of abstinence but also its allocation of agency.

ALTERNATIVE UNIVERSES: THE DEATH OF BELLA

The deviation from the canon that the death of a main character represents has consequences for other characters, not only in terms of events, but in terms of personality development and actions. Alternative Universe stories (AUs) do not, as the category's name might suggest, place canon characters in completely different settings, or universes. They are rather "what if" stories which, more or less subtly, change conditions presented in the canon. A number of fan fictions in this category are based around the idea that Bella dies, which, in turn, frees other characters from their canon behavior. SnowWhiteHeart's humorous AU *Dear God* depicts Edward far removed from Forks as the sweet scent of Bella's blood has proven too delicious to resist and he has killed her.[28] The internal (if brief) battle with bloodlust Edward reminisces about results in his view of himself as a monster and the realization that there is no God: "Only a world without a holy guardian could allow such a monster to do something so utterly brutish and indulgent to an innocent." In the absence of such a deity, Edward himself takes on the role of God and his canonical ability to hear peoples' (and vampires') thoughts is utilized by SnowWhiteHeart as her protagonist, in atonement for his sins, listens in on thoughts and wishes, granting those he can.

In this fanfic, Edward is portrayed in ways that can be characterized as OOC (Out Of Character): that is, an image is presented that is far removed from the canon. He is self-reflexive and sarcastic, and a sense of humor is added to his musings. Everyday expressions connected to deities, for example, such as "*God, he's hot*," get a twist as Edward, in his self-professed role thinks: "Again, she's not wrong. God is indeed hot, especially today, with my navy polo, collar popped." In addition to this noncanon sense of humor, SnowWhiteHeart recuperates the vampiric bite. Edward here is a creature to be feared and unabashedly uses his superhuman powers and feeds on human blood. Significantly, however, his victims are described as either deserving of this fate, or in need of it (with Bella as an exception). He "murders stalkers of women" and performs "mercy-kills" of people who either cannot survive or do not want to live. In this, Edward resembles other contemporary variations on the vampire trope. Fred Botting observes, in connection with Anne Rice's *Interview with a Vampire*, that contemporary "vampire mythology requires adaptation: vampire lore moves closer to a natural justice."[29] Like Rice's vampires, SnowWhiteHeart's Edward is adapted to a more humanized state in comparison with the traditional vampire. Still, contrasted to the good vampires in Meyer's canon, he exhibits an unusual brutality.

Edward's OOC characteristics do not, paradoxically it may seem, completely divorce *Dear God* from the canon. Rather, by questioning Edward's self-control in situations involving both bloodlust and sexual lust, downplaying his canon desire to blend into human society, and eliminating his serious approach to his own existence, SnowWhiteHeart subverts one-to-one associations to established conventions in the canon while simultaneously drawing attention to these. The "new" Edward added to the archive, then, is clearly recognizable, not because he is described in ways that repeat canon characteristics, but because these characteristics are turned inside out.

The death of Bella is in *Dear God* is used to authenticate Edward's vampiric nature but bloodlust is not the only desire he gives into. He meets an author with writer's block and decides to inspire her by amending her lack of a perfect hero. "She wants someone complicated, handsome, dark, fascinating, tormented, unforgettable," Edward realizes and, posing as her new neighbor, inches closer to the struggling artist. The story ends with a graphic sexual scene in which Edward seduces the budding novelist. The superhuman speed that Edward uses in the canon to traverse forests is here used in cunnilingus, and, naturally, reveals to the female protagonist that he is something not altogether human. This realization gives her the hero she needs and *Dear God* ends with the author busily working away at her computer.[30]

Characters' alternative sexual proclivities and a reconfiguration of their desires are explored in shoefreak37's AU, *The Strange Design of Comfort*, where Bella's death results in the pairing of Edward and Jacob.[31] Homoerotic stories about male characters who are not romantically linked in the canon are labeled slash, a fanfic category that has received a lot of critical attention. In early criticism, slash was often touted as subversive[32]; however, more recent studies, following on the more varied output of popular culture texts, suggest that this is not necessarily the case. Christine Scodari, for example, warns against "broad generalisations about the resistive character and potential" of both slash and fan fiction in general, and argues that although some texts can certainly be said to be "counter-hegemonic" others "serve hegemonic ends."[33] Further, slash often follows conventional romantic structures and depicts characters in fairly traditional roles, and there is, at times, a hesitation to let the homoerotic relationship have any future outside the specifically created situation, thus casting doubt on the possibilities of successful same-sex relationships.[34] Despite these caveats, authors' homoerotic pairings of noncanon couples clearly question the heteronormativity of the canon and provide alternative depictions of desires.

Most slash builds on an already intimate relationship between the male characters, described by Elizabeth Woledge as "a homosocial world in which the social closeness of the male characters engenders intimacy."[35] The social closeness often starts from a professional relationship, for example, that between *Star Trek's* Captain Kirk and Mr. Spock (whose initial pairing signaled by their names separated by a slash—Kirk/Spock—is what gives name to this fanfic category), but a deep friendship is also likely to spark slash authors' interest. Meyer's canon depicts very few homosocial relationships outside of family-like structures, and so, when slashing Jacob and Edward, shoefreak37 pairs two characters who in the canon are tied together (and simultaneously separated) by nothing more than their love for Bella. Her death in childbirth in *The Strange Design* unites Edward and Jacob in grief. The characters are further linked by the promise made by Jacob to kill Edward if anything happens to Bella. This promise features also in the canon, but has a different consequence here as Edward, after Bella's death, sees it as a boon as he is unable to end his own life. However, Jacob finds himself incapable of fulfilling his promise because if Bella loved Edward, so must he. Jacob also takes on roles and responsibilities Bella has previously had, since he is capable of human emotion: "*I know you can't cry, but I can do it for you…*"

Although the homoerotic attraction itself results in OOC characterizations, given the *Twilight* canon's portrayal of exclusively heterosexual couples and desires, Jacob and Edward are kept "in character" in a number of other aspects. The traits that characterize Edward's and Jacob's superhuman (and true) selves in the canon come to the fore in the fanfic when the comfort of the shared tears gives way to erotic feelings. The physical strength both the vampire and the shape shifter possess puts them on equal terms, which can be juxtaposed with the constant worries Edward in the canon harbors for hurting Bella. In contrast, in *The Strange Design*, "Edward is not afraid to let his overwhelming *need* take control because Jacob will not break." In this pairing, Edward does not have to limit or restrain what he is and what he desires.

In a discussion about slash and romance, Anne Kustritz argues that:

> Slash does not deal in the careful presentation of one's self in order to show a desired partner an ideal image, but rather in the revelation and acceptance of actual faults. This brings to the surface an individual's desire to be recognized completely by another, to drop the pretense of an image, and to be accepted as a total human being, complete with imperfections and infractions.[36]

With the substitution of "vampire" and "shape shifter" for the word "human" in the last sentence, one can see that shoefreak37's AU illustrates this recognition of faults and pretenses. In contrast to the canon, where Edward's and Bella's inequality in terms of physical strength leads to an imbalance in power over what actions are performed, Jacob and Edward here meet as equals, as themselves, and share responsibilities for the choices made. The equality between them is contrasted to their body temperatures, another intertextual link to the canon in which Edward continuously chills Bella's skin and Jacob provides needed superhuman heat. In the fanfic, the lovemaking is literally protected by this difference.

> The heat of Jacob's skin meeting the cold temperature of Edward's causes a cloud of steam to rise over their coupling, shielding them from the outside as they continue to thrust and moan. All the loss, all the sorrow and pain ebbs away in the cleansing fog, and all they see and feel is each other.

The physical and psychological meeting between the two disperses their grief and while the characters' relationship outside the specific situation is not explored further, a return to their previous roles is not suggested.

Despite the alternative pairing and the different events leading up to lovemaking, there are strong affinities between *The Strange Design* and the previously discussed *Love Man*. Equality between characters is in both stories reached through an acknowledgment of their true selves and the validity of their desires. Stress is put on their shared responsibility, which serves as a contrast to the canon where Edward is in control of the couple's abstinence, often against Bella's expressed wishes. Both fanfics thus evidence how readers question the power imbalance in the canon, adding more evenly matched couples to the archive.

Endless Love

Despite the prevalence of *Twilight* fan fictions describing sexual scenes (to varying degrees of detail), the most powerful emotion described is romantic love, the foregrounding of which establishes close ties to Meyer's canon. Bella and Edward's relationship is the core of the saga, but the novels are filled with images of other couples, similarly destined to be together forever (in the case of vampires), for an unusually long life (in the case of shape shifters), or at least through high school (in the case of humans). The texts analyzed in this chapter demonstrate that despite the numerous alterations made in fanfic, the central love story from the canon is an element endlessly repeated in ways that do not necessarily add to the archive. SnowWhiteHeart's *Dear God* is the only text in the sample that does not hinge on romantic closure and, significantly, it is the text that most clearly illustrates OOC behavior. The other four stories all explore and provide resolution to physical and romantic desire. *Soul Searching* and *Vanquish* effect this by sowing the seeds of Edward's decision to turn Bella, thereby ensuring their continued relationship. *Love Man* stages a love scene between the central characters and emphasizes their closeness by the parallel to another popular culture couple, and *The Strange Design* portrays intense homoerotic emotions that enable the characters to meet as equals.

The love between Bella and Edward permeates the entire *Twilight* saga. It structures the plot as the main characters' actions are propelled by love, whether expressed through enticement, protection, betrayal, or lies. Events that move the action forward (such as James' attack and interactions with the Volturi) are similarly connected to Edward and Bella's love for each other. The main characters define themselves in relation to the love they harbor for each other, and the changes they go through, the choices they make, are all motivated by their love. In itself, the Bella/Edward story is, of course, a reiteration of the star cross'd lovers theme with different species standing in for feuding families. The prevalence of narratives—both classical and contemporary—focused on incommensurable, unstoppable, and eternal love teach readers and viewers that everlasting togetherness is to be strived for, and that tales about this quest deserve to be told. This may be one reason for the endlessly repeated story line. Another reason, particularly tied to fan products such as fan fiction, is the imitative act itself as a tribute to the text world of which the author is a fan. When publishing a fanfic, the writer offers up the imitative act for scrutiny and feedback. While many readers may applaud both subtle and profound differences between canon and fanfic, a certain amount of fidelity to the central theme of love is encouraged and lauded.

In the conventional romance format, success hinges on eventual closure; the lovers will get each other, and in the case of *Twilight*, not just for a few decades, but for all eternity. The *deferment* of this closure, however, might be seen as a final reason for the masses of romantic fan fiction connected to the *Twilight* saga. The lack of resolution in popular culture texts can be of different kinds, but seems to be a prerequisite for fandom activity. Esther Saxey discusses how the extended story arches in the *Buffy* television series blur the boundaries between action and closure. While the action-packed middle segment of the episodes may further threats, most shows end with temporary closure: the threat is averted, the vampire is slayed, or the demon defeated. At the same time, however, viewers know that the process and structure will be repeated in the next episode. Exploring fan fiction produced in the Buffyverse, Saxey notes a "general . . . interest in the middle of shows over their closure,"[37] which demonstrates that the possibility of repetition (in the next instalment, or in the next story) is of central importance.

The *Twilight* saga is not an extended series in the same sense as *Buffy*, but it similarly resists closure, and specifically *romantic* closure, in the first three texts. In *Twilight*, Bella has to be content with a kiss, despite her wish to be turned and be with Edward "forever."[38] While their relationship is well established in the following two novels, there is still a distance between human and vampire precluding the consummation of their relationship, and possible jealousies are obstacles that prevent a complete resolution to the romance. The sustained "middle" that the first three novels constitute is particularly noticeable when seen in relation to the last pages of *Breaking Dawn,* where the characters are completely united. Bella can lift "the shield" that has previously prevented Edward from accessing her mind and memories, the kiss bears no traces of hesitation, and they walk "blissfully" into their joint "forever."[39] The fanfics on *Twilighted* set after *Breaking Dawn* often depict a new romance structure focused on the next generation, commonly revolving around Bella and Edward's daughter. Fanfic authors thus seize on and expand the endlessly deferred closure to a new romantic core story: another "middle" of an extension of the *Twilight* saga.

CONCLUSION

In the mix between subversions of canon elements and the recycling of the central romance, many fanfics illustrate a conflation of what Hutcheon claims defines an adaptation—"wanting to tell the same story over and over again"—and what she argues it is not: "never wanting a story to end."[40] Often, the two criteria are inseparable, with narrative elements, plotlines, and characterizations undermined, thus altering the story and expanding the archive, *and* the love story endlessly repeated. To view fan fictions as "written readings" of the canon gives valuable insight into a contemporary form of creativity and into sometimes very complex intertextual links between narratives in different media.

Fan fiction further illustrates that boundaries between authors and readers are becoming increasingly blurred in a media landscape characterized by participation, and that texts are increasingly seen as communal pools of inspiration. Even canon authors may create what can be termed fan fiction, and Meyer's most recent publications serve as interesting examples. Her novel draft *Midnight Sun* corresponds to the many fan fictions that alter the narrative perspective of the canon: while the plot of *Twilight* is repeated, events are narrated from Edward's point of view.[41] The recently published novella *The Short Second Life of Bree Tanner* expands on the story of a minor character from the canon, a teenager who appears briefly in *Eclipse*, and has countless analogues in fan fiction; to develop storylines centering on a character perceived as insufficiently explored constitutes a continuous pull for fanfic authors.[42] Writers appropriating and developing their own material are not labeled fanfic authors (at least not openly) and are perhaps less likely to question and subvert canon elements. Still, examples such as Meyer's draft and novella evidence, like many fan fictions do, the twin desires of offering alternative readings and perspectives and of recycling the story, again and again.

NOTES

1. February 2011. In the book section on the same site, the number of *Twilight* fanfics is surpassed only by texts connected to *Harry Potter*, of which there are, to date, over 500,000.
2. The fan fiction *Dear God* was retrievable from the site in November and December of 2009, but has subsequently been removed from *Twilighted*.
3. Linda Hutcheon, *A Theory of Adaptation* (New York: Routledge, 2006. Print), 9.
4. Abigail Derecho, "Archontic Literature: A Definition, a History, and Several Theories of Fan Fiction," *Fan Fiction and Fan Communities in the Age of the Internet*. Eds. Karin Hellekson and Kristina Busse (Jefferson: McFarland, 2006. Print), 63.
5. A common way to signal overt ties to the canon is by prefacing the fanfic with a disclaimer. *The Strange Design of Comfort*, for example, opens with the following statement: "*Twilight* and all characters herein belong to Stephenie Meyer. No copyright infringement intended."
6. Derecho, 65.
7. As an example of the complexity of the archive, Derecho mentions Jane Austen's *Pride and Prejudice*. The archive in this case consists not only of the novel, but "usable artifacts [such] as Elizabeth Bennett [sic], Fitzwilliam Darcy, the sprawling estate of Pemberly [sic], and Austen's particular version of English manners and morals" (65).

Add to this adaptations in different media, prequels, sequels, and the thousands of fan fictions in existence.

8. Sheenagh Pugh, *The Democratic Genre: Fan Fiction in a Literary Context* (Bridgend: Seren, 2005. Print), 92.

9. The traditional reasons for using a pseudonym are varied and can range from desiring to, through the name, establish a connection with the canon, to limiting risks involved in the use of copyrighted material, or simply preventing recognition from "real life" coworkers or friends, especially if writing sexually explicit or (intentionally) bad fanfic. However, in contemporary fanfic, the use of pseudonyms is established convention.

10. 5by5creations, *Soul Searching*. Web. Accessed December 5, 2009. www.twilighted.net and *Vanquish*. Web. Accessed December 5, 2009. www.twilighted. net.

11. Fan fictions are categorized in different ways on different sites to indicate what type of text they are. The category AU (Alternative Universe), for example, indicates what relationship the story has to the canon, whereas slash denotes a homosexual pairing. Crossovers means stories that feature characters from two (or more) fictional universes. Fanfics can also be categorized according to the genre they belong to; angst, for example, denoting a story where characters wrestle with existential (or other) doubts, or according to story length or rating. Ratings commonly correspond to the MPAA ratings, but a fanfic author can also simply signal that the material is not intended for young readers by assigning labels such as "adult" or "mature." Registration at the site is often required to access adult stories, and *Twilighted* is a case in point.

12. Chapter 3: "Fight." Forthcoming references to *Soul Searching* indicate what chapter quotations are taken from. The other fanfics analyzed are not divided into chapters and will instead be referred to by the stories' titles.

13. Chapter 3: "Fight," and *Vanquish*. Structurally, these aspects bring the fanfics closer to the TV series the author remediates than to the *Twilight* canon. Characters in *Buffy* and *Angel* are used to new forms and genealogies of vampires, and developing strategies for how to slay them is an integral part of the narrative structure of episodes in both series.

14. Milly Williamson, *The Lure of the Vampire: Gender, Fiction and Fandom from Bram Stoker to Buffy* (London: Wallflower Press, 2005. Print), 31.

15. Williamson, 188.

16. To create an image of a human-sembling family, Emmett, Edward, and Alice Cullen pose as adopted, and Rosalie and Jasper Hale as foster children. The pairings of Emmett and Rosalie, and of Alice and Jasper do not, therefore, represent biological incest. However, as Bella's friend Jessica exclaims, with a voice full of "shock and condemnation," the romantic relationships are still perceived as breaking a social taboo: "They're all *together*...And they *live* together." Stephenie Meyer, *Twilight* (2006; London: Little, Brown book, 2007. Print), 18.

17. Chapter 3: "Fight." The substitution of animal blood for the human equivalent is not exclusive to Meyer's vampires. Anne Rice's Louis, for example, attempts to survive on a diet of rats rather than take human lives. Charlaine Harris' Vampire Bill (and many of his kind) subsists on synthetically produced blood that even further diminishes the threat to humans.

18. Chapter 2: "Los Angeles."

19. Chapter 3: "Fight" and Chapter 7: "Neither here nor there."

20. Chapter 5: "To Hell and Back."

21. Chapter 6: "Today."

22. starshinedown and pogurl, *Love Man*. Web. Accessed December 5, 2009. www.twilighted.net. *Dirty Dancing*. Dir. Emile Ardolino. Perf. Jennifer Grey, Patrick Swayze, Jerry Orbach (Great American Films Limited Partnership, 1987. Film.)

23. Stephenie Meyer, *New Moon* (2006; London: Little, Brown book, 2009. Print), 12 and *Breaking Dawn,* (2008; London: Little, Brown book, 2009. Print), 45.
24. Caitlin Flanagan, "What Girls Want," *Atlantic Monthly* (Dec. 2008. Print), 117.
25. Christine Seifert, "Bite me! (Or Don't)," *Bitch Magazine* (nd). Web. Accessed January 10, 2010, np. http://bitchmagazine.org/
26. *Breaking Dawn,* 90.
27. Seifert, np.
28. SnowWhiteHeart, *Dear God.* Web. Accessed December 5, 2009. www.twilighted. net
29. Fred Botting, *Gothic Romanced: Consumption, Gender, and Technology in Contemporary Fictions* (London: Routledge, 2008. Print), 77.
30. Although no other similarities beyond the superhuman intervention should be inferred, the inspiration Edward gives the novelist can be read as an extratextual reference to Meyer's professed dream inspiration for the *Twilight* saga. Stephenie Meyer homepage, (n.d), Web. Accessed Januart 10, 2010. http://www.stepheniemeyer.com/
31. shoefreak37, *The Strange Design of Comfort.* Web. Accessed December 5, 2009. www. twilighted. net
32. See Patricia Frazer Lamb and Diana Veith, "Romantic Myth, Transcendence, and Star Trek Zines" *Erotic Universe: Sexuality and Fantastic Literature.* Ed. Donald Palumbo (New York: Greenwood, 1986. Print), 235–55, and Henry Jenkins, *Textual Poachers: Television Fans and Participatory Culture* (New York: Routledge, 1992. Print).
33. Christina Scodari, "Resistance Re-Examined: Gender, Fan Practices, and Science Fiction," *Popular Communication* (1:2. 2003. Print), 125.
34. See Maria Lindgren Leavenworth, "Lover Revamped: Sexualities and Romance in the Black Dagger Brotherhood and Slash Fan Fiction," *Extrapolation* (50. 2009. Print), 442–462.
35. Elizabeth Woledge, "Intimatopia: Genre Intersections Between Slash and the Mainstream," *Fan Fiction and Fan Communities in the Age of the Internet,* 100.
36. Anne Kustritz, "Slashing the Romance Narrative," *The Journal of American Culture* (26. 2004. Print), 379.
37. Esther Saxey, "Staking a Claim: the Series and its Slash Fan Fiction." *Reading the Vampire Slayer: the New Updated, Unofficial Guide to Buffy and Angel.* Ed. Roz Kaveney (London: Tauris Parke, 2004. Print), 206.
38. *Twilight,* 433.
39. *Breaking Dawn,* 699.
40. Hutcheon, 9.
41. Stephenie Meyer, *Midnight Sun,* Web. Accessed January 10, 2010. http://www.stepheniemeyer.com/
42. Stephenie Meyer, *The Short Second Life of Bree Tanner* (London: Little, Brown, 2010. Print).

CHAPTER 6

TRUE BLOOD WAITS: THE ROMANCE OF LAW AND LITERATURE

MEREDITH WALLIS

As STEPHENIE MEYER WOULD HAVE IT, the *Twilight* saga is not much of a romance, or rather, "it's a romance more than anything else, but it's just not that romance-y."[1] Certainly, something (actually a lot of something) romance-y is happening at the level of description—"my personal miracle...Time had not made me immune to the perfection of his face"[2]; "my mouth glued to his...answering every unspoken question his asked."[3] And in dialogue: "Before you, Bella, my life was like a moonless night...you shot across my sky like a meteor. Suddenly everything was on fire."[4] In genre romance, the principles' love story does the work of the narrative: whether or not the protagonist loves and is loved, to what extent and how drives the plot to a comedy of errors or a deceptive confusion, later explained, still later forgiven. The climax, preceded by what *Pride and Prejudice*'s Elizabeth Bennett explains as the removal of "former prejudices," is the confession: where Mr. Darcy tells Elizabeth "of feelings, which, in proving of what importance she was to him, made his affection every moment more valuable."[5] On the level of narrative form, then, the *Twilight* saga arrives at something like genre trouble as it departs decidedly from the structure: the climax is not Edward and Bella having (or not having) sex or a lingering, gothic death followed by a marriage, as in the much referenced *Wuthering Heights*. Instead, suspense is ultimately provided by and resolved through a courtroom drama, Perry Mason–style with a surprise witness (Alice!) and shocking testimony (more dhampirs!). Moreover, the central conflict of the novels—whether or not Bella will become a vampire—is decided not by love or choice but by various species of juridical wrangling: first in the form of the Volturi's edict, then legislatively, when Bella calls for a vote of the Cullen family, and finally legitimated with an amendment to the Quileute/Cullen treaty. What drives the conflicts is the vampire secrecy law from which any and all other laws stem and which, like any good foundational taboo, seems to be defined by nothing more than constant violation. The real villains of the series are the black-robed Volturi, the "ruling class . . . [who] have assumed the position of enforcing [vampire] rules—which actually translates to punishing transgressors."[6] To complete the saturation of legal metonyms, Bella's father, the most important nonsupernatural character, is a cop. So there is something romance-y here, in the genre sense. The series centers around a relationship rebelled against, challenged, and ultimately reconciled, with both parties changed—a change of jurisprudence rather than sensibility, or perhaps more accurately, a change of jurisprudential sensibility. The business of *Twilight* is still, obviously and unabashedly, desire (a skim of the back-covers is sufficient to make this point). The difference is in the object choice: the romance of the *Twilight* saga turns out to be with the law.

This is a chapter about that romance, about what is between law and literature. For the late jurist Robert Cover, the relationship, like Bella believes of her vampire love, is one of inextricable entanglement. The inseparability is, at its most abstract and perhaps most obvious level, ontological: law is not, as Justice Holmes wrote in 1881, "the axioms and corollaries of a book of mathematics," but rather a set of narratives or, to paraphrase Holmes, the embodiment of a story.[7] Cover's meaning, here, is both more expansive and more specific: "No set of legal institutions or prescriptions exists apart from the narratives that locate it and give it meaning. For every constitution there is an epic."[8] The creation of legal meaning is cultural and collective, a process Cover terms *jurisgenesis*, and law comes into being not through pronouncement, but through interpretation, that is, at the moment of an interpretative act, or using Cover's more evocative word, *commitment*, official or private: acts which hold together a given *nomos* and become laws of the *polis*. Each part of a written constitution (or statute) has no meaning outside the narratives used to explain it, outside of the interpretations of the epics used to support a given hermeneutic (i.e., the divergent usages of Biblical text to either uphold or reject capital punishment as an appropriate interpretation of the Eighth Amendment injunction against "cruel and unusual punishment"[9]). The heart of Cover's project is a plea for a richer hermeneutic field, and as such his most salient political critique is about a praxis of resistance—a refusal to cede legal meaning to the exclusive province of the state (even given discrepant power distribution). For this reason, he focuses on *conscious* commitments made from communities who actively produce oppositional legal meaning, for example, abolitionists, religious sectarians, civil disobedients. His ethical thrust is this: "We ought to stop circumscribing the *nomos;* we ought to invite new worlds."[10]

Theories of resistance, then, must also invite new worlds. What follows is not precisely a critique but an expansion: all jurisgenesis requires commitments, but most commitments are something less than conscious. These less-than-conscious commitments derive from the cultural productions, including but not limited to literature, that go into making "sense" make sense, that is, making *sense* common, which is also to say, making specific meanings *popular*. All narratives—and thus, all cultural media engaged in producing such narratives—have the potential for jurisgenesis, but a commitment must be made to this nominally extralegal text (the epic) as well as to a sanctioned legal text (the constitution), and the simplest and most direct index of such a commitment would be the popularity of the work, the quantity and quality of consumption. Thus, while Cover selects the *Torah* and Attic dramas like the

Oresteia for his epics, I've picked Meyer's commercial juggernaut about the trials of a clumsy teenager in love with a glittery, century-old vampire.[11] *Twilight* does legal work because it has been chosen (i.e., has been committed to) above and beyond similar texts, but it is also chosen because of the work it does, that which allows the audience, to use a teen colloquialism, "to relate" to the text.[12] The formulation—every constitution is an epic— includes implicitly a relationship not just of influence but of equivalence: that is, that every epic is a constitution. Thus, I am making a claim not for *Twilight* as merely a text of legal socialization or regulation (though it is these things) but *as law itself*, or as Desmond Manderson puts it, as "a source of law," a site of production for structures of legal subjectivity. The romance under investigation here is not precisely the intratextual one of literature with law, but the intertextual romance of law with literature. The legalistic themes and genre trouble of *Twilight* matter here not as evidence of why *Twilight* is a jurisgenerative text (it could be one without explicit legal tropes as Manderson demonstrates of *Where the Wild Things Are*, more on which later), but as evidence of a *nomos* saturated by juridical language, which tells us less about a relationship to a particular jurisprudence and more about the production of a specific subject.

As the specific historical subject of youth is defined as both a transition *from* and *to* another subjectivity, what makes texts from the marketing category-cum-genre of "young adult (YA) literature" relatable is not just some accurate mimetic identification of the experience of being a teenager but a narrative continuity with the preceding literature. Teasing out the relationship to law advocated by the structure of *Twilight*, then, requires locating the narrative predecessor in children's literature of the juridical subject YA literature is assumed to have acquired. Though *Twilight* is often grouped with the YA genre of horror or fantasy, it might be usefully understood as part of a subgenre or category that I will call the teen monster story. From a jurisprudential point of view, the logical precursor for the teen monster story is the magical journey narrative. The magical journey traditionally begins with a disorderly or disobedient act: either implicit—like Dorothy's inability to follow her Aunt Em's command or Alice's impetuous rabbit hole choice[13]—or explicit like Max's wolf-suit and cannibalistic threats in Maurice Sendak's *Where the Wild Things Are*. After the disorderly act, the child enters a fantasy land of different rules, populated by monsters and wonders. The child usually attempts in some way to replicate the (recently disobeyed) legal order of his or her own world—Max's commands to the wild things, Alice's attempts to impose British manners. In so doing, the child begins retroactively to obey, which precipitates the return to the ordinary world, often understood, as Susan Honeyman puts it, as a way to "explain away the inaccessibility of childhood and spaces invented for it by having children grow out of them."[14] Honeyman's (horizontal) spatial use of grow *out* instead of the (vertical) temporal grow *up* is key: the end of the fantasy narrative is seldom adulthood. Children grow out of the fantasy land like growing past interest in a puzzle—through sufficiently exhausting their own interpretations of the game and learning the "proper" one.

In his analysis of *Where the Wild Things Are* as a source of law, Desmond Manderson identifies the return as a kind of learning, a representation of the child-protagonist's choice to be responsible for and to law.[15] In returning, the child learns to love the law by transitioning from a position of being subject *to* its regulation to one of becoming a legal subject. Drawing on Levinas, Manderson defines this subjectivity as "our sub-jection through responsibility to others," and by this, he means that Max makes an ethical choice for responsibility rather than obedience.[16] The monsters remain behind in the fantasy world, literally wild *things*, prelegal objects set in contrast to the rapidly *civilizing* protagonist. The door to the magic land generally only swings one way, meaning only the child is eligible to become a subject, to enter the new legal order through a rejection (of the Wild) and a choice to follow law by subjugat-ing desire. The benefit of this practice of restraint—that is, the reward for not just following but loving law—is readily apparent at the conclusions of these narratives: explicitly parental love is offered and implicitly protection is provided from the vio-lence of disorder, of things that don't make sense.

In the magical land narratives, the child might start out displaying monstrous tendencies toward disobedience, but he makes (duly rewarded) choices to accept the legal order, to put away wildish things. In the transition to an older audience, monsters come out of the closet, as it were: they attend high school, worry obses-sively about crushes and controlling their monster-hormones, dramatize each anxiety as one of mortal peril, and "sometimes…have a problem with [their] temper."[17] In short, monsters are teenagers. Or rather, the narrative shift from fantasy land to teen monster story highlights how the discursive representation of adolescence is monstrous.

Contributing to this conflation, the favored monsters are also humanoid or half-human—vampires, werewolves, faeries, angels—torn between two sets of norma-tive commitments and belonging to neither.[18] The ubiquitous "rules scene," where the human is taught the rules of the real monster world as opposed to the mythic one, dramatizes this tension—that growing into a teenager is also a process of gain-ing access to knowledge about rules of the adult world which challenge conceptions formed in childhood. *Twilight*'s rules scene comes in the first book as Edward debunks a series of Bella's assumptions based on vampire lore, replying "myth" to each. Meyer's vampires are neither burned by the light nor sleep during the day, and almost a hun-dred pages later when he steps into the sun, Edward supplies *Twilight*'s contribution to *vampir* mythology, more My Little Pony than nosferatu: "he…literally sparkled, like thousands of tiny diamonds were embedded in the surface."[19]

If the essence of what it means to be a vampire is to be one who drinks the blood of humans, then the "vegetarian" Cullens are not quite vampires, but can never be human, as pages (and pages) of description of their unearthly beauty and power attest. They inhabit a liminal state between two legal orders. I want to make a distinc-tion between this claim to liminality and a more general description of the vampire as liminal, as for example *undead* (neither alive nor dead).[20] The Cullens make a moral choice to live in this state in order to be good. The choice shares more with vegetarianism than Meyer might have intended as it is not a revolutionary position, but, to borrow a phrase from the 1990s, an alternative lifestyle, meant not to disrupt or challenge the system but to negotiate an alternative normative space within it. In jurisprudential terms, the Cullens' vegetarianism does generate a legal meaning but not a radical or (as Cover terms it) *redemptive* one; the Cullens' lifestyle is fully compatible with the legal norms of both the vampire and human societies. Edward explains his vegetarianism to Bella in terms of personal desire: "I don't *want* to be a monster."[21] For the monster, being good, then, requires (1) a desire not to desire (and thus a severing of desire from pleasure) and (2) a practice of restraint, which explains why Edward considers himself rebelling by simply allowing himself to sit with Bella in the first book: "I'm giving up...trying to be good. I'm just going to do what I want now."[22]

Shifting restraint and the subjugation of desire away from the protagonist to the monster complicates the implied relationship between authority and desire. In the magical land narrative, the child accepts authority as if she had the power of a choice between discrete entities: the legal order or the chaotic *id*. Bella, on the other hand, lives in a world in which her choices are seldom if ever respected and where she frequently is unsure whether she has the possibility of selection: "I could do nothing different....I didn't know if there ever was a choice, really."[23] If we take Bella's statements of her lack of choice literally for a moment, instead of reading them as an adolescent excuse or an archetypal feminine pathology, then we might read her as demonstrating a real understanding about the effect of relations of power on the process of jurisgenesis. The child is empowered to make a choice regarding authority and to come to understand its purposes. But notice the passive nature of *em*powered—by whom? For what purpose? Bella has the ability to create meaning—jurisgenesis—and she does, by radically reinterpreting Edward's understandings about what it means to be a vampire, by refusing to cede to the official interpretation of vampire-as-damned. But Bella has neither the power to make herself a vampire nor that which would prevent her from being killed by the Volturi for knowing their secrets. Put in Cover's language: "The conclusion emanating from this state of affairs is simple and very disturbing: there is a radical dichotomy between the social organization of law as power and the organization of law as meaning."[24] Manderson sees the legal child subjectivity produced in *Where the Wild Things Are* as one that acknowledges the choice to take on the responsibilities that are passed down to us from benevolent authority figures. In contrast, following Cover, the legal adolescent subjectivity produced in *Twilight* is one that challenges the relationship between benevolence and authority and acknowledges the consequences of this relationship on the possibility of choice.

The possibility of having your legal meaning elected depends not on your will, but on that of the judicial power. Courts, including vampire ones, do not adjudicate truth, but a quantum of interpretation, a selection between competing narratives under a rubric that asks not *which is more truthful* but *which is more convincing*. The final adjudicative authority does not create legal meanings, but kills them—what Cover terms the *jurispathic* function of judges— naturalizing, through the appearance of some sort of equally weighed contest of literary hermeneutics, the violence of the enterprise, "the shadow of coercion."[25] The drama of the court room, then, is not one of finding the interpretation closest to Law, but one of marketing the most convincing interpretation to those who have the power to enforce commitments with the violence of the state or, in the case of the Volturi, the martial resources of the aristocracy. The menacing Volturi, in fact, makes clear what the decorum and civility of the courtroom are meant to obscure: that the most *convincing* narrative does not achieve this status through logic, but through power. Bella's predicament—her lack of choice—shows law to be a process and practice of interpretative commitments located and given meaning through the diffuse and often contradictory narratives that make up a *nomos* and weighed by respective access to capital (economic but also symbolic, institutional, cultural).

The consequence of this weighing—that some interpretations, and thus some legal meanings, are more equal than others—tends to overwhelm the other consequence—that our cultural narratives generate these meanings—with the result of reinforcing the fetishization of law, that is, reproducing the mythologies that order and naturalize inequitably structured relations of power by fixing (hegemonic) meaning and animating the law as subject (e.g., "this building is closed by law"; "it's the law"). Roland Barthes describes the function of myth as emptying reality: "literally, a ceaseless flowing out, a hemorrhage, or perhaps an evaporation, in short a perceptible absence."[26] This absence becomes perceptible at moments of fissure, where an occurrence or speech-act resists being brought under reigning schemas of intelligibility. Consider, for example, the following propositions from *Twilight* law: (1) *all immortal children are illegal* and (2) *immortal children born and not made are not illegal.* The prior law—all immortal children are illegal—sits alongside the amendment—except those born—creating a fissure, which in turn, shows the idea of legality as a known, uncontested concept to be mythic. The meaning chosen turns out to depend on those who, most visibly in the context of a climax of gathering vampire armies, have the power to define it.

But Bella does make choices, and what Bella is able to choose, what she *desires*, is just as revealing jurisprudentially as what she is not. To love the good monster in such a way that he stays good means Bella must desire his restraint, his abstinence, and thus her own subjectivity is defined not by abstaining but by waiting. In a switch from the teen romance formula of dramatizing temptation and waiting for desire (the someday-my-prince-will-come model), the teen monster story dispenses with the pretense of fighting temptation and eroticizes the state of waiting. In the context of consumerism, Honeyman tracks a similar shift in Hansel and Gretel retellings: "Whereas premodern stories indicate that blame, thus agency, resides with the kids lured (as clarified by their responsibility to resist temptation), consumerist revisions of such mythologies involve relocating agency in the lure itself. Consumers are increasingly depicted as willing victims of a manipulation wherein deeper structure is concealed, agency being reimagined as externally located (impossibly) in ephemeral confections."[27] Although Honeyman is specifically speaking to the affect necessary to produce docile consumers, this stage of late capitalism needs a legal subjectivity as well, and what better way to produce one than a *desire for waiting,* the exact legal situation of the twentieth-century construction of adolescence.[28]

Manufactured adolescence-as-waiting—to work, to vote, to graduate, to consent to sex, etc.—betrays another legal quandary of this temporal construction, namely, that neither the privileges nor regulations of the states that it is constructed out of and against—childhood and adulthood—apply fully. Like monsterhood, then, adolescence is characterized by its own moral ontological impossibility—that is, the good teenager, like the good vampire, is one who is not a teenager at all.[29] Thus, Bella's version of the Cullens' "vegetarianism" is a (very) quiet rebellion against being a teen girl (i.e., a refusal to be a teenager), typified by her disengagement, by her status as a loner who doesn't "relate well to people [her] age."[30] Bella is not great at school or sports, barely reads, and has no hobbies. She is also dutiful—volunteering for chores, serving as her father's maid and cook, and doing all her homework. She is, at best, a reluctant consumer, indifferent to shopping, clothes, cars, and nonvampire-related gossip. Her ennui is continually set in contrast to the bubbling normalcy of the other human girls that she can barely bring herself to make friends with, interacting with normal teenagers with about as much gusto as the Cullens bring to their five hundredth repetition of high school. Here, the pattern should be more recognizable as part of a familiar genealogy, that of the anti-teenage teen girl: Bella is the next generation (or perhaps next, next generation) of *Pretty in Pink*'s Andie Walsh—lower middle-class, a mother figure for her distraught, abandoned father, adored by her male best friend, and in love with a seemingly unattainable rich guy who is associated with the endless consumption (cars, clothes, colleges) that she initially shuns but is allowed to accept through the obligations of love. Thus Honeyman's willing victim of consumerism meets the legal subjectivity of the "good" teenager to produce a story that is less the *Wuthering Heights* that Meyer aspires to than *Emma*, and less that than *Clueless*: what it is that Bella is waiting for is not a star-crossed love, but the make-over into the legal subject she aspires to be.[31] Bella might be a subpar human, but by the end of the series, we learn that she's a really, really excellent vampire, whose main power turns out to be the resistance that had originally been located in Edward. The jurisprudential value of the make-over narrative is in how the transition to the new subject inevitably requires a transition of sensibility (i.e., Mr. Knightley proclaiming Emma "materially changed"[32] or *Clueless*' Cher attempting to become socially conscious), which is, simultaneously, a transition of the rules governing the subject (Emma becomes the type of girl who *would marry*, Cher becomes the type of girl who interests her former step-brother).

In Manderson's reading, part of how Max learns responsibility is by transitioning "from being an object obliged to follow orders, to a legal subject who feels a genuine sense of obligation to the law."[33] Bella is a teenager, though, and the inquiry she presents is one of radical jurisprudence: just what is the law to which she is to be obligated? Her relationship to the laws is one of production within a field of constraint, and her desire is for (new) law. It is here where Bella's character distinguishes herself from other characters in the romantic subgenres. The human girl in vampire romances rarely if ever *wants* to be a vampire, and even in the adult monster romances, her resistance to becoming undead usually provides much of the drama.[34] Bella not only wants to be a vampire, but pursues this goal with the single-minded tenacity usually reserved in teen girl culture for getting the boy, the pony, or Harvard. Being a vampire is, in colloquial terms, her (un)life-goal. If children are like lawyers, as Manderson suggests, in their search for proper (read: accepted by authority) interpretations of rules, then Bella is like a lawyer in what is perhaps the least popular sense: zealous advocacy. The level of advocacy required for lawyers is an ethical responsibility, here, from the Model Rules of Professional Responsibility: "As advocate, a lawyer zealously asserts the client's position under the rules of the adversary system."[35] Bella's advocacy is set in contrast jurisprudentially to both Edward—her inaugural authority into the new law—and the Volturi—the ruling class of the new order.

Edward is a rule hound, worrying constantly about the law of monsters, of humans, and of the divine (no sex before marriage, no turning Bella into an undead beast who might feast on the faces of her family, blah, blah, blah). In *Eclipse*, we have a typical scene of Edward condescending to Bella's interpretation of rules. She's arguing for sex before marriage, and he counters with this: "Now, there's a world full of dissension about this, but the vast majority seem to think that there are some rules that have to be followed."[36] Cleverly, Bella counters using the technique of conflict of laws: "Vampire rules aren't enough for you? You want to worry about the human ones too?"[37] The "rules" of which Edward speaks require no interpretation because he has ceded legal meaning to whatever qualifies as the state in the order sovereign to his particular inquiry, for example, Christianity for marriage, vampiric consensus for damnation. Whereas Bella's zealous advocacy makes her a resister, a revolutionary, who puts forth legal meanings in direct contrast to the state, who claims she can have no life outside her interpretation, Edward is a voice piece for the status quo, or in more class-specific terms, middle management.

The Volturi, in contrast to Edward, are management, of course, and appropriately appear to favor legal formalism—there is a Law beyond law that gives meaning to any given rule (conveniently the meaning that most favors the class making the rules)—particularly in the first "court" scene in *New Moon* when they make clear that per the secrecy rule, Bella's life is forfeit if she is not either killed at the end of her use or granted immortality. The animation of law as subject by Caius is a typical trope of formalism; here, speaking of Edward and Bella's violation of the secrecy code: "The law claims them."[38] In the second court drama, Aro again demonstrates formalist logic by disregarding Carlisle's defense that he did not intend to create an immortal child: "how can your intent possibly matter, dear Carlisle, in the face of what you have done."[39] The solution to this challenge in *Breaking Dawn* seems to rest at first in a battle of interpretations, the traditional problem of "meaning" in law. Aro is the judge; Caius, the prosecution; Edward, the defense. The legal issue before the court: does a rule outlawing vampire children extend to a child born of a vampire and a human who will grow for a period of time and then maintain immortality? The issue of Renesmee—immortal child or dhampir—again points to the contrast between the social organization of law as power and as interpretation: jurisgenesis cannot be unhinged from the relations of power that code the jurispathic function of selection. But set, as it is, in contrast to Bella's redemptive interpretations of legal meaning, the very idea of formalism—that there is a Law outside of law—is challenged. This jurisprudence goes beyond hermeneutics to look at power, which Aro betrays when he switches the issue before the court: "No broken law...does it follow then that there is no danger?...That is a separate issue."[40] The nomadic vampire Garrett also affirms this emphasis on power in his speech, claiming the Volturi have come to protect their rule by destroying the "good" vampires: "These ancient ones did *not* come here for justice as they told you."[41] To no great surprise, the *Twilight* saga's jurisprudential approach is one that matches the adolescent subjectivity it also produces—one which recognizes the power of law's regulation while challenging, not the idea of law, but its representative source.

This court scene betrays another myth, one of temporal ordering, to which Edward is susceptible and the Volturi are strategic: violation appears to proceed in an orderly fashion from law; in other words, you choose whether to obey or disobey and get punished by law accordingly. The logical flaw in this ordering is clear from the outset as a problem of the origins: law must begin, as revolutionaries and martyrs are so keen to remind us, in illegality, in a founding violence that relies on temporal displacement that, as Jacques Derrida explains, justifies "recourse to violence by alleging the founding, in progress or to come, of a new law, of a new state. As this law to come will in return legitimate, retrospectively, the violence that may offend the sense of justice, its future anterior already justifies it."[42] This temporal paradox is not simply one of origins, but a problem inherent to language that occurs at each instance of interpretation. If we understand law to be acts of textual interpretation, then the problem of retroactively justified violence exists in every moment of law. Law is made out of its perceived violation; wherein, judgment is a retroactive application of meaning, an exercise of choice whose justness is promised by a future perfect and can therefore only be determined by its confirmation thereafter.

The temporal ordering myth, understood in conjunction with law as an interpretative commitment, should not be read as dystopic. Quite the contrary: that the interpretative commitment of jurisprudence comes out of perceived violation is what frees up consent from its unsightly marriage to state obedience. One may, as Bella does, consent to an interpretation that is not that of the ruling class in accordance with another narrative, and one's violation and violence, like that of the Volturi's, has the opportunity to be justified in a future anterior. Consent-related resistance, then, should be understood not as *civil disobedience* but as *uncivil obedience*—obedience to something not fully included nor fully excluded by the civil. By resisting Edward's middle-management nagging and the imperial edicts of the Volturi, Bella does a specific kind of legal work, one which is often framed dismissively (and paternalistically) as "teenage rebellion," that is, a temporally bound resistance to good sense. By obeying her own fully formed interpretation of vampires as different but not evil, Bella resists, to paraphrase Antonio Gramsci, not good sense but common sense.

However, the sophistication of this jurisprudential methodology is undercut by its substantive goals. Although the Volturi are questioned as kings, the Cullens do not revolt, wishing only to be left alone to pursue their lifestyle, more Amish than evangelical in their juridical approach. In the same way, Bella's radical interpretation is belied by the content of her desires. She's certainly a zealous advocate; she might even be one precisely within the definition proposed by the Model Rules. But who is her client? This, I think, rather than some nostalgic fondness for '90s-style "girl power," is the true contrast to *Buffy the Vampire Slayer*: Buffy (like Nancy Drew or Veronica Mars or the Power Puff Girls) is chosen for a job, and not just any job, but a job of saving others. (Even Harriet was a spy.) Keeping in mind that Bella's pregnancy was not only unplanned but inconceivable to our protagonist, Bella's desire to become a vampire has nothing to do with labor of any sort; rather, the transformation centers on a fantasy of leisure, a life lived with the sole purpose of loving a man and becoming part of his family. The vampire family, like representations of particularly fervent immigrants, is described as über-American. Their favorite pastime is baseball. They have a car for all seasons. They eat a lot of red meat and enjoy hunting. But they are also the idle aristocracy of *Gossip Girl*, wealthy parasites with endless leisure time whose only real drama seems to be whom they might sleep with, what they will have for dinner, and whether those things will be the same.[43]

The text raises the stakes of Bella's decision, not by transitioning her into a legal advocate for a cause or client beyond her own social climbing, but by highlighting the vampires' perception of humanity, which initially brings the text more in line with the traditional constructions of adolescent subjectivity as having to do with loss. The Cullens' abstinence, what Aro terms their "unorthodox path," comes out of a belief in the great, irreversible loss of their humanity. Edward and Rosalie, in particular, see their nonconsensual transition to vampirism as one of damnation, of the loss of their souls, and thus Bella's consenting and (worse) overwhelming desire for this violence has to be read in an interpretative framework where Edward and Rosalie's beliefs might turn out to be true, thus making Bella, like many teenagers (and adults), wrong about the consequences of attaining the desire she so zealously pursues.

This qualification about Bella's interpretation of vampirism should be read as distinct from the popular critique of the series that locates the problem of Bella's desire in an inability to appreciate the danger Edward's unapologetically obsessive and physically damaging behavior towards Bella (e.g., watching her sleep, stalking her, blaming her "smell" for his desire, roughing her up during sex). This framing reproduces the sexism it seeks to critique by assuming that this aspect of the story is the one which is *fantasy*. Clearly, part of what one is waiting for in the manufactured space of adolescence is to escape the regulation and surveillance which defines the category (demonstrated most grotesquely by phenomena like Dateline's *To Catch a Predator* or new technologies like human-implantable radiofrequency identification), to transition out of a legal subjectivity that requires an acceptance of authority qua authority.[44] Read in this way, Edward's behavior attains a sort of metonymic verisimilitude. Far more disturbing than the idea of abuse as a secret desire that must be squelched by a vigilant feminist critique is a reality of abuse that we misdiagnose as desire.

Bella's radical jurisprudence and the law that emerges from the *Twilight* saga point toward a different fantasy, one which is more utopic impulse than romantic escapism. Meyer gives us a transition without loss, transforming the traditionally sentimentalized end of childhood into a gift, into that which, through persistent advocacy, makes a boring, clumsy teen into an unusually strong, exceptional vampire, who, significantly, becomes more powerful than those who previously threatened her safety, including the two legal authorities of the new order: Edward and the Volturi. Taking seriously the ways in which adolescents might enjoy *The Twilight Saga* as a fantasy that they relate to means understanding how what seems most problematic about the series might in fact be what is most normative and not necessarily what is most appealing. In other words, the "fantasy" at work here—but also the one to be worked for—might be a world where adolescent pleasure and hermeneutic strategy possess the potential for jurisgenesis, that is to say also, the potential for juridical integrity. If becoming an adult necessitates a linguistic and metaphoric death of the child, we can look at a work like the *Twilight* series as grappling quite literally with the anxiety that motivates being a teenager, the space we have set aside to deal with the question at the heart of this violent transition: how do you get out of childhood alive? And, less metaphorically, and more jurisprudentially: how do you get out of childhood *good*?

NOTES

1. Meyer in an interview with Gregory Kirschling, "Stephenie Meyer's 'Twilight' Zone," *Entertainment Weekly* (5 Jul. 2008), Web. Accessed September 8, 2010. np.
2. Stephenie Meyer, *Eclipse* (New York: Little, Brown and Company, 2007. Print), 17.
3. Ibid., 618.
4. Stephenie Meyer, *New Moon* (New York: Little, Brown and Company, 2006. Print), 514.
5. Jane Austen, *Pride and Prejudice* (New York: Dover Publications, 1995. Print), 247. *Pride and Prejudice* is useful here both as a text marked as an originary point for contemporary genre romance form and as one cited by Meyer specifically as an inspiration for her work, in particular for the first book. From a 2008 interview: "All of the books in the *Twilight* Saga have a classical inspiration. With *Twilight*, it was *Pride and Prejudice*. Very loosely related." Meyer, Little, Brown and Company, 2008, Web. http://www.youtube.com/watch?v=UVEvEtF08S8&feature=player_embedded.
6. Meyer, *New Moon*, 429–30.
7. Oliver Wendell Holmes, *The Common Law* (New York: Dover Publications, 1991. Print), 1.
8. Robert Cover, "Nomos and Narrative," *Harvard Law Review* 97, no. 68 (1984): 4.
9. In one of the most famous cases on the death penalty and the Eighth Amendment—*Furman v. Georgia*—each of the nine Supreme Court Justices filed a separate opinion. In his dissent from the ruling that the death penalty in the cases did constitute "cruel and unusual punishment," Chief Justice Burger expressed the problem of multiple, conflicting narratives thus: "[t]he widely divergent views of the Amendment expressed in today's opinion reveal the haze that surrounds this constitutional command" 408 U.S. 238 (1972), 376 (Burger, C.J., dissenting). For a comprehensive layout of the different arguments, see Daniel A. Rudolph, "The Misguided Reliance in American Jurisprudence on Jewish Law to Support the Moral Legitimacy of Capital Punishment," *American Criminal Law Review* 33 (1996).
10. Cover, 68.
11. Certainly, the *Twilight* saga can be considered epic in the sense of scale. If taken as one text, which I will do, the four-parter clocks in at 2,443 pages, longer than the almost never-published unabridged juggernaut of *Les Misérables*, though with considerably larger font. In the J.K. Rowling school of series-writing (or perhaps more accurately marketing), Meyer follows the reverse nesting doll practice, each book bigger than the one that came before.
12. Obviously, Meyer was not filling some void of vampire young adult fiction or even a more specific void of YA vampire romance between a human girl and an unbearably hot gentleman-vampire—L.J. Smith had a successful run mining this theme decades earlier in her *Vampire Diaries* series, now a television show on the CW—and the year before *Twilight*'s release, publishers promoted the thematically similar *Vampire Kisses* series and *Touched by a Vampire*. The idea that popularity causes legal influence relies on an assumption about the working of trends in capitalism that analyzes fads qua fads, unhinged from any substantive content that might make a difference in a popular object's appeal to a specific audience at a specific moment. The question of why, given a set of similar market variables, promotion and theme, Meyer's *Twilight* succeeds over something like Mari Mancusi's *Stake That* must turn for its answer in what Franco Moretti calls "a process of deliberate reduction and abstraction," to details smaller than the text proper —here, jurisprudential sensibility—and larger—here, genre. See Moretti, *Graphs, Maps, Trees* (New York: Verso, 2005. Print), 1.

13. Two roughly contemporaneous film versions of older classics—*Peter Pan* and *The Wizard of Oz*—both feature explicit disobedience not appearing in the book versions.

14. Susan Honeyman, *Elusive Childhood: Impossible Representations in Modern Fiction* (Chicago: Ohio State Press, 2005. Print), 69. Honeyman goes on: "the writer must negate the fantasy with the dream motif, realistically engineer a return to 'reality,' or leave that child and space accessible, somehow balancing an impossible illusion of entry despite its accessibility" (73).

15. Desmond Manderson, "From Hunger to Love: Myths of Source, Interpretation, and Constitution of Law in Children's Literature" *Law & Literature* 15 (2003).

16. Ibid., 135.

17. Stephenie Meyer, *Twilight* (New York: Little, Brown and Company, 2007. Print), 164.

18. See Michel Foucault, here, from *Abnormal*: "Thus the monster is said to be a being in which the mixture of two kingdoms can be seen...We look for a breach of human and divine law in their progenitors." *Abnormal: Lectures at the Collège de France*, 1974-1975 (New York: Picador, 1999. Print), 64.

19. Meyer, *Twilight*, 260.

20. For a clear working of this argument, see K. A. Nuzum, "The Monster's Sacrifice—Historic Time: The Uses of Mythic and Liminal Time in Monster Literature," *Children's Literature Association Quarterly* 29, No. 3 (2004): 217–227.

21. Meyer, *Twilight*, 187.

22. Ibid., 88.

23. Ibid., 139.

24. Cover, *Nomos*, 18.

25. Ibid., 40.

26. Roland Barthes, *Mythologies* (New York: Straus and Giroux, 1972. Print), 143.

27. Susan Honeyman, "Gingerbread Wishes and Candy(land) Dreams: The Lure of Food in Cautionary Tales of Consumption," *Marvels & Tales* 21, no. 2 (2007): 196.

28. For a detailed description of the "discovery" of American adolescence, see Steven Mintz, *Huck's Raft: A History of American Childhood* (Cambridge: Harvard University Press, 2004. Print),154–199.

29. Meyer makes this easier by having Bella turn 18 and say things like: "Nobody has custody of me. I'm an adult." *Eclipse*, 48.

30. Meyer, *Twilight*, 11.

31. *Clueless* involves more normative references to law: Cher's father is a lawyer, her love interest works for her father, and she consciously emulates her father's profession in order to get what she desires. (Delightfully, given Honeyman's thesis, Cher discovers the truth about her feelings while on a shopping spree.)

32. Jane Austen, *Emma* (London: J.M. Dent & Company, 1892. Print), 247.

33. Manderson, 117.

34. See Laurel K. Hamilton's popular Anita Blake series or Charlaine Harris' Sookie Stackhouse one (the basis for HBO's *True Blood*).

35. John Dzienkowski, Ed., *Professional Responsibility Standards, Rules & Statutes 2006–2007* (St. Paul: Thomson West, 2006), 6.

36. Meyer, *Eclipse*, 453.

37. Ibid.

38. Meyer, *New Moon*, 477.

39. Stephenie Meyer, *Breaking Dawn* (New York: Little, Brown and Company, 2008. Print), 686.

40. Ibid., 715

41. Ibid., 717; original emphasis.

42. Jacques Derrida, *Acts of Religion* (New York: Routledge, 2002), 269.

43. The *Gossip Girl* vampire is also, of course, Marx's capital, "dead labour, which, vampire-like, lives only by sucking living labour, and lives the more, the more labour it sucks." *Capital,* Volume 1 (Norwalk: Easton Press, 1992. Print), 257. The relationship between this metaphor and vampire fiction has been thoroughly worked through. As a model, see Franco Moretti, *Signs Taken for Wonders* (London: Verso, 1988. Print), 83-108. And for contemporary fiction, Rob Latham, *Consuming Youth: Vampires, Cyborgs, and the Culture of Consumption* (Chicago, IL: Chicago University Press, 2002. Print), np.

44. From an early twentieth-century primer on adolescence, part of a rash of advice books that corresponded with the rise of high schools: "When rationalistic parents and teachers ask me when they should cease to command and when begin to explain common grounds of morality, I am almost tempted to the extravagance of replying that there are things for which no reason should be given till the youth is strongest and can whip his elders... argument is sometimes a poor and cheap substitute for respect to personal authority." G. Stanley Hall, *Adolescence, Its Psychology and its Relations to Physiology, Anthropology, Sociology, Sex, Crime Religion and Education* (New York: D. Appleton and Company, 1905. Print), 534.

PART II

GENDER AND SEXUALITY

CHAPTER 7

WAKE UP, BELLA! A PERSONAL ESSAY ON *TWILIGHT*, MORMONISM, FEMINISM, AND HAPPINESS

TAMMY DIETZ

I AM A LITTLE JEALOUS. I'll start there to get it off my chest. First-time novelist makes it big. No graduate school, no writing classes, no queries and rejections, no years and years of writing and editing, and quitting and restarting. According to the bio at the author's website, it took Stephenie Meyer under a year to whip a whimsical dream into a mega-selling series of books.

As is the nature of envy, I am critical. *Twilight* is the most entertaining of the four-book series, but none are well written. It may be in poor taste to dwell on the flaws in an artistic endeavor, particularly when the craft of writing is not the focus of this essay. Suffice it to say that in the rush to take the story from hazy dream to bound page, literary finesse does not seem to have been Meyer's priority. But petty envy and literary style criticisms aside, I found reading *Twilight* to be engaging and also curiously bothersome.

I bought the novel at a Rite Aid during a family vacation at the Oregon coast. While my husband and children played Frisbee and dug tunnels and castles in the coarse northwestern sand, I unfolded a camp chair and angled my floppy hat to shade the pages of my book. Occasionally other women passed me and commented that they were *Twilight* fans, too. I smiled and nodded. I wasn't sure that I was ready to count myself as a fan. Still, like many readers, I finished the first book in a matter of days and when I was done, I couldn't quite tell why I had been compelled to turn each page.

The story seemed so familiar to me, so believable and easy to swallow, and I am not typically a reader of fantasy or romance. But something about *Twilight* struck an old bone that I struggled to identify.

At first, I suspected Meyer's religious affiliation to be the culprit. I was once a Mormon, too, and the surface similarities between *Twilight* and Mormon theology are noteworthy, if usually unnoticed by non-Mormon readers. But I soon discovered there was more to the root of my discontent than the whiff of a harmless religion ambitious to convert new (and stray) members. In *Twilight*, like in Mormonism, buried behind gleaming stories and rituals that spotlight powerful human emotions such as desire, faith, devotion, and love, a disturbing message pulses to a familiar beat. *Twilight* does not just reflect Mormonism, *Twilight* positively glows (or dare I say, sparkles) with Mormonism's least appealing aspect: the subtle but powerful message its worshippers receive that men are superior and women are subordinate.

To see the heart of the matter, however, we must first peel back the layers of similarity beginning with seemingly innocuous common themes in *Twilight* and Mormon ideology.

TWILIGHT AND MORMONISM: ON CHASTITY

First and foremost, Meyer promotes the notion of chastity in the *Twilight* series with a flourish. It is fair to say that *Twilight* succeeds largely because Bella is chaste and Edward abstains—for a very long time. The primary conflict in the lean and simple plot of the first three books rests squarely on the sexual tension between withholding lovers. This tension is emphasized further by the nature of vampire bloodlust. Edward wants Bella in an even more potent (and threatening) way than typical human sexual desire, and Bella's power to tempt Edward is more than ordinary magnetism. The control they must both display, Edward in particular, is symbolized by Edward's vampirism and Bella's humanity.

In the Mormon faith, premarital chastity is paramount for both girls and boys, but particularly for girls, who are viewed as the ones with the power to tempt. For girls, chastity is considered more important than life itself. In *The Book of Mormon*, Jacob recites that the Lord specifically "delights[s] in the chastity of *women*" (Jacob 9:28, emphasis added), and later in the book of Moroni, the purity of the Lamanite daughters is identified as "most precious and dear above all things" (Moroni 9:9). Control of sexual urges prior to marriage is a core idea for many fundamental Christians, and Mormons are no exception. Chastity is a requirement for a temple wedding, which, in the Mormon faith, grants women entrance to the highest levels of heaven. The pressure young Mormon women receive to remain chaste cannot be overstated. Perhaps a personal story captures it best.

In the summer of 1979, I turned twelve and I also attended my very first annual Young Women's conference. It was the largest young adult event I had ever attended, with hundreds of young women from all over the region, and I was not sure what to expect but was overwhelmed by the size of the gathering. The meeting was predictable, for the most part. Singing by the congregation, a few musical solos by particularly talented young women from other Wards, talks about love and honesty, the trueness of our gospel, obedience to the living prophet, all pretty much the same kinds of things I had heard in Sunday School, from which I had just graduated. Until the closing talk. The grand finale.

The Relief Society president stepped up to the podium and cleared her throat. "Girls," she began, "I want you to consider this rose."

Her blouse was baby blue. Ruffles at the neckline. She also wore white gloves, an unusual but striking accessory. In a gloved hand, she held a single long-stemmed red rose with petals just beginning to open.

"What a beauty to behold," she said into the microphone, and then paused. "Now. What if I were to remove a petal from this rose. Just one petal won't make a difference, right?"

She plucked a petal, the red of the rose garish against the white of her gloved hand. "What if I remove another?" She removed another petal and waited a moment for us to see the slight change in shape, the imperfection. She continued removing petals until only one remained, attached but compromised. Twice she attempted to hold the last petal upright, but it slumped back down each time. She set the mutilated rose on the podium, removed her gloves, and silently clasped her bare hands.

"Girls, *you* are this rose," she said. "This rose could be *you*."

I was stunned and rapt by the gravity of her message and I waited for clarity to follow. She told us that just as the rose is perfect in the Lord's sight, so, too, were we. But if we allowed ourselves to be spoiled and defaced, such sins could be forgiven but never recovered. Once our flower was plucked, it was no more. It would not regrow its petals. It could not regain its beauty. Its lovely scent would be but a memory. It would be useless.

My heart thudded in my chest. At the time, I was not even quite sure I understood what she was talking about, but felt ashamed anyway.

To conclude the evening, roses were handed out. Each and every girl received her very own long-stemmed *white* rose along with a note that read: "You are pure. You are chaste. You are special."

By the time I received my rose, its silky soft petals had already begun to show the tattered signs of age, and its small white head drooped like an apology. The message to us girls was a powerful one. Our beauty, our relevance, our worth was tied directly to our ability to remain chaste. The message to boys was similar, but with a slightly different flavor: while girls had the power to force the wait, boys had the power to choose the possibilities. Either way, nothing sexual was to occur prior to marriage in a Mormon temple.

In *Twilight*, abstinence from premarital sex is so much a part of the story's suspense that there would not be much left without it. Abstinence is not just a side note or a character trait. For Bella, more literally, but just as importantly as for many young women who adhere to strict Bible-based thinking, abstinence is a matter of life and death.

ON FAMILY

Mormons value family very highly. In the *Twilight* series, the importance of a strong family unit is promoted through the affectionate characterization of the Cullen clan. They are vampires, yes, and that sets them apart from inferior humans, but among their own, they are superior because they have found one another and have formed a group headed by a calm, wise, governing patriarch named Carlisle.

Mormons are well-known for idealizing traditional, patriarchal families. In 1995, Mormon president Gordon B. Hinckley spoke at a General Relief Society meeting where he delivered a proclamation inspired by God.

> By divine design, fathers are to preside over their families in love and righteousness and are responsible to provide the necessities of life and protection for their families. Mothers are primarily responsible for the nurture of their children.[1]

Carlisle and company, in many ways, represent the Mormon ideal of how a family should operate, and this representation is that much more striking against Bella's less traditional, divorced parents.

ON LIFE AFTER DEATH

Many of Meyer's ideas about immortality seem inspired by Mormonism. For example, the Cullens deny themselves their base desire—to drink the blood of humans—and for that reason they are depicted as spiritually, or at least ethically, advanced. They have also continued to increase their education and knowledge while immortal. In other words, Meyer characterizes the Cullens with higher virtues than other vampires and higher knowledge than the humans, eternally evolving in spite of their situation. They may be immortal, but they do not stop improving themselves.

Similarly, Mormons believe that God was once a man and men will one day be Gods, that all of our time on earth and in the hereafter is spent growing and evolving toward that end. In Mormon afterlife, spirits can continue to progress, learn, grow, and advance, continually bettering themselves until they reach a state of god-like perfection after which men will receive appointment to watch after planets of their own. Mormon immortality, like vampire immortality, is in many ways only the beginning.

ON PREORDAINED PARTNERSHIP

Meyer also fictionalizes deeper theological tenets with the idea of "imprinting." In New Moon and Eclipse, imprinting is explained as mating for eternity: no matter the age of his soul mate, the one who imprints knows for certain, and so he "marks" her for good keeping. While attributed to the werewolves, Edward and Bella appear to share this imprinting somehow, though it is not fully explained. He craves her blood more than the blood of other humans and the implication is that perhaps Edward imprinted on Bella. But in the case of Jacob, Bella's werewolf friend, there is no question. In Breaking Dawn, Jacob imprints on Renesmee, Edward and Bella's daughter, just after she's born. He will care for her as a sibling until such time as she is old enough to unite with him more intimately. In the Twilight series, males do the imprinting (choose), females receive the imprint (wait), and the bond is accepted as paranormal, destined, and preordained, as if controlled by God.

Thinking back to what it was like to grow up Mormon, I recall two doctrines that stuck with me most: that chastity was my best virtue and that when the time was right, giving it up to my "Chosen One" after a temple marriage would be the most important thing I could ever accomplish during this lifetime. Though it is not directly preached and cannot be found in Mormon scripture, many Mormons believe in and encourage this idea of a single individual with whom we have a preearthly bond. The idea is that our spiritual lives extend this one—on the front end and the back end and we have probably met our partner God or Goddess before this life. The most righteous and faithful Mormons whose minds and hearts are open will know the instant they meet their Chosen One. It would be a sacrilege to deny the partnership.[2]

In *Breaking Dawn*, Bella and Edward finally wed and much like in a Mormon wedding, their bond is meant to extend beyond this life into the afterlife. With their marriage this earthly life becomes irrelevant. Marriage and immortality are interwoven ideas for the primary characters in the *Twilight* series. One does not exist without the other, as in the Mormon faith both are the key to reaching God. Unlike traditional Christianity that recognizes the pinnacle of the Adam and Eve story as a fall from grace, Mormons recognize a holy marriage and subsequent sexual intercourse to be just the opposite: the surest way for humans to become Gods themselves.

THE BAIT AND SWITCH

Mormonism and *Twilight* have many things in common, but more than any other religious similarity, it was Meyer's portrayal of Bella's character that struck an old nerve in a way I could not quite explain at first. I felt as confused about what bothered me as when I was a young woman receiving subtle messages that undermined my worth. Why did Bella's love-struck character feel so familiar? I am decades beyond my teens but could it be that Bella reminded me of how I once was? Why did her passive nature and Edward's fatherly dominance irritate me so? Furthermore, why were these mediocre books such an enormous commercial success? And more personally, why did I find their success so disturbing? *Twilight* is a love story and stories of unfulfilled or forbidden romance are almost always a hit. Most of us can relate to the experience of wanting someone who is out of our reach for whatever reason. Am I such a curmudgeon that I cannot even appreciate a good love story anymore? Or was there something else I recognized hidden behind the provocative veil of desire?

It was a brilliant, sunny day when I finished reading *Twilight* and set it in the sand between my bare feet. I squinted at white-crested waves, wondering again what it was that pestered me so, when a woman and two small boys walked toward me from the shore on their way to the staircase leading up to the street. The woman carried a beach blanket and a white cane outstretched before her as she tapped at the sand and urged her boys to stay close. A blind woman, unassisted, with children. A blind woman taking her children to the beach to play. My jaw dropped. How could I ever complain about the challenges of motherhood again?

As they passed, the woman asked one of her children if he still had his sandals. He said yes at precisely the same moment that one of his shoes slipped from his fist and dropped without a sound. I popped out of the chair to jog up behind them and fetch the lost shoe. I tapped her shoulder and she stopped and turned, her eyes shielded by dark glasses.

"He dropped his shoe," I said, almost worshipfully. "I didn't want it to get lost."

"Oh," she said reaching out, her cane dangling from a wrist strap. "Thank you so very much." She grabbed at the space around my hand until she caught the shoe. And then, like any other mother, she added, "Like I need another trip to Target for yet another pair of flip flops!"

"Right," I agreed as I watched her gather her boys and head toward the sandy staircase. I returned to my camp chair and picked up my book. For a moment, I considered the blind woman while studying *Twilight's* striking red and black cover with those pale, feminine hands outstretched and cupping a perfectly ripened red apple. This is when it came to me in a flash. I realized, right at that moment, that it was not small jealousies or jaded romanticism or the religious parallels that reminded me of a church I had long since left behind that pestered me. *Twilight* bothered me on a much deeper level that had to do with what makes a heroine: Bella and the woman on the beach are opposite kinds of blind, one a champion of self-respect and the other a sheep in disguise.

Bella's worth is only realized through companionship and subordination to a male partner and protector, a vampire in Meyer's story but any righteous man according to the fundamental beliefs of Meyer's religion. She is presented as awkward, bumbling, and full of self-reproach no matter her advantages and intellect. Her only actions are those that contribute to her own dependency and subordination while the woman from the beach seemed brave and more than self-sufficient regardless of her challenges. One woman seems to do much with little; the other does little with much. Bella, a character made to appear romantic and desirable, is a model of ineptitude.

Only moderately disturbing is *Twilight's* success among adult women. We have all been bred on the notion of happily-ever-after as characterized by Cinderella, Snow White, Sleeping Beauty—you name the damsel. Look good, snag a protector, escape into marriage, and never worry about independence and self-sufficiency. Though many of us have lived to learn the realities of this fantasy, we may still feel, at times, nostalgic for at least the easy idea of it—that having someone to look after us, care for us, and provide for us like a father will make our lives ideal.

More deeply disturbing is *Twilight's* success among younger women. Meyer has captivated millions of young readers with a story about subordination, dependency, and self-sacrifice to the point of self-collapse. She portrays Bella as childlike and helpless, incomplete without her love interest, entitled to protection and in the end, willing to stunt her own development in exchange for the perception of security.

But Meyer does not portray the realities of a life spent leaning on another, nor does she reveal the myth of security. She herself has become insanely *in*dependent[3] by writing books that represent, at their very core, the trick that has been played on females for centuries, a classic bait and switch. The bait: claim a life of dependency and realize happiness. The switch: dependency on anything is an obstacle, not a vehicle, to happiness. And happiness, as it turns out, is maddeningly within our own control.

BELLA THE HELPLESS

In *Twilight*, the "trick" begins with Bella characterized as incapable, childlike, and in need of a father. Bella's *real* father, Charlie, is largely inept: the sum of his involvement in Bella's life is to provide a bed in which she can rest, to listen to her stories from time to time, and to eat the food she prepares. In essence, she has no father: "Charlie had left for work before I got downstairs. In a lot of ways, living with Charlie was like having my own place...."[4] Though Bella is seventeen years old when the story begins, the reader sympathizes with the father gap and in this way is primed for a replacement.

At the same time, though, Bella seems remarkably independent. She is intelligent and does well in school. She spouts off in biology and complains about the misogyny of Shakespeare's women in English. She has moved away from her mother to a new town. She is taking care of her less-than-involved father, rather than him taking care of her. But perhaps Bella's most identifiable individual trait is her self-proclaimed clumsiness. Bella is, evidently, a klutz: "Possibly my crippling clumsiness was seen as endearing rather than pathetic, casting me as a damsel in distress."[5] And that's just one example. There are literally dozens, perhaps hundreds, of references to Bella's uncanny knack for being in the wrong place at the wrong time and tripping all over herself to scramble out. She is continually falling, slipping, swooning, fainting, or somehow winding up in harm's way without the prowess to escape.

Meyer's use of language further relays her protagonist's insecurities and inabilities. The words "helplessly," "feebly," "unwillingly," and the like are used by the narrator ad nauseam.

Thank goodness for Edward, for without him, Bella would surely be dead. Unfortunately, he also lusts after her blood, and thus her life. Cleverly, such a dynamic creates undeniably high stakes for Bella. Behind door number one: danger of injury, pain, and hardship as she outgrows her "clumsiness." Behind door number two: death by vampire bite. But instead of facing the uncertainty, risk, and adventure of learning, growing, and successfully escaping this no-win scenario, Bella takes door number two and readers accept this because it seems to be what Bella wants. Perhaps somewhere in the deepest recesses of their psyches, readers remember wanting something similar.

BELLA THE INCOMPLETE

For centuries, women have been regarded as inferior to men and deficient without them. In *Twilight*, in the few scenes where Bella and Edward are apart, Bella does nothing but think about being with Edward. Nearly all of *New Moon* is devoted to Bella's incompleteness without him. The reader latches onto Bella's core desire for Edward and reads 643 pages of very little action other than the protagonist's yearning for her vampire love.

Early on in the *New Moon* narrative when she thinks she spies his car in her driveway, she claims to feel an "overwhelming, heady" sense of relief.[6] And later, while looking through a set of photos including one of herself and Edward, she says: "The contrast between the two of us was painful. He looked like a god. I looked very average, even for a human, almost shamefully plain."[7] This sentiment of inequality is perhaps most poignantly expressed when Bella is attempting to converse with Jacob on the matter. Without Edward, she describes herself as an "empty shell" and as "uninhabitable" as a "condemned house."[8] Even if it means complete self-sacrifice, she sees her partnership with and vampire transformation by Edward as her only chance for equality with him.

It's not so unusual. I am over forty, and now I regard myself as equal to men, but it is not difficult to recall feeling differently when I was a girl. It was a subtle thing. Inferiority was deceptively provocative. I longed for something better even if I did not understand what, and it felt a lot like ambition. But not. Somehow, I did not feel quite whole and it was more a matter of completing myself than it was about rising to the possibilities. Growing up Mormon, I received this message in hundreds of ways, from direct messages in stories and scripture to understated suggestions in art and rituals.

A mini-movie that I saw many times growing up tells it best. *Johnny Lingo* (1969) had been shown so often at church functions that I knew it by heart. In the story, a Polynesian trader named Johnny Lingo visits a neighboring island to trade cows in exchange for one of the landowner's daughters. Johnny surprises the islanders by choosing a sullen and plain-looking woman named Mahana. None of the islanders, including Mahana's father, Moke, think she is of much value and prior to the bargaining, there is gossip about how very few cows Mahana will fetch for Moke. One, it is agreed. Mahana is worth only one cow. All are so convinced that one cow is a reasonable expectation that a local advisor in these matters suggests to Moke that he ask for three so that there is room for negotiation downward. Johnny surprises everyone by upping the ante and offering Moke an unheard of eight cows for his daughter's hand in marriage. Johnny and Mahana leave the island and months later when they return, Mahana has been transformed into a stunning Polynesian beauty complete with a brilliant red hibiscus tucked behind an ear. All agree she is now worth *more* than eight cows. Johnny says that her worth was never determined by what others saw but by what she truly was.

The film was always shown, as I recall, to coed groups. There I sat, a rather plain girl myself, amongst a dozen or more Mormon tweens all on the cusp of puberty. The message to boys was clear. The plain girl was beautiful inside and all that was necessary for her beauty to surface was for a boy to notice her. By opening their minds to the possibilities, boys could use their power to raise a girl's sense of self-worth and claim a lovely mate at the same time. Boys could choose, but what was a girl to do?

As a young person, I determined that Mahana was transformed from plain to stunning because someone loved her, which I found frustrating. She could not claim her worth independently and in the end, beauty was still the ultimate display of her value. The fact that someone saw a diamond in the rough seemed arbitrary and beyond her control, which made me feel terribly self-conscious about my own appearance but more importantly, unclear as to what action I could take. Boys could choose. I got that. But girls could do what? Wait with a smile?

And the cows. Mahana, a human being, had been traded like a slave. The central conflict of the story was her price.

The film represented an important lesson toward subordination: that my worth was tied to recognition from and partnership with a man. Once I ingested that, the next lesson was easier to accept and also had a way of snuffing out the indecencies of the first lesson.

Motherhood. One day I would reach what was preached as my full earthly potential and become a mother. It was not only that a man would make me complete, but that I needed one in order to become a mother. And absolutely nothing should compete with motherhood. David O. McKay, Mormon president in the 1950s, famously once said, "No other success can compensate for failure in the home."[9] There was never any question that these words were directed primarily at young women and implied that any pursuit of success outside the home was not worth the risk. And Mother's Day celebrations in our Ward were always the same. A troupe of young girls carried pink carnations through the high-ceilinged chapel while the organist played "Home Can Be a Heaven on Earth." Each mother was given the same number of carnations as she had children. The mother with the most carnations would be asked to remain standing for additional adulation and praise.

Being a woman meant being a mother. There simply is no other way I could have understood it. To be a woman was to be a mother but also, in a way, a child. Beginning at age twelve, all Mormon males are ordained as members of the priesthood, which gives them the authority to give blessings of health and reform to others, baptize nonmembers, and deliver prophecies on God's behalf. Technically speaking, the twelve-year old son of a Mormon woman would outrank her in many matters of health and family welfare. By turning twelve and receiving the priesthood, a mother's son becomes more like an older brother. Therefore, even when she reaches her earthly potential of motherhood, her worth is tied directly to her attachment to men—first her father and brothers, then her husband, and then her sons.

Why wouldn't she, then, and Bella in turn, feel entitled to attachment?

BELLA THE ENTITLED

It was not only the Mormon faith, of course, that taught me I was entitled to safety and protection. Like many girls, Mormon or not, I was bred on fairytales. To be so beautiful that a prince would sweep me away to a castle in the distance where peasants carried the burden of life's hardships was the dream of this little girl.

But I left home just as I finished high school. Because I had to, I battled my way through housing challenges, cockroaches, unemployment, sleazy bosses, self-funded college, legal troubles, and more before I found my way to responsible adulthood. And I resented it almost the whole time.

Because I am female, a part of me felt entitled to be taken care of and watched over. When I found myself on the streets, sleeping in my car, and begging for jobs, it seemed to me that a great injustice was underway.

In her groundbreaking book, *The Cinderella Complex: Woman's Hidden Fear of Independence*, Collette Dowling writes that the consequences of choosing dependency can be dire, especially for older, widowed, or divorced women:

> This, then, is the bitter truth on which younger women—still romantic, still in love, still cushioned by the dream that women can safely allow others to take care of them— turn their backs. The myth is that security, for women, lies in remaining forever and permanently attached, coiled within and stuck to "the family" like mollusks with their shells.[10]

But the consequences for the dependent woman may not be realized right away, which is why Bella is such an important and dangerous role model for young women. Bella represents this precise moment in a woman's life when she psychologically prepares to leave childhood. A conditioned sense of inequality accompanies natural feelings of childhood incompetence as she prepares for adulthood. Here at this juncture, she will either fall for the myth and seek out a protector, or realize her blind spot, adjust, and discover self-worth. In *New Moon*, as Bella begins to purposefully put herself in danger in order to draw her love interest to her rescue, the reader begins to realize that she has fallen for the myth; in essence, she orchestrates her own imprisonment. The only hope we can have for her well-being is for him to indeed come to her rescue, and then prove to be a compassionate jailor.

Bella the Anesthetized

As a vampire, Edward represents more than a man: he is practically a god. He appears godlike to Bella, speaking to her mind as if a conscience, and he represents eternal life. Because he *is* superior and she is so desperate to be as close to his level as possible, she manipulates and lies to get there. It is as if she is in a trance, hypnotized, and asleep, and only assertive passively, through manipulative actions and self-deprecating remarks intended to harness secondary power, the power of the subordinate. While pining over his absence in *New Moon*, she says, "Losing track of time was the most I asked from life."[11]

By this time in the *Twilight* series, not halfway through the second of the four books, Bella has confessed the truth of things. Time is not worth her attention; life is not worth living without her man. *She* has nothing to offer of herself without him. Without Edward, our protagonist is incomplete. But with him, is she truly complete? Or is her self-esteem merely anesthetized and numbed by his presence?

In *Breaking Dawn*, Bella gets what she wants and becomes a vampire. The situation demands it. But as romantic and empowering as this may seem—humanly vulnerable woman turned particularly controlled and graceful vampire—I suggest that Bella's transformation represents an ideal of women forever sleeping through opportunities for their own personal development in this life. When Bella literally gives up her life so that she can become Edward's partner and find her identity and grace solely through her attachment to him, it is as if the real Bella has simply gone to sleep. Instead of sleeping while lying in wait for a prince, the sleep begins when Bella finds him.

But the sleep can be a restless one. In *Kill the Princess: Why Women Still Aren't Free from the Quest for a Fairytale Life,* Stephanie Vermeulen writes:

> With major changes in our lives, many women now desire more than the happy-wife-and-mother role. Often those who are discontented in the role, but continue to play it, find themselves severely depressed. Rarely do they understand why. After all, society promises girls that marriage (preferably to a wealthy prince), with a good home and a bunch of children, will be fulfilling. But what the depression is showing is that the notion of prince and red roses can only exist in a fairytale.[12]

When I was a child, I did not understand my mother's illness, if that is what it was. At church, she clutched her purse with both hands and pursed her lips shut. At home she complained almost incessantly about her disappointments with our father. She had picked the wrong prince. Or rather, the wrong prince had picked her.

She cried daily, spent enormous amounts of time receiving "counsel" from our Ward bishop, lost enthusiasm for homemaking and childcare, and by the time I reached puberty, she spent most of her time in a bathrobe sitting in her bedroom with her papers and books.

I remember her eyes. Everything I knew about my mother I learned by watching her eyes. I remember her looking down at her papers and books or looking out beyond my face, but rarely making eye contact. I remember the vacancy in her eyes that also at times appeared distraught as if a remarkable intelligence were trapped within. I remember her tears. I remember her distance. I could not get close to her, partly because I did not want any part of her misery but also partly because she seemed more like a ghost than a person to me. Shadowy, troubled, repeating her woes as though she were talking in her sleep, she was often unable to respond to prompts from others.

After a therapist advised my father to sell his antique rifles because he was not safe in a home with both my mother and shotguns in it, she begrudgingly began to take antidepressants. While these medications lightened her mood, she still remained a mystery. The real person beneath her exterior still seemed lost.

We all began to label my mother as mentally ill. The medication seemed to help. I felt better about her thinking that a physical illness was the cause of her inattentiveness as a mother. My father could relax and let the pills take the edge off his wife's anger rather than examine the ways he was contributing to her suffering. And my mother could, in essence, rest through her rage.

As a grown woman looking back, however, I realize that my mother's great sleep is a much more complex, sad, and tragic story. I will never know how much of her "condition" is biological and how much is circumstantial, and I cannot help but acknowledge that the latter is an important factor. She is indeed a victim, but at least in part by her own choices and mindset, her own willingness to sleep.

Only once did I dare an attempt to wake her.

I am writing a memoir and one of the ideas I had been considering was weaving my mother's coming-of-age story with my own. So I sent her a list of questions about the time in her life when she made the choices that would map her future. What she enjoyed studying in high school and college, if she had ever had any jobs and how she liked them, when she chose to marry and have children and so forth. She returned a short list of responses and from it, I learned more about my mother than I had ever known before.

I always knew she had married young, but I did not know that she had finished college two years before my father did, though he was almost ten years her senior. I didn't know that right after graduating with a degree in music and a state credential, Mom secured a job teaching music at an elementary school. Within the first six months she took it upon herself to form a stringed instrument program for the entire school district. My father worked at a grocery store and continued to tinker with college. His dismayed parents strongly encouraged him to finish his education, get a career, "be a man." My mother's teaching success further magnified my father's disgrace in his parents' eyes. She therefore quit working her job after that single academic year and never worked outside the home again.

I asked her once why she stopped teaching. She changed the subject, which in our family was the usual method for avoiding communication while still speaking. But this time, I did not let it go. I had never been more curious to know.

"But why did you quit that job, Mom?"

"You can look up where the school district is online, they have a website, I think," she said.

"Yes, but did you like working there? Did you enjoy working outside the home?"

She was silent and a twinge of guilt struck me.

"I mean, I know times were different," I said, unintentionally providing a lead to an easy answer.

She was silent.

"Are you there, Mom?" I asked.

"Yes. Do you want to talk to your father again? He's right here?" she said.

"No, Mom, I want to talk to you. Why did you quit that job?"

Silence. So I gave her another nudge. Another out. One that would make both of our stories easier to tell, more convenient to live with. The easiest out of all.

"Dad didn't like you working? Is that it?" I asked.

"No," she said immediately but quietly. "But I can't talk much when he's right here next to me."

"I don't understand, Mom. If Dad didn't mind you working then what problem would he have hearing why you quit?"

Silence. And then in the dimmest of voices, almost inaudible, she spoke.

"His parents, as I recall, felt very strongly that your father should be the man of the house."

"So you quit because of his parents?"

More quietly she said, "Not exactly, no."

Like a reporter grilling a politician, I felt opportunistic, mean-spirited even. What would happen to my mother if she rose from sleep now, when her hair had gone white and her hands had lost their steady?

I had questioned her into a corner, which is not what I wanted. I wanted to truly understand why my bright mother, who finished college expediently and with exceptional grades, who found employment immediately after graduation working in a highly specialized and desirable salaried job, who had the vision and ambition to spearhead organizational improvement right from the start, I wanted to know why this woman did not continue to work at least until she had children.

After a long pause that tugged at an age-old heartache, my profoundly unfulfilled mother said that she did not know why she quit working. She could not remember. And she did not want to think about it anymore.

I told her I loved her, words we rarely said out loud. In a faraway voice, she said she loved me, too.

Wake Up, Bella!

It is not easy to give up the fairytale. The rewards of a self-sufficient life are not always obvious. But this reader of *Twilight* has seen a *real* life lost to female dependency.

Twilight troubled me at my core, for Bella reminded me of my own conservative upbringing and the pressures my mother faced fifty years ago. I wanted to reach through the pages and shake Meyer's protagonist awake, perhaps take her on a Dickens-like journey to my mother's present and hover over the bed where my mother now spends most of her days. I'd take Bella's arm and point to my sad, frustrated, clinically depressed and either tearful or drugged-into-silence mother who cannot acknowledge that she has helped build her own cage by agreeing to the lopsided terms of patriarchy and submitting to total dependence on a man.

In *The Dance of the Dissident Daughter*, Sue Monk Kidd takes the reader on her journey of feminist awakening from rigid patriarchal Christian beliefs to notions of the divine feminine. But it is not a straight shot. Kidd must first recognize the pitfalls of a belief-system she embraced so wholly that she became a writer of Christian material. Her awakening later in life threatened her marriage, her career, and even her faith. About the fact that it took so many years for her eyes to open, she writes: "It's a peculiar thing, isn't it, that a woman can prefer the safety of cages to the hazards of freedom?"[13]

Many of us break out. Somehow or other, by circumstances that at the time felt terribly unfair to me, I grew up, made a career for myself, and escaped the prison of dependency that I thought was what I wanted. Other women do the same. But many do not. Because of this, I say: *Twilight* is not a love story; it is part one of a tragedy. In all of our efforts to bring feminine equality to the world stage, the fact that so many millions of women can identify so wholly with passive and dependent Bella makes me wonder: have we really broken free? Perhaps all we've done is raise the height of the cage.

Twilight may be the hour in which vampires rise. But it is also the time in a woman's life when she, too, may wake from sleep to discover an entire day has passed without her action or involvement, her influence and intelligence, without her vital contribution to the evolution of humankind. And if it truly is sunset before her eyes peel open, she will soon realize that the day can never be reclaimed.

Stephenie Meyer has capitalized on the human vulnerability toward dependency, especially for a population of young women already primed since birth by social messages of what it means to be female. With the help of her own religious conditioning, she has made millions selling us the oldest and most useless story ever told.

NOTES

1. www.lds.org, Web. Accessed July 5, 2010. np.
2. Those familiar with the colorful history of the Church of Jesus Christ of Latter Day Saints might be wondering about polygamy. It is a well-documented fact that the church founder and its most influential leader, Joseph Smith and Brigham Young respectively, were polygamous many times over. Might there be more than One for some faithful members of the church? The answer is yes—polygamy is accounted for deep in the more controversial teachings of the church and in its lesser-known scripture called *The Doctrine and Covenants*. Polygamy as divine may also be fictionalized in Meyer's fifth book intended for adult audiences, which did not reach anywhere near the success of *Twilight*. In *The Host*, one married woman's body is sometimes occupied by an alien woman's spirit creating a polygamous triangle involving two females

engaged in an intimate relationship with one male. But that is a topic for another essay.

3. In some estimates, Stephenie Meyer has earned more than $300 million dollars from the sale of *Twilight*. As a Mormon in good standing, she has likely tithed 10% of that—$30 million dollars—directly to the LDS church.

4. Stephenie Meyer, *Twilight* (New York: Little, Brown and Company, 2005), 54.

5. Meyer, *Twilight*, 55.

6. Stephenie Meyer, *New Moon* (New York: Little, Brown and Company, 2006), 76.

7. Meyer, *New Moon*, 85.

8. Meyer, *New Moon*, 254.

9. J.E. McCullough, "Home: The Savior of Civilization," *Conference Report* (1995), 116.

10. Colette Dowling, *The Cinderella Complex: Woman's Hidden Fear of Independence* (New York: Simon and Schuster, Inc., 1981), 40–41.

11. Meyer, *New Moon*, 127.

12. Stephanie Vermeulen, *Kill the Princess: Why Women Still Aren't Free from the Quest for a Fairytale Life* (New York: Anchor Books, 2005), 156.

13. Sue Monk Kidd, *The Dance of the Dissident Daughter* (New York: Harper Collins, 1996), 83.

Chapter 8

"When you kiss me, I want to die": Arrested Feminism in *Buffy the Vampire Slayer* and the *Twilight* Series

Rhonda Nicol

No doubt due to the surface similarity of the romance narrative—teenage girl falls in love with a vampire—comparisons between Buffy Summers of *Buffy the Vampire Slayer* (*BtVS*) and Bella Swan of the *Twilight* series are ubiquitous. One comparison, Jonathan McIntosh's widely viewed (over a million hits on YouTube) mash-up, *Buffy vs. Edward: Twilight Remixed*, imagines a universe in which Edward Cullen attempts to woo not Bella Swan but Buffy Summers, vampire slayer and feminist darling. McIntosh sees his work as an argument against the specific way in which romance and gender roles are constructed in the *Twilight* series, praising *BtVS* for its resistance to gender stereotypes and condemning *Twilight* for its "antiquated, sexist" constructions of gender.[1]

McIntosh, a self-described "aspiring feminist guy," claims that *BtVS* and *Twilight* represent "the metaphorical battle between two opposing visions of gender roles in the 21st century."[2] His construction of Buffy as the "good" feminist and Bella as the "bad" feminist is typical of Bella/Buffy comparisons. Dana Stevens, for instance, speaks for many *Twilight* critics when she proclaims, "Bella Swan is the anti-Buffy,"[3] and texts pitting Buffy against Bella, asking how well each heroine measures up to a monolithic, authoritative (yet oddly ill-defined) version of feminism, abound.

Buffy/Bella comparisons often tout Buffy as a good, progressive feminist role model[4] and Bella as an anachronistic throwback to prefeminist conceptions of a feminine ideal. They generally fail to give serious consideration to the reasons behind the phenomenal popularity of the *Twilight* books, often simply vilifying them and implying that fans (and sometimes even Stephenie Meyer herself) are naïve dupes of the patriarchy who have not been appropriately "enlightened" by feminism. Joanne Hollows and Rachel Moseley note that feminist critiques of popular culture often assume that "feminism, or the feminist, can tell us about popular culture, but [do] not examine what popular culture can tell us about feminism" and that a feminist critique should "judge and measure feminism's success or failure in making it into the mainstream."[5] Certainly feminist critiques of the *Twilight* phenomenon tend to manifest this impulse. For example, media critic Lucy Mangan deems the series "depressingly retrograde, deeply anti-feminist, [and] borderline misogynistic"; she dismisses fans as generally "young, inexperienced and underinformed" and therefore too naïve to choose their pleasure reading wisely.[6] The brisk sales of all the *Twilight* books, however, suggest that the trope of the unapologetically, unambiguously happy ending, complete with rescuing Prince Charming, maintains its allure for women of all ages. How might we account for the continuing popularity of a romance masterplot that would seem to run counter to feminist ideals? Given the acknowledged breadth of the *Twilight* series' fan base, it seems disingenuous in the extreme to characterize the fans en masse as "inexperienced and underinformed." Surely at least some of them have heard of feminism.

I suggest that instead of regarding *BtVS* and the *Twilight* arc as oppositional texts, regarding the former as a triumph for feminism and the latter as an embarrassment, it might be productive to consider both in terms of their similarities in order to explore what *BtVS* and the *Twilight* stories, both artifacts of popular culture, can tell us about the state of contemporary feminism. Rachel Fudge observes that for young women, "a certain awareness of gender and power is ingrained and inextricably linked to our sense of identity and self-esteem—call it feminism's legacy";[7] both Buffy *and* Bella certainly express beliefs and exhibit behaviors that mark them as inheritors of this legacy. However, "feminism's legacy" is riddled with contradiction and conflict. Ariel Levy posits that the mid-twentieth-century schism between the women's movement and the sexual liberation movement resulted in a kind of stalemate with regard to the relationship between feminism and women's sexuality, thus leaving unresolved questions about the definition of "sexual liberation" and the forms that a woman's engagement with and performance of sexuality could and should take.[8] Jennifer Baumgarder and Amy Richards argue that the young women coming of age during feminism's third wave, inheritors of this ongoing conflict, struggle to resist "the false impression that since women don't want to be sexually exploited, they don't want to be sexual"[9] and have embraced both a belief in basic feminist tenets (social, political, fiscal, and sexual equality for women) and a performance of gender that unabashedly embraces more traditionally "feminine" and sexualized aspects of gender performance.

BtVS had its broadcast premier in early 1997, which was an interesting moment for third wave feminism. At this point, the messy, angry Riot Grrl movement of the early-to-mid-1990s had largely given way to the Spice Girls craze of the mid-to-late-1990s; "girl power" had gone from a fringe movement to a full-blown mainstream phenomenon.[10] The integration of feminism as "girl power" into the mainstream ushered in conflicting social pressures; suddenly young women were told both to allow themselves to revel in their sexy girliness and simultaneously to resist being sexualized and objectified, resulting in a tension between a persistent fetishization of female as a sex object and a celebration of an idealized "girl power" that remains unresolved. Jessica Valenti, founder of feministing.com, distills this contradiction to its simplest terms: "We're too slutty. We're not slutty enough."[11]

The mainstreaming of a sexualized "girl power" feminism that created a space for a performance of gender both "feminine" and assertive has given rise to an equal and opposite movement to bring back the ever-popular "traditional values" and to reinscribe femininity as modest and chaste rather than bold and aggressive. As Valenti puts it, "[S]exualized pop culture and a conservative movement to reinforce traditional gender roles are colliding to form a modernized virgin/whore complex. We're getting abstinence-only education during the day and *Girls Gone Wild* commercials at night."[12] Feminist rhetorics spent many years situating discussions of sex and sexuality in terms of a woman's right to say "no," but the integration of "girl power" feminism's message of sexual empowerment and autonomy reframes the discussion, telling women that they should say "yes" to their own desires and thereby claim the cultural and personal power to which contemporary feminism tells them they are entitled.

Levy argues that many young women, caught in a culture that tells them to act like sexual beings even as they are discouraged from actually having sex, "are conceiving of sex as a performance you give for attention, rather than something thrilling and interesting you engage in because you *want* to."[13] And although the *Twilight* series has been criticized for implicitly advancing an abstinence-until-marriage agenda (Christine Seifert calls it "abstinence porn"[14]), both Meyer's novels and *BtVS* are refreshingly sex-positive in at least one important way: they both configure female sexual desire as intrinsic rather than performative. Bella may wait until marriage to have sex with Edward, but waiting until marriage to have sex *isn't* her idea, nor does she seem to be concerned with maintaining her chastity. However conservative the series might be in other respects, Bella is never criticized, either implicitly or explicitly, for her sexual curiosity. When she and Edward kiss for the first time, Bella's physical reaction is passionate and visceral: "Blood boiled under my skin, burned in my lips. My breath came in a wild gasp. My fingers knotted in his hair, clutching him to me. My lips parted and I breathed in his heady scent."[15] Buffy, too, experiences desire for and curiosity about sex, and even though her choice to have sex with Angel results in some unforeseen (and very unfortunate) consequences, she is never vilified for her decision to have sex. Her friends and family may wish she had picked a different partner, but none of them suggests that she deserves censure simply because she has sex. Giles, her Watcher and substitute father figure, tells her, "If it's guilt you're looking for, Buffy, I'm not your man. All you will get from me is my support and my respect."[16]

Both *BtVS* and *Twilight* deviate from a historical tendency for popular fictions to manifest a "reluctance to treat girls as active in their own sexual pleasure" and to construct them as "enforcers of the traditional code of sexuality that limits sexual expression"[17] Sexual activity is not specifically maligned in either series, but, as Roberta Seelinger Trites observes, "reassurances to teenagers that their actions are normal still start from the assumption that someone thinks their actions are not."[18] Certainly the boundaries of acceptable sexual expression are very tightly policed in each series, and neither *BtVS* nor the *Twilight* books offers a truly revolutionary perspective on sexual relations between young adults. Both locate sexual activity as something that should only transpire within the context of a narrative of romantic love and as the culmina-tion of the process of courtship; sex is only sanctioned as an expression of love. When Giles reassures Buffy that her decision to have sex with Angel, although "rash," was not unreasonable, he tells her, "I know that you loved him, and he has proven more than once that he loved you."[19] In *Twilight*, choosing to have sex outside of a stable romantic relationship is not entertained as a possibility. As far as we know, Bella is the only (human) teenager in Forks who is even considering having sex, and neither Bella nor Edward regards sex as an activity engaged in primarily for sheer physical pleasure. After they have made their declarations of eternal love, Edward asks her if she is a virgin, to which Bella replies, "I told you I've never felt like this about anyone before, not even close." When Edward points out that "love and lust don't always keep the same company," Bella counters, "They do for me."[20]

Bella and Buffy manifest the belief that sex and love ideally should go hand-in-hand, and they believe this not only because they are "good girls" but because they are good at *being* girls. To be female is to be *not* male, and despite feminism's challenges to the dominant cultural script of females as vigilant guardians of virginity and to the practice of stigmatizing female sexual desire, the cultural script of male sexual desire remains essentially the same; it is still constructed as predatory and dangerous. Brad Perry argues that males are socialized to view their sexuality as "characterized by action, control, and achievement" and to view sex as "the get-some game."[21] While females are still socialized to see sex primarily as an expression of love, males are encouraged to construct sex as conquest, and both males and females understand not only their role but also the role of the other in the dance of courtship. This paradigm perpetuates a power imbalance between males and females in intimate relationships and affirms heterosexual sex as a locus of male domination and control.

Not surprisingly, both series repeatedly construct men as inherently sexually aggressive and rapacious, casting women in a position wherein they must *re*act to sex-ual advances rather than initiate them. Both Buffy and Bella are obligated to defend themselves against unwanted advances, especially when they enter the public sphere. Fudge suggests that Buffy challenges the paradigm of girls' vulnerability in public spaces, observing, "With her preternatural strength and supreme confidence, she can literally go wherever the hell she pleases. Her domain is a traditionally male, con-ventionally dangerous one: the darkened streets, abandoned buildings, and stinking alleys that girls have long been cautioned to beware of."[22] However, the overwhelming majority of the vampires that Buffy stakes are male. Over the course of the series, she finds herself pinned to the ground by a male vampire in a missionary-position tableau during countless vampire/Slayer skirmishes, thus implying that every time she makes a foray into the "darkened streets," she is putting herself at risk for rape, metaphori-cally if not literally. Bella, too, is, as Edward tells her, "a magnet for *trouble*." He notes, "If there is anything dangerous within a ten-mile radius, it will invariably find you,"[23] and, truly, whenever she ventures outside of Edward's protection, she frequently faces the threat of sexual violence. Not only is she nearly gang-raped[24] by a mob of human males but she is also bitten by James, which functions as a metaphorical rape; fortu-nately Edward is able to suck out the venom, thus rendering the act of penetration, if not incomplete, then at least sterile.[25]

Additionally, both Bella and Buffy must deal with unwanted sexual advances from trusted members of their own respective social circles. When Jacob forcibly kisses Bella, Bella's reaction underscores her perceived helplessness and her sense of the encounter as an assault: "I opened my eyes and didn't fight, didn't feel...just waited for him to stop."[26] Later, Jacob abuses Bella emotionally when he obliquely threatens suicide in order to coerce her into asking him to kiss her.[27] Buffy is also repeatedly forced to defend herself against implicit and explicit threats of sexual assault from friends and even lovers. She is not only sexually harassed by a hyena-spirit-possessed Xander[28] but also, in one of the show's most disturbing turns, by Spike, a vampire with whom she had been having a consensual sexual relationship[29] (and who becomes a legitimate romantic interest *after* the near-rape incident) despite regarding him as "an evil, disgusting thing."[30]Strikingly, Buffy characterizes her first sexual encounter with him as "the most perverse, degrading experience of my life."[31] When she inadvertently admits to Tara that she's been having a sexual relationship with Spike, Tara assures her that she does not need to be in love in order to have sex, but Buffy rejects this possibility, begging Tara, "Please don't forgive me."[32] When Spike attempts to rape her, it seems like an inevitable consequence of her poor decisions and thus a punishment she believes she deserves.

Disturbingly, both *BtVS* and *Twilight* imply that sexual assault often carries with it a degree of culpability on part of the female victim. Buffy makes "poor kissing decisions"[33] that lead to her assault by Spike. Bella chooses not only to remain friends with Jacob despite his repeated assaults but even asks Edward to punish her for having been coerced into kissing Jacob. She tells Edward, "I want you to tell me that you're disgusted with me and that you're going to leave so that I can beg and grovel on my knees for you to stay."[34] The *Twilight* series offers an additional example of a young woman being sexually assaulted and internalizing blame for the assault: Rosalie, Edwards's "sister," tells Bella she was raped and left to die by her fiancé and some of his friends. Rosalie implies that she was victimized due to her own desirability; she tells Bella she came to see her beauty as a "curse."[35] She also implies that her own vanity and her own pleasure in her sexual desirability made her a target for abuse, noting that before the assault, she was "[p]leased that men's eyes watched me everywhere I went, from the year I turned twelve."[36] Before Royce (her fiancé) and his friends rape her, Royce rips her clothing in an attempt to expose her to the other men, turning her vanity and pleasure in her own body against her, the objectification that she had found pleasurable and empowering becoming a justification for her rape.[37]

Both *BtVS* and *Twilight* illustrate how sexual assault can be used to enforce a male/female power differential, but even when sexual acts are mutually welcomed, a power differential still persists. As Heather Corinna points out, "the young woman who is provided with a sexual awakening by a paternal male partner remains an ideal, common fantasy,"[38] and this fantasy is definitely perpetuated in both Bella's relationship with Edward and Buffy's relationship with Angel. The figure of the powerful, authoritative male provokes in each heroine a commensurate desire to submit and to be consumed. Since both Edward and Angel are vampires, this desire to be consumed by love could possibly literally come true; for both Bella and Buffy, their fears of the actual physical risks of sex with their paramours (sex with a vampire might result in death) symbolize young women's fears of being damaged (emotionally and/ or physically) even should they willingly choose to engage in physical intimacy.

This association of fear with desire underscores the point that although sex might be dangerous for young women, that edge of danger is not only expected but eroticized in romance narratives, and when one's love interest is a vampire, the stakes are raised considerably. While contemplating her romantic history, Buffy wonders, "Can a nice, safe relationship be that intense? [P]art of me believes that real love and passion have to go hand-in-hand with pain."[39] Early in their relationship, Angel tells Buffy their romance is a bad idea and it "could get out of control." He warns, "This isn't some fairy tale. When I kiss you, you don't wake up from a deep sleep and live happily ever after." "When you kiss me, I want to die," Buffy replies.[40] Bella, too, seems to subscribe to this view of romance; she indicates her willingness to risk her life to be with Edward at least as many times as he warns her that he's a danger to her. Very soon after their first meeting, Bella realizes that Edward "thirsted for my blood" but that she is "unconditionally and irrevocably in love with him,"[41] thus making the risk irrelevant to her and possibly even part of Edward's appeal. "[T]he romance-novel script of ravishment"[42] has demonstrated considerable staying power, perhaps because it implicitly acknowledges young women's not-unreasonable fears about acting upon their own sexual desires.

It may seem paradoxical, but I suggest that the figure of the virtuous vampire lover dominates the currently wildly popular urban fantasy/paranormal romance movement—a sort of hybrid genre *Salon*'s Laura Miller characterizes as "eschewing the conventional 'happily ever after' ending and depicting romantic relationships as uncertain and ambiguous"[43]—precisely because it both installs and subverts "the romance-novel script of ravishment." The (male) vampire body both makes the dangers of male sexuality overt and obvious and pathologizes the male body rather than the female body; it is the male vampire body that is unruly and must be subject to discipline. A romantic relationship with a vampire might be characterized by ambiguity and uncertainty, but the understanding that he is dangerous and the specific reasons why he is dangerous are never the slightest bit ambiguous. Additionally, these "good" vampires *know* that they are dangerous, that their bloodlust is tied to their sexual impulses, and that their sexual impulses are therefore suspect and must be rigorously policed. Edward warns Bella repeatedly that her life is at risk by being with him, telling her, "It's not only your company I crave! Never forget that. Never forget I am more dangerous to you than I am to anyone else."[44] Angel, too, warns Buffy that he's dangerous, even before he turns into Angelus. Shortly after their first kiss, during which his face morphs into its demon visage, thus reminding Buffy that Angel is a vampire, he tells her, "I can walk like a man, but I'm not one. And I wanted to kill you tonight."[45]

Both *BtVS* and *Twilight* make male sexuality less frightening by offering a strategy of separation and containment for dealing with predatory male sexuality via the figure of the vampire lover. If your boyfriend is a vampire, then his "otherness" (read maleness) can be qualified and therefore made manageable. Fang-equals-penetrating-phallus is a time-honored metaphor, and the vampire love interest with control over his vampire nature also leashes his aggressive male sexuality. Sarah Seltzer suggests that the "good" vampire boyfriend offers female consumers of paranormal romance "a real fantasy:

a world where young women are free to describe their desires openly, and launch themselves at men without shame, while said boyfriends are the sexual gatekeepers."[46] The vampire lover's self-awareness imposes a burden on him to bear the primary responsibility for reining in his own darker impulses, ironically making him less of a threat than a human male. If the "good" vampire love interest can simply restrain the overriding vampiric impulse (to penetrate/bite, to consume), then his paramour is free to explore her sexual desires without fear of degradation.

However, this shift of responsibility from the female to the male is not absolute in either *BtVS* or *Twilight,* and in a variation on the old "blame and shame" script, both Angel and Edward struggle with their own impulses and then punish Buffy and Bella for their own failings, using both young women's naïveté as a mechanism for this punishment. Interestingly, Bella and Buffy are shamed for not being worldly enough to suit their more experienced paramours.

Edward implies that when he was turned seventeen, his sexual impulses became permanently conflated with his thirst for blood, thus making it virtually impossible for him to experience sexual desire as something separate and distinct from blood-lust.[47] Therefore, his period of adolescent rebellion, during which he parted ways with Carlisle and chose to feed from humans, can be read as a period of sexual exploration. Edward tells Bella, "I wasn't sold on his [Carlisle's] life of abstinence, and I resented him for curbing my appetite."[48] Even if he is virginal in the strict sexual sense of the word, Edward has indeed sated his carnal appetites. When Edwards ends their rela-tionship in *New Moon,* he knows exactly how to hurt Bella; he configures her body as the inadequate one. He tells her, "I'm . . . *tired* of pretending to be something I'm not, Bella. I'm not human. I've let this go on much too long, and I'm sorry for that."[49] Because Bella understands that bloodlust and sexual desire are inexorably intertwined for Edward—he cannot allow himself to become physically intimate with her for fear that he will drain her—when he criticizes her for forcing him to control his predatory impulses, she understands that he is implicitly criticizing her for being an inadequate sexual partner. Ironically, she is quite willing to risk her safety to satisfy her sexual desires; Edward is punishing her for his own inability to control his vampire nature.

Angel, like Edward, was not always a "good" vampire; as Angelus, he tortured his (usually female) victims with relish until he was "cursed" with a soul, and when he and Buffy have sex, his moment of untrammeled bliss revokes his soul, at which time he loses the ability to control the darkest aspects of his nature. Although the condi-tions of the curse were supposed to ensure that Angel would remain in torment for-ever, it is primarily Buffy who suffers when Angelus reemerges. Angelus taunts Buffy mercilessly, and his first line of attack is to belittle their sexual encounter, ridiculing her for her sexual inexperience and characterizing it as cause for humiliation. He tells her, "You've got a lot to learn about men, kiddo. Although I guess you proved that last night." After demeaning her sexual performance, he also denigrates her for her choice to have sex with him, sneering, "You know what the worst part was? Pretending that I loved you. If I'd known how easily you'd give it up, I wouldn't have bothered."[50]

The fact that both Buffy and Bella are subject to this particular kind of humili-ation underscores the extent to which changing sexual mores have introduced even more possibilities to fail in performing one's gender role adequately. Failure to have sex can result in being labeled "frigid" or "uptight," and choosing to have sex, even under the "right" circumstances, exposes one to multiple risks: being labeled a "slut" or "easy" and/or being found sexually inadequate. Joss Whedon claims when he was writing the script for the confrontation between Buffy and Angel, "I actually felt like an ugly person. I don't know how I was able to write this so easily. It felt icky that I could make him say these things. It felt icky and kind of powerful. It was very uncomfortable and very exciting for me to do it."[51] The scene is excruciating to watch (and, I would speculate, was so easy for Whedon to produce) precisely because Angelus' emotional evisceration of Buffy so perfectly reflects an all-too-familiar cultural script that doubly damns women for acting upon their sexual desires.

By changing the stakes for women's sexuality—no longer is there a simple dividing line between the "good girl" who does not have sex before marriage and the "bad girl" who does—a young woman of the third wave struggles with a peculiar kind of performance anxiety: she must be concerned not only with when to "do it" and with whom but also with her prowess as a sexual partner once she does have sex. Women are conditioned to believe that they must negotiate a complex set of social codes in order to perform sexuality adequately; excess of any kind results in social censure. If there are more possibilities available to young women than ever before, there are equally more opportunities for failure, and unwise choices carry penalties. Both *BtVS* and *Twilight* provide foil characters as a model of what one should avoid becoming: the mad/bad woman whose promiscuity reads as indicative of larger pathologies. In *BtVS*, Faith's disdain for sexual monogamy is symptomatic of her emotionally and psychologically damaged state. Renee, Bella's mother, is portrayed as slightly "boy crazy" (she marries a much younger man), which is presented as indicative of her overall irresponsibility: her ditziness is a running joke in the series, rendering her powerless.

Valenti notes that women's "morality is defined by our sexuality"[52]; for women, choices about their sexual behavior are just about what they do but about who they are. Sex is always a risky proposition for a woman; both Buffy's and Bella's stories tell us that women are defined by the acts of their bodies and that those acts are read and interpreted by men. When Edward and a still-human Bella finally do have sex for the first time, Bella's bruised and battered body sets off another round of Edward's self-flagellation. Somewhat disturbingly, Bella can only resist the narrative that Edward imposes upon her body and assert her bodily autonomy by defending her right to be battered.[53] In Buffy's case, after she has sex with Angel, he is quite literally no longer the person she fell in love with, and when Angelus belittles her, the normally confident and assertive Buffy doubts her own worth. At least when Angel returns to his virtuous, ensouled self, Buffy's choice of lovers—and thus her own judgment— is validated. Her attempts to engage in sex *without* love and commitment end in either a near rape (c.f. her relationship with Spike) or, in the case of her brief relationship with Parker, her first college boyfriend, in humiliation. Ironically, Parker persuades Buffy to have sex with him by utilizing rhetorics of empowerment and bodily autonomy that are clearly influenced by third wave feminism. After they have sex, however, he avoids her, and she finds him giving the same speech to a different girl.[54] When he hears of her romantic woes, Spike mocks her, sneering, "Did he play the sensitive lad and get you to seduce him? That's a good trick if the girl's thick enough to buy it."[55] In every case, when Buffy's relationship fails, she internalizes its failure; she effectively pays for her "poor kissing decisions" over and over again.

Bella manages to avoid the perils of serial monogamy by marrying her vampire and embracing the promise of a literally eternal love. However, she too recognizes that sex equals danger for women. On her honeymoon night, she thinks, "How did people do this—swallow all their fears and trust someone else so implicitly with every imperfection and fear they had—with less than the absolute commitment Edward had given me? If it weren't Edward out there, if I didn't know in every cell of my body that he loved me as much as I loved him—unconditionally and irrevocably and, to be honest, irrationally—I'd never be able to get up off this floor."[56] Although Bella initially objects to Edward's demand that they marry before having sex, she eventually comes to see its appeal, positing that Edward's value system, rooted in his late-nineteenth-century/early-twentieth-century human life, comes from "[a] world where it would surprise no one if I wore his ring on my finger. A simpler place, where love was defined in simpler ways."[57]

Little wonder that such a worldview, with its promise of an easily navigated morality, holds such appeal for Bella (and for legions of *Twilight* fans) given the complexities of female sexuality for women in the twenty-first century. As long as women continue to receive contradictory messages about sex, romance, and gender performance, a masterplot of romantic love, with its promise to mitigate the emotional and social risks of sexual activity by providing young women a socially sanctioned space in which to explore their sexual desires, will maintain its power and its allure in the popular imagination due to its promise of safety, however illusory.

NOTES

1. Jonathan McIntosh, "What Would Buffy Do?: Notes on Dusting Edward Cullen," *Bitch: Feminist Response to Pop Culture*, August 12, 2009. Web. http://bitchmagazine.org/post/what-would-buffy-do-notes-on-dusting-edward-cullen. Accessed September 11, 2009.
2. Ibid., n.p.
3. Dana Stevens, Review of *Twilight*, directed by Catherine Hardwicke, *Slate*, November 20, 2008. Web. http://www.slate.com/id/2205013/. Accessed January 6, 2010.
4. However, I should note that there are many critiques of Buffy as feminist role model. For an excellent overview of such critiques, see Patricia Pender's article "I'm Buffy and You're . . . History" in *Fighting the Forces: What's at Stake in Buffy the Vampire Slayer*, eds. Rhonda V. Wilcox and David Lavery (Lanham, MD: Rowman & Littlefield, 2002. Print).
5. Joanne Hollows and Rachel Moseley, "Popularity Contests: The Meaning of Popular Feminism," in *Feminism in Popular Culture*, eds. Joanne Hollows and Rachel Moseley (Oxford: Berg, 2006. Print), 1.
6. Lucy Mangan, "Dangerous Liaisons," *The Guardian*, December 4, 2008. Web. http://www.guardian.co.uk/film/2008/dec/04/twilight-film-vampire Accessed January 10, 2010.
7. Rachel Fudge, "The Buffy Effect," *Bitch: Feminist Response to Pop Culture*, Summer 1999, no. 10,. Web..http://bitchmagazine.org/article/buffy-effect Accessed January 3, 2010.
8. Ariel Levy, *Female Chauvinist Pigs: Women and the Rise of Raunch Culture* (New York: Free Press, 2006. Print.), 54–60.
9. Jennifer Baumgardner and Amy Richards, *Manifesta: Young Women, Feminism, and the Future* (New York: Farrar,Straus, and Giroux, 2000. Print), 137.

10. The phrase became so ubiquitous that the Oxford English Dictionary added it in 2002. "*Girl Power* Enters the Oxford English Dictionary," *Ask Oxford*, Web. http://www.askoxford.com/pressroom/archive/oedjan02/ Accessed January 9, 2010.

11. Jessica Valenti, *Full Frontal Feminism: A Young Woman's Guide to Why Feminism Matters* (Berkeley, CA: Seal Press, 2007. Print), 6.

12. Jessica Valenti, "Purely Rape: The Myth of Sexual Purity and How It Reinforces Rape Culture," in *Yes Means Yes: Visions of Female Sexual Power and a World Without Rape*, eds. Jaclyn Friedman and Jessica Valenti (Berkeley, CA: Seal Press, 2008. Print), 300.

13. Levy, *Female Chauvinist Pigs*, 163.

14. Christine Seifert, "Bite Me! (Or Don't)," *Bitch: Feminist Response to Pop Culture*, Winter 2009, no. 42, 23. Print.

15. Stephenie Meyer, *Twilight* (New York: Little, Brown, 2005. Print), 282.

16. "Innocence," episode no. 14, *Buffy the Vampire Slayer: The Complete Second Season on DVD* (January 20, 1998; Los Angeles, CA: Twentieth Century Fox Home Entertainment, 2002).

17. Linda Christian-Smith, *Becoming a Woman Through Romance* (New York: Routledge, 1990. Print), 34;41.

18. Roberta Seelinger Trites, *Disturbing the Universe: Power and Repression in Adolescent Literature* (Iowa City: University of Iowa Press, 2000. Print.), 88.

19. "Innocence," *Buffy the Vampire Slayer*.

20. Meyer, *Twilight*, 311.

21. Brad Perry, "Hooking Up with Healthy Sexuality: The Lessons Boys Learn (and Don't Learn) About Sexuality, and Why a Sex-Positive Rape-Prevention Paradigm Can Benefit Everyone Involved" in *Yes Means Yes: Visions of Female Sexual Power and a World Without Rape*, eds. Jaclyn Friedman and Jessica Valenti (Berkeley, CA: Seal Press, 2008. Print), 200.

22. Fudge, "The Buffy Effect."

23. Meyer, *Twilight*, 174.

24. Ibid., 156–162.

25. Ibid., 454–457.

26. Stephenie Meyer, *Eclipse (*New York: Little, Brown, 2007. Print), 331.

27. Ibid., 525.

28. "The Pack," episode no. 6, *Buffy the Vampire Slayer: The Complete First Season on DVD* (April 4, 1997; Los Angeles, CA: Twentieth Century Fox Home Entertainment, 2002).

29. "Seeing Red," episode no. 19, *Buffy the Vampire Slayer: The Complete Sixth Season on DVD* (May 7, 2002; Los Angeles, CA: Twentieth Century Fox Home Entertainment, 2004).

30. "Smashed," episode no. 9, *Buffy the Vampire Slayer: The Complete Sixth Season on DVD* (November 20, 2001; Los Angeles, CA: Twentieth Century Fox Home Entertainment, 2004).

31. "Wrecked," episode no. 10, *Buffy the Vampire Slayer: The Complete Sixth Season on DVD* (November 27, 2001; Los Angeles, CA: Twentieth Century Fox Home Entertainment, 2004).

32. "Dead Things," episode no. 13, *Buffy the Vampire Slayer: The Complete Sixth Season on DVD* (February 5, 2002; Los Angeles, CA: Twentieth Century Fox Home Entertainment, 2004).

33. "Smashed," *Buffy the Vampire Slayer*.

34. Meyer, *Eclipse*, 534.

35. Ibid., 166.

36. Ibid., 155.
37. Ibid., 159–160.
38. Heather Corinna, "An Immodest Proposal," in *Yes Means Yes: Visions of Female Sexual Power and a World Without Rape*, eds. Jaclyn Friedman and Jessica Valenti (Berkeley, CA: Seal Press, 2008. Print), 184.
39. "Something Blue," episode no. 9, *Buffy the Vampire Slayer: The Complete Fourth Season on DVD*, (November 30, 1999; Los Angeles, CA: Twentieth Century Fox Home Entertainment, 2003).
40. "Reptile Boy," episode no. 5, *Buffy the Vampire Slayer: The Complete Second Season on DVD* (October 13, 1997; Los Angeles, CA: Twentieth Century Fox Home Entertainment, 2002).
41. Meyer, *Twilight*, 195.
42. Corinna, "An Immodest Proposal," 184.
43. Laura Miller, "Buffy Fans: Read This," *Salon*, June 23, 2009, Web. http://www.salon.com/books/feature/2009/06/23/ vampire_fiction/index.html Accessed September 14, 2009.
44. Meyer, *Twilight*, 282.
45. "Angel," episode no. 7, *Buffy the Vampire Slayer: The Complete First Season on DVD* (April 14, 1997; Los Angeles, CA: Twentieth Century Fox Home Entertainment, 2002).
46. Sarah Seltzer, "*Twilight*: Sexual Longing in an Abstinence-Only World," *The Huffington Post*, August 9, 2008, Web. http://www.huffingtonpost.com/sarah-seltzer/twilight-sexual-longing-i_b_117927.html, Accessed January 10, 2010.
47. Meyer, *Twilight*, 278.
48. Ibid., 342.
49. Stephenie Meyer, *New Moon* (New York: Little, Brown, 2006. Print), 70.
50. "Innocence," *Buffy the Vampire Slayer*.
51. Joss Whedon, Commentary on "Innocence," *Buffy the Vampire Slayer: The Complete Second Season on DVD* (Los Angeles, CA: Twentieth Century Fox Home Entertainment, 2002).
52. Jessica Valenti, *The Purity Myth: How America's Obsession with Virginity is Hurting Young Women* (Berkeley, CA: Seal Press, 2010. Print), 147.
53. Stephenie Meyer, *Breaking Dawn* (New York: Little, Brown, 2008. Print), 86–98.
54. "The Harsh Light of Day," episode no. 3, *Buffy the Vampire Slayer: The Complete Fourth Season on DVD* (November 30, 1999; Los Angeles, CA: Twentieth Century Fox Home Entertainment, 2003).
55. Ibid.
56. Meyer, *Breaking Dawn*, 83.
57. Meyer, *Eclipse*, 325.

CHAPTER 9

"ONE IS NOT BORN A VAMPIRE, BUT BECOMES ONE": MOTHERHOOD AND MASOCHISM IN *TWILIGHT*

MERINNE WHITTON

> *"I tried to visualise the Cullen family without their creator, their center and their guide— their father, Carlisle. I couldn't see it."*
>
> —Bella, *Breaking Dawn*

STEPHENIE MEYER'S *TWILIGHT* SAGA has been a runaway success with its target market of prepubescent girls; however, the series has proved less popular with feminists, who have expressed concern about the marginalized role Bella plays within her own narrative, and the messages her story is sending to a generation of young women about relationships, families, and gender roles. Meyer has stoutly defended her vision from all attacks, claiming that theories about Bella being an antifeminist character "are usually predicated on her choices."[1] Her implication is that true feminism supports a woman's right to choose her own path, even one that limits her whole purview to marriage and babies. This may well be the case; however, it is disingenuous of Meyer to imply that Bella really has a "choice." At the periphery of the overarching plot of the intermale struggle for dominance—over females, territory, knowledge, and, ultimately, the self—the female characters in the saga create a feminine narrative in which motherhood is the only licit objective of womanhood. This theme returns with increasing frequency through *New Moon* and *Eclipse*, reaching its apotheosis in the final installment, *Breaking Dawn*, by which point the subtext has become overt—that in the *Twilight* universe, mothering is what women are for, and that it is the only role in which they can find true fulfilment. Furthermore, the models of motherhood we are exposed to in the saga combine to suggest a maternal ideal in which self-sacrifice amounting to masochism is inherent. However, far from being a reification of the mother's role, this theme supports a paradigm of parenthood that is patriarchal in the most literal sense. As we will see, Meyer uses the mythological framework of the vampire to uncouple the biological links between the mother and the child, in favor of a father-centered family model that represents a regressive yearning for preindustrial gender roles.

MARTYRED MOTHER OR FAILED FEMALE: WOMEN IN *TWILIGHT*

The saga both begins and ends with a mother. Bella Swan's motive in leaving Arizona and moving to the rainy and uninviting town of Forks is to free her "erratic, harebrained mother" Renee from her parental responsibilities, allowing her to follow her young lover.[2] This sacrifice sets Bella on the path that will ultimately lead to her own accession to motherhood; along the way, she will collide repeatedly with the question of what it means to be a mother.

The ideal is introduced by its antithesis, Renee, whose most notable feature in the saga is her absence. It is apparent from the first that there has been an inversion of the mother–child relationship, with Bella adopting the parental role over her impulsive young mother. Bella has spent most of her life "taking care of Renee"[3]; her move to Forks is only her latest self-sacrifice, in which she makes the break so crucial in post-Freudian models of parenting: "you have to let them go their own way eventually…you have to let them have their own life."[4] Bella, however, remains unable to relinquish her nurturing role, and lavishes care on her father—cooking, cleaning, and keeping house, sheltering him from the harsh realities she herself is exposed to, and anticipating his every desire. Even at this early stage in the narrative, Bella already has the insignia of Meyer's model of motherhood—martyrdom.

This trait is represented more literally in the seemingly innocuous character of Esme, the "mother" of Edward, Emmett, Jasper, Rosalie, and Alice. Always a peripheral character, on the surface, it seems that Esme is included by Meyer only as a device to emphasize the traditional "perfection" of the Cullen "family"—which is to say their adherence to the formula of heteronormative, monogamous married pairings (as compared to Bella's own "broken" home). Bella describes Esme admiringly as "a fairy tale—Snow White, in the flesh,"[5] which is an uncannily accurate assessment. Esme's entire existence is oriented around her own vampiric version of the Seven Dwarves. She arranges their home, encourages their talents, and tenderly curbs their excesses, every inch the devoted mother figure. When, in *New Moon*, Alice updates Bella on the activities of the Cullen family, Esme's husband and "children" variously teach, learn, and travel, while Esme herself is restoring a seventeenth century house—ever the home-maker.[6]

However, like the protagonists of many fairy tales, the almost cartoonishly maternal Esme has a darker subtext—through her, we get our first intimation of how deep the ideal of self-sacrifice runs in Meyer's model of the perfect mom. We learn, almost as an aside, that Esme attained immortality via suicide—she jumped off of a cliff after her "first and only baby," a son, died a few days after his early birth.[7] The gender of the child is by no means insignificant, as we will see later on—throughout the saga, a marked preference is shown for male children (or children imagined to be male). The fact that this detail is given so little weight when it arises (for no one ever questions the legitimacy of Esme's extreme reaction to her bereavement) veils its importance—death as devotion is a theme that recurs frequently in the series, particularly with regard to mothers and sons.

Certainly the devotion of Emily (the de facto mother of the La Push pack) to her mate and his dependents borders on the suicidal. Emily, like Esme, is a fairy-tale mother: living in the woods in her idyllic little house, she is "a cheerful person who never sat still…and always cooking, too."[8] The association of Emily with the provision of endless nourishment is pronounced—the first we hear of her is Embry's confident assertion that "you know she'll have food waiting."[9] In this sense, she represents the fantasy of the infant subject of psychoanalysis, the breast that is never withdrawn, and she is presented as being completely fulfilled in this role.[10] However, Emily performs her maternal duties at constant risk of assault—she is already permanently scarred from an angry encounter with Sam early on in their relationship. Disturbingly, this assault is deemed to have marked the turning point in her previously ambiguous attitude to her destiny, suggesting an element of either masochism or sublimated coercion in her self-sacrifice.[11]

This fantasy of motherhood as intrinsically masochistic is finally attributed true mythic status by Meyer when it is incorporated into the Quileute tribe's ancient werewolf legends, in the person of The Third Wife. The Third Wife sacrifices herself for her children in the most explicit way, fatally stabbing herself to provide a momentary distraction during a fight between her aged husband Taha Aki and the terrible Cold Woman. It is interesting to note that the death of their mother allows The Third Wife's immature sons to make the transformation into werewolves (a process that usually first takes place in adolescence), allowing them to fight alongside their father. To a psychoanalyst, this turn of events would seem strongly reminiscent of the resolution of the male Oedipus complex, in which the boy renounces his mother in order to identify with his father (a crucial step without which healthy psychological development is impossible).[12] Bella's admiration for and attempted emulation of The Third Wife's sacrifice in *Eclipse* symbolizes the perpetuation of an ideal where good motherhood entails ultimate sacrifice—in effect, the only good mother is a dead mother.

Bella continues to follow this model upon finding herself pregnant with Edward's child. She is determined to proceed with the pregnancy in spite of the risk to her own soon-to-be-immortal life. This is a complete reversal of her previous viewpoint, in which she "didn't care about giving up children for [Edward]."[13] In an uncharacteristic break from her usually submissive behavior, Bella defies the male authority figures who call for her to terminate her pregnancy, and in what could generously be interpreted as a feminist move, invokes Rosalie's aid to help her retain control of her body. Bella is certainly made to suffer for her obstinacy: her unnaturally strong baby breaks her ribs with its kicks, requires that she drink human blood to feed it, and, in a birth scene so horrifically graphic that it has drawn comparisons to *Alien*, gnaws its way out of her womb, accompanied by anime-style fountains of blood, and snaps her spine for good measure.[14] To add insult to injury, when placed upon her breast, the half-vampire baby immediately bites her. Throughout this ordeal, Bella never expresses anything but worshipful devotion toward her "angel-faced baby."[15] In effect, like The Third Wife, she "dies" for her child, and is only revived through the miracle of vampirism (necessitating yet more agony).

In summary, ideal motherhood in *Twilight* is a fairly daunting prospect. However, Meyer presents it as not simply the best, but the *only* path to fulfilment for women. She hammers this point home with the stories of both Rosalie and Leah, whose lives are apparently blighted by their infertility. In Rosalie's case, this misfortune is the only thing about the character that makes her sympathetic to the reader. The desire for children is her most enduring memory of humanity, and the cause of her intense bitterness about being made a vampire (and thus, unable to have them). Rosalie openly admits that she chose her lover Emmett due to his resemblance to her old friend's baby, which she coveted in her mortal life.[16] Her obsessive drive to preserve the life of Bella's child, in spite of the risk to Bella's life, is figured as the direct consequence of her own thwarted maternal instinct. Rosalie's desperation is tragic; but the full weight of Meyer's moral message regarding the imperative of motherhood is brought to bear in the character of Leah.

In a deeply moving scene in *Breaking Dawn*, it is implied that the cause of all Leah's suffering is her barrenness. It is the reason her lover Sam imprinted on her symbolically fertile cousin Emily instead of on her; it is why she has become "the girlie-wolf" of the deeply masculine La Push pack—she is, as she describes it, "good for nothing else."[17] Leah confesses that before she became aware of her infertility she had not given motherhood a second thought; this is reminiscent of Bella's Road-to-Damascus conversion from disinterest in to obsession with maternity upon discovering her pregnancy. In the contrast between Bella and Leah, Meyer presents a parable, a veiled warning to a generation of modern young women (many of whom share such ambivalent attitudes to motherhood) of the threat to their ultimate fulfilment, to their very femininity, posed by delaying or denying their maternal destiny. Bella's happy ending is the reward Meyer promises from motherhood; the tragic figure of Leah represents the grim fate Bella has escaped. In Meyer's paradigm, in which the role of women is limited solely to mothering, Leah is "not as female as she should be"—only mothers can be female, and females can only be mothers.[18]

It is telling that even beyond denying her Sam, Meyer continues to punish Leah for her failure to be a "real" woman by refusing to allow her to enjoy the privileges of an honorary man. Leah is excluded from the "brotherhood" shared by the males in the pack, who find her feminine mentality intrusive (their intolerance for her pain over Sam is contrasted with their seemingly boundless patience with Jacob's agony over Bella), and her physicality embarrassing. Moreover, although she has become a werewolf, as "the girlie-wolf," she is denied the full benefits of wolfhood. While one of the common characteristics of new male werewolves is a sudden increase in physical mass and strength in human form (which is reflected in their wolf incarnations) no corresponding change in Leah is remarked upon before the change, and her wolf incarnation is relatively small.[19] In the battle with the newborns in *Eclipse*, she has to be rescued by the males of the pack after, as Jacob caustically puts it, "trying to prove she's as tough as the rest of us"—clearly, she can never be "as tough."[20] In addition, while the male wolves are happy to "eat raw"—that is, to hunt and kill their food, overcoming their human aversion by channelling their animal instinct—Leah remains squeamish about this aspect of wolf life, putting her at frequent disadvantage.[21] Leah is left neither fish nor fowl, barred from her designated female role and unable to enjoy the compensations of a male one.

The maternal moral extolled by these central characters is shored up by the context Meyer creates. In the *Twilight* universe, we meet remarkably few women who do anything other than mother (or yearn to). Successful career women with independently derived authority certainly do not feature largely in the text. It seems extremely improbable that not a single one of Bella's teachers mentioned in the books is female, nor any of the doctors who treat her after her many and varied mishaps.

WHERE'S MOMMY? FOREGROUNDING FATHERS

Despite Meyer's limitation of viable female identity to the role of nurturing mother figure, she does not attach any important status to this role. In fact, despite its ubiquity among the female characters, the state of motherhood is marginalized throughout, with mother figures either absented from the text altogether, or elided with a patriarch from whom they draw legitimacy but no authority. This trope is certainly assisted by the series' previously mentioned glut of dead or absented mothers. Bella's mother Renee makes a few cameos, but the parental authority in the protagonist's life is her father, Charlie. Jacob's mother, we learn, was killed in a car crash when he was an infant, leaving him to be parented by his father, Billy.[22] Carlisle's mother died in childbirth, and he was raised by his authoritarian pastor father.[23] The most explicit example of this transfer of parental authority from the inadequate figure of the mother to the more capable male is when Edward's dying human mother Elizabeth literally hands over her son to the superior custody of Carlisle.[24] Even when a mother figure is present, she is secondary to the father or representative authoritative male (the key examples being Carlisle and Sam). The patriarch ultimately makes all decisions unilaterally, and the rest of the family adheres to his decisions. It is significant that when, in *New Moon*, Bella canvasses the Cullens on the issue of her becoming a vampire, Carlisle's is "the vote that mattered most, the vote that counted more than any majority."[25] In the case of Sam, as the Alpha wolf his word is literally law.

This is not simply a division of spheres along chauvinistic lines, wherein the father is the locus of power, the mother of care. Beyond the material elements of nurturing (Esme's homemaking and Emily's perpetual cooking) the mother's parenting role is marginalized—the father is the source of guidance and support, and is far more involved with his charges' inner lives and personal struggles. Sam guides the new werewolves through the traumatic experience of the change, and patiently helps them to control their new impulses. It is even implied that only an authoritative father figure can fulfill this role: when Leah and Seth become wolves, their widowed mother needs Billy's help to deal with this "trouble with her kids," in spite of having always been presented as a strong character throughout the series.[26] Carlisle performs a similar role with newborn vampires, training them to control their urges in a way that mimics the early socialization of infants usually assumed to be a part of mothering.

So, since she has already restricted licit female identity to motherhood alone, what motivates Meyer to construct the family as father-centered? Far from being a progressive reflection of the current Western fashion for "new men" who are more emotionally available and hands-on with their offspring, Meyer's model recreates that which would have been the norm from the Classical period, and which was only disrupted relatively recently by the exigencies of the Industrial Revolution. This cataclysmic cultural shift resulted in a rift between people's families and their working lives, as it became necessary for people to work for wages outside of the home. In families with the option to have a single breadwinner, it made practical sense that the mother (who physically bore and nourished her children) was the one who stayed at home. This transformation in family life magnified the connection between a mother and her children from a matter of biological necessity to one of almost mythic importance. After the propagation of the ideal of the "angel at the hearth," and the popularization of psychoanalysis, the mother was no longer considered a mere incubator, but the primary caregiver and a major developmental influence upon the child.[27] The pervasiveness of this new orthodoxy is such that at the dawn of the twenty-first century, we find it difficult to comprehend that the trend of the last two hundred years has been the exception rather than the rule, and that hitherto, the father was the parent who mattered.

In the early modern period, when Western society first began to grow introspective about childcare, all the parenting pamphlets produced were addressed to the father, on the assumption that he would be the main guiding influence on the child.[28] Going back further to the ancient Greeks and Romans, the paterfamilias had ultimate authority over his young—deciding if a pregnancy should be brought to term, and choosing whether to accept or expose any children born. Mothers had no rights over their own children, nor was their input required much beyond weaning—boys would be educated by male tutors chosen by the father, and girls were usually married off at a young age to much older men. The mother's status in the household, given the frequency of a significant disparity in age between husband and wife, was not much greater than that of her children.

Not for Meyer the post-Industrial exaltation of the mother as the lodestone of domestic life; she figures the Cullen family as a pre-Industrial utopian ideal, with the father as both ultimate authority and primary caregiver. This reflects her religious background; the Church of Jesus Christ and the Latter-Day Saints, while mandating motherhood for women, lays heavy emphasis on the responsibility of a father to provide "spiritual and physical support for all other family members," asserting that "giving Christ-like service as a husband and father is the most important work a man can perform during mortality."[29] On various inspirational websites, Mormon leaders lament the "growing cultural confusion about the roles of parents" and admonish fathers to lead a "family-centred life," in obvious reaction to the post-Industrial state of affairs in which fathers more often than not work long hours outside the home, delegating parental power to mothers.[30]

In the *Twilight* saga, Meyer manipulates elements of the vampire myth in order to further her representation of the Cullens as the father-focused Mormon ideal of the "eternal family." However, her symbolic neutering of female generative power goes far beyond the reinstatement of an idealized social order; it speaks directly to the deep-seated psychological motivations of that initial idealization. She taps into an ancient seam of male jealousy and fear of women's reproductive and nurturing capacities, and reflects a consequent cultural theme of the male appropriation of meaningful parenting.

"No mother gave me birth":
Meyer's Myth of Male Mothering

The myth of male mothering has roots as old as civilization itself. Indeed, Robert McElvaine has argued that the two are concomitant—that the shift in human societies from the nomadic hunter-gatherer model to ones based around agricultural settlement is what first alerted humankind to the male role in procreation (previously believed to be a unilateral effort on the part of the mother).[31] What McElvaine calls the "seed" metaphor fostered the mistaken belief that man contributed all the necessary materials for life, while women provided only the environment in which the child grew. We can see this trope running through Western culture, as mother goddess religions are superseded by those dedicated to a father god, as Eve is born of Adam in a mythic reversal of nature, as Aphrodite springs from the foam of Cronos' castrated testicles and Athene bursts forth from Zeus's head. So powerful and enduring was the belief articulated by Apollo in *The Eumenides* that "the mother is not the true parent of the child which is called hers,"[32] that when sperm was first examined under a microscope, the male observers asserted in all seriousness that they could see the tiny child fully formed within.[33] Even now that the dual nature of procreation has been proved beyond a shadow of a doubt, we can observe the hangover of this male appropriation of creative power in our very language: as Shari Thurer notes in her historical study of motherhood, "'to father' means 'to generate'; 'to mother' means 'to nurture.'"[34]

The post-Freudian psychoanalyst Karen Horney reversed Freud's concept of penis envy by giving the myth of male mothering the diagnosis of "womb envy," attributing the appropriation of meaningful parenting by the father, and the exaltation of other modes of creativity from which women are disbarred, to a prevalent and intense male envy "of pregnancy, childbirth, and motherhood...and of the act of suckling."[35] Anthropologists have also identified this as the motivation behind cultural practices of diverse societies in which men imitate both menstruation and childbirth,[36] or effect the "rebirth" of male adolescents into an exclusively male society by the dispensation of "male milk."[37] McElvaine theorizes that womb envy is stronger at those points in history when what are perceived as male social roles are under threat of disenfranchisement and obsolescence, heightening male awareness and resentment of their reliance on women for the essential act of procreation. Thurer's research substantiates this theory with the example of the Industrial Revolution, when men—complacent in their vital new role as provider in the capitalist labor market—allowed mothers more significance in child rearing.[38] Following this line of reasoning, Meyer's reinterpretation of vampire mythology to eradicate the mother's role is timely, reflecting the growing participation of women in the workforce, especially in the previously masculine bastions of industry and warfare; this increase in women's opportunities seems critically related to the lessening importance of stereotypically "male" strengths, such as physical power and aggressive instinct.

The myth of vampirism easily lends itself to alternative parenting possibilities. Since its absorption from folktales and penny-dreadfuls into literary culture proper via Bram Stoker's classic *Dracula* (1897), a great part of the vampire's terror and appeal has been his ability to transform others, a transformation that is always likened to a rebirth. This capacity for creation is often invested in a powerful male, with the prime example being Dracula himself, "a father-figure of huge potency."[39] However, the actual *process* of transformation has traditionally borne the hallmarks of motherhood, with a characteristic fixation on the mutual pleasures of suckling. When Dracula attempts to transform Mina Harker into a vampire, he does not simply drain her blood—he "open[s] a vein in his breast . . . and press[es her] mouth to the wound," forcing her to drink his own blood in an obvious parallel to a mother suckling her infant.[40] This reciprocal blood exchange has provided the basic template for contemporary renditions of the vampire, from Anne Rice's *Vampire Chronicles* to *Buffy the Vampire Slayer* and *True Blood*. In Rice's version of the process, the blood exchange is explicitly linked to the act of suckling one's infant—the author uses a vampiric framework to present the prelinguistic, preoedipal pleasures of infant intimacy with the mother, most transparently when her hero Lestat is changed by the ancient Magnus:

> I drew with all my power upon that great fount that I knew would satisfy my thirst *as it had never been satisfied before* . . . it was not merely the dry hissing coil of the thirst that was quenched and dissolved, it was all my craving, all the want and misery and hunger that I had ever known . . . all the desperate desires of my life were a thousand-fold fed . . . love you, I wanted to say . . . love you, love you, this is what I had always so wanted, *wanted and could never have*, this, and you've given it to me! [emphasis added][41]

While Janice Doane and Devon Hodges read this scene as a feminist reification of motherhood, in fact it is nothing of the sort—the whole tenor of the passage is not that "father is really mother,"[42] but that father is a *better* mother than mother ever was. As the highlighted phrases suggest, the superior nourishment he gives redeems the unsatisfying experience of maternal nurturance, catering to fantasies (prompted by the rudeness of weaning) of an idealized mother who does not withdraw the breast.[43] That the vampire myth in this case is used to appropriate the mother's awesome preoedipal powers is made evident by the passage in which Lestat makes his own mother a vampire, reversing the power dynamic of their relationship by assuming the role she had so inadequately performed: "there was no mother anymore, no petty need and petty terror."[44] This theme is found throughout the *Chronicles*; another example can be found in *Interview With The Vampire*, Lestat and Louis "adopt" the child Claudia, taking her from the corpse of her mother who, like Elizabeth in *Twilight*, has failed her child by dying and must cede parental power to the two immortal "fathers."

Meyer's version of the vampire myth goes far further than either Stoker or Rice to transfer meaningful parenting from mothers to fathers. Whereas these earlier authors used vampirism to allow male characters to access maternal models of generation and nurturing, Meyer adapts the myth's methodology to efface such models altogether.

The figure of Carlisle Cullen is the lynchpin of Meyer's neutering of maternal power. As the undisputed patriarch of the Cullen clan, his role is compounded by the fact that it is he, not Esme, the mother figure, who has chosen and "made" all of their "children." In fact, Esme herself, although Carlisle's nominal consort, was made a vampire by him as well, and thus shares the same subordinate status as the "younger" Cullens in relation to her husband/father. Her "son," Edward, is in fact several years "older" than her, and has far more authority within the family—although he too defers to Carlisle. Esme's claim on her "children" is an indirect one, deriving legitimacy only through her submissive relationship to the patriarch who is their "real" parent. A similar situation can be observed with Emily, who is only able to find her family in the wolf pack through the disempowering experience of being imprinted on by Sam.

The method by which Meyer's vampires are made continues this effacement of maternity by departing from the tradition established by Stoker and Rice, in which the new life is acceded to by an exchange of blood reminiscent of a mother suckling her child. In Meyer's version of vampirism, transformation is achieved solely by the overtly phallic bite and consequent injection of "venom," a method that recreates McElvaine's "seed" metaphor, in which life is seen as the consequence of the active male element (sperm/seed) in the passive female one (womb/earth).[45] By this method, Carlisle can "mother" his children without attaching any value, even by appropriation, to female methods of generation and nurture—this is male mothering in which mother is entirely eclipsed.

That creative power in Meyer's world is the rightful preserve of the male is subtly emphasized in the text. The vast majority of vampires whose origins we are given to know were created by powerful males. Even Rosalie, whose desperation to mother is evidenced above, abides by this custom—having chosen a child for herself in the form of Emmett, she does not presume to create him herself, but carries his mauled and dying body hundreds of miles back to Carlisle to seek the sanction and parenting of the patriarch.[46] Those female vampires who do create others are not presented in a favorable light. Jasper's immortal "mother," Maria, creates children to serve her own ends, destroying them when they are of no further use.[47] Victoria creates an army of savage newborns, again for the purpose of waging war, and fails to "bring them up" appropriately—as a result, both she and all her "children" are destroyed by the father-led Cullen clan.[48] Finally, we hear the second-hand tale of the Denali clan's "mother" Sacha, who wilfully creates an "immortal child" in defiance of the Volturi's law, endangering her daughters by her crime and ultimately traumatizing them by dying with the boy.[49] Vampire mothers in the literal sense—as opposed to father-approved surrogates like Esme—are selfish and inadequate, and more often than not come to a bad end.

It seems perverse that after going to such lengths to erase the physical link between mothers and their children by adapting the traditional vampire myth, Meyer should, at the last, decide to bend her own newly minted mythology to its breaking point in order that Bella should become pregnant. Certainly Bella's potential for giving life (as opposed to keeping house) is not an issue frequently addressed in the series. Until her period fatefully fails to arrive, we are given no indication that she has a menstrual cycle—an issue that would surely have arisen during her three-year relationship with a vampire hypersensitive to the smell of her blood. However, far from being a last-minute return to natural, mother-centered patterns of parenthood, the conception and birth of Renesmee are merely a tool with which Meyer hammers the last nail into the coffin of the maternal connection to the child.

From the moment she knows that she is pregnant, Bella is in love with her unborn child. However, this love is not expressive of the power and joy of maternity that Horney posited as the source of male womb envy: "the blissful consciousness of

bearing new life within oneself…and the ineffable happiness of the increasing expectation of the appearance of this new being."[50] Bella does not experience the life inside
her as being something new; rather she imagines it as a perfect facsimile of the father,
a little Edward (she instantly presumes the child is male). She actively hopes to have
as small a part in the end product as possible: "I hoped he would have Edward's face
exactly, with no interference from mine."[51] When Edward, fearful for Bella's life,
tries to bargain with her to abort the mysterious fetus in exchange for another baby
conceived either with Jacob or via IVF, she is revolted—not, as one might expect, at
the chauvinism that she farm her uterus out to her friend, but because her desire is
not for a child of her own, but for "Edward's child,"[52] in a classic recreation of Freud's
conviction that what a woman desires is not the child in its (and her) own right, but
to receive from the father a "penis-baby."[53]

Other aspects of Meyer's mythological framework further facilitate the theme of
Bella as a passive incubator. Although it takes its toll on her mother, Renesmee's
sped-up gestation minimizes the input Bella can claim to have had in her child's
development by truncating the period of pregnancy. This also falls in with the father-
focused keynote of antiabortion rhetoric—that life proper begins at conception,
rather than being a gradual process taking place over many months in the womb.
Although Renesmee's amniotic sac is impenetrable to ultrasound, it is not immune
to Edward's mind reading skills, which allow him greater intimacy with the child
inside Bella than she has herself. Bella's knowledge of her child's needs is mediated by
the father, in a preternatural parallel with what feminists have decried as the disempowering medicalization of pregnancy, whereby what used to be a natural process,
administered by other, experienced women, has fallen under the aegis of a medical
establishment controlled predominantly by men.

Renesmee's birth is gratuitously gruesome, and Bella is unconscious from the outset, her depersonalized body "worked over" by Jacob and Edward (Carlisle is absent
when labor begins, fortuitously clearing the way for Edward to assume the role of
patriarch as he ascends to the role of father/husband in his own vampiric family
unit).[54] Both of these men will ultimately express a superior claim over Bella's child,
Jacob by imprinting on Renesmee and Edward by dint of Renesmee's predominantly
supernatural nature—it is later remarked that her special gift "could only have come
from a very gifted father."[55]

Having delivered his daughter, Edward turns to the matter of creating his wife as
a newborn vampire. The hypermedicalized process, in which he sedates Bella with
morphine and then injects his venom into her heart by dint of a syringe, is a further
sophistication of Meyer's adapted creation method, divorcing the male creative force
still further from anything smacking of fleshly, female generation.[56] The transformation process absents Bella from the narrative for several days, during which time
Renesmee develops at an unprecedented rate, due—we are to infer—to her hybrid
nature. Meyer never addresses why the offspring of a human and an unchanging
creature, who will eventually cease developing entirely, should as an infant grow so
rapidly, but the plot device serves to further divorce Bella from a primary relation to
her child. As nursing Renesmee would be impossible even if Bella were conscious (her
only attempt at "breast-feeding" is swiftly intercepted by Edward) the child is instead
fed by a series of bottle-wielding "wet-nurses" authorized by Bella's father.[57]

By the time Bella finally meets her child (an encounter which is delayed as much as possible) Renesmee's talent is already widely known: by touching someone and looking deep into their eyes, Renesmee can communicate her inchoate perceptions and emotions in a powerful connection that evokes the preoedipal state of identification between mothers and infants.[58] In Meyer's mythology, however, this talent is not exclusive to mother and child; it is a general means of communication, invalidating any idea of a unique connection between Bella and Renesmee. Renesmee is no more her mother's child than she is Edward's, Carlisle's, Rosalie's, or any of the other substituted caregivers whose connection to her is through the father. Bella's own father is not permitted to touch his grandchild, in case he discovers her talent.

Renesmee's name—a combination of the names of her maternal and paternal grandmothers—is an interesting device, suggesting the inevitability of her own eventual accession to the state of motherhood (an event already foreshadowed by her predestined relationship with Jacob). The fact that this name (chosen for her by her mother) is, against Bella's protestations, shortened to "Nessie" (a contraction invented by Jacob and quickly picked up on by the rest of the family) is just another example of how Bella's authority as a mother is sidelined by authoritative males, and offers little hope for Renesmee's own eventual control of her future. Just as Bella's "choice" to sacrifice herself for her child was made for her by the patriarchal context Meyer creates, Renesmee's identity and choices appear to be equally circumscribed—in the *Twilight* universe, unequal monogamy and castrated maternity are the limits of female destiny.

NOTES

1. Stephenie Meyer, "Breaking Dawn: Frequently Asked Questions," *Stephenie Meyer's Official Website*. Web. http://www.stepheniemeyer.com/bd_faq.html, Accessed 22/05/10.
2. Stephenie Meyer, *Twilight* (London: Atom, 2007. Print), 4.
3. Stephenie Meyer, *Eclipse* (London: Atom, 2008. Print), 40.
4. Ibid, 40.
5. Meyer, *Twilight*, 282.
6. Stephenie Meyer, *New Moon* (London: Atom, 2007. Print), 352.
7. Meyer, *Twilight*, 321.
8. Meyer, *New Moon*, 308.
9. Ibid, 289.
10. Ibid, 297.
11. Ibid, 110–1.
12. Sigmund Freud, "The Dissolution of the Oedipus Complex" (1924), *On Sexuality* (London: Penguin, 1991. Print), 316–8.
13. Stephenie Meyer, *Breaking Dawn* (London: Atom, 2008. Print), 119–20.
14. "Five Scenes That MUST Be in *Breaking Dawn*," *Eclipse Movie website*. Web. http://www.eclipsemovie.org/five-scenes-that-must-be-in-breaking-dawn/, Accessed 22/05/10.
15. Meyer, *Breaking Dawn*, 344.
16. Meyer, *Eclipse*, 149.
17. Meyer, *Breaking Dawn*, 91.

18. Ibid, 291.
19. Meyer, *Eclipse*, 354.
20. Ibid, 525.
21. Meyer, *Breaking Dawn*, 240.
22. Ibid, 136.
23. Meyer, *Twilight*, 289.
24. Meyer, *New Moon*, 34–7.
25. Ibid, 472.
26. Meyer, *Eclipse*, 284.
27. Janice Doane and Devon Hodges, *From Klein to Kristeva: Psychoanalytic Feminism and the Search for the "Good Enough" Mother* (Ann Arbor: The University of Michigan Press, 1992. Print), 2–3.
28. Shari L. Thurer, *The Myths of Motherhood: How Culture Reinvents the Good Mother* (New York: Penguin, 1995. Print), 166, 263.
29. Lynn Scoresby, "LDS Perspectives on Fatherhood," *Light Planet*, Web. http://www. lightplanet.com/family/fathers/fatherhood.html, Accessed 22/05/10.
30. Kim Crenshaw Sorensen, "A Latter-Day Father's Guidebook," *The Church of Jesus Christ and the Latter Day Saints, Gospel Library Magazines website*, Web. http://www. lds.org/ldsorg/v/index.jsp?vgnextoid=2354fccf2b7db010VgnVCM1000004d82620a RCRD&locale=0&sourceId=8b323ff73058b010VgnVCM1000004d82620a____& hideNav=1, Accessed 22/05/10.
31. Robert McElvaine, *Eve's Seed: Biology, the Sexes, and the Course of History* (New York: McGraw-Hill, 2001. Print), 122–5.
32. Aeschylus, *The Oresteian Trilogy* (Harmondsworth: Penguin, 1968. Print), 169.
33. McElvaine, 124.
34. Thurer, 213.
35. Karen Horney, *Feminine Psychology* (New York: W.W. Norton, 1993. Print), 60–1.
36. Thurer, 37.
37. McElvaine, 122.
38. Thurer, 183–4.
39. Maurice Richardson, "The Psychoanalysis of Count Dracula" in Christopher Frayling (ed.), *Vampyres* (London: Faber & Faber, 1991. Print), 419.
40. Bram Stoker, *Dracula* (Oxford: Oxford University Press, 1996. Print), 288.
41. Anne Rice, *The Vampire Lestat* (London: Sphere, 2009. Print), 101–2.
42. Janice Doane and Devon Hodges, "Undoing Feminism: From the Preoedipal to Postfeminism in Anne Rice's Vampire Chronicles," *American Literary History*, 1990, 2 (3), 422–42.
43. Doane and Hodges, *From Klein to Kristeva,* 17.
44. Rice, 174.
45. McElvaine, 125.
46. Meyer, *Twilight*, 252.
47. Meyer, *Eclipse*, 264–5.
48. Ibid, 22.
49. Meyer, *Breaking Dawn*, 30–2. It is interesting to note here the preference shown for boy children that will later be shown by Bella when imagining her unborn child— Sacha prefers to die for her male child than to live for her three "daughters."
50. Horney, 60.
51. Meyer, *Breaking Dawn*, 119.
52. Ibid 120.

53. Sigmund Freud, "On Transformations of the Instinct as Exemplified in Anal Eroticism" (1917), *On Sexuality* (London: Penguin, 1991. Print), 297.

54. Meyer, *Breaking Dawn*, 326.

55. Ibid, 545.

56. Ibid, 325.

57. Ibid, 328. This too is a customary trope of pre-industrial societies, where choosing an infant's wet nurse was "a task assigned to the biological father and jealously guarded by him." Thurer, 127.

58. Ibid, 411–2.

OF MONSTERS AND MEN: TOXIC MASCULINITY AND THE TWENTY-FIRST CENTURY VAMPIRE IN THE *TWILIGHT SAGA*

TRACY L. BEALER

THE PHENOMENAL POPULARITY OF STEPHENIE MEYER'S *TWILIGHT* saga among women and girls has generated a concurrently passionate response from feminist critics and cultural analysts. By and large, the most positive reaction from this community has been to applaud the way the films in particular encourage studio executives to recognize and respect the purchasing power of women.[1] Aside from this market-centered endorsement, the writers find the material itself, especially its treatment of gender, "retrograde...infuriating,"[2] and "cringe-worthy."[3] The critics tend to locate their critiques on an unfavorable reading of heroine Bella Swan, finding her a "submissive,"[4] "obsessive and self-destructive"[5] character who passively depends upon her stable of male admirers for validation and survival. Put most succinctly by Kate Harding, feminist commentators are asking, "What *is* it that makes girls go nuts for this crap?"[6] The purpose of my chapter is not to answer Harding's question—I imagine every fan would have a different response—but to counter the premise of the criticism.

Dismissing Meyer's novels as antifeminist "crap" because Bella does not consistently challenge normative gender roles ignores the many ways Edward Cullen, her vampire soul mate, does. Nina Auerbach, in her seminal study of literary vampires *Our Vampires, Ourselves*, argues that "every age embraces the vampire it needs."[7] Since Edward has been unquestionably embraced by twenty-first-century readers, what does he give us that we need? I think one answer lies in the way his love for Bella transforms his understanding of what it means to be a man by and through challenging his definition of what it means to be a vampire. As recent gender theorists have argued, investigating and subverting normative masculinity is a crucial component of the feminist project. By situating Edward's reluctant and fraught evolution from a patronizing and callous loner to an empathetic and vulnerable romantic partner in a supernatural context, the novels hyperbolize and thoughtfully address the trials of negotiating a progressive male identity in a masculinist world. As Trevor Holmes notes, "one of the purposes of vampires in general [is] the displacement of real social relations onto the fantastic in order to foreground the fault lines in what is taken as natural in any particular social sphere."[8] In this chapter I will explore the ways that *Twilight*'s supernatural male hero both exposes and challenges normative masculinity.

Beginning in the 1980s, feminist theorists started to look at the way gender norms that promote and perpetuate submissive roles for women depend upon complementary and similarly reductive identities for men. The theoretical term "phallic masculinity" began to circulate in the literature, referring to the privileged ("normative") version of manliness that encourages emotional hardness and physical and social dominance, and perpetuates a collective social fantasy that men are active subjects positioned against women, who are figured as passive and penetrated. It should be clear from this brief description of what Kaja Silverman calls the "dominant fiction" of late twentieth-century Western gender politics[9] why this rigid and dangerous version of masculinity is called "phallic." French philosopher Jacques Lacan identified the phallus as the emblematic symbol of power in the psychological and social makeup of modern Western subjects (think of the Washington Monument, the architecture of skyscrapers, or most ancient and contemporary weaponry).[10] Though Lacan was careful to insist upon maintaining the distinction between the body part belonging to human beings gendered male and the way that marker of sexual difference is mythologized in the mind and the social world, Silverman and others show how that distinction persistently collapses.[11] When the phallus and the penis are equated, male subjects will always already be associated with and expected to wield dominating and oppressive social and sexual power. Therefore, one feminist theoretical and political goal becomes unhinging the social symbols of power from the male body, and imagining new ways of inhabiting a masculine identity that do not reflect and encourage the emotional hardness and impenetrability associated with masculinist domination. What makes this psychoanalytic theory relevant for a discussion of Edward is the way the physical markers of his vampirism conflate with and encourage him to embody phallic masculinity, and how he learns to resist this predilection with Bella.

The male vampiric bodies in the *Twilight* saga are in many ways a literalization and intensification of this toxic version of masculinity.[12] Their phallic (and in *Twilight* mythology, venomous) fangs are fatally penetrative while their preternatural strength renders them capable of brutal physical violence. Bella repeatedly describes the feel of their bodies as cold, solid, and inflexible as stone. Even the series' innovation of vampiric skin sparkling in the sunlight like diamonds emphasizes physical appeal at the cost of an adamantine hardness. These characteristics seem to suggest that Edward conforms to the hypermasculinization that cultural historian Michael Kimmel identifies as endemic to representations of supernatural masculinity in the late twentieth century. Citing the film versions of *Bram Stoker's Dracula* (1992) and *Interview with the Vampire* (1994), he writes that "the masculinist descent to the primitive has resurfaced in another guise—the return of the monster as hypermasculine beast."[13]

However, there are several complications in Edward's character and storyline that suggest he is at the vanguard of contemporary vampires who will challenge and reimagine the toxicity of their phallic bodies by and through romantic love.[14] Nina Auerbach shows that throughout the nineteenth and twentieth centuries in the United States and Britain, literary vampires "shape themselves to personal and national moods."[15] This chapter argues that in the twenty-first century, Edward Cullen is not only shaped by but shapes the individual and social conception of masculinity through his disgust for the very traits that make him hypermasculine, and his attempt to love Bella in spite of (not through) his physical and psychic compulsion to dominate.

Edward, perpetual seventeen-year-old and romantic hero of the series, distinguishes himself from other Byronic protagonists in his literary lineage (Heathcliff from Brontë's *Wuthering Heights*, Mr. Darcy from Austen's *Pride and Prejudice*, Lestat de Lioncourt from Anne Rice's *The Vampire Chronicles*) by the depth and power of his self-loathing.[16] I argue that his initial attitude and behavior toward Bella—condescending, dominative, angry—that some critics have designated as "emotionally abusive"[17] and that seem to conflate with descriptions of phallic masculinity, derive from a profound hatred of himself stemming from his dangerous body. In the first volume of the series, Edward articulates a psychiatric self-analysis that pathologizes his desire to pursue a relationship with Bella despite the constant temptation to devour her. By calling himself a "*sick*, masochistic lion" (emphasis added),[18] Edward reveals not only that he is suffering, but more crucially that he understands himself to be wicked and contaminated because his vampirism renders his body inherently predatory. However, his second defining term, "masochistic," is both insightful and misapplied. It is not his masochistic desire to expose himself to the temptation Bella embodies that actually causes Edward's torment. As I will argue later, this masochism is actually his salvation. He has convinced himself that his transformation into a vampire has cost him his soul, and he has internalized this perceived loss by identifying himself as a "monster"[19] doomed to destroy Bella. Therefore, a more accurate diagnosis of Edward's psychic suffering is Freudian melancholia.

In "Mourning and Melancholia," Freud theorizes that loss can prompt two divergent psychic responses in human beings. Mourning the lost object (which can be a person, an idea, or an aspect of the self) involves discovering a substitute to which the person's feelings can reconnect. A melancholic, conversely, refuses to psychically surrender what has been lost, and instead wholly internalizes that loss, directing inward the conflicting feelings of anger and love that were originally attached to the object.[20] Though this diagnosis is no longer current in psychiatric discourse, Freud's theory can help illuminate the origin and makeup of Edward's self-loathing. For him, the lost object is his humanity. When Carlisle Cullen transformed his dying body into a vampire, Edward lost many of the physical characteristics of human beings—first and foremost mortality, but also the necessity to sleep and eat; he simultaneously gained strength, speed, and senses incommensurate with a human body. And, most significantly, he acquired the desire to hunt and kill people for food. Edward links this loss of his human body to the loss of any capacity to *be* human—compassionate, vulnerable, and most of all, innocent.

Rather than mourning the changes that vampirism wreaked on his life and body and moving forward to embrace the possibilities his preternatural self affords (the way

Carlisle does through continuing to practice medicine), the beginning of the series finds Edward not only abstaining from human blood, but also from any meaningful relationships with human beings. His venomous fangs, superhuman strength, and bloodlust give him the capacity for brutal violence, and he initially misreads these *physical* traits that are endemic to vampirism as *behaviorally* prescriptive. Though he and the rest of the Cullen family are "vegetarians" who have sworn off human blood and feed only on animals, the opening chapters of *Twilight* describe an Edward convinced that the poisonous lethality of his body has a direct connection to an equally noxious internal self. After Bella discovers the truth about him and his family and reaffirms her interest in a relationship anyway, his perplexed question, "You don't care if I'm a monster? If I'm not *human?*"[21] reveals that at this point for Edward, the categories are mutually exclusive. Edward's immortal and supernaturally strong body, a hyperbolic manifestation of an idealized masculinity that privileges dominative power, is inextricably linked for him to a bloodlust that he understands as both the symptom and the proof of his inherent monstrosity—a conviction that his attraction to Bella will force him to revaluate.

Ironically, it is precisely his "masochistic" impulse to engage with Bella despite the pain it causes him that provokes him to revaluate the unbreakable link he has forged between vampirism and evil, and thereby enables him to inhabit a more empathetic and intersubjective model of masculinity. Bella's arrival at the high school Edward and his vampire "siblings" attend exposes him to a test he did not expect. Because the scent of Bella's blood is overwhelmingly alluring to him, she receives the full force of his defense mechanisms. Whereas other students complain of the Cullen siblings'— and Edward's in particular—relatively benign aloofness and disinterest in participating in the social life of the school, Bella is treated to an intense and sustained dose of the disdain, arrogance, and remoteness he adopts to keep humans at a distance, and therefore "safe," from him. Edward's initial interactions with Bella exemplify the most toxic physical markers of his vampirism: he acts as if not only his body but also his self is cold, hard, and impenetrable. Bella's first-person narrative account describes him as "hate-filled,"[22] "patronizing,"[23] and "cold [and] indifferent."[24] He later admits he initially dismissed her as an "insignificant little girl."[25] However, an episode following Edward's rescue of Bella from a runaway van suggests that though his attitude is intolerable in content, it springs from a deep fear and uncertainty about who he is and what he is capable of.[26] When Bella confronts him at the hospital following the near-fatal accident, demanding that he explain the supernatural speed and strength that allowed him to deflect the van from crushing her, Edward initially responds with language that mimics the aggression of which he knows his body is capable: a "cutting" tone, a "defensive" posture, and an overall attitude of dismissive "derision." However, Bella refuses to submit to his posturing by backing down—she "scowl[s]" back at him and "frigidly" demands he account for his behavior. This replication of Edward's own rhetorical display of strength momentarily breaks through his defenses and reveals the uncertainty and conflict that drive his unpleasant behavior. When Bella asks why he even "bother[ed]" to save her, "for a brief moment his stunning face was unexpectedly vulnerable. 'I don't know,' he whispered." Edward is frightened by his attraction to Bella and his seeming inability to distance himself from her. He is shaken by the conversation, and the vulnerability and doubt he communicates physically and verbally to Bella suggest that his harsh façade is beginning to shatter. In a provocative reversal, here Edward's emotional shell is in fact "penetrated" by Bella's incisive and direct questioning.

As their relationship progresses, Edward reveals another characteristic, aside from the particularly seductive scent of Bella's blood, that draws him to her: she alone is immune to his telepathy, introducing another aspect of Bella that forces him to renegotiate his strategies for interacting with her. Edward is one of the vampires in the *Twilight* universe gifted with abilities above and beyond strength, speed, and near-immortality—he can read human and vampire (and werewolf) minds. This mental invasion is a complement to and intensification of the hypermasculine penetration signified by his fangs. Aside from the obvious advantages telepathy gives him in combat, he also relies on the skill to cement and rationalize his detachment from anyone outside his family. Edward's ability to read minds makes any social interactions with humans beyond the superficial literally unnecessary. His inability to see into Bella's mind, therefore, both frustrates and attracts him. He can only know what she consciously chooses to articulate about her thoughts and feelings. To the novels' credit, the series uses this device to demonstrate that Edward's desire for Bella is not only motivated by the scent of her blood, a trait over which she has little control. In the course of talking to her, he discovers he genuinely likes her personality. As he puts it in their revelatory discussion in the meadow, she is "too interesting"[27] to stay away from, and that fascination derives from her intelligence and refusal to let Edward hide behind his defenses, what he calls "that flash of intuition in your eyes when you see through my pretenses."[28] The supernaturally tinged dynamic between Edward and Bella again rewrites normative gender positions. Edward is "seen through," penetrated, by Bella, and the inversion makes the duo more attracted to each other, and more attractive to contemporary readers.

As Bella's body and mind prompt Edward to continue interacting with her, the novel catalogues a concurrent dismantlement of his posture of defensive detachment. His developing affection for Bella leaves him vulnerable to feelings that consistently belie emotional impenetrability. When he begrudgingly admits that Bella's collapse during a blood typing activity in biology class "scared" him, she relates that "his tone made it sound like he was confessing a humiliating weakness."[29] While explaining his decision to remain in contact with Bella despite earlier pronouncements that he would stay away, he alludes to the vampirisim he has not yet confessed. When she expresses confusion, he admits, "I always say too much when I'm talking to you—that's one of the problems."[30] Edward degrades his increasing capacity for emotional engagement as "weak" and a "problem" while simultaneously finding himself quite unable to interrupt it as he has presumably done before. His willingness to care about Bella enough to be frightened by her collapse contradicts his foundational assumption that as a vampire, he is only and always threatening to human beings. Additionally, his evolving desire for intimacy with Bella demonstrates that his condescension, aggression, and remoteness were expressions of a misguided understanding of what it means to be strong. For Edward, what will require real emotional and physical strength is not concealing his inner self, but exposing it to Bella by and through revealing himself to be a vampire and pursuing the relationship anyway.

When he shows her his bare skin in the meadow's sunlight and finally confirms his supernatural status, the novel also reveals the method by which he will be able to activate his masochism to transform his understanding of the relationship between vampirism and humanity. This conversation is a turning point in Bella and Edward's relationship, but not yet in his self-conception. He decides to pursue a romance with Bella despite the pain of constant temptation, but still believes himself to be depraved and damned for doing so. He calls himself a "deplorable creature"[31] for having the instinct to feed on Bella's blood, but he also identifies and begins to honor the competing and complementary impulse to touch and, crucially, be touched by her, in a nonlethal but still pleasurable and satisfying way. Though "conflict rag[es] in his eyes," Edward allows himself to touch Bella tenderly, "swiftly brush[ing]the length of [her] cheekbone with his fingers,"[32] and realizes that he is capable of mediating his strength and interrupting his thirst in order to enjoy a sensory experience that is mutually enjoyable and gratifying. Whereas feeding is the vampiric equivalent of phallic domination, with the pleasure and desire located only on the penetrative partner, Edward and Bella's careful touching is a model of intersubjectivity in which both participants give and receive pleasure. When Bella touches Edward, he allows that even his cold, hard skin responds to the affectionate touching he has denied himself since his transformation, sighing, "You can't imagine how that feels."[33] Edward's decision to be emotionally and physically intimate with Bella reveals that the one way to harness his bloodlust is to, surprisingly, indulge in a very different kind of lust. In interesting ways, the novels seem to conflate what Edward calls his "human instincts...buried deep, but they're there"[34] with a conception of heterosexual desire that is not predatory and dominative but empathic.

Sexual expression becomes a way for Edward to reclaim the tenderness, empathy, and compassion that he felt was lost along with his human soul. In order to touch Bella in a way that won't kill her, he *must* imagine himself in her weaker and more vulnerable body. He alludes to this projection through his repeated anxiety about losing physical "control" when around Bella[35] and his later justification for delaying the consummation of their relationship until she is "less breakable."[36] Kaja Silverman argues in *Male Subjectivity at the Margins* that masochism—a fair designation for Edward's choice to endure the pain of thwarted sexual desire and bloodlust—is not debilitating, but rather liberating. Her study suggests that in order to undo phallic masculinity, men must discover within themselves and accept the characteristics that have been termed "feminine" in order to challenge a social fiction that masculinity is commensurate with impenetrability, coldnesss, and domination. According to Silverman, this identification with an "other" that has been socially devalued can be painful, but it is painful in a way that is potentially restorative for the male subject. What she calls "heteropathic identification"—feeling with and for a socially devalued other—is "pleasurably painful" because "it represents a refusal...of the imperialism of the 'self'...it represents the ultimate divestiture...of 'self.' "[37] Silverman's use of scare quotes around "self" indicates her poststructuralist skepticism about the concept of a coherent self, but her analysis of male masochism is still relevant without this philosophical move. What Edward divests is his conception of an irredeemable monstrous self, created in order to compensate for the loss of his human body, and, according to him, soul.

Because Edward is a vampire, as long as Bella is human he must repeatedly submit himself to the pain of denying his desire to consume her or consummate their relationship physically. He must suffer every time he sees her. What makes male vampires who fall in love with humans, and Edward in particular, potentially politically progressive is precisely the *repetition* of this masochistically painful disavowal of the hypermasculine penetrativeness and lethality of the vampiric body. Discarding normative gender roles is not something one does once. Social expectations are as pernicious and powerful as Edward's bloodlust, and must be constantly challenged and negotiated. Edward and Bella model this negotiation through continually navigating the practical challenges of their progressing sexual relationship.

Edward's development of a more empathic masculinity differs from a similar move in literature and some social groups in the 1970s. Michael Kimmel's sociological history of American manhood cites the emergence of "men's liberationist" movements[38] that sought to challenge normative masculinity by embracing "decency, sensitivity, and liberal values."[39] Auerbach traces a concurrent reevaluation of Dracula in film as a "non phallic man" motivated by love, not hunger, who passively accepts his own destruction.[40] Both the social and the fictional movements aimed to obliterate the phallic connotations of manhood, and both failed. Kimmel cites the rabid cultural and social counterattack against "new men" in both media representations and cultural commentary,[41] and Auerbach traces the reclamation of phallic vampirism in the 1980s through films like *The Lost Boys* and novels such as Brian Aldiss's *Dracula Unbound*.[42] What makes Edward's character different and possibly immune to the backlash chronicled by Kimmel and Auerbach is that Meyer's novels do not have him either by choice or authorial intervention surrender the phallic aspects of his physical self once he begins to soften his emotional self-expression and explore intersubjectivity.[43] Because he is a vampire, his body is irrevocably phallic, with all the danger and toxicity that designation implies. He carries that lethal capacity to harm along with an empathic desire to love until Bella is changed into a vampire in the fourth novel, rendering the necessity to mediate his preternatural strength from concern for her physical frailty unnecessary. Until that point, though, Edward models a way of being that does not obliterate the latent danger of phallic masculinity, a move that would be impossible for him, but rather seeks to drain his phallic body of the lethal potential it houses. As Edward moves through the second and third books of the series, his and Bella's attempts to negotiate this balance speak to the compromises and challenges inherent in inhabiting a body that is designated as powerful in a way that is alluring but also toxic and dangerous.

The second novel in the saga, *New Moon*, chronicles how Edward's persistent refusal to surrender a binary understanding of good and evil, monster and human, intensifies his self-loathing to the degree that he deserts Bella for most of the novel. In *Twilight*, Edward communicates a gendered worldview that divides those with preternatural abilities into "superheroes" and "bad guys,"[44] and places himself squarely in the latter category. He bemoans the way his attraction to Bella creates a "chasm between what I knew was *right*, moral, ethical, and what I *wanted*."[45] This chasm widens in the early chapters of *New Moon* when his desire to integrate Bella more completely into his life results in a near-attack on her from his brother Jasper. Edward's explanation for leaving Bella soon after, which she hears as a rejection and withdrawal of his love, is actually a coded repetition of his refusal to create and inhabit an identity that includes both his vampirism and the capacity for empathic love that he tentatively exhibited at the conclusion of *Twilight*: "'I'll always love you…in a way. But what happened the other night made me realize that it's time for a change. Because I'm…*tired* of pretending to be something I'm not, Bella. I am not human.' He looked back and the icy planes of his perfect face were *not* human."[46] As Edward reveals after their reunion, he never stopped loving Bella. But by leaving her, he does abandon the masochistic mediation of his sexual and vampiric desire for her—the very negotiation between phallic masculinity and intersubjectivity that reawakened his "human instincts"[47] in *Twilight*. Because he thinks such empathy and tenderness is a fantasy and doomed to fail, Edward's departure can be understood as a relapse into the self-loathing he exhibited at the beginning of the previous novel, with its attendant cruelty. His body again replicates the inhuman coldness he feels he must demonstrate to hurt Bella sufficiently to make her forget him. However, the despair both Edward and Bella endure as a result of their separation is intolerable, and prompts Edward to again renegotiate his fraught understanding of what it requires to be "good" in a "bad" body.

Edward leaves Bella because he believes it is wrong for a vampire to expose a human to danger by the physical proximity a romantic relationship requires. The effects of the separation on both of them—Bella is driven into self-destructive thrill-seeking in order to hallucinate Edward's disapproving face and voice; Edward isolates himself from his family and attempts suicide when he hears a rumor of Bella's death—prompts him to articulate a more subtle, complicated, and difficult ethical stance:

> I lied, and I'm so sorry—sorry because I hurt you, sorry because it was a worthless effort. Sorry that I couldn't protect you from what I am. I lied to save you, and it didn't work. I'm sorry…I could see it in your eyes, that you honestly *believed* that I didn't want you anymore.…When I told you that I didn't want you, it was the very blackest kind of blasphemy.[48]

What Edward regrets here is the way an ethical rigidity based in abstract ontological categories results in a breakdown of intersubjective empathy. Because he was so committed to the wrongness of a vampire loving a human, he failed to perceive how rejection and separation from him would hurt Bella, would not liberate or protect her but in fact endanger and harm her physically and emotionally. The near-disastrous consequences of this mistake result in an upheaval of Edward's conception of who he is and what is right. Rather than understanding himself primarily according to the category of "vampire," he adjusts his existential self-conception to center on his love for Bella. Dismissing as ridiculous her belief in his rejection of her, he exclaims, "The most absurd, ridiculous concept—as if there were any way that *I* could exist without needing *you*!"[49] Edward's self-accusation of "blasphemy" now derives not from a belief in the evilness of vampirism but in his disavowal of love. Translated into an argument about gender, Edward has shifted his primary self-conception from a rigid category— phallic male, to a relational model—lover of Bella not only abstractly, but also physically.

His pronouncement toward the conclusion of the novel that "right and wrong have ceased to mean much to me"[50] indicates he has jettisoned the type of categorical imperatives that philosopher Kelly Oliver argues are incompatible with what she terms "hyperbolic ethics." This conception of moral behavior "holds us all responsible not only for our actions, beliefs, desires, values, and the other's response, but also for our unconscious bodily drives and affects."[51] Translating Oliver's theory into the supernatural context of Meyer's novels highlights the way Edward's denial of his "bodily drives"—his physical desire for Bella—actually results in unethical behavior. Oliver argues in *The Colonization of Psychic Space* that "traditional moral theory holds individuals responsible for their actions within the limits of their reason."[52] Reason in fact dictates that a vampire wishing to abstain from eating humans should not spend time with them much less fall in love with them. However, as the first two novels demonstrate, such "reason" excuses behavior from Edward that is antisocial at best and cruel at worst. The separation detailed in *New Moon* reveals that it is not enough for Edward to love Bella in the abstract—for the sake of their mutual survival, he must also touch and be touched by her. Oliver argues that ethical behavior requires a belief "that our bodies and behaviors require incessant interpretation," necessitating subjects "to continually question our own motives and desires."[53] By committing themselves to pursuing a sexual relationship despite the danger, Edward and Bella engage in the delicate and continual interrogation that Oliver proscribes.

The third novel in the saga finds Edward and Bella's relationship negotiating the complication not of physical separation, but that of competition. The boyish crush that werewolf Jacob Black develops on Bella in *Twilight* deepens into a deep and mutually affectionate relationship in *New Moon*, and their dynamic represents another way Meyer's novels investigate masculinity and sexual expression in a supernatural context. Jacob's lycanthropy in some ways renders him just as dangerous as Edward (as evidenced by alpha wolf Sam Uley's accidental mauling of his fiancée Emily[54]), but with several crucial differences in terms of how their physical and emotional intersubjectivity would play out in a romantic relationship. Werewolves do not correspond to phallic masculinity in precisely the same way vampires do. The hairy pelts, pointed teeth, and predatory instincts of their lupine counter-selves are undeniably a commentary on the expectations and anxieties that center on the male body,[55] but the temporary nature of their time in bestial form makes the type of repeated physical renunciation Edward chooses to suffer unnecessary. Therefore, Jacob's pursuit of Bella lacks the opportunity for heteropathic identification that Edward's masochistic denial encourages.

Eclipse translates the physical characteristics of vampires and werewolves in the *Twilight* universe into contrasting articulations of the way Bella's relationship with Edward and Jacob require intersubjective emotional and physical negotiation. The novel establishes Edward and Jacob as diametrically opposed romantic possibilities for Bella by and through their different preternatural characteristics. Edward's icy skin not only corresponds to his initial chilly demeanor, but also points toward the literal and conceptual space he must maintain between his craving for Bella's body and blood and his emotional desire to create a lasting relationship with her. Jacob's high body temperature serves as a physiological metonym for his anger-induced shifting into wolf form and his passionate pursuit of Bella despite her love for Edward.

Eclipse cannot be said to chronicle a love triangle in the classic sense, as all three parties acknowledge that Bella wants to be with Edward. The nature of the conflict is not situated on Bella's feelings, but rather her future.

In the chapter entitled "Fire and Ice,"[56] Bella overhears Edward and Jacob discussing the way their different bodies afford different opportunities for loving her. As the trio waits out a freezing night outdoors in a tent, Jacob's body is better able to accommodate Bella's human need for warmth, and he uses this lycanthropic characteristic to make his case to Edward that he would better suit her as a romantic partner: " 'You know, she could still change her mind,' Jacob taunted him. 'Considering *all* the things I could do with her that you can't. At least, not without killing her, that is.' "[57] Jacob's emphasis on "*all*" carries a double entendre when paired with the qualification of not killing her. The pointed remark refers to both the sexual consummation Jacob's human form could manage without fear of lethal injury, and the more "normal" human life he could provide Bella without "killing" her human body and making her a vampire. As Jacob further explains, with a less acerbic tone, "I really think I could make her happy. She's stubborn, no one knows that better than I do, but she's capable of healing. She would have healed before. And she could be human, with Charlie and Renée, and she could grow up, and have kids and ... be Bella."[58] Life with Jacob would not require the type of intense physical and emotional denial that her relationship with Edward entails. However, the very necessity of this complicated and painful give and take require Bella and Edward to engage in the sort of compromise, compassion, and acceptance that mark the best of empathic relationships, and eliminate the domination and impenetrability of which Edward's phallic body is constantly capable.

Late in *Eclipse*, Bella attempts to seduce Edward, prompting a negotiation that leads Edward to an uneasy acceptance of his humanity by and through a willingness to make love to Bella before her transformation into a vampire. To this point in the novels, Edward has linked penetrating Bella's body sexually with surrendering control to his vampiric body. Though they have engaged in heavy petting since *Twilight*, Edward has refused to consummate their relationship for fear of the lethal damage his body could wreak on Bella's human form when his mind is distracted by sexual passion. His heteropathic identification with her "breakable"[59] body leads him to refuse her advances, whispering, "Bella, I could kill you." Her response, "I don't think you could,"[60] introduces the possibility that Edward's phallic body could be overcome by his empathic will.

Bella suggests that Edward's love for her would prevent his body from harming her, no matter the circumstances. "Obviously not that you aren't physically able to hurt me, if you wanted to ... More that, you *don't* want to hurt me ... so much so that I don't think that you ever could."[61] Edward persistently casts his romantic pursuit of Bella as evidence of the selfishness and depravity he associates with vampiric bloodlust, insisting, "I had no right to want you—but I reached out and took you anyway."[62] But Bella unhinges the consummation of their physical relationship from dominative violence by reframing sex as a way to deepen and extend the mutual pleasure of their emotional connection: "You said I could have any part of you I wanted. I want this part. I want *every* part."[63] The bargain they strike, to make love when Bella is still human but after they've married, evidences Edward's apprehensive acceptance of his capacity to control his dangerous body through faith in the human connection he has forged with Bella.

The narrative arc of the four novels argues for the significance of this triumph of the empathic will over the phallic body, but Edward's faith in his ability to manage his penetrative body remains tenuous and uneven. Although their first night together as a married couple in *Breaking Dawn* leaves Bella's body slightly bruised but relatively unharmed, Edward tortures himself over these minor injuries in a return to the self-loathing of *Twilight* and *New Moon*.[64] This sexual act, however, results in the birth of Renesmee, whose unique powers prompt the alliance of a global network of vampires against the scheming Volturi, as well as causing the erosion of Jacob's romantic love for Bella, which dissipates when he imprints on her daughter. This textual evidence makes it difficult to support Edward's accusatory judgment that he was "a monster for having agreed" to their bargain.[65]

It is significant that Edward's struggle to reconcile his loathing of his phallic body with his desire to love Bella empathically is neither a smooth nor unitary process. In fact, the issue is not completely resolved until Edward transforms Bella with his venomous fangs in a scene that, in Jacob's unsettling narration, merges violent injury with sexual touch: "It was like he was kissing her, brushing his lips at her throat, at her wrists, into the crease at the inside of her arm. But I could hear the lush tearing of her skin as his teeth bit through, again and again, forcing venom into her system at as many points as possible."[66] *Breaking Dawn* confirms that Bella's transformation enables more physical and emotional intersubjective connection between the two, as her heightened senses allow her to experience his body in a more complete way, "as if the touch of his skin, his lips, his hands, was sinking right through my smooth, hard skin and into my new bones. To the very core of my body. I hadn't imagined that I could love him more than I had."[67] However, this resolution on the level of plot forecloses a *practical* portrayal of what a constant negotiation between a phallic body and an empathic will might look like. Edward's character is therefore a tentative and incomplete version of the male vampire's capacity to consistently challenge phallic masculinity, but a truly progressive one just the same. Meyer sustains Edward's masochistic denial for over two thousand pages, documenting the mental energy required to manage a body capable of lethal force and penetrative domination.

What are the implications of Edward's checkered progress from cruelty and self-loathing to empathy and faith in his humanity for masculinity studies? Nina Auerbach, writing of the waning political progressivity of supernatural fiction at the end of the twentieth century, argues that vampires can allow us "to envision lives beyond the constraints of death and social expectations";[68] a vision she saw diminishing with the reimposition of patriarchal norms in late-twentieth-century vampire fiction. However, Edward's uneven evolution in the *Twilight* saga reactivates the possibility of challenging social constraints not by transcending them, but rather by recognizing their enduring power and learning to subvert them through masochistic denial. Edward's powerful and penetrative body remains a recognizable metonym for idealized masculinity in the late twentieth century. His vampirism reemphasizes, not rejects, that particular social expectation. However, his desire to overcome and deny his body's enduring potential to harm Bella, and his reliance on intersubjective negotiation and heteropathic identification to harness this bloodlust, models one way for men to live empathically in a twenty-first-century world still partially structured by masculinist assumptions. The phenomenal response from women and girls to Edward as a romantic hero creates a space and a market for twenty-first-century vampires who do not drain their female victims of blood, but rather their own vampiric bodies of the will to dominate.

NOTES

1. Kate Harding, "Could 'New Moon' be a feminist triumph?" *Salon.com* (December 9, 2009), Web. Accessed December 9, 2009. np; Sady Doyle, "Girls Just Wanna Have Fangs," *Prospect.org* (November 19, 2009), Web. Accessed December 14, 2009. np.
2. Caitlin Brown, "Feminism and the Vampire Novel," *Thefword.org* (September 8, 2009), Web. Accessed December 14, 2009. np.
3. Rachel Simmons, "You Asked for It: How to Talk to Girls About the Messages of New Moon." *Rachelsimmons.com* (December 2, 2009), Web. Accessed December 14, 2009. np.
4. Brown, "Feminism."
5. Simmons, "Messages."
6. Kate Harding, "Why not Team Bella?" *Salon.com* (December 2, 2009) Web. Accessed December 14, 2009. np.
7. Nina Auerbach, *Our Vampires, Ourselves* (Chicago, IL: University of Chicago Press, 1995. Print), 145.
8. Trevor Holmes, "Coming Out of the Coffin: Gay Males and Queer Goths in Contemporary Fiction," *Blood Read: The Vampire as Metaphor in Contemporary Culture.* Eds. Joan Gordon and Veronica Hollinger (Philadelphia: University of Pennsylvania Press, 1997. Print), 182.
9. Kaja Silverman, *Male Subjectivity at the Margins* (New York: Routledge, 1992. Print), 15–16.
10. Jacques Lacan, "The Signification of the Phallus," *Écrits: A Selection*. Trans. Bruce Fink. (New York: WW Norton & Co., 2005. Print), 575–84.
11. See also Luce Irigary, *This Sex Which Is Not One*; Judith Butler, *Bodies That Matter: On the Discursive Limits of "Sex"*; and Jane Gallop, *Reading Lacan*.
12. The female vampires in the series also obviously share these same physical markers of vampirism. However, the way the plot is constructed (all the women are already matched with male vampires when the books begin) makes Edward's conflict about the dangers his vampiric body poses to Bella particularly productive for a reading that translates the vampire/human dyad to a commentary on human gender roles.
13. Michael Kimmel, *Manhood in America: A Cultural History* (New York: The Free Press, 1996. Print), 325.
14. Both Chelsea Quinn Yarbro's Count Saint-Germain and Angel from Joss Whedon's television series *Buffy the Vampire Slayer* and *Angel* are Edward's forerunners in using vampirism to interrogate normative masculinity. However, any attempt to maintain a meaningful romantic relationship is foreclosed for both of these characters: Saint-German because once his love for a human woman is consummated by making her a vampire, they can no longer be lovers, and Angel because the gypsy curse that restored his human soul to his vampiric body stipulates that if he experiences a moment of "true happiness" (i.e., a sexual relationship with his true love Buffy), he will return to a solely demonic consciousness. The *Twilight* saga does not include these structural prohibitions on vampire–human relationships, and instead uses the first three books of

the series and the beginning of the fourth to explore how Edward and Bella can have a physical relationship despite the practical challenges. It also must be noted that all of these relationships are heterosexual, although it is outside the scope of my argument to comment on how these fictional representations either challenge or reinforce heteronormativity. See Holmes's essay in *Blood Read* for an investigation of male vampires and homosexuality.

15. Auerbach, 5.
16. Many studies have discussed the emergence and implications of the "sympathetic vampire" in literature (see Auerbach; Milly Williamson, *The Lure of the Vampire: Gender Fiction and Fandom from Bram Stoker to Buffy* [London: Wallflower Press, 2005. Print]; Tomc and Zanger essays in *Blood Read*), but I see the innovation in Edward's character being his initial *resistance* to sympathy because of the way his self-hatred manifests as antisocial disdain for Bella. He does not appear vulnerable or ask for pity because of what has happened to him or because he hates feeding on humans (as does, for example, Louis in *Interview with the Vampire*), but articulates and operates from a disgust with his *self*, not only his vampirism.
17. Harding, "Team Bella."
18. Stephenie Meyer, *Twilight* (New York: Megan Tingley Books, 2005), 274.
19. Ibid., 184.
20. Sigmund Freud, "Mourning and Melancholia." *The Freud Reader*. Ed. Peter Gay (New York: W.W. Norton & Co., 1989. Print).
21. Meyer, *Twilight*, 184.
22. Ibid., 27.
23. Ibid., 62.
24. Ibid., 86.
25. Ibid., 271.
26. Ibid., 64–65.
27. Ibid., 272.
28. Ibid., 273.
29. Ibid., 98–99.
30. Ibid., 88.
31. Ibid., 277.
32. Ibid., 220.
33. Ibid., 261.
34. Ibid., 278.
35. Ibid., 225, 310.
36. Stephenie Meyer, *Eclipse* (New York: Megan Tingley Books, 2007), 446.
37. Silverman, 264–65.
38. Kimmel, 281–82.
39. Ibid., 294.
40. Auerbach, 145.
41. Kimmel, 294.
42. See chapter 4, "Grave and Gay: Reagan's Years," in which Auerbach describes the privileging of the patriarchal family in Joel Schumacher's film, and the diseased and destructive vampires in Aldiss's novel.
43. Though Edward, like the kinder, gentler versions of Dracula Auerbach describes, is motivated by love, his hunger is always present, powerful, and discussed by the characters.
44. Meyer, *Twilight*, 92.
45. Ibid., 303.

46. Stephenie Meyer, *New Moon* (New York: Megan Tingley Books, 2006), 70.

47. Meyer, *Twilight*, 278.

48. Meyer, *New Moon*, 510.

49. Ibid., 510.

50. Ibid., 514.

51. Kelly Oliver, *The Colonization of Psychic Space: A Psychoanalytical Theory of Oppression.* (Minneapolis: University of Minnesota Press, 2004. Print), xxiii-xiv.

52. Ibid., xxiii.

53. Ibid., xxii.

54. Meyer, *New Moon*, 331.

55. For example, see Chantal Bourgault du Coudray, *The Curse of the Werewolf: Fantasy, Horror, and the Beast Within* (London: I.B. Tauris & Co., 2006. Print).

56. A reference to the Frost poem that serves as the novel's epigraph, indicating the cataclysmic implications of Bella's decision between the icy vampire and the fiery werewolf.

57. Meyer, *Eclipse*, 495.

58. Ibid., 501–2.

59. Ibid., 446.

60. Ibid., 447.

61. Ibid., ellipses Meyer's.

62. Ibid., 454–55.

63. Ibid., 535–36.

64. Stephenie Meyer, *Breaking Dawn* (New York: Megan Tingley Books, 2008), 88–89.

65. Ibid., 88.

66. Ibid., 354–55.

67. Ibid., 426.

68. Auerbach, 192.

CHAPTER 11

THE *OTHER* EDWARD: *TWILIGHT'S* QUEER CONSTRUCTION OF THE VAMPIRE AS AN IDEALIZED TEENAGE BOYFRIEND

JOSEPH MICHAEL SOMMERS AND AMY L. HUME

> *About three things I was absolutely positive. First, Edward was a vampire. Second, there was a part of him … that thirsted for my blood. And third, I was unconditionally and irrevocably in love with him.*[1]

GUIDED BY THESE FUNDAMENTAL PRINCIPLES, Stephenie Meyer's *Twilight*[2] saga stands at the forefront of a popular resurgence in the genre of vampire literature since its debut in 2005. These three tenets, culled from the thoughts of Isabella Swan, Meyer's adolescent protagonist, function as more than mere obiter dicta to both Bella and an audience built primarily of young adult women. These rules lay the foundation for a rather unusual reconceptualization of the vampire mythos, where passion still remains tied up in blood, but the desire for blood is not tied up in sex—at least for the vampire in question above. In a conventional sense, this idea seems somewhat paradoxical: the penetration of the victim's skin inflicted by traditional vampires has long been associated with the penetration of sexual intercourse; sating the vampiric yearning for blood reads as parallel to gratifying sexual lust. Thus, Edward's behavior is just plain queer.

When critics such as Judith Halberstam read and decipher vampiric desire, they remind us that the nature of the "vampire is not lesbian, homosexual, or heterosexual; the vampire represents the *production of sexuality itself*" (emphasis added).[3] Therein, a vampire such as Edward Cullen seems to represent a queer agency in vampiric literature, not because of any sexual preference, but because his relationship to sexuality as desire challenges the dominant societal norms for vampires.[4] In a vulgar sense, his behavior is deemed "odd," or queer, given what is commonly accepted as normal. For example, consider two seemingly concupiscent teenagers who are eager to engage in sexual intercourse but, for some reason or another, abstain. Or, to repack the metaphor, consider one seemingly teenage male vampire who is eager to find a mate deciding to deny himself by choosing *not* to bite the throat of the woman he claims to love. Without stretching the boundaries of vampirism too greatly, something seems quietly amiss. Or at least unstated. If a teenage reader were to state it, however, we suspect the question might be, "What's the deal with Edward? Bite her already!"

Psychologists and psychoanalysts from Sigmund Freud to Camille Paglia generally agree on one thing concerning the idea of the Westernized vampire: since even before Bram Stoker's 1897 *Dracula*, "the attack of the vampire is [symbolic] of rape"; the draining of the blood, since Dracula slaked his own thirst, was a "sexual matter ... a perversion of heterosexual activity" where drinking it "symbolizes sexual intercourse" and such pleasure was forbidden, "evil" and "erotic."[5] Freud, not unlike Mina Harker in *Dracula*, thought that humanity had always found consorting with the dead (or undead) to be "unclean," and cannibalism was outright repulsive.[6] However, Freud also felt that consuming one's prey, which is essentially what Bella is to Edward—a "snack," as another vampire puts it—makes her a *possession* and not merely a foodstuff.[7] Interestingly, Bella's friend, Mike Newton, who aspires to be more than just her male comrade, intuits in a moment of jealousy that Edward looks at her "like [she's] something to eat."[8] However, instead of devouring her and symbolically consummating the sexual act, Edward suggests that it is Bella who possesses *him*, making that fate of being consumed, either literally or figuratively—according to Freud at least—highly improbable. Edward is thus "queered" by his rhetorical construction of the dynamic. Not unlike falling in love with the best cheeseburger in the world or a *very* rare slice of Kobe beef, Edward's love for Bella empowers him to withstand his mixed cravings for both the satisfaction of sexual desire and sustenance.

Meyer recuperates the vampire mythos from even the steamy, seedy world of Anne Rice's *Vampire Chronicles* where it has been argued that "the kill is sexual."[9] She locates her vampires to the cold, perennially damp state of Washington where lust appears to boil both Bella and Edward's blood, but even the most intense passion during a kiss is enough to chill Edward's already cold lips to "unresponsive stone."[10] Gregory Waller has suggested that no matter what monstrous form the vampire typically takes in literature, Meyer casts Edward as a "seductive siren" to Bella and a "romantic hero" to Meyer's audience.[11] Yet, an elephant lingers in the room: if Bella's humanity inhibits their affection, why not just change Bella into a vampire? Why not let their young romance reach fruition sooner, and let them live a perfect life together for all eternity?[12]

When James, the antagonist of the first novel, bites into Bella's hand, Edward forces himself to taste her blood to remove James' venom and stop the transformation; Bella asks why he stopped it. This is a perfectly reasonable question from a perfectly willing candidate for transformation. Edward replies, "I can't do it, Bella. I *won't* do that to you" (emphasis added).[13] Edward claims that he does not want to infect her with what Martin Wood has called the "disease" of vampirism,[14] but given the emotional and psychological commitment Bella has made to Edward, as shown in our epigraph, she obviously does not have the problem with it that he does. Therein lies Meyer's striking addition to the vampire mythos. She transforms lust into love and creates a romance of piety and restraint. In doing so, she constructs Edward as a vampire who is queer: he "can't" and "won't" consummate the act of biting the woman he loves.

TRAPPED IN A COFFIN OR A CLOSET: EDWARD'S PUBLIC PARADOX

Many questions have arisen concerning Edward's reluctance to transform Bella and his appeal to her, let alone to the actual breathing population of Meyer's readership, in general. Recently in *Esquire*, Stephen Marche, perhaps channeling Anne Rice through Eve Sedgwick,[15] suggested a rather simple solution to the apparent problem of Edward's reluctance to transform Bella.[16] He claimed that Edward appears to be gay, and this identity fascinates young women:

> Edward... is a sweet, screwed-up high school kid, and at the beginning of his relationship with Bella, she is attracted to him because he is strange, beautiful, and seemingly repulsed by her. This exact scenario happened several times in my high school between straight girls and gay guys who either hadn't figured out they were gay or were still in the closet. *Twilight*'s fantasy is that the gorgeous gay guy can be your boyfriend, and for the slightly awkward teenage girls who consume the books and movies, that's the clincher. Vampire fiction for young women is the equivalent of lesbian porn for men: Both create an atmosphere of sexual abandon that is nonthreatening.[17]

The argument is slightly reductive to say the least. We ourselves acknowledge that while Edward's behavior may be queer for a vampire, he is not marked as disinterested in Bella sexually; on the contrary, his interests lie in a monogamous, stable relationship that creates a sensitive, considerate, and patient character—the heteronomative female's idealized mate. In essence, he possesses all the vampire's traditional strengths and none of his shortcomings. What young, twenty-first century woman could resist that? Elements of Marche's claims do not go unsubstantiated, however. The construction of a mysterious and unattainable "other," which Edward is to both vampires and humans alike,[18] appeals to all sorts of fantasies of romantic or sexual desire.

Given a history so imbued with blood and sexuality, why would a mythology as old and manifold as the vampire legend not also explore the complications that might occur if desire subverted need (read: heterosexual reproduction) and a vampire and a human found love where their conditions ostensibly inhibited any sort of meaningful relationship between them? And as David Denby, a reviewer for the *New Yorker*, aptly points out: "teen-age girls don't want intercourse; they want romance."[19] Therein, it appears that Meyer constructs in *Twilight*, which Denby colorfully describes as "an abstinence fable that's sexier than sex," a partnership in which Edward and Bella must maintain boundaries by preventing physical intimacy, regardless of the forces—whether these be social conventions or biological drives—propelling them toward it. As most readers view the couple as heterosexual (i.e., "male" plus "female"), their relationship dwells in the domain of the heteronormative. As we see it, however, Edward and Bella represent the "other" to the rest of society—humans, vampires, and werewolves alike—in their vampire-plus-human joining. Their desire for one another, then, is more accurately read as a queer agent of social change in Meyer's series.

The dangers the characters pose to one another and the taboos against their queer coupling—a vampiric predator who seeks a monogamous relationship with a human victim *without* killing her or transforming her into a vampire—do not go without precedent. Marginalized characters who consider themselves similarly othered by larger communities often find comfort and even romance together. Queer desire, such as Edward and Bella experience, can be mapped throughout representations of vampiric lore in Western literature, although more traditionally in cases of same-sex couples. Samuel Taylor Coleridge's eighteenth-century poem "Christabel," for example, enacts a narrative viewed by those such as Paglia replete with "sexual ambiguity" between Geraldine and the eponymous Christabel.[20]

Thus, while Edward might be *queer*, we argue, not unlike Sadie Stein, that the character is neither "gay" nor "asexual"; he clearly harbors a physical desire for Bella. To Bella, however, Edward Cullen is definitely a very queer figure within *Twilight*—even so simply as is displayed when her adolescent construction of vampires brushes up against the reality of the Cullens' ethics of a peaceful and concomitant existence with humans.[21] This governing *ethos,* in turn, severely limits the capacity for the couple's physical relationship in *Twilight.* Edward's restraint from blood-draining violence against humans and his sexual desire for Bella come into conflict with the unconditional love he feels for her, inhibiting the capacity for their relationship to progress beyond certain points. His subject position blankly removes the sexual construction and metaphor of "blood" from the reader's traditional concept of the romantic vampire.

What Marche dubs "an atmosphere of sexual abandon that is nonthreatening," we call Edward cast as the gay, or impossibly idyllic, boyfriend: Edward represents everything Bella wants in a mate but cannot obtain. Edward offers the type of emotional maturity and physical security that Bella's father would like to offer—except Edward *can* protect Bella from harm whereas paternal or patriarchal law falls short or simply fails. The relationship between the two that Meyer creates in the series duplicates youthful romantic fantasies of male heroism without even the most remote threat of sexual intimacy. As such, what seems so unconventional about employing the romantic mode in this work obviates its use as a sort of supernatural problem novel that can only be solved by Bella accepting her fate and being transformed at the saga's end.

QUENCHING A YOUNG WOMAN'S THIRST
FOR THE IDEALIZED MATE

While the ages of the audience may vary, adolescent women constitute the majority of *Twilight*'s readership. Why, exactly, Meyer's series appeals to young women, though, remains up for some debate. A recent article in *Psychology Today* suggests that women may be drawn to Meyer's depiction of the vampire because it fits the ideal, Westernized male image:

> Women are genetically programmed to respond to males who have the best chances of successfully fathering and rearing children. [*Twilight's*] vampires are often depicted as

tall and handsome, a combination that signals good genes and high testosterone. They
are also frequently portrayed as wealthy and powerful [and] the fact that vampires are
novel and dangerous only adds to their attraction.[22]

And while we cannot speak toward the science of a woman's genetic program-
ming, Edward certainly seems to easily fit that description: the Cullens, through
Carlisle's medical practice, are exceedingly wealthy, owning a spacious mansion and
several expensive vehicles. To count the number of times Bella refers to Edward as
"beautiful" would be redundant; however, Bella's first remarks about the Cullens
identify them as "all devastatingly, inhumanly beautiful [with] faces painted by an
old master as the face of an angel."[23] Interestingly enough, although there are an
endless variety of words synonymous with "beautiful" that Meyer could have used,
she chose to paint them, men and women, in either feminine or asexual ways. As
Stein points out, they appear to have been "airbrushed" from a "fashion magazine,"
with eyes that radiate the dark and gothic as if with eye liner. She even refers to
Edward as a "Greek god" and Adonis:[24] tellingly, he is associated with Aphrodite's
lover more than Ares, god of war, Zeus, god of thunder, or any of the more "masculine" Greek mythological incarnations. Add to that construction the fact that
Edward dresses exceedingly fashionably for a high schooler (even if it is Alice who
dresses him), possesses the maturity one might expect of an adult pushing ninety
years old, and seems, from Bella's perspective, to be excessively oblivious to the
throngs of young women who covet him. Furthermore, Bella speaks of Edward
in the discourse of television advertising when she describes his voice as "quiet"
and "musical."[25] Given that, generally, "regular"[26] teenage males have been found
by critics to be "common as household dust" to the young adolescent female[27] it
makes sense that Bella's fascination with Edward's exogenous factors might paint
him as naturally Other and potentially queer, outside of and superior to the norm
of what she finds surrounding her. It really does not push the boundaries of the
imagination, for someone existing within the narrative itself, to consider or believe
in Edward's homosexuality.[28]

A *QUEERY*: WHAT IS THE OTHER SIDE TO EDWARD CULLEN'S CHARACTERIZATION?

Edward functions as a queer figure in *Twilight* on a variety of different levels. Queer
desire in Edward and Bella's relationship refers primarily to their similar subject positioning as Other, essentially denoting their position and status as outsiders to what
or whoever constitutes the norm in Forks: though Bella was born in Washington, she
lived most of her life in the American Southwest. Edward, a Chicago native, is a vampire; essentially, this others and queers him from living things in general. However,
the Cullens are also cast as "vegetarian" vampires who do not subsist on the blood
of humans and are equally outsiders in Meyer's cosmology from the established base
of formerly human sanguisuge.[29] John Allen Stevenson reminds us that, in no less
than *Dracula* itself, Van Helsing refers to Dracula as "the other."[30] Both Stoker and
Stevenson refer more to the taboos associated with coupling between vampire and
human that equate to an interspecies relationship; however, Stevenson notes that this

can easily be seen within contemporary perspectives as well, where an "inter*racial* sexual competition" is illustrated metaphorically through vampires and humans.[31] Using the term *queer* in Meyer's very heteronormative addition to the cult of vampire fiction may be best understood as it applies to those already marginalized in dominant society by their race, ethnicity, sexuality, gender—and, yes, vampirism.[32] This is primarily due to the fact that *Twilight* is an adolescent narrative—a "maturation" or "coming-of-age" story[33]—where operating as the outsider trying to fit in is a reliable and sturdy trope.

The struggles exhibited by Bella and Edward are easily relatable to an audience that has both lived through the difficulties of problematic relationships and more than likely read more than their share of coming-of-age narratives. And while we do not discount the arguments concerning the idea of vampires as a race, we are particularly invested in looking at them as a culture with supposed, accepted heteronormative tropes and schemes. What is interesting about Meyer's method, however, is that by structuring Edward from the subject position of the so-called gay boyfriend, she avoids what some have called the "hostility" that exists between the male vampire and his young, female prey.[34] Edward's case is queer, indeed.

Interestingly, Michael Warner explains that the "trouble with normal" hinges on the fact those othered by dominant cultural discourse get *defined* solely by their sexual/societal deviancy:

> Even after years of resistance, loathing for queer sex, like loathing for gender nonconformity, remains powerful enough to make the lesbian and gay movement recoil, throwing up its gloved hands in scandalized horror at the sex for which it stands. The movement has never been able to escape some basic questions: How is it possible for example, to claim dignity for people defined in part by sex, and even by the most undignified and abject sex?[35]

The popularity of Meyer's book series presents an interesting response to Warner's query. The Cullens not only reintegrate themselves into human society, but, in spite of their queer existence as vampires, they maintain and even promote the dignity to which Warner refers. When Charlie castigates Bella for behaving like a townie for questioning the Cullens, he refers to them as an "asset to the community."[36] Charlie, an officer and respected public official of the town, though initially skeptical of the Cullens himself, becomes highly impressed by the clan. Importantly, in terms of sexuality, he singles out Carlisle and Esme for their capacity as parents to "those adopted teenagers."[37] Charlie does not consider it at the time, but the fact that the Cullens adopt, and, probably to his mind, are unable to reproduce, seems to only foster greater respect from him. Generally, representations of Western vampires from *Dracula* to Justin Cronin's recent *The Passage* repeatedly center around the fear of their monstrous desire to drink blood and promulgate the furthering of their species by infecting their otherwise "normal" prey. Meyer's vampires are no different, with their venom that comingles with their victims' blood upon biting into them. Yet, Edward's defining characteristic remains not his potential to "turn" Bella and thereby produce vampiric "offspring," but rather his ability to abstain from drinking her blood, despite having a peculiar taste for it.[38] This kind of cool control over physical desire and hunger does not occur without *significant* difficulty, but it does primarily define Edward and his family by their refusal to reproduce. As a vampire, Edward must, therefore, be understood to be inherently queer in relation to humanity.

MORE ON THE TROPE OF "THE GAY BOYFRIEND"

Vampires bear the burden of the fear their identities incite due to the cultural baggage of their mythology. Some have said that these trepidations shift in different cultural moments so that figures such as vampires embody the paranoias of a particular historical time and place, allowing us to read culture through the abjection of the monster.[39] Yet, the forbidden romance between Edward and Bella that Meyer constructs for her young female readership lacks fear. Edward explains that "most humans instinctively shy away from us, are repelled by our alienness," but social distance seems to be the only indication of fear or suspicion in Forks.[40] Even while discussing her possible death, at any number of intervals, Bella remains remarkably fearless in the presence of her otherwise chaste protector. In fact, the protagonist's private description of Edward as a "vampire who wanted to be good—who ran around saving people's lives so he wouldn't be a monster" aligns him with Superman, Spiderman, Batman, and other representations of messianic figures, if only to her.[41] Categorizing him as more of a superhero than anything else, Bella makes a lucid remark about the oft ill-considered loneliness and outsider status of the superhero. In regard to the aforementioned "Superman" example, Kal-El[42] is the actual person, the alien in question; Clark Kent is the secret identity created so that Superman can have a normal life. Superman, depending upon which incarnation of the character one reads, can do veritably anything, and yet, his abilities inhibit him from even the smallest social graces, let alone having a relationship with Lois Lane, who he feels would be exploited by his rogue's gallery as a weakness (akin to what James does to Edward when he threatens Bella's life[43]). Either Bella must be, as she calls herself, a "stupid lamb"[44]—too innocent or duped to properly be afraid of her theoretical boyfriend's lion-like strength and hunger—or Edward's vampirism is not what primarily defines his queer otherness in this text. We gravitate toward the latter interpretation as it seems to explain, to some degree or another, the audience's fascination with someone they might otherwise fear.

The way romantic desire functions in this human–vampire relationship makes Edward queer on a different level—as a metaphorical portrait of "the gay boyfriend." That term should not be seen as a sexual practice so much as a social construct of the boyfriend every young, heteronormative woman desires: the perfect boyfriend who is so perfect that he actually cannot be attainable (and thus is classed as "gay"). In order for Edward to maintain control over his vampiric impulses, he must practice "mind over matter," meaning that no matter how much Bella's blood boils over with fantasies of sexual intimacy, Edward must remain strong and resistant to them lest he might tear her apart. While the couple certainly does share intimate spaces together, caressing one another's faces, and even, with some difficulty, limited kissing, Edward's construction as her boyfriend, less in any sort of traditional sense and more in name only, lies in his unwillingness to consummate Bella's wishes. He must frustrate her for her own good. As mentioned earlier, he claims to fear that sex would "break" Bella, noting: "If I was too hasty…I could reach out, meaning to touch your face, and crush your skull by mistake."[45] Talk of lovemaking *cum* human mutilation seems odd pillow talk if not simply overtly unappealing. And Edward's descriptions seem purposefully vivid. The choices to abstain not only from drinking human blood but also from sexual intimacy and the means of achieving these goals offer a very different perspective on Edward's desire.

As one critic has noted, "the sexual nature of the vampire's desire—the embrace, the kiss [i.e. the bite]…the longing glances—are all as symptomatic of sexual desire as they are if bloodlust. That nature is relegated to the climax of the narrative."[46] As such, when the climax of *Twilight* leads to what amounts to an anticlimax of *not* seeking to sup upon the blood of the prey but, rather, to remove the venom and inhibit the transformation, one could easily define Edward as queer within his community, although heteronomative in meeting the needs and desires within Bella's heart. Edward, severely agitated by the Bella's infected condition when James bites her, cries out: " 'Bella, Bella, oh please, no, no!' … A howl of rage strangled on his lips."[47] His emotional state, words, and actions seem to reject his own biological imperatives as a vampire as well as the actions of a man in romantic love when he resoundingly refuses Alice's prompt to bite Bella and save her life from both James's bite and her injuries. Carlisle offers an alternative: simply remove the venom by sucking it out. Edward is hesitant here as well, but he does eventually accede as a last resort. Bella remarks: "his head bent over [me] and his cool lips pressed against my skin."[48] As Gomez indicates, not only is the bite sexual, but so is the kiss. And pressing his lips upon Bella is simultaneously heteronormative and queer: it is a sign of stupendous intimacy for Edward and one that precludes the intercourse he will deny her until they are wed.

Because of the frantic state in which Edward has found Bella—nearly dead and certainly broken by James—some readers might argue that it is not so unusual that Edward is not in the mood to perform a tender mercy upon her, let alone publicly. Further, since Carlisle is a physician and the person who suggests the procedure, it actually makes *more* sense for him to bestow the "kiss" that removes the venom. However, Carlisle's lament that he "can't help" Edward perform this task, seemingly because he must staunch Bella's bleeding, also seems to smack of the idea that Carlisle considers the act a moment of great intimacy as well. As such, Carlisle forces Edward into the heteronormativity of Bella's world despite his "son's" resistance: she's your girlfriend, you have to kiss her—PDA[49] or not.

Whether the coupling be same-sex or not, the bite exhibits itself as a "queer sexual practice" because, according to Case, it remains "ultimately out of the category of the living."[50] Her statement mainly refers to the ability for queer couples to reproduce, which defines gay and lesbian relationships less and less today; it certainly does not remain an impediment for Edward and Bella later in the series.[51] But, in *Twilight,* Edward can be read as a gay boyfriend because an intimate relationship with Bella seems, to him, like an impossibility, or at least a physical impasse, due to his inability to connect with her either through the practice of the vampiric bite or regular romantic and sexual heteronormative practices. His otherness as a gay boyfriend, though, typically flies under the radar of most readers, largely because Meyer's audiences and characters both inhabit an overwhelmingly heteronormative culture. Even in the

Cullens' queer household in which Carlisle chose Edward as his first "companion," most family members pair themselves off in heterosexual couplings—except, prior to the saga's start, Edward. Very much like what Terry Castle names the "apparitional lesbian," the gay boyfriend appears to be "from the start, something ghostly."[52] As a gay unobtainable other who serves as the object of Bella's romantic fantasies, Edward appears to be a sheer heteronormative illusion. She wonders if he is actually real or possibly imagined, and whether their relationship is real or even possible. In many ways, chasing Edward is akin to chasing the phantasm of him in Bella's dreams. And, unfortunately for Bella, she seems to always wake up.

THE VAMPIRE-PROBLEM NOVEL

Roberta Trites has made emphatic comment on the possibilities that are allowed to the young gay male in the so-called "problem novel":

> Books about gay male teenagers superficially seem to promise the reader freedom from past constraints, freedom from continued repression, freedom from narrow-minded discourse—but simultaneously, such books often undermine that alleged liberation, as if the very existence of the genre gay YA literature depended on repression. And indeed, the existence of the genre very well may depend on this double-voicedness, for mainstream YA publishing still acts as if it were threatened by the idea of homosexuality. As a result, in gay young adult literature, homosexuality seems at once enunciated and repressed.[53]

Of course, what she classes as the "gay male," we apply to the young, othered vampire, Edward, who has been critically considered in this chapter as emblematic of the homosexual despite his assuredly heterosexual markers of hetero- or metrosexuality. Nevertheless, our queering of Edward vis-à-vis Meyer's heroic construction of him allows the character to become a sympathetic figure in the eyes of both Bella and the reader. This is revolutionary simply because part of the allure of the vampire in most early fiction is that they are *vilified* figures who happen to make terrific romantic *antiheroes*, not heroes. Colloquially speaking, vampires have a history of occupying the "bad boy" subject position where women become enraptured with them in spite of themselves in a sort of cannibalistic Stockholm syndrome. By contrast, Edward provides the reader with the desexualized construct of the "good" vampire,[54] capable of being a hero without qualifications.

Edward accomplishes this in many ways. He is selfless. Though it took him a decade to appreciate Carlisle's respect for humanity, Edward embraced Carlisle's purview and allowed his adoptive father to teach him how to "curb his appetite" from the blood of living people to game animals.[55] Likewise, although Edward is remarkably powerful, he prefers to remain unassuming and does not use his strengths—physical or mental—indiscriminately to lethal ends, even when prompted and seemingly within his right. For example, when Bella is about to be attacked by ill-meaning thugs bent on acts not specifically mentioned by Meyer but implied as sexual assault, Edward simply uses his skills at mind-reading and being adroit with an automobile to rescue her from the scene.[56] Edward describes a desire to inflict violence although he does not succumb to it: "I heard what they were thinking... It was very... hard—you can't imagine how hard—for me to simply take you away, and leave them . . . alive."[57] Here, the reader and Bella are entranced by his maturity, evident in his decision not abuse his gifts.

It may seem odd to couch a vampire in problem novel discourse, or narratives of the gay boyfriend. Wood argues, however, that reengineering old forms is actually quite necessary for the evolution of the genre in contemporary times; he believes that the old "codes" of the vampire mythos "have become obsolete."[58] In his mind, for the vampire to exist and be successful in the current day and age, the figure must "translate mythic truth by means of *new*, powerful codes" (emphasis added).[59] Others have made the same argument for the retelling or remytholgization of vampire mythology.[60] The idea crystallizes in our consideration of flipping traditional perspectives on the sexuality of the kill in vampire fiction through those that might otherwise seem to embrace the Victorian repression that inspired the eroticization of the blood in the first place.[61] It is really not that hard to imagine; Paglia notes that overt calls for piety in periods of sexual repression seemed to construct the need for the counterbalance.[62] In the 2000s, Meyer seems to have capitalized on the idea that, in an era where sex and sexuality are nothing more than a few keystrokes or TV channels away, passion could be created through restraint: yes, Edward *could* taste Bella; he *could* transform her and make love to her endlessly without damage. However, much more compelling is reading Meyer's construction of Edward Cullen as a lonely, selfless, and self-imposed Other. When Bella declares that she is, indeed, ready for her senior year of high school "to be the twilight of [her] life, though [her] life has barely started," Edward declares, "It's not worth it."[63] We would argue that he says "It's" but he means "I'm." What's not to love about the beautiful queer vampire who renders himself undesirable and inaccessible, refusing to kill or seduce, in order to finally find the love of his afterlife.

NOTES

1. Stephenie Meyer, *Twilight* (New York: Little, Brown & Co, 2005. Print), 195.
2. Simply for purposes of clarity, when we discuss *Twilight,* we refer only to Book I of the *Twilight* saga. When referring to the larger corpus, we will use the term *Twilight* saga.
3. Judith Halberstam, *Skin Shows: Gothic Horror and the Technology of Monsters* (Durham: Duke University Press, 1995. Print), 100.
4. David Halperin has suggested that being queer is "by definition, whatever is at odds with the normal, the legitimate, [or] the dominant. There is nothing in particular to which it necessarily refers. It is an identity without an essence. 'Queer' then, demarcates not a positivity but a positionality vis-à-vis the normative." David Halpern, *Saint Foucault: Towards a Gay Hagiography* (Oxford: Oxford University Press, 1995. Print), 62.
5. Lorrah 1999, 31; Bentley 1972, 28–29; Wood 1999, 59. This list of critics would be incomplete if the work of Nina Auerbach was not mentioned. Auerbach's work does not supplement the work of critics mentioned as much as provides foundation for it. However, in our discussion, she supplements these ideas by noting (in a discussion of Stoker) how, in sexually metaphoric terms, a vampire's consumption of blood does not "drain vitality" so much as "bestow it." (1995, 96). Our understanding of the transaction of blood as a metaphor for sex, and often rape, also comes from historical

depictions of the vampire's bite. See, for example, Luise White's *Speaking with the Vampires* for further reading.

Contemporary stories of sanguinivorous behaviors further complicate the notion that the hunger for blood always signifies a lust for sexual pleasure. Meyer joins a new generation of fiction writers, including Jewelle Gomez and Charlaine Harris, who describe alternative motivations for drinking blood. Some do it to "give birth" or to adopt a new member into a vampire family or queer community. Others, like Carlisle Cullen, drink blood to save humans from a death (Meyer, 341). Note, however, that in *Twilight* Carlisle's decision to save Edward from Spanish Influenza comes from his desire for a companion: "He acted from loneliness" (288). Yet, even though Edward was Carlisle's first companion and surrogate child, Meyer suggests that the Cullens prefer heterosexual pairings.

6. Sigmund Freud, *Totem and Taboo* (New York: W.W. Norton & Co, 1950), 65.
7. Freud, 102; Meyer, *Twilight,* 379. Edward complicates this notion somewhat when he flatly states that it is rather "difficult" not to drink from Bella when his hunger rises. Meyer, *Twilight,* 188.
8. Meyer, 221.
9. Martin Wood, "New Life for an Old Tradition: Anne Rice and Vampire Literature," *The Blood is the Life,* eds. Leonard Heldreth and Mary Pharr (Bowling Green, OH: Bowling Green SU Popular Press, 1999, 59–78. Print), 73.
10. Meyer, 282.
11. Gregory A. Waller, *The Living and the Undead: From Stoker's Dracula to Romero's Dawn of the Dead* (Urbana: University of Illinois Press, 1986), 3.
12. The astute and no doubt thorough reader of the *Twilight* saga will likely point out that the Volturi, a sort of vampire royalty in Meyer's cosmology, make the same edict to Edward when they learn that Bella knows of vampires. Near the end of *New Moon* (2006), they issue their proclamation that Bella will be transformed or perish (478). In *Breaking Dawn* (2008)*,* this finally comes to pass *only* in order to save Bella's life by injecting his venom into her heart (375–80).
13. Meyer, 474.
14. Wood, 3.
15. In *The Epistemology of the Closet,* Sedgwick openly considers questions pertaining to how one, be it the reader or some other, recognizes a homosexual when one sees one. As Ellis Hanson notes, she, not unlike Rice, does this frequently throughout her work (378).
16. It should be noted that, in *New Moon,* when Edward understands that Bella will be transformed at some point, he actually goes so far as to initially suggest that Carlisle do it (535).
17. Stephen Marche, "What's *Really* Going on With All These Vampires," *Esquire Online,* October 13, 2009. http://www.esquire.com/features/thousand-words-on-culture/vampires-gay-men-1109. Web.
18. The Cullens, as a family, are othered to vampires as they will not take human life. Edward is othered to Bella given their different species.
19. David Denby, "Twilight," *New Yorker,* December 8, 2008. http://www.newyorker.com/arts/reviews/film/twilight_hardwicke . Web.
20. Camille Paglia, *Sexual Personae* (New York: Vintage Books, 1991), 321.
21. In another theoretical framework, Sue-Ellen Case interprets vampires as queer because they stand outside dominant culture and "attack," in a literal sense, "the dominant notion of the natural," or heteronormative (1991, 3). From this perspective, vampires incite fear less due to their traditional hokum as monsters or creatures of the

night bastardized from their once human person; rather, they are demonized largely because of the ways their supernatural powers and sexual ambiguity subvert societal norms. Worse still, they can pass for the heteronorm and invade their territory. "Like the Phantom of the Opera," Case notes, "the queer dwells underground, below the operatic overtones of the dominant" (3). Such instigators of social change often get characterized as monstrous, regardless of their intentions or practices, because the very existence of the Other threatens to break the boundaries of the normal. The reader finds this situation throughout *Twilight* as the Cullens are painted as the literally picture-perfect family whose members "pass" for "normal," despite their otherworldly good looks.

22. Sophie Chen, "Bloodlust: Why women are suckers for bloodsuckers." *Psychology Today* 42 (Nov–Dec 2009), 18.
23. Meyer, 19.
24. Ibid., 18–19, 206.
25. Ibid., 43.
26. 'Regular' meaning normatively heterosexual.
27. Paglia, 479.
28. Meyer writes *Twilight* entirely from Bella's perspective, and the narrative reads as exceedingly insular and internal since Bella is not excessively chatty by her own admission (36). Part of the allure of young adult literature is that its narrators are constructed for the purpose of creating psychological bonds with the reader of associations and empathy; in this way, Bella's narrative perspective allows her to connect with other young girls who can empathize with her situation. Sommers has written on this phenomenon before (Sommers 2008), where "the sororal bonds the young female protagonist seeks with the audience member represent [the locus of] an isolation, though not necessarily an alienation, only rectifiable through a dialogic connection with some Other" (267). In this particular case, Bella's position as othered in her school matches Edward's position as vampiric Other; readers simultaneously connect with Bella because they relate to her situation: a desire for bonding that is problematic, by virtue of being taboo or forbidden, making it all the more enticing.
29. Meyer 188.
30. Quoted in Stevenson 1988, 140.
31. Ibid., 139.
32. The distinction between various uses of the word queer seems necessary, most importantly because critics often use it as a denotation of same-sex desire. While Edward and Bella find themselves both in a position of the other, their courtship revolves around heteronormative impulses. Eventually, as noted, these impulses manifest themselves as one might expect a passionate, heteronormative relationship to—for vampires.
33. Russell 2009, 239.
34. Roth 1977, 113.
35. Michael Warner, *The Trouble with Normal: Sex, Politics, and the Ethics of Queer Life* (Cambridge, MA: Harvard University Press, 1999), 48.
36. Meyer, 36.
37. Ibid., 36.
38. Ibid., 275.
39. Cohen 1996, 4.
40. Meyer, 275.
41. Meyer, 89–92, 204.
42. Kal-El is Superman's given Kryptonian name.
43. Meyer, 445.

44. Ibid., 274.
45. Ibid., 310.
46. Gomez (1997), 85.
47. Meyer, 453.
48. Ibid., 456.
49. An acronym for: Public Display of Affection.
50. Case, 4.
51. Yet, it must be noted that, once again, Edward is, essentially, forced into action. When the Volturi learns of Bella's humanity in *New Moon*, Edward is instructed to turn her, or she will be destroyed (2006, 478). Edward later agrees only the grounds that they marry first.
52. Terry Castle, "From The Apparitional Lesbian: Female Homosexuality and Modern Culture," *Feminist Literary Theory and Criticism*, eds. Sandra M. Gilbert and Susan Gubar (New York: Norton, 2007. 757–72, Print), 757. Castle argues that the repression of lesbian sexuality can be noted by the absence of lesbians in literary history. The "lesbian apparition" simply has not received the status of cultural recognition. The presence of the gay boyfriend seems to suffer the same kind of invisibility. Yet, the cover of going unnoticed seems to be something that vampires and Edward as a gay companion to Bella enjoys. Unlike the lack of recognition, or outright denial, that the lesbian receives in Castle's reading of her, Edward's beauty makes him a prime target of young heterosexual desire, as noted by his popularity among young female readers.
53. Roberta Trites (1998), 143.
54. Carter (1999), 166.
55. Meyer, 342.
56. Ibid., 161–164.
57. Ibid., 176.
58. Wood, 59.
59. Ibid.
60. Gomez 87, Waller 9.
61. Wood 73.
62. Paglia, 221.
63. Meyer, 497.

Part III

Class, Race, and Green Space

CHAPTER 12

"EMBRACED" BY CONSUMPTION: *TWILIGHT* AND THE MODERN CONSTRUCTION OF GENDER

MICHAEL J. GOEBEL

THE CULTURAL IMPACT OF THE *TWILIGHT* SAGA HAS BECOME INESCAPABLE. A Google search of the phrase "*Twilight* saga," for example, results in over 40 million pages containing everything from officially sanctioned merchandise to fan pages to events such as the *Twilight* Alaska cruise "priced at $1,049 per person, pre-tax, for an inside cabin, plus a $150 '*Twilight* registration fee.'"[1] Within these pages, there are also an extraordinary number of sites where fans openly express their desire to become vampires and look for "real" vampires who will "embrace" or "turn" them. The people on these sites plead to be a part of something special or different, or want to experience the love that Bella and Edward share. Although the concept seems extreme, it is not surprising that American culture, driven by material consumption, gravitates toward a figure like the vampire, particularly when the most popular reenvisioning of this mythic character looks like Robert Pattinson or Kristen Stewart. What most people do not see, however, is how these characters illustrate one-dimensional reductions of personality that only allow for individuation through materiality. They embody a new conception of quintessential masculinity and femininity based on the acquisition of material wealth that, in Meyer's texts, quickly translates to ideas of beauty, as well as social and economic class. The author reveals this by directly depicting consumption as a means to achieve idealized beauty. Further, the *Twilight* saga creates a layering between the text, audience, and capitalist ideology, enacted by the characters and reflected/confessed/represented by the throngs of fans who engage in its economy, which allows them to align themselves with these newly constructed versions of masculinity and femininity. The immediacy of the formidable impact surrounding this phenomenon is tantamount to the automation seen in Fordist production.

In the United States, the principles of Fordism entirely reinvented industry through the process of automation and the eradication of skilled workers in favor of machines operated by unskilled expendable laborers. This ideological and technological shift is responsible for the version of capitalism in existence today, based on the intense accumulation of mass-produced commodities. Most cultural theorists who analyze Fordism have done so within the scope of the economy, the perpetuation of labor, and wage relations, but have not fully theorized these principles in relation to gender construction.[2] Over the last century, capitalism has created dynamic shifts in gender roles in order to open new markets for groups whose strict adherence to traditional mores would otherwise prohibit them from becoming an active purchasing group. American masculinity is a perfect example of this, originally formulated on a dichotomy that placed men in the role of active/producer and women in the role of passive/consumer. The feminization of everyday consumption that resulted from this rigid duality restricted the scope of buying to one segment of the population and alienated the other, thereby limiting the general consuming segment of the population, making the process of capital accumulation for businesses more difficult. This cultural "error" took generations to change as men were slowly evolved into a consuming class so as not to short-circuit their cultural hardwiring, which would lead to a defensive antagonistic stance toward the powers that encouraged this change. As each generation gradually shifted its perception of what constituted masculinity, consumption took on a more asexual quality, allowing men to partake in the act and still remain "masculine." In the past these shifts have temporarily solved the issue of immediate capitalistic gains, but never solved the larger problem of how to create a generation of consumers who have no boundaries or prohibitions constructing their identity through consumption. This problem is addressed and resolved in the *Twilight* saga, which I will explain further shortly.

What is most important to note here is the sheer length of time it took to move men from solely occupying one role (producer) to being comfortable also inhabiting its antithesis (consumer), and how resistance is still evident in certain parts of the male population today. Proof can be found in advertising strategies for products where the male figure in the advertisement expresses extreme disinterest or emasculation in shopping. The act of consumption in these commercials is performed by a woman, and highlights the antiquated notion that shopping and consumerism is a feminine characteristic, all the while aligning the product with the reticent male viewer.[3] The limitations of this outmoded dichotomy clearly still resonate even today, which is why it is paramount that capitalist interests irrevocably tie *all* ideas of gender and the act of gender construction to the defining characteristic of the prevailing economic system—consumption. By doing so, they effectively eliminate the problem of saturation (or reduced demand for consumables) by making the penalty of nonconsumption, regardless of gender, an identity crisis that entirely destabilizes the individual. Consumption, in this configuration, becomes a necessity of far greater consequence than ever before, since the need to consume shifts from the realm of desire to that of sine qua non in the form of an unquenchable thirst that dictates every facet of an individual's existence.

Stephenie Meyer's *Twilight* saga illustrates and reinforces this dynamic shift in capitalist constructions of gender, through the metaphor of the vampire, the very definition of uncontrollable consumption, driven mad by insatiable thirst, yet rendered docile and sedate directly following acts of consumption. Economic class is stratified in her work, placing the vampire at the highest echelon of society and wealth (including striations between vampire clans), while relegating both humans and werewolves to subordinated impoverished classes in the text. Meyer's fictional world may, on the surface, be about romance and unrequited love, but below this façade lies something far more sinister than fictitious vampires: the inculcation of desire to embody the vampire's wholly consumptive nature as a means to define *every* facet of a person's real life, including their gender.

From the very first moment the Cullens are introduced to the reader, there is no equivocation as to just how perfect they are—beautiful in every way, impeccably dressed, driving brand new high-end cars, and maintaining a socially and intellectually privileged position in their high school. The way minor characters in the novel speak about them immediately places them in a mythic realm where their actual presence is preceded by a flurry a commentary and sidelong glances, as if a famous person just set foot on school grounds. Although it can be argued that most teenage melodramas position the "popular" students similarly, there is usually no doubt that these people are as human as the rest of the characters in the narrative. This is intrinsically different in *Twilight* and is one of the few successful literary moments in Meyer's first book. Popular students in most teenage fiction have stories and history that everyone knows about; they make themselves the center of attention, but ultimately have the same worries, fears, and goals as those around them. The Cullens, however, are draped in speculation and although they are the center of attention, it is not of their own accord. Because of their aloofness, which is equated with "cool" by the other students, they are elevated into the limelight as those around them long to know who they really are and why they are cloaked in mystery. The Cullens, again unlike characters in traditional narratives, only engage with their supposed peer group when it is absolutely necessary and never address any of the questions or speculation surrounding them. Meyer uses this voyeurism and isolation to begin the class stratification between the Cullens and everyone else, which is only further substantiated when it becomes clear they are vampires.

Once this hierarchy is defined, Meyer creates an especially interesting relationship for readers/viewers, who, because they are human, are immediately allied with the humans in the text, yet are given the privileged position of being able to see inside the secret world of the Cullen family. Because humans reside beneath vampires in Meyer's hierarchy, this secret access into the life of the vampire elite results in an ongoing comparison, which continually depicts inexhaustible wealth against everyday mediocrity. Each time the reader/viewer enters the Cullens' home (a palatial estate of architectural artistry rife with art, lavish furniture, and modern electronics) or one of their many exotic cars, it bolsters the hierarchical divide Meyer creates and causes a desire to dissociate with the humans of the text and identify with the vampires. This moment of identification with the vampire sets the process of automation—a central component in the capitalist process of construction—into motion: here, in the construction of gender ideals.

Under the system of Fordism, the principles of automation and mechanization are key in creating a system where labor is transformed and "the relationship between workers and means of labor is reversed…[i]nstead of wielding tools, the workers become appendages of the machines," thereby increasing the efficiency of production and increasing surplus value for the capitalist class.[4] Extrapolating this Fordist process beyond the confines of economic theory, the process of gender construction has also become automated in the same fashion, beginning with the inversion of the traditional means of identity formation. In other words, instead of gender identity being constructed by an individual through engagement with the social world around them, there is now a bevy of products inextricably infused into children's lives from the very earliest stages of infancy and these shape gender. Based on the sex of the child, a parent needs only plug them into this system and the child becomes immersed in the dictates of that gender at that moment in time through the products that surround him/her. It is of little consequence to the economy what form gender representation takes at any moment, so long as it is contained within the broader ideological foundation that product choice defines one's gender. In Volume One of *Capital*, Marx clearly details how the success of automation is predicated on early introduction into the system, stating: "the workman should be taught from childhood, in order that he may learn to adapt his own movements to the uniform and unceasing motion of an *automaton*."[5] As the infant grows up, she (or he) internalizes that she can continue to align herself with societal gender norms at any given point in time simply through the act of purchasing that which (re)defines gender at any given moment. The inculcation of children into this process removes a tremendous number of obstacles for capitalist growth, because it is not what is being purchased that controls the individual, but the act of consumption itself and how it shapes identity. Corporations can then rely on marketing to shape a new image of masculinity or femininity based on trends that create the most surplus value, and the individual who receives these images will be more attuned to embrace them as culturally accepted and begin purchasing to accomplish this personal transformation, aligning himself with this culturally valued image of gender. This process by its very nature is automated; individuals become locked in this mind-set, from their earliest memory, having had products, clothes, and toys used to convey appropriate gendering, so when they reach the point where they begin to outwardly express their own gender, they automatically use the same means of definition: consumable goods.

Time becomes an enormous factor in this equation, and with each new generation successfully taken through this process of automation, the more time collapses in all respects: the process of redefinition and appropriation of culturally accepted gender norms quickens, allowing for more cycles to occur. The ideology is reinforced, and the distance between childhood and adulthood becomes shortened. This is not to say that children physically mature into adulthood sooner, only that they are pushed to become autonomous consumers earlier because autonomy equates to choice and decision-making abilities and subsequently, within the scope of a capitalist economy, to brand recognition and allegiance. The sooner people make choices about products they desire for themselves, the stronger the connection becomes between created desire and what satisfies that desire. By striating the consuming class and the marketing surrounding them into a larger set of possibilities (infant, toddler, child, tween, teenager, late teenager/young adult, adult, twenty-something, etc.), manufacturers can track the effectiveness of brands and target their marketing at later points to connect with the nostalgia of branding choices made earlier on. This reduction of human nature to mathematics through restricted variables allows companies to create more products that connect with their consumer base and determine within more stringent parameters what their expected profitability and capital increases will be as a person moves through each of these categories.

Within the *Twilight* saga, the compression of time and automation of consumption is figured by the bite. In the texts, the bite as transformational process is treated like a religious ceremony, where the participants understand the outcome and significance, but only certain vampires understand how the process really works. In this regard, Carlisle takes on a pseudochastened, priest-like role, having performed this rite many times. Though he denies himself *full* indulgence in the pleasures of human flesh to accomplish each transfiguration, the very process itself is predicated on consuming as a transformative means. Adding to the air of piety surrounding this ritual, each time Edward begins to explain a new piece of the puzzle to Bella about how his family members became vampires, his posture changes, surrounding the topic with reverence and mysticism; deep breaths, long pauses, and a softening of his tone to a near whisper always inflect his explications.[6] Moreover, the religious iconography inherent with a three-day transformation resulting in resurrection betrays an overt conflation of Christianity and capitalism where salvation is aligned with consumption. Even the pain involved in this transformation is downplayed by Meyer's overly positive portrayal of the resulting vampiric life, with only Rosalie ever really lamenting the fact that she was "turned." This relegates the need to endure pain to a classic literary device, the hero's trial. The limitless power that ensues after being bitten is immediately tied to gender and cultural ideas of beauty, illustrated by the gender ideals in the first book. As Edward notes, "everything about me invites you in—my voice, my face, even my *smell*."[7] After being subjected to the myriad variants of just how beautiful Edward is for hundreds of pages, it is impossible to leave this scene without understanding that he *is* the image of masculinity women embrace. For men to meet the expectations of the opposite sex they will need to enhance their outward appearance to become this new masculine ideal—an ideal based on consumption and achieved by the same means.

To further reinforce this ideology, it is essential to make sure that—without ambiguity—generally held conceptions of gender are equated with the tenants of capitalism. Meyer makes these connections repeatedly, beginning with her first introduction of the Cullens. The representation of the Cullen family across the *Twilight* books and films can be boiled down to a simple idea: benevolent bourgeoisie. Their aristocratic stature is softened by their overt intentions to protect Bella and keep her safe from the myriad forces that seem to continually conspire against her. This includes helping her transcend the need for human consumption and opt for what they consider a "vegetarian" lifestyle. The idea of vegetarianism in the text is absurd, because they still kill animals and drink their blood, but their "choice" mirrors modern, class-driven trends in food consumption, where wealthier families can afford healthier food and fully organic or vegetarian lifestyles, which are substantially more expensive than eating mass-produced food. In this sense, Bella is offered the same warmth that corporations offer consumers: the freedom to choose which brand or style accurately reflects them, thereby creating the illusion of free will, yet never allowing for the possibility to alter the perception that consumption *itself* is necessary and absolute.

At the same time, the Cullen family represents a classic portrayal of upper class domesticity: a doctor husband paired with a stay-at-home wife and children who are closely engaged with their parents and whose autonomy allows them to experience their every desire, while always keeping their family well-being paramount. Through these endlessly reiterated descriptions, it is easy to let the conspicuously consumptive nature of the family fade into the background as a nuance that highlights the American ideal that hard work will bring you happiness, but this is precisely where the narrative becomes dangerous. The naturalization of the Cullens' near limitless wealth and continual consumption in forms that range from excessive (purchasing a luxury car to use as a bribe) to the categorically absurd (purchasing an island as an anniversary present) are highly romanticized in the texts, and with this romanticization comes a deeper connection between the act of consumption, ideas of beauty, and identity formation.

The beginnings of this connection are apparent in the very first chapter of *Twilight* when Bella attends her first day of school in Forks. Just before she encounters the Cullens for the first time, she describes two of her classmates, a boy named Eric and a girl she does not name. The descriptions of these two individuals are unflattering at best as she points out various flaws in their physical conditions—for him, an unpleasant voice, skin problems, and general awkwardness, and for her, wild curly hair that actually increases her height.[8] After reciting details of the beauty of the Cullens to a point where the reader assumes they are almost painful to look at they are so perfect, she encounters Mike Newton. Of all the depictions of humans throughout the book, Bella is most kind to Mike, but different from every other person's description, he is contextualized within the economic hierarchy. Bella takes most students at face value, describing their maladies as expected, but Mike is described as a "cute, baby-faced boy, his pale blond hair carefully gelled into orderly spikes, smiling at me in a friendly way."[9] A few pages later, Meyer accounts for the positive portrayal by situating him in terms of his family and their business, which is successful, and he appears to be part of one of the wealthier families in Forks: "Nice kid—nice family. His dad owns the sporting goods store just outside of town. He makes a good living off all the backpackers who come through here."[10] In *New Moon*, Bella revises her description of Mike, positively highlighting his development over the summer. Within three paragraphs of this initial comment, Bella makes a reference to how she works in his family's sporting goods store to save money for college.[11] This again keeps his physical attributes closely tied to his socioeconomic status. The repetitive nature of Meyer's comments clearly delineates between two diametrically opposed classes, with vampires maintaining an elevated position to humanity, and also creates a hierarchy amongst humans in which only those humans with any sort of wealth are sketched in positive terms. Meyer mitigates even these more favorable descriptions, however, with endless hyperbolic depictions of Edward.

This formula applies to Bella, as well, who (outside of Edward's view of her) is not consistently portrayed as terribly beautiful, but more average, and often described as pallid and skinny—a direct correlation to her family's lower middle class standing.

What is different about Bella earlier on, however, is that she longs for the world of the vampire and is willing to do anything to attain acceptance therein. Unlike those humans around her, because of her privileged view into the world of the Cullens, she can see the banality of human existence and understands that differentiation comes by elevating herself into a class that has a profoundly different relationship with consumption. Particularly in *New Moon* and *Eclipse*, this is illustrated by her frequent diminution of being human, using modifiers like "only" and "merely" to describe herself.

Meyer's tendency to conflate beauty and wealth as defining characteristics of quintessential ideas of masculinity (portrayed predominantly through Edward and Carlisle) and femininity (through Alice, Rosalie, Esme, and later Bella, after her vampiric transformation) is particularly problematic. It lends itself to a reinforcement of the idea that gender is constructed through acts of consumption and the more ability one has to consume, the more ideally masculine or feminine they are. The way Bella introduces Mike Newton is the subtlest example of this conflation of gender/beauty/ consumption in the books. A far more obvious example occurs in *Breaking Dawn* when Bella finally becomes a vampire and is at last *fully* entrenched in the Cullen family. Almost immediately after Bella resumes consciousness from her transformation, she is placed in front of an enormous mirror so she can look upon her new form, which she describes as "indisputably beautiful... flawless... a carving of a goddess."[12] It is telling that as soon as Bella surrenders completely to a life of consumption her image changes and she becomes uncannily beautiful.

This tendency does not simply apply to the descriptions of these characters; the author is equally vivid when commenting on the beauty of the *objects* the Cullens own. In a move that subverts gender conventions but still stresses consumption, she highlights particular tastes that illustrate a nonconformist frame to traditional gender stereotypes. A clear example of this is Alice's penchant for cars and Rosalie's ability to fix them. It is not just that these women like automobiles because they look sporty; they understand them at a different level, more on par with connoisseurship. Clearly, the desire to amass sports cars is something not typically associated with women, but it serves to illustrate the point that gender, when built on the premise of consumption, becomes more amorphous than in previous generations. Anything can be used to express this construction. Bella's incorporation into the Cullen family and the realm of conspicuous consumption in *Breaking Dawn* provides a perfect example: she is given a Mercedes Guardian to replace her 1953 Chevy pickup after she and Edward are engaged. Significantly, the protagonist does not understand the noteworthiness or rarity of the car she drives. This is only brought to her attention when someone asks to take a picture of the car while she is at a gas station. At this point she still resides in the world of humans, but this gift remains a symbol of her crossing into the world of consumption. Her lack of recognition of what she drives stems from her not residing entirely in the consumptive world of the vampires. Later in the book, following her transformation into a vampire, Edward gives her an even more ostentatious and conspicuous car, a Ferrari F430. Each time she is further immersed within the Cullen family, her proof of acceptance into this world is marked by an act of overtly conspicuous consumption predicated on the conception that the expressions of gender espoused by the elite become the dominating ideas for the masses.

When individuation is defined through material possessions, those with wealth are the only ones who can truly illustrate originality. This is evidenced in the individualized special powers designated to the vampires compared with the homogenized powers of the Quileute werewolves. It is further emphasized each time the Quileutes enter the narrative, as Meyer makes sure to reference their poverty in some way—for example, the many references to the miniscule size of the Black's house, especially when compared to the Cullen's palatial estate, and Jacob's beat up VW Rabbit juxtaposed against the Aston Martin Vanquish Edward uses to drive Bella to the prom. Each time the Quileute/werewolf poverty is situated alongside the Cullen/vampire wealth, it reinforces the hierarchy Meyer has created and illustrates the *actual* role of the Quileutes in the text, which is to serve as a point of comparison between modern and classic (as well as racial) versions of masculinity. Their impoverished state and visible hulking strength are indicative of working class labor and the outmoded conception of masculinity as equated with physical strength. In Meyer's world the vampires have equal, if not greater, strength than the werewolves, yet they do not need to embody the same physicality that the werewolves/Quileute men do. The vampire's effete, trend-conscious image situated within the realm of consumption becomes the de facto illustration of modern masculinity, which is why Jacob, as beautiful as he is, can never be a viable love interest for Bella.

In this formulation, Emmett clearly seems to stand out as an exception to the rule. However, it is important to note the inconsistency of the character, particularly how he is depicted in the films. First, though he is larger in size than the other members of the Cullen family, he is still not as large as the werewolves. Furthermore, in the films he is given a hip, urban edge that displaces the simple, rural version of the character from the novels. In the movie version of *Twilight* when he is first introduced, he enters the cafeteria completely adorned in white. He wears a white-hooded Henley, white pants and white sneakers, more along the lines of hip-hop chic than country farmboy. His stark white clothes are contrasted against his dark, cropped hair, angled sideburns and a large black leather bracelet on his right arm. Each time he enters the film after this he continues to embody urban trendiness, later donning a puffy down vest, and during the baseball scene a dark track suit with the jacket zipped halfway up to expose his chest and a fitted hat cocked to the side and back. In the *New Moon* film, during Bella's birthday party, he is dressed in a dark green shirt, again buttoned up only enough to bare part of his chest, along with a dark vest that exudes both high fashion and style. Consequently, his comment about his gift to Bella—"finally a decent sound system for that piece of crap [truck]"—reveals his affinity for upper end consumables and completes his alignment of masculinity, wealth, and consumption.

This intrinsic connection between idealized gender portrayal and material wealth is by far one of the most damaging conflations reiterated ad nauseum throughout Meyer's novels. Her overt materialist tendencies result in the mediation of individuals through the objects they own, where it becomes impossible to separate the person from the brand: Edward and Volvo, Carlisle and BMW, Alice and Porsche. This inseparability is particularly well demonstrated in the movie *New Moon*, when Bella sees a specter of Edward in the parking lot of her school: when he appears, his Volvo appears with him, and when he vanishes, the car evanesces as well.[13] What is created is a vertiginous spiral that inculcates the audience into this same ideology through their emotional connection to the characters. Because these characters are so heavily mediated throughout the text by the cars they drive, the clothes they wear, and the lifestyle they can afford, the audience connects as much with these components as they do with the emotional elements of the characters. Looking over the scores of web pages where teenage girls discuss how they want to be Bella Swan and want to find their own Edward Cullen, it is clear that these popular culture icons have efficiently reconstructed modern ideas of masculinity and femininity for the next generation of consumers in the United States and beyond.[14] Because fans are so deeply invested in the fantasy that Bella and Edward embody,[15] they elevate this fantasy from fiction to the level of reality by turning the actors in the film into movie stars, who now must embody this consumptive persona in real life through their new wealth and status. And now that the actors evince this ideology, it becomes even more dangerous because it no longer resides in the world of fantasy, but exists in reality, and is therefore theoretically achievable. Fans confess their acceptance of the concepts of gender constructed through consumerism in these texts and as they mature they will look for partners who adhere to this image and define their gender through the same means, creating a society dominated by automaton consumers who only understand self-definition as an outward expression of materialism.

Notes

1. Blackbook.com, "*Twilight* Fans Sell Out Alaskan Vampire Cruise," *Blackbook Magazine*, Web. http://www.blackbookmag.com/article/twilight-fans-sell-out-cruise/8069.

2. For critical analysis of Fordism and post-Fordism and the economic ramifications on culture see: Michel Aglietta, Robert J. Antonio, Alessandro Bonnano, Alain Lipietz, David Harvey, Bob Jessop, Max Koch.

3. An excellent example of this appeared in a 2010 Superbowl advertisement for Flo TV, where the male figure in the commercial has to miss watching a sporting event to shop with his female significant other. The bored look on the male actor's face is paired with the announcer's pitch, which draws further attention to his emasculation while imploring him to take part in the very same act of consuming: "Jason, get yourself the Flo TV personal television. It's live mobile TV so now live sports goes where you go. Change out of that skirt Jason." YouTube.com, "Superbowl XLIV TV Commercials – FloTV," Web. http://www.youtube.com/watch?v=3M-KybkB_XU.

4. Michel Aglietta, *A Theory of Capitalist Regulation: The U.S. Experience* (Verso Classics: London, 1979. Print), 113.

5. Karl Marx, *Capital,* Volume One, in *The Marx-Engels Reader*, ed. Robert C. Tucker (New York: Norton, 1978. Print), 408. Italics mine.

6. Stephenie Meyer, *Twilight* (New York: Little Brown, 2005. Print), 286, 336, 341, 473.

7. Ibid., 263–264. Edward's confession reestablishes the point of comparison between the human and the vampire, and betrays the longing people feel to have this same power: who wouldn't want to be endlessly rich, impeccably dressed and entirely irresistible?

8. Ibid., 15–17.

9. Ibid., 25.

10. Ibid., 36.

11. Stephenie Meyer, *New Moon* (New York: Little Brown, 2006. Print), 12–13.

12. Stephenie Meyer, *Breaking Dawn* (New York: Little Brown, 2008. Print), 403.

13. *New Moon*, DVD, directed by Chris Weitz (Santa Monica, CA: Summit Entertainment, 2010).

14. This revision of gender ideology in the *Twilight* saga represents the next step in the naturalization of gender construction and consumption, particularly as it relates to men. Though the concept of "metrosexual" existed well before Meyer's series became popular, the term was coined during a liminal period to signify a fraction of the population that did not adhere to the generally held ideas of normative, heterosexual masculinity. Now that men's interest in their appearance and lifestyle, and subsequent use of consumption to define these attributes, are becoming normalized, the designation metrosexual has lost cultural relevance and has fallen out of general parlance.

15. The direct influence of these characters on modern conceptions of gender can be seen very tangibly already. For example, when the Social Security Administration released the most popular baby names of 2009, the most popular girl's name was Isabella (Bella's full name), the most popular boy's name was Jacob, and Cullen was the fastest rising name on the list, moving up 297 places. USAToday.com, "Twilight Influences Most Popular Baby Names of 2009," *USA Today*, Web. http://content.usatoday.com/communities/entertainment/post/2010/05/twilight-influences-most-popular-baby-names-of-2009/1.

CHAPTER 13

FASHION SUCKS...BLOOD: CLOTHES AND COVENS IN *TWILIGHT* AND HOLLYWOOD CULTURE

ANGIE CHAU

IN LATE SEPTEMBER 2009, the online shopping website Bluefly ran a web promotion for vampire-inspired fashion titled "Fashion sucks...blood." In the opening sequence to this shoot, shoppers were shown a series of photographs. The first featured an elegant brunette in a long red gown. The second image was a close-up of the face in the third photo, which highlighted a blonde-haired young woman with dark eye shadow, staring pensively into the distance, wearing layers and layers of silver chain necklaces and bracelets. The detail that struck me the most was the slender trickle of blood dripping down from the corner of her left eye. The next few photographs presented young couples—the men with black slimcut suits and peacoats or dark jeans, the women in black leather and dark ruffles, always accessorized with lots of silver and rhinestone studded jewelry (even a spider ring). The last shot was of a sultry brunette, drinking what appeared to be blood out of a straw stuck in a soda bottle labeled "Tru Blood"—presumably part of the viral campaign for Tru Blood, the synthetic blood nourishment beverage created to promote the popular HBO series *True Blood* back in fall 2008. Online shoppers could then click on a link to watch the YouTube video "Killer Vampire Fashion," a one-minute, forty-second documentary of the fashion shoot, or they could purchase the items spotlighted in the session.

My initial reaction to this marketing strategy was one of utter incredulity. Would any shopper be motivated to buy jewelry just because it was mysteriously labeled "vampire inspired"? More pressing, do vampires bleed from their eyes? Despite my cynicism, I had to admit that the Bluefly promotion caught my attention enough for me to click on the icon and view the slideshow a few times, if only to try to solve the puzzle of what constituted "Killer Vampire Fashion." Presented with the opportunity to write about the apparent cause and effect of *Twilight* and other contemporary vampire fiction's popularity, I began to reflect on the disparity between fashion as portrayed in Stephenie Meyer's novels and the corresponding films, and the so-called vampire fashion of the clothing industry. This chapter looks at how fashion works as both a commodity and a symbolic marker in the *Twilight* series and its film adaptations, spilling over into the sphere of celebrity culture. I will demonstrate how the ambivalent attitude about fashion conveyed by the books' characters allows for the optimal manipulation of their on- and off-screen counterparts by marketers and popular media: as both the key characters in the novels and their celebrity actors insist on their fashion ineptitude, they become the ideal, interchangeable blank slates for fashion marketing.

Drawing from a variety of popular consumer sources, ranging from the marketing materials of online shopping sites to celebrity gossip magazines, the first part of my chapter establishes the trend of vampire fashion as a widespread phenomenon in popular culture, spurred on or perhaps even instigated by fictional multimedia productions like *Twilight* and HBO's *True Blood*. I then turn to the novels themselves and examine how Bella's contradictory attitude about fashion is centered on her (mis)understanding of fashion's sole purpose as inciting male vampire desire. Finally, I look at how actors Kristen Stewart ("Bella") and her costar Robert Pattinson ("Edward") carry over this same ambivalent disdain for fashion in the media's portrayal of their fashion sense, and how this, in turn, shapes marketing strategies. Similar to the manner in which the Cullen family is able to dress expensively and shop outside inherently human economic constraints without appearing to be overly enthusiastic consumers, Stewart and Pattinson are able to adopt a blasé attitude about fashion yet still serve as walking advertisements for high fashion.

Using Roland Barthes' *The Fashion System* as a starting point, I am particularly interested in his assertion about fashion production and consumption:

> Calculating, industrial society is obliged to form consumers who don't calculate; if clothing's producers and consumers had the same consciousness, clothing would be bought (and produced) only at the very slow rate of its dilapidation; Fashion, like all fashions, depends on a disparity of two consciousnesses, each foreign to the other. In order to blunt the buyer's calculating consciousness, a veil must be drawn around the object—a veil of images, of reasons, of meanings...[1]

In Barthes' study of "Fashion" with a capital "f," which he defines as the written description of clothing found in French magazines like *Elle* and *Le Jardin des Modes*, he explains that "financial constraints do not weigh upon the Woman of Fashion, precisely because Fashion is omnipotent to thwart them: the high price of a garment is mentioned only to justify it as 'outrageous': money problems are never invoked except insofar as Fashion can solve them."[2] For Barthes, the obfuscation of price that the veil provides is absolutely crucial to the perpetuation of consumer desire. In the case of the *Twilight* phenomenon, there is a hyperconsciousness of financial constraints that appears around every corner, contributing to a new kind of consumer that calculates, and a new kind of marketer that strategizes accordingly.

To illustrate the extent to which the *Twilight* saga has permeated into mainstream popular culture, the original film in the series, which was released in November 2008, grossed $383.8 million worldwide.[3] According to Nielsen SoundScan, the sound-track to the first film sold 2.2 million copies,[4] and the four books in the series sold over 70 million copies.[5] Beginning in the fall of 2008 and lasting well into the fall of 2009, newspapers ranging from the *New York Daily News* to the *New York Times* fea-tured articles on vampire fashion. Although in the books the concept of stereotypical "vampire fashion" is ridiculed (in Volterra, Bella, noticing Volturi members Felix and Demetri wearing normal clothes underneath their cloaks and hoods, recalls Edward's ridicule of black satin cloaks and plastic fangs[6]) popular media reached the consensus in the last two years that indeed vampire fashion was "in," and all fingers pointed to *Twilight* as the source of inspiration.

As early as spring 2009, the website Trendhunter.com featured an online video montage of Top 10 recent vampire moments titled "Vampire Couture." Ruth La Ferla, writing for the *New York Times*, cited examples of vampires dominating the fashion scene in the June 2009 issues of *W* magazine and Italian *Vogue*, although her piece focuses less on fashion than the enigmatic and purposely vague vampire style. La Ferla writes, "The style world, too, has come under the vampire's spell, in the shape of the gorgeous leather- and lace-clad night crawlers who have crept into the pages of fashion glossies."[7] For an article about clothing chic, actual garments figure surprisingly little into the picture; instead, La Ferla, summarizing the photo spreads in *W* and *Vogue*, calls attention to facial details such as "killer glares," "chalky pallor," and a "smear of scarlet" on a model's cheek. Both the *Daily News* and *Los Angeles Times* remarked on the goth trend hitting fashion houses like L.A.'s Rodarte.[8]

But how did the trend start? La Ferla credits *Twilight*: "What began with the Twilight Saga, the luridly romantic young-adult series by Stephenie Meyer, followed by 'Twilight,' the movie, has become a pandemic of unholy proportions."[9] Mark Ellwood concurs, beginning his article on vampire chic and gothic glamour, "The mass hysteria over the new movie 'Twilight' is just one hint that combination of the erotic and the macabre is back—front and center—in pop culture."[10] Popular media was quick to pick up on the irrefutable connection between marketing and *Twilight*, whose reach extended far beyond the scope of fashion. Brooks Barnes, writing for *The New York Times*, informs readers, "You can now buy 'Twilight' makeup (staining lip balm, $18); a Barbie-like Bella action figure; and the themed Volvo (the pitch: 'What drives Edward Cullen May Soon Drive You')."[11] *Twilight*-themed merchandise, from official retailers Hot Topic and Nordstrom to unofficial web retailers capitalizing on the same craze, found a captive consumer base in dedicated fans commonly referred to as "Twi-hards," and *The Los Angeles Times* even reported Beverly Hills beauty salon Gavert Atelier offering "Twilights," a "process that gives clients the same highlights as their idols [Pattinson and Stewart], framing the face in a way that casts that other-worldly glow."[12]

Ironically, what is imagined and promoted by marketers as vampire-inspired human clothing has little to do with the novels, despite the fact that fashion occupies a crucial part in the novels and the films. For human Bella, her lack of high fashion sense is an indication of her own failing to measure up to the glamour of the Cullen family. The earliest textual clue of the significance of clothing's role in the series occurs in the very first paragraph of the first book, as Bella describes her physical move from Phoenix to Forks in terms of her summery top and the parka she carries onto her flight. While this detail is important to the plot of the narrative—Bella's move from the perpetually sunny southwest to the typically overcast northwest means she will come into regular contact with vampires who must stay out of direct sunlight—it is also an indication of Bella's down-to-earth and practical clothing style. Not surprisingly then, Bella's first impression of the Cullens at school never once directly refers to what they are wearing. However, her narration is full of hints related to fashion: one sister is described as reminiscent of a cover girl for the *Sports Illustrated* swimsuit issue, and the entire family is described as able to be featured on the "airbrushed pages of a fashion magazine."[13] It might be argued that the beauty of the Cullens is in their remarkable faces and bodies rather than any material display, but it becomes clear that this is a short-lived oversight on Bella's part.

As a mere mortal, Bella is not immune to mundane concerns, although she is a far cry from the teenage shopaholics her classmates resemble. On her first day at Forks High School, she is self-conscious about the used Chevy truck her dad Charlie has bought for her as a welcome gift. She feels slightly reassured only after she scopes out the school's parking lot and sees that "most of the cars were older like mine, nothing flashy"[14] (although she is still self-conscious enough about the "thunderous volume" of her engine to stop her car as soon as possible). The only exception in the parking lot is Edward's "shiny Volvo," and later in the saga, we see Rosalie's BMW M3, the Porsche that Edward bribes Alice with, Bella's Mercedes and "after" Ferrari, all of which stand in stark contrast to Jacob's auto mechanic work on his VW Rabbit and the old motorcycles. These class markers help the reader to situate human Bella as in between the elite luxury and high sense of style of the vampires, as represented by the Cullens, and the lower working class Quileutes.

Bella's status as an outsider surfaces frequently in her ambivalent attitude toward fashion. During the prom dress shopping trip to Port Angeles with her classmates Jessica and Angela, Bella is shown as just barely fashion-competent as she dutifully doles out sage advice to the other two girls about what colors and styles complement their eye and hair color. But the narrator points out that despite her own need for new shoes, Bella only watches from the sidelines since she is "not in the mood to shop" for herself.[15] This outing reveals Bella's role in the margins, unwilling to participate in the most normative teenager girl activity, and also shows her to be more down-to-earth and less materialistic than her friends. She is simultaneously benevolent yet sophisticated: the "limited choices" in Port Angeles make for a much easier shopping trip than back in a big city like Phoenix.

Readers are introduced to her timidity about fashion during her pajama dilemma, since her bedtime attire takes on new significance once she finds out that Edward sits next to her every night watching her sleep. Her raggedy T-shirt and sweats make her feel self-conscious and thus she laments never packing the Victoria's Secret silk pajamas her mother gave her (tags still on two years later!), suggesting that she is not impervious to girlish insecurities, despite her reluctance to subscribe to society's ideals of femininity. Moreover, Bella's resistance to wearing brand name sleepwear that in real-life boasts a retail cost of nearly $60, and her subsequent regret of not doing so, highlights her financial insecurity and class-consciousness around Edward. Chapters later in *Twilight* when she visits the Cullen residence for the first time she struggles: "It was hard to decide what to wear. I doubted there were any etiquette books detailing how to dress when your vampire sweetheart takes you home to meet his vampire family . . . I ended up in my only skirt—long, khaki-colored, still casual. I put on the dark blue blouse he'd once complimented."[16] Bella manages to both stay true to herself ("still casual") at the same time wearing what Edward likes her in.

When the subject of Bella and Edward's wedding arises in *Eclipse*, Edward's sister Alice is, of course, ready with the dress. " 'Perrine Bruyere has a waiting list, you know,' she said, defensive now. 'Fabric masterpieces don't happen overnight. If I hadn't thought ahead, you'd be wearing something off the rack!' "[17] Bella is shown characteristically stammering in response, "Per—who?" The reader is left to assume that fictional dress designer is so high-end that Bella is too ignorant to recognize her name despite Bruyere's popularity, which warrants a waiting list. Once Alice presents the gown though, Bella reveals her criteria: "It's beautiful. It's just right for him."[18] Alice is the one who has to gently correct Bella's constant pandering to Edward, asking Bella if, more importantly, the dress is right for her, and in the end, Bella gets the best of both worlds—she reaps the benefits of having a friend with impeccable taste, not to mention unlimited funds, but without having to be branded herself as superficial and high maintenance. At the same time, she is forced again to confront the error of her misjudgment—that the purpose of high fashion is not to please Edward but to serve as an indicator of class. Bruyere's wedding gown is desirable precisely because it is so hard to attain, because of the waiting list, because of its elite status in contrast to being off-the-rack.

Bella's clothing choices are always based on what she thinks will incite Edward's desire. During their honeymoon on Isle Esme, Bella tries to use the sexy sleepwear given by Alice to seduce Edward: "I'd started slow with innocent ivory satins, worried that revealing more of my skin would be the opposite of helpful, but ready to try anything. Edward seemed to notice nothing, as if I were wearing the same ratty old sweats I wore at home."[19] Bella's willingness to dress uncharacteristically stems from her misconception of the relationship between fashion and vampire desire. Well aware of the potential power of lingerie on mortal men, Bella's experiment reveals that Edward is not attracted to Bella for her outward charms, and the failure of fashion as a force of enticement confirms that vampire desire is based on more intrinsic qualities such as scent. Bella's misunderstanding of fashion does, however, allow ample room for interpretation and manipulation in the novels.

If the concept of vampire fashion were accurately construed from passages describing Edward's and Bella's preferred outfits, runway models would be wearing long khaki skirts, blouses, khaki pants, and pullovers. Bella's description of Edward's clothing in the novel is exactly the opposite of glamorous: "if I hadn't seen him undressed, I would have sworn there was nothing more beautiful than Edward in his khakis and beige pullover."[20] Unlike Edward, however, who, as the quintessential vampire, is immune to the costly temptations of high fashion, Alice is clearly obsessed with haute couture and serves as an exception to the general rule that vampires are not susceptible to earthly consumer desires. In *Breaking Dawn*, when Edward volunteers to donate clothes to Jacob and Leah, he explains, "Alice rarely allows us to wear the same thing twice. We've got piles of brand-new clothes that are destined for Goodwill."[21] This confession allows readers to understand that Edward and the rest of the Cullens' impeccable style is not voluntary but instead forced upon them by wasteful Alice. Consistently throughout the series, the narrator can only make sense of her expensive tastes by portraying them in a derogatory light. However armed with her unique power of foresight, she is repeatedly depicted in the series as vapid and childlike, always in connection to her inclination for high fashion, which, it should be noted, serves a seemingly purely aesthetic purpose as opposed to Bella's attempts to dress "for" Edward or to please him.

For instance, on Bella's first hunting trip with Edward after her transformation in *Breaking Dawn*, Alice is to blame for the impractical fashion choice: "this dress—that Alice must have put me in sometime when I was too lost in the burning to notice—was not what I would have picked out for either jumping or hunting. Tightly fitted ice-blue silk? What did she think I would need it for? Was there a cocktail party later?...Well, Alice always seemed to treat clothes as if they were disposable and meant for one-time usage."[22] Bella's stiletto heels, too, are the result of Alice's work and Bella blames her initial clumsiness on her: "The ground seemed to move toward me so slowly that that it was nothing at all to place my feet—what shoes had Alice put me in? Stilettos? She'd lost her mind."[23] But according to Alice, Bella's poor fashion sense is an indication of her former human inadequacies: "Her fashion sense hasn't improved as much as her balance."[24]

Bella's transformation allows her access to the world of vampire fashion and high couture, although she insists upon remaining in the margins to a certain extent. Miraculously, however, it does not change Bella's simple down-to-earth taste. Presented with her new closet, Bella enlists Edward's olfactory help in finding her "artfully faded blue jeans" and "long-sleeved white t-shirt," foregoing a "floor-length silk gown inside—baby pink" and swearing to avoid all satin and silk.[25] Bella as vampire is still the same old Bella: although she is a vampire, she is a practical one like Edward and has retained her human tomboyishness. Moreover, since she now has unrestrained access to Alice's outlandishly fanciful fashions, her decision to stay practical and minimalist is even more admirable.

Jacob's outwardly demonstrative indifference to clothing serves as a telling contrast to Bella's fashion ineptitude and Alice's shopaholic tendencies. If Alice is the epitome of fashion to the excess, Jacob seems to be all about practicality and function. After his transformation, he is usually depicted as topless, never wearing anything more than cut-off sweats and T-shirts. Bella finally asks him, "Is it really so impossible to wear clothes, Jacob?...I mean, I know you don't get cold anymore, but still."[26] His explanation is that life without "a complete outfit" is easier: "My clothes don't just pop in and out of existence when I change—I have to carry them with me while I run. Pardon me for keeping my burden light." Asked by Bella about the black cord he wears around his calf, he exclaims proudly, "That's more than just a fashion statement—it sucks to carry jeans in your mouth."[27] For Jacob, whose only concern is practicality, fashion is seen as a frivolous waste of time; he insists on setting the record straight, so that even accessories such as the black cord for tying on his jeans so that he doesn't lose them as he changes into his werewolf form, which could be misconstrued as fashionable, serve a crucial function. In contrast to Bella, whose desire to please Edward often serves as a motivating force in the pursuit of fashion, Jacob uses his practicality and anti-fashion to impress Bella.

In real life, actors Stewart and Pattinson's self-proclaimed clothing habits are more werewolf than vampire. Amidst the Edward-craze back in the fall of 2008, Pattinson, at an Apple-sponsored appearance in Soho, New York, was described as sporting a "tatty ski cap" and wearing nothing more exciting than "gray jeans, vintage tee, oversized coat, and black Nike sneakers."[28] Asked by *Vanity Fair*'s Cassandra Handley in a Q&A about his trademark style, Pattinson answers, "Looking terrible. Truly, I wear the same thing every day. I don't know how to use a washer machine."[29] A year later, for *Harper's Bazaar*'s November 2009 cover story, Pattinson again admitted to never doing laundry and the writer explained that, "When his clean laundry runs out, he steals socks and underwear from sets."[30] In the cover story for *Vanity Fair*'s December 2009 issue, Pattinson repeated, "I don't have any material desires at all. I wear the same clothes every single day. I don't buy anything."[31]

Similarly, in a video filmed at *Allure* magazine's November 2009 cover shoot, Kristen Stewart responded to a question about her sense of fashion, "How would I describe my personal style? T-shirts—my favorite T-shirts are my brothers' old T-shirts that they've worn out. Jeans and sneakers—I'm like a sneaker fanatic, I have a fetish, it's weird." In the *Harper's* article, she is described as wearing "her uniform of jeans, a white tank under another tie-dyed one, and a hoodie," and writer Laura Brown notes, "Ask her who made her top and she has no idea." Following Bella's down-to-earth everygirl image and Jacob's ultrapracticality, Stewart and Pattinson are constantly lauded for and self-consciously proud of their grunginess as part of the general campaign to garner more fans, who presumably would be more attracted to accessible, relatable characters or actors like themselves.

Yet in the *Harper's* article, Brown does manage to squeeze in the following line, albeit in parenthesis: "(While she will admit to one girlish thing, a love of Chanel, her dream outfit is a custom Brooks Brothers suit.)."[32] Despite the stars' image of being low-maintenance and fashion-unconscious, popular media insists on the opposite, resulting in a convoluted message of the celebrities wearing affordable clothes yet deep down harboring expensive tastes, a marketing strategy that works remarkably well on consumers.

In many of the strategies employed by marketers to sell their "vampire clothing," the concept of vampire fashion is left deliberately vague in order to accommodate styles from as diverse a range as designer couture to the grunginess of actors like Stewart and Pattinson. The ambiguity surrounding vampire style allows substantial flexibility; therefore Stewart can claim to be both fashion naïf, as she often does in interviews, and inadvertent fashion ingénue. Like the Cullens, the celebrity actors function as extraordinarily glamorous, good looking characters that project the message, "Hey, I don't care about fashion either," but are always dressed in high fashion, for which they conveniently do not have to suffer the financial consequences. In turn, consumers (normal people, noncelebrities, nonvampires) look at them and think, "I can look like that guy, he doesn't care, he doesn't have expensive tastes," yet cannot actually afford the very same high fashion items. Consumer desire thus hinges on what is ostensibly attainable and affordable, but at the same time perceived to be elitist due to either high cost, or being sold out and unavailable to obsessive fans.

In a video clip taken from the *New Moon* photo shoot for *Entertainment Weekly*'s August 14, 2009 issue featured on the magazine's website, an off-camera interviewer asks actor Stewart, "A lot of the clothes you wear are sold out of stores as soon as they are identified…and sometimes re-released. Do you keep anything for your own closet?" Stewart, dressed in a faded gray T-shirt and black leggings with black boots, and shown posing with her costar Taylor Lautner ("Jacob") responds, "The things that have been sold out have been like, like, the things that people are actually able to get like the things that are semi-cheap. So yeah, those things like sweatshirts and jackets—those are all mine which is bizarre to have people go out and buy, um, but like the really cool stuff—I never get to keep any of that like, um, anything like for an event or anything like that it's all…it's just I'm not important enough yet I think." Stewart pointedly differentiates between what is accessible to her fans ("things that are semi-cheap," such as her sweatshirts and jackets) and "the really cool stuff," the haute couture given to her for celebrity events.

Later, when asked about her fans' responses to her appearing in movies as diverse as *Twilight* and *Adventureland*, she insists, "I'm so not Bella—you know, that's such a different aspect of me." Stewart's reluctance to being identified as her onscreen persona is not particularly unusual, but what is remarkable is the way that popular media has repeatedly insisted on her resemblance to Bella Swan, most noticeably in style of dress. In the off-camera exchange, Stewart discerningly points out the discrepancy between the official perception of her high fashion (designer special-event wear) and what is perceived as her everyday wear, and the multilayered process of consumerism that surrounds her clothing choices. In order to close the distance between what is imagined by the fashion industry as vampire fashion and what is being touted both in the novels and in Hollywood, popular media must therefore rely on the conflation of actor and character: to her fans Kristen Stewart is at once alternative teen idol *and* relatable Bella. A perfect example of this is *InStyle*'s report titled "Kristen Stewart Steals Bella's Style," as a promotion for Converse sneakers: "Kristen Stewart took a break from the Italian set *of New Moon* to attend the MTV Movie Awards, but she didn't leave her character's comfy-casual style far behind. While she looked stunning in a red Yigal Azrouel dress, she made a statement by pairing it with a pair of Converse Chuck Taylor sneakers. JustJared.com has reported it was a last minute replacement for pumps after she twisted her ankle, a trick she must have picked up from her *Twilight* character, Bella. In the film Bella injures her leg before prom and accessorizes her dress with a walking cast and Converse sneaks."[33] The act of wearing sneakers with a designer dress is first interpreted as a throwback to Bella's "comfy-casual style," but once rumor of the injury surfaces, is then re-interpreted as even more of a specific textual reference. This of course works in favor of both Converse and Yigal Azrouel, the former now deemed red carpet worthy, the latter's conservative hoity-toityness offset by a smidgen of teenage rebelliousness.

Like Stewart notes, many of the clothes she appears in are not affordable for the average fan. But at the same time that she is proclaiming the accessibility and affordability of her everyday clothes, she is repeatedly photographed outfitted in designer pieces. For instance, when she appeared on the cover of the November 2009 issue of *Allure* magazine in time for the film release of *New Moon*, features inside the issue included a "Style Timeline" of Stewart's metamorphosis from tomboy child actor to red-carpet screen siren and "8 Hair and Makeup Tricks Inspired by *Twilight*," as well as a spread featuring Kristen Stewart in what else?—a black leather jacket and a leather-and-lace Rodarte dress. In the 2009 *Allure* interview Stewart is asked "What was your favorite outfit and why?" She answers haltingly, "I like the leather jacket that I wore, it just felt good on, it was just a good jacket." Along the lines of the quote in parentheses from the *Harper's* article, here Stewart must again reconcile her purported indifference for high fashion with its inescapable impact on her life.

If the most common marketing approach is appealing to fans' celebrity fervor, consumers can choose between dressing like the actors in real life and dressing like the actors in the films. *InStyle* magazine has the first option down to a formula, reporting, for example, on December 2, 2009, "*Twilight* Stars Love J Brand Jeans": "The cast of the *Twilight Saga* spend a lot of time together and it shows—in their style! The stars all rely on a jeans-heavy look perfect for traveling the globe and their current go-to label for cool denim is J Brand. Ashley Greene was recently spotted in their dark pencil-leg style tucked into boots, while Kristen Stewart paired their skinnier style in ghost with edgy oxfords. Even the boys are getting involved—Taylor Lautner dressed up J Brand Denim Co.'s slim straight-leg jean in outlaw with a vest for a red carpet appearance." The assumption is that if the stars are wearing it, it must be good. However, given the fact that celebrities can afford more expensive clothing than the average moviegoing fan, Hollywood fashion magazines like *InStyle* provide an easy alternative for advertising designer jeans that run close to $200.

The second option, to actually dress like the characters in the film, is also possible. Asked about clothing in the film, *Twilight's* costume designer Wendy Chuck reveals that most of the costumes came from discount shops like Loehmann's, Nordstrom Rack, Internet outlets, and local Portland, Oregon, shops due to budgetary restraints, although she admits that the one "high-end item was Edward's Gucci jacket for the prom."[34] In the same article, Chuck elaborates on each main character's style, which means listing a series of name brands for each actor. For instance, Edward's style "is formed by a mix of American Apparel T-shirts, jackets from G-Star, H&M shirts, Chimala jeans, and A-life sneakers or vintage boots."[35] She claims: "I used a lot from G-Star for Jasper, he's wearing a G-star jacket and Levi's and always has Western boots on." *New Moon's* costume designer Tish Monaghan tells *Entertainment Weekly* that the wolves' clothes came mainly from Levi's, American Eagle, Old Navy, and Wal-Mart, and Jacob's T-shirts from The Gap, Banana Republic, American Apparel, Levi's.[36] While technically these affordable wolf items from widely accessible lower-end stores are not part of the ever-elusive vampire style, publicizing the retailers used on-set has been a successful way of permitting the characters' and actors' down-to-earthiness while still stimulating the fans' need to buy.

The contrast between vampire fashion as reported by popular media and Stewart and Pattinson's noncommittal attitude toward fashion demonstrate that in the contemporary moment of advanced consumer capitalism, marketers have carefully constructed a direct connection between the film actors and their onscreen roles in order to appeal to consumer-fans. This connection relies on the consumer's intersecting desires to be able to afford fashionable clothing and to dress like celebrities; the latter, which arises from the privilege, or at least illusion of privilege, of being free from economic constraints, a characteristic shared by celebrities and vampires alike. And the concept of "vampire fashion," rather than being a completely ambiguous or empty label, has instead been strategically used by the fashion industry and popular media to encompass a wide range of contradictory clothing styles. The *Twilight* series is unique in being the primary force behind this trend, yet just based on the novels or films alone, the idea of vampire fashion remains deliberately hazy. Bella's tomboyish style is offset by her insecurity and incessant desire to please Edward, just as Edward's tastefully expensive clothing is tempered by his professed disgust at wastefully ostentatious Alice. By viewing the public personae presented by actors Stewart, Pattinson, and even Lautner, in popular media in conjunction with the texts, however, we can see how the conflation of fictional character and celebrity profile works in favor of fashion marketing's appeal to fans. For the new breed of calculating consumer, Kristen Stewart and Robert Pattinson's fashion sense, or self-glorified lack thereof, is even more appealing than Bella's and Edward's reluctance to waste money on the latest must-haves: celebrities who are too cool (and too cheap) to care about fashion wear these brands, so you should too.

Notes

1. Roland Barthes, *The Fashion System*, Trans. Matthew Ward and Richard Howard (Berkeley: University of California Press, 1990. Print), xi.
2. Ibid., 261.
3. Patrick Goldstein, "'The Twilight Saga' puts Summit in the mega-franchise business," *The Los Angeles Times*, "The Big Picture" Blog, November 24, 2009, Web. NP.
4. Todd Martens, "'Twilight Saga: New Moon' and its vampy sounds," *The Los Angeles Times* "Hero Complex" Blog, October 26, 2009, Web. NP.
5. Brooks Barnes, "Media Vampires Beware," *The New York Times* (November 13, 2009. Print), AR1.
6. Stephenie Meyer, *New Moon* (New York: Little, Brown and Company, 2006. Print), 492.
7. Ruth La Ferla, "A Trend With Teeth," *The New York Times* (July 1, 2009. Print), E1.
8. Mark Ellwood, "Vampire chic: Gothic glamour rules, from fashion to makeup," *New York Daily News*, November 22, 2008, Web, NP, and "Top 10 fashion moments of 2008," *The Los Angeles Times*, Web, NP.
9. La Ferla, "A Trend With Teeth."
10. Mark Ellwood, "Vampire chic: Gothic glamour rules, from fashion to makeup," *New York Daily News* (November 22, 2008, Web), NP.
11. Barnes, "Media Vampires Beware."
12. Melissa Magsaysay, "Oh, that seductive 'Twilight' merchandise," *The Los Angeles Times*, (November 15, 2009. Print), A4.
13. Stephenie Meyer, *Twilight* (New York: Little, Brown and Company, 2005. Print), 18.
14. Ibid., 14.
15. Ibid., 154.
16. Ibid., 318.
17. Stephenie Meyer, *Eclipse*, (New York: Little, Brown and Company, 2007. Print), 612.
18. Ibid., 614.
19. Stephenie Meyer, *Breaking Dawn*, (New York: Little, Brown and Company, 2008. Print), 100.
20. Ibid., 488.
21. Ibid., 273.
22. Ibid., 408–409.

23. Ibid., 409.

24. Ibid., 409.

25. Ibid., 488.

26. Meyer, *Eclipse*, 215.

27. Ibid., 216.

28. Andi Teran, "A Spotlight on Twilight at the Apple Store," *Vanity Fair* (November 4, 2008. Web), NP.

29. Cassandra Handley, "Q&A: *Twilight's* Robert Pattinson," *Vanity Fair* (November 5, 2008. Web), NP.

30. Laura Brown, "Robert Pattinson and Kristen Stewart's Wild Ride," *Harper's Bazaar* (November 2009. Web), NP.

31. Evgenia Peretz, "*Twilight's* Hot Gleaming," *Vanity Fair* (December 2009. Web), NP.

32. Brown, "Robert Pattinson and Kristen Stewart's Wild Ride."

33. "Kristen Stewart Steals Bella's Style," *InStyle*, June 1, 2009, Web, NP.

34. "*Twilight* Fashion," *InStyle*, Web, NP. http://www.instyle.com/instyle/package/general/photos/0,,20241149_20231628_20536039,00.html

35. "*Twilight* Fashion," *InStyle*, Web, NP. http://www.instyle.com/instyle/package/general/photos/0,,20241149_20231628_20523541,00.html

36. Mandi Bierly, "'New Moon' costume designer Tish Monaghan on Edward's suit and Jacob's cut-offs," *Entertainment Weekly* (November 28, 2009. Web), NP.

CHAPTER 14

Trailing in Jonathan Harker's Shadow: Bella as Modern-Day Ethnographer in Meyer's *Twilight* Novels

Joo Ok Kim and Giselle Liza Anatol

> It was on the dark side of twilight when we got to [our destination]...Being practically on the frontier...it has had a very stormy existence, and it certainly shows marks of it.
>
> —Bram Stoker, *Dracula*[1]

Stephenie Meyer's *Twilight* saga situates itself within a tradition of vampire narratives, or a "vampire canon," constituted by a wide range of texts including novels like Bram Stoker's *Dracula* (1897) and films like the South Korean *Thirst* (2009). Meyer's series consequently invites comparisons to the existing body of work, while creating its own disruptions and possibilities within that larger body. In this chapter, we trace some of the racial and ethnic discourses in the *Twilight* series. We will demonstrate how, much like Stoker's Jonathan Harker, Isabella Swan operates as a type of ethnographer—she is almost scientific in her observations of the vampire and werewolf cultures in which she finds herself immersed, and she is compelled by the Pacific Northwest like Harker is drawn into the mysterious "East"—both of which are problematically rendered as nearly mystical, especially in the depiction of Native/native peoples.

Ethnography, a branch of cultural anthropology, grounds itself on the principle of gaining a holistic picture of the culture being studied—not just recording descriptions of the physical environment in which a people live (landscape, weather, types of

_, etc.), but ways of life, past and present; the range of people's interactions ₁n one another—formal and informal, civic, familial; their spiritual practices; their beliefs; etc. The *Oxford English Dictionary*'s definition of ethnography—"the scientific description of nations or races of men, with their customs, habits, and points of difference"—suggests objectivity in its allusion to science, but simultaneously hints at how bias often enters the narrative: the observed culture is approached as one of difference from the "normal," "standard" culture of the observer.

The power relations implicit in *Twilight* as an ethnographic work are complicated. Edward Cullen's extrahuman vampiric power is the ability to conduct surveillance on the humans around him. He gains access to all this knowledge because he can read minds. Bella alone is inaccessible to him, which informs part of his attraction to her. More interesting for our argument here, however, is that because Edward cannot "read" Bella's mind or the narratives she spins for herself, she is ideally positioned to enact the role of an ethnographer. She has exclusive outsider access to communities of vampires and werewolves, which she observes and reports to the saga's readers.

Ethnography has long been considered the purview of European male writers—those privileged enough to be educated, moneyed enough to travel, and free to leave the domestic space. As Joan Pau Rubiés explains:

> Although the emergence of an academic discourse based on comparison, classification, and historical lineage called ethnology is a nineteenth-century phenomenon, in reality both ethnography and ethnology existed within the humanistic disciplines of early modern Europe in the primary forms of travel writing, cosmography, and history, which often informed specific debates—about the capabilities and origins of the American Indians, the definition of "natural man," the influence of climate on national characteristics, or the existence of stages in the history of civilisation.[2]

Although seemingly powerless when it comes to fighting off vampiric attacks, Bella has progressed far beyond the Victorian-era "Angel in the House" and occupies positions inaccessible to both Edward and Jacob, who both function in different ways as racialized "others." As American Indian subjects, Jacob and the rest of the Quileute characters in Meyer's novels appear sequestered on the La Push Reservation. And although Edward and his family are white and wealthy, their secret identity as vampires suggests a type of passing narrative, where characters attempt to blend into the dominant culture despite possessing the blood of another race.[3] Bella is—at least until her vampiric transformation—a heteronormative white human and citizen, who unquestioningly belongs to the nation-state, if not to Forks. In this way, the novel opens up interrogations of the relationships between power, dominance, subjugation, and sovereignty.

THE ETHNOGRAPHIC IMPULSE IN STOKER'S *DRACULA*

Because many people are unfamiliar with the wide array of vampire novels and short stories that preceded *Dracula*, as well as the myriad vampire tales from cultures outside of Europe, Bram Stoker typically receives the majority of credit for developing the paradigmatic bloodsucker: an aristocratic man who hails from Transylvania, possesses the ability to transform into a bat, and shows vulnerability to garlic and crosses.[4] Yet all of the eighteenth- to late nineteenth-century vampire texts, from Heinrich Ossenfelder's "Der Vampyre" (1748) to Rudyard Kipling's "The Vampire" (1897), reveal cultural attitudes not only about evil and superstition, but also about the social and political issues of the time, be it nationalism, evolution, disease, power, and/or gender and sexuality. Thus, although Stoker's novel is often approached as a universalist "classic," it cannot truly be separated from its historical and cultural contexts—details and discourses that are hinged on considerations of race and gender.

The Romantic writers of the late eighteenth to the mid-nineteenth century were largely opposed to slavery, for example, and late eighteenth-century travel texts tended toward sentimentality in their representations of exchanges between British explor*er*/ Self and foreign explor*ed*/"Other."[5] These early imperialists can be understood as depicting "the Other's voices in dialogue with the voices of the self and tender[ing] the Other some credibility and equality."[6] However, as time wore on, an increasingly self-centered trend developed: Patrick Brantlinger describes a set of nineteenth-century British writing in which authors such as Carlyle and Dickens condemn harsh treatment of the poor but do not express the same attitudes toward the racially oppressed. From the eighteenth to the nineteenth centuries, "blame" shifted from the barbaric slave owner, who exploited the African slave, to the brutal and savage African who required European salvation. British explorers traveling to Africa from the late 1850s onward—among them Speke and Burton, Livingstone and Stanley—provided compelling narratives of this sort for the residents back home: Henry Stanley's *In Darkest Africa*, for example—published seven years before Stoker's *Dracula*—sold more than 150,000 copies in English and was identified as "read more universally and with deeper interest than any other publication of [1890]."[7] Brantlinger argues, "such accounts of African exploration exerted an incalculable influence on British culture and the course of modern history."[8] One could easily surmise that Stoker—whose text we explore here in detail simply because it is the most widely read—would have been influenced by these narratives and perspectives.

Africa was not the only landscape that British subjects viewed as wild and foreboding yet worthy of further study. Numerous critics have commented on the anxiety created by Dracula's movement from the "barbaric" East to the "civilized" West. Bram Dijsktra reads Stoker's novel as Victorian England's obsession with the "forces of bestiality and degeneration" that threatened British evolutionary progress. He argues that evidence of Dracula's "unevolved" state—his hairiness, his bestial blood drinking, the location of his castle—and his Semitic facial features—the "beaky nose" black moustache and pointed beard—all render him as "emphatically Eastern European."[9] Auerbach and Skal also mention the "penetration of England by aliens" in the 1880s: groups of immigrants to the nation, especially Jewish settlers, meant that "the boundaries of England and Englishness became less clear-cult, [and] racial purity became a new fetish."[10] In the novel itself, the vampire hunters' mission is linked with the Christian Crusades. Van Helsing proclaims, "we go out as the old knights of the Cross to redeem more. Like them we shall travel towards the sunrise."[11] The language of glorious West and barbarous East is clearly reinforced.

For Stoker's character Jonathan Harker, the displacement of western European civilizing forces begins when he leaves Munich on his travels to Dracula's Transylvanian homeland. A punctual man, he notes that his train should have arrived in Vienna at precisely 6:46, but was an hour late.[12] In Buda-Pesth, he feels as though "we were leaving the West and entering the East"[13]—a sensation that suggests a physical border between the hemispheres, the cultures, the people. And Jonathan is about to delve even farther into the interior: business takes him to "the extreme east of the country...one of the wildest and least known portions of Europe."[14] And Jonathan's narrative abounds in quasiethnographic descriptions of the foods he eats, how they are prepared, and the precise names of the dishes. "I had for dinner [...] a chicken done up some way with red pepper, which was very good but thirsty. (*Mem.*, get recipe for Mina.) I asked the waiter, and he said it was called 'paprika hendl'...."[15] His attentions to food serve two functions: to situate the exotic—that is, inferior—nature of "other" cuisines in a normative hierarchy, and to foreshadow the fact that Eastern Europeans may be so "backward" in their consumption practices as to include blood-drinking at the far edge of civilization.

Like Burton, who casts the African peoples he recounts in his 1861 *The Lake Regions of Central Africa* as childish, idle, morally deficient, and superstitious, Jonathan identifies Dracula's homeland as harboring "every known superstition in the world."[16] The population does not seem aware of advances in medicine, as the people are plagued by conditions not typically seen in England's capital: "we passed Cszeks and Slovaks, all in picturesque attire, but I noticed that goitre was painfully prevalent."[17] Jonathan further identifies the population of Saxons, Wallachs, Magyars, and Szekelys as "savages," with the Slovaks being "more barbarian than the rest." Interestingly, however, he quickly suppresses any fears that might arise out of his description: "They are, however, I am told, very harmless and rather wanting in natural self-assertion."[18] These strange foreigners might be uncivilized, but they are no match for the superior British agent. Jonathan, with his imperialist eye, notes that the Transylvanian population would be easily conquerable by more "assertive" nations—Great Britain being a prime example.[19]

Whereas the geographical, nationalistic, missionary, and/or economic goals of the writer-explorers examined by Brantlinger, Pratt, and others may not exactly apply in Jonathan's case, his visit to Castle Dracula ends up in the same way: "[the] goal...turns out to include sheer survival and the return home, to the regions of light."[20] England is his cultural light and Mina is his romantic light; ironically, Lucy, whose name literally means light, turns out to be one that dims before his return to Britain. The other male protagonists who fight valiantly to save her help to reinforce the imperialist agenda of the novel. In a letter to Arthur Holmwood, Lucy's fiancé, the American Quincey Morris identifies Jack Seward as "our old pal at the Korea"—a contested imperial site in the 1890s, when Britain and the United States attempted to halt Japan's cornering of trade markets.[21] Stoker's threesome has also shared adventures in the prairies—ostensibly in the States, during the period of Manifest Destiny—as well as in the Marquesas Islands in the South Pacific and on the shores of Lake Titicaca. In other words, they have the money to travel to North America, Asia, and South America, but also an imperialist interest in the "unspoiled" regions of the world. At one point in the novel, Jonathan attacks Dracula with "his great Kukri knife," a weapon used by the Gurkhas of Nepal, who were allies of the British army in their conquest of India.[22] Renfield, one of Dr. Seward's mental patients, alleges that Arthur's father was "the inventor of a burnt rum punch"—a likely allusion to the British colonial presence in the "West Indies"—and also extols the official statehood of Texas, Quincey's home territory, and the Monroe Doctrine.[23] This praise of US westward expansion echoes with his fanatical desire for Dracula's invasion of western Europe.[24] The juxtaposition poses both as threatening, but this might just be Stoker's point: the patient cannot distinguish "good" from "evil," and Stoker's apparent admiration of US ingenuity and action—Quincey often moves and acts when the other men are simply standing and speaking—suggests that he admires Americans rather than condemning them.

Critic Talia Schaffer points out that Stoker's narrative can be read as one of "the first epidemiological horror novels," tied to late nineteenth-century fears of infectious diseases like syphilis and the concurrent discovery of germs.[25] As a demon in the shape of a man, however, Dracula reads much more like the threatening foreigner who will "batten on the helpless" in attempts to conquer a new land.[26] Terror arises from his practice of sucking blood—his foreign habits—but that is not the only reason. Everyday citizens are unable to *see* the source of danger—Dracula confesses to Jonathan that he wants to be "like the rest, so that no man stops if he sees me, or pause in his speaking if he hear my words, to say, 'Ha, ha! a stranger!' "[27] Stoker hints at the threat of an assimilation that is too perfect: it does not allow easy distinctions between those who "belong" to the nation and those who do not.

Stephen Arata lays out how Dracula's vampirism is "interwoven with his status as a conqueror and invader"; Stoker links the vampire to racial anxieties precipitated by the workings of empire, especially its imminent collapse. In other words, the core of terror in *Dracula* resides in the fact that the crumbling of British civilization is not generated by the invasion of foreigners, but rather that the bodies of Others massing inside England's boundaries are the result of the initial imperial move outward. Thus, British expansion leads to its own demise. Further, Dracula does not attack and kill, but rather "appropriates and transforms" his victims: "Dracula imperils not simply his victims' personal identities, but also their cultural, political, and racial selves." Thus, despite resistance to the lure of the Other, perhaps best signified in the scene of Mina's symbolic rape by Dracula, "one literally 'goes native' by becoming a vampire oneself."[28] While this is not the immediate threat in Meyer's series—the plot is designed so that readers *want* Bella to "go native" and succumb to the lure of the vampire—Edward and his kind are othered nonetheless. Part of what seems to make them more attractive than the werewolves is that they have more fully assimilated the "human" (in other words, dominant culture's) values, material aspirations, and social behaviors.

THE INTERSECTION OF RACE AND GENDER IN *DRACULA*

Besides generating anxieties about the racial and cultural boundaries of the nation, the late nineteenth century also brought about crises in the definitions of "femininity." New modes of female subjectivity and the rise of the "New Woman" were partly responsible for the depictions of vampiric women, both on and off the pages of contemporary fiction. Independent *and* sexualized, the New Woman was a reaction against Victorian sensibilities. As Mina proclaims in Stoker's text, however: "Some of the 'New Woman' writers will some day start an idea that men and women should be allowed to see each other asleep before proposing or accepting. But I suppose the New Woman won't condescend in future to accept; she will do the proposing herself."[29] Mina's attitude is telling: although she once entered the working world as a schoolteacher, and is now prepared to support herself financially through her typing and shorthand skills, as well as with her intellect and highly rational mind, she resists the label that generated so much anxiety in England and elsewhere.

For more socially conservative members of turn-of-the-century British society, intellectual and economic power were deemed to be the purview of middle and upper class white men. Sexual power and desire in women were also often regarded as dangerous. Thus, the character of Lucy in Stoker's novel becomes horrific when her "purity" transforms into "voluptuous wantonness."[30] Part of the horror that Lucy generates centers around her sucking children's blood rather than being a "naturally" maternal influence; perhaps more significantly, however, is that she desires to suck blood from *men*.[31] Her fangs allow her to pierce the skin, breaking the bodily boundary that is meant to contain, and she becomes the penetrator rather than the penetrated. Her staking can thus be construed as an act of purification, allowing her "holy calm"[32] despite its gruesome violence, which invokes an active male sexuality that punishes the demonic woman for straying from established sexual roles.[33] The policing of Lucy's sexuality by all three of her suitors as well as Van Helsing and Mina reveals the strict regulation and obsessive construction of normative western bourgeois womanhood.

While considering how Lucy is cast as troubling the boundaries of sexuality, one must also examine how Stoker employs racial discourses to further complicate her character: Lucy is repeatedly represented in conjunction with another fraught literary character—Shakespeare's Othello. In one of Stoker's numerous references to Shakespeare throughout the novel, Lucy writes of her encounter with Quincey Morris: "I sympathize with poor Desdemona when she had such a dangerous stream poured in her ear, even by a black man."[34] The anxieties surrounding Lucy's dangerous sexuality are thus inseparably linked to the hint of miscegenation, even as Lucy is literally of "mixed blood," receiving blood from all of her suitors and Van Helsing during the course of her transformation into vampire. Lucy's self-alignment with Desdemona in a letter describing the intents of her suitors suggests that questions about gender, sexuality, and the construction of the "universal" bourgeois woman are inextricable from the racializing forces of the British and American empires.

That the racial and gendered intersections between *Dracula* and *Twilight*—written more than a century later—similarly designate certain participants in British and American empires as "civil" and others as "monstrous" or "savage" suggests the ongoing power of the vampire genre to influence readers' perceptions of nation and national belonging.

TWILIGHT AND THE CAPTIVITY NARRATIVE

The imbrications of gender, sexuality, race, and empire are certainly echoed in the *Twilight* series as Meyer recycles the stereotypical images of American Indians, especially in the second book of the series, *New Moon*. In this novel, Sam Uley finds Bella in distress in the forest after Edward leaves her. As Sam carries her home, Bella thinks:

"I hung there, limp, as he loped swiftly through the wet forest. Some part of me knew this should upset me—being carried away by a stranger. But there was nothing left in me to upset."[35] This passage contains resonances of early captivity narratives, fitting the theme of the "civilized" white woman taken prisoner by an "uncivilized" American Indian man. By describing Sam as loping, Bella/Meyer evokes thoughts of animal traits as much as human ones. Readers familiar with captivity narratives might recall Mary Rowlandson's 1682 "Soveraignty & Goodness of God...," which likens indigenous peoples to wolves, "hell-hounds, roaring," "barbarous creatures," and "ravenous beasts."[36]

This scene in *New Moon* relies on not just one specific narrative, but rather isolates a reoccurring theme from an entire genre that does the tactical work of establishing the inferiority of Indians and justifying colonialism. And thus, although she is two centuries away from the Western edge of the American "wilderness" or frontier—very similar to the edge of the frontier mentioned by Jonathan Harker in *Dracula* and cited in the epigraph of this chapter—Bella maintains the trope of American Indian lowliness and European/American superiority and reinforces her own racial dominance. She appears very much like the early captives who claimed power despite the apparent *disempowerment* of being carried away.

More fitting, perhaps, is a connection to be made between the *Twilight* series and popular historical romance novels—an entire subgenre of which has evolved from American captivity narratives. Scholar Kate McCafferty notes that "[t]he basic story formula is as follows: young, beautiful, white, affluent woman meets young, handsome, Native American man. Eighty percent of the time, players meet along border spaces.... All women make their erotic interests known to the chosen Native male, initiating and authorizing his sexual pursuit, if not directly pursuing him," suggestive of Bella's employment of her own sexuality for the purpose of gathering Quileute legends from Jacob, discussed further below.[37] Meyer restakes a variation of the captivity narrative romance novel in order to stage longstanding fantasies in American literature between white women and indigenous men. In this way, her representations are captive to narrative forms and conventions that continue to erase historical violence.

STUDYING THE QUILEUTES AND THE CULLENS: BELLA AS ETHNOGRAPHER

To return to our earlier assertion: the power relations implicit in ethnographic work are complex, and thus, although Bella might be interpreted as disempowered along gender lines, she definitely occupies a superior racial position to both Jacob (literally) and Edward (figuratively). In her ethnographic role, Bella constructs as much as she "discovers" their otherness, firmly within the tradition of Western imperial and colonial ethnographic methods. Bella the Discoverer is evident in *Eclipse*. Worried that the other guests at a La Push bonfire will scorn her for her close affiliation with the Cullens and romantic involvement with Edward, she expresses anxiety about her outsider status: "Would they be angry with Jacob for inviting me? Would I ruin the party?" She is greeted warmly, however, by male and female, old and young: Billy Black, Old Quil, and Sue Clearwater are present; the adolescent Quil jumps up to give her a kiss on the cheek; Sam's girlfriend Emily squeezes her hand. "I was treated like someone who belonged"—not simply to a party on the reservation, but a gathering of "La Push's most secret society." Apparently, she is not only the first non-Quileute allowed to hear "the stories of how we [wolf shape-shifters] came to be," but she is allowed to participate in this history lesson with Quil, Seth, and Leah—recent additions to the "pack."[38]

The session has an almost sacred quality—Billy serves as priest, Emily as scribe, and the listeners as the rapt and respectful congregation—and yet Bella is distinctly a witness, not a convert. She is afforded a unique space in the session—not only as a mediating force between white and First Nations peoples but between the tribe and vampires, albeit as a particularly situated, or subjective, rather than neutral, mediator who shapes readers' notions of the Quileutes. She is a translator of culture—an ethnographer.

As an ethnographer, Bella carefully un-/dis-covers the doubly Othered: the Quileute people as well as the werewolf shapeshifters. She also participates in the *construction* of otherness by reinforcing and materializing new stereotypes of American Indians. According to Ward Churchill, "not only is the Indian-in-American-literature genre alive and well, but [...] it has undergone something of an arithmetic progression, assuming a position occupying simultaneously both fictional and nonfictional frames of reference."[39] In Meyer's novels, Jacob occupies a semisovereign space on the reservation, but is made to be an exotic, foreign-seeming racialized minority. When the hot-tempered Paul flies at Emmett Cullen during the chase after Victoria, Jake defends his wolf-brother's actions to Bella: "The vampire was on our land."[40] The phrase echoes with the history of broken treaties and could be interpreted as an assertion of Native sovereignty; however, without that specific language, the racial, historical, and political elements are lost to most casual readers.[41]

This is not to say that Meyer's work functions as a social studies textbook, but rather that her representation of the Quileutes relies on and reinforces "the persistent image of the Indian as a sort of subhuman, animal-like creature who was a danger to hardy Anglo frontiersmen."[42] The author remixes her protagonist's ethnographic—and therefore putatively legitimate—approach to the Quileute nation with a longstanding US literary tradition of dangerous and often willful misrepresentation, obscuring the sediments of institutional, cultural, and economic violence that are the layered legacies of conquest and colonialism.

According to Churchill, systematic and institutionalized acts of brutality against indigenous populations are often "purged through a reconstitution of history as a series of tragic aberrations beginning and ending nowhere in time. The literal [...] events [...are also] voided by sentiment and false nostalgia rather than treated as parts of an ongoing process. The literal is rendered tenuously figurative, and then dismissed altogether."[43] Here Churchill refers to intentional acts of colonial aggression including series of forced removals, massacres, and wars that must be rendered as exceptions rather than as deliberate and sustained violence against indigenous populations; he identifies these acts as an essential part of US nation building. Meyer's series also participates in an ongoing reconstitution of history, not by cloaking massacres and cultural extermination with retroactive regret and tragedy, but by materializing the figure of the "noble savage" as

Jacob—an obscenely consumable cultural franchise that obscures the centuries-long process of colonization.

Indeed, when focused through the lens of comparative British and US empires, both *Dracula* and *Twilight* can be seen as employing the vampire genre to project the anxieties of "being practically on the frontier"—whether that be on the European or North American continent—onto the bodies of the natives, and at the same time ghosting the violent histories of conquest. In other words, if Dracula both reflects and constitutes certain racialized anxieties over both penetrating the boundaries of empire and the literal bodies compelled to migrate through or to the imperial "center," the *Twilight* series can be seen as playing a similar role in both reflecting and constituting the nationalist (and racialist) anxieties of the United States. One only needs to think of some Tea Party members' recent and unabashedly racist statements, Arizona's xenophobic SB 1070, and aspects of the larger debate on immigration and labor in the present moment in the United States.[44]

In her role as ethnographer, Bella activates existing epistemological frameworks that purport to know and to represent the Other, presuming her own subject position as normative. Bella charges gaps in her own knowledge not with *critical possibility*, which might mean taking advantage of her particular subject position to seek and create narratives that brush against ingrained ways of thinking about race, gender, and empire, but instead she recirculates historically powerful stereotypes. Her methodology consists of two flawed approaches: interviews with the vampire and the werewolf, and online research.

During her interview with Jacob, a process that extracts knowledge while simultaneously constructing Jacob as Other, Bella is very self-aware of her methodology, which intentionally directs her unskilled sexuality toward Jacob, as she "mak[es] an effort to smolder at him."[45] She explicitly capitalizes on Jacob's attraction to her in order to gain information that might reveal truths about Edward. In La Push, on Quileute land, after Bella acquires from Jacob the genealogy that binds the Quileutes to the existence of vampires, Jacob also self-consciously tests Bella's incredulity by asking, "So do you think we're a bunch of superstitious natives or what?"[46] Jacob's query calls attention to the very specific ways they are both situated, destabilizing the notion of a detached, objective ethnographer. Jacob's question reveals that he is an active agent in this interview, and that he is absolutely (and ironically) aware of the stereotypes reproduced in US mainstream culture. In the movie, however, Jacob is much less concerned with the possibility of Bella constructing the Quileute characters as "a bunch of superstitious natives," as he reassures her evident fear by telling her " 'It's just a story, Bella.' "

In *Twilight*, Bella attempts to distance herself from the "new age" bookstore, noting that "it wasn't what I was looking for. The windows were full of crystals, dreamcatchers, and books about spiritual healing. I didn't even go inside...There had to be a *normal* bookstore in town" (emphasis added).[47] Bella refuses association with the "fifty-year-old woman with long, gray hair worn straight down her back, clad in a dress right out of the sixties," in order to distinguish the "real" problems she is having with vampires from the "fake" narratives and tools sold in the bookstore.[48] However, the *Twilight* movie shows Bella Googling "Quileute legend," through which she finds the link for the "new age" bookstore. She takes the shop seriously, and purchases a book that provides much of the global historical information that authenticates vampires. The Internet and the New Age bookstore thus stand as equally credible resources in her search for reliable, accurate information.

Either way, Bella's investigation leads to her "discovery" of vampire legends—tellingly recorded in a published book—an act that traces back to Bram Stoker's depictions in *Dracula* of the overwhelming anxiety and obsession with ordering knowledge and recording truth. Stoker renders knowledge as distinct from memory, and fact as distinct from fiction. Knowledge is documented, codified, verifiable. Even before the Table of Contents, an anonymously penned statement (we later find the author to be Mina Harker) declares:

> How these papers have been placed in sequence will be made made [sic] manifest in the reading of them. All needless matters have been eliminated, so that a history almost at variance with the possibilities of later-day belief may stand forth as simple fact. There is throughout no statement of past things wherein memory may err [. . .].[49]

The reader *should* inquire exactly which elements were deleted, by whom, and upon what grounds, but the writer's insistence on the narrative as "history"—a set of written documents simply placed in order rather than crafted, reconsidered, revised, and rewritten—seems to preempt this line of questioning and establish objectivity and credibility. Like Bella in her acts of "discovery" and construction of information, the "sequencer" of the *Dracula* papers absents herself from a position of control. Similarly, when Jonathan Harker finally begins to articulate his suspicions in Castle Dracula, he writes in his diary, "Let me be prosaic so far as facts can be; it will help me to bear up, and imagination must not run riot with me."[50] Writing and facts will sustain him where imagination will tear him asunder. And again, later: "Let me begin with facts—bare, meager facts, *verified by books and figures*, and of which there can be no doubt. I must not confuse them with experiences which will have to rest on my own observation or my memory of them" (emphasis added).[51]

One might be reminded of Aro's words near the end of Meyer's *Twilight* series, when discussing the differences between the Quileute werewolves and the European Children of the Moon: "Though the [former] creatures think of themselves as werewolves, they are not. The more accurate name for them would be shape-shifters. The choice of a wolf form was purely chance."[52] He attempts to control the Quileutes' identity—their self-representation and their perception by others—through the control of discourse. Similarly, Meyer's novels enact a form of control. Although obviously fiction, they are tangible texts holding written accounts of Quileute and vampire legends. For many readers, they thus have the potential to be read interchangeably with fact.

As a contemporary ethnographer, Bella does have some consciousness of the separate cultural identities of different Indian nations. She notices that Sam "made a brief comment in an unfamiliar, liquid language—I could only be positive that it wasn't French or Spanish, but I guessed that it was Quileute."[53] Her "standard" is European languages—she has been either taught or exposed to English, French, and Spanish—but she knows enough to distinguish (in her mind, if not in her ear) between the language of Quileutes as opposed to Iroquois or Navajo. However, in many other ways, she (and Meyer) constructs all of the Indigenous characters as being exactly the same. The "pack" is a homogenous group, physically indistinguishable from each other. Bella states, "they reminded me of brothers, quadruplets. Something about the way they moved almost in synchronization to stand across the road from us, the way they all had the same long, round muscles under the same red-brown skin, the same cropped black hair, and the way their expressions altered at exactly the same moment."[54]

Furthermore, Bella repeatedly comments on the "exotic" features of the Quileute, marking and fetishizing racial difference within an operative construct of whiteness as normative.[55] This constitutes an odd move of making indigenous into "foreign," displacing ongoing indigenous erasure to an association that is absolutely "non-native": white Americans are shifted to the privileged space, coming to occupy the phenotypic, geographical, and cultural claims of belonging to North America.

Although he is othered in ancillary ways, Edward is consistently described in terms of his whiteness, which in most cases reinforces the beauty ideals of the dominant culture since he is constantly portrayed as alluring rather than eerie or frightening. In *Eclipse,* his complexion and facial features are linked to ancient Greco-Roman sculptures: Bella comments, "My eyes traced over his pale white features: [. . .] the straight line of his nose, the sharp angle of his cheekbones, the smooth marble span of his forehead."[56] In *Breaking Dawn,* she swoons, "I never got over the shock of how *perfect* his body was—*white*, cool, and polished as marble" (emphasis added).[57]

Furthermore, Meyer constantly employs imagery of precious and semiprecious stones and metals to heighten the sense of allure of the vampires. Edward's hair is repeatedly described in terms of its "bronze" hue, as is his daughter Renesmee's.[58] Jasper's "honey hair [appears] *silver* in the weak moonlight," while Rosalie's "*golden* hair piled up in a soft *crown* on top of her head," which connotes wealth and royalty.[59] Edward's eyes are depicted as "liquid gold," "burning gold," and "jewel-like"; similarly, Carlisle possesses "golden eyes, almost the exact shade of his fair hair."[60] And lest the reader believe that this imagery comes from Bella's idealization of Edward and his family, Meyer reveals that Jake, too, can see the golden hues of the vampire's eyes. He observes Esme's "wide, dark gold eyes on my face" and Alice's "gold eyes wide and burning."[61]

And so, when Bella laments to Edward and Jake, "Why can't you both just be civilized?"[62] the long history of American Indian stereotypes means there are different implications in this statement for the white-skinned vampire than there are for the Quileute shapeshifter. At the same time, however, Edward's coloring, and that of the rest of the Cullens, always sets them apart. Because their identity can be read through their *unnaturally* white skin color, they serve as members of a metaphorical Other race. This again places Bella in a position of authority in contrast to the vampires— one that readers focused solely on the gender implications of the novels might be inclined to overlook.

One would hope that in the three hundred years since the publication of the original captivity narratives and the nearly two hundred years since the most prominent examples ethnographic travel writings from the British empire, racial dynamics might have changed more drastically than is evident in the *Twilight* series. The novels serve not only to perpetuate the dominant social order, but they also contain the historical and cultural reverberations of empire, and ongoing expressions of global capitalist violence. We have seen the continuities, and so must persist at interrogating the stakes.

NOTES

1. Bram Stoker, *Dracula,* eds. Nina Auerbach and David J. Skal (New York: W.W. Norton, 1997. Print), 11.
2. Joan Pau Rubiés, "Travel Writing and Ethnography," *The Cambridge Companion to Travel Writing.* Eds. Peter Hulme and Tim Youngs. (New York: Cambridge University Press, 2002. Print), 243.
3. For those unfamiliar with passing narratives, a classic example would be Nella Larsen's Harlem Renaissance novella, *Passing* (1929).
4. In fact, in the same year that Stoker published *Dracula,* Rudyard Kipling published "The Vampire" and Florence Marryat published *The Blood of the Vampire.*
5. Cultural critic Mary Louise Pratt cites the work of Mungo Park and John Stedman as examples of the former ideology. Park authored *Travels in the Interior Districts of Africa* (1799), which documented his mission to locate the Niger River and assess its potential as a trade route. Stedman travelled to the Caribbean in the 1770s to help quell slave insurrections in the Dutch colony of Surinam. His exploits—military, cultural, and sexual—are detailed in *Narrative of a Five Years Expedition Against the Revolted Negroes of Surinam.* Pratt, "Scratches on the Face of the Country; or, What Mr. Barrow Saw in the Land of the Bushmen," in *"Race," Writing, and Difference,* eds. Henry Louis Gates, Jr. and Kwame Anthony Appiah (Chicago, IL: University of Chicago Press, 1985, 1986): 138–62.
6. Pratt, 151.
7. Brantlinger, 195, quoting M.E. Chamberlain's *The Scramble for Africa* [1974]. Patrick Brantlinger, "Victorians and Africans: The Genealogy of the Myth of the Dark Continent," in *"Race," Writing, and Difference,* eds. Henry Louis Gates, Jr. and Kwame Anthony Appiah (Chicago, IL: University of Chicago Press, 1985, 1986): 185–222.
8. Brantlinger, 195.
9. Bram Dijsktra, "Dracula's Backlash." In Bram Stoker's *Dracula, A Norton Critical Edition,* eds. Nina Auerbach and David J. Skal (New York: Norton, 1997), 460.
10. Auerbach and Skal, xi. Joseph Valente, on the other hand, suggests that the anxiety about Eastern European invasion can be read in tandem with feelings about the colonization of Ireland. Stoker's mixed ethnicity (his father was Anglo and his mother, Celtic) resulted in an uneasy identification with both "conquering and a conquered race, a ruling and a subject people, an imperial and an occupied nation" (4). According to Valente, the Eastern threat could represent *both* Transylvania/Eastern Europe *and* England; the invaded Western space would then relate both to England and to Ireland. Joseph Valente, *Dracula's Crypt: Bram Stoker, Irishness, and the Question of Blood* (Urbana: University of Illinois Press, 2002).
11. Stoker, 278.
12. In Dracula's castle in the "far" east, he completely loses his sense of time.
13. Stoker, 9.
14. Stoker, 10. This description resembles Joseph Conrad's depictions of the wilds of Africa—the "heart of darkness" that holds the power to corrupt Mr. Kurtz. Like Kurtz, Jonathan also appears to be morally corrupted by his contact with Dracula and thus "go native": he adopts Dracula's nocturnal schedule, scales the castle walls, and almost submits to the vampiric women.

15. Stoker, 9.
16. Stoker, 10.
17. Stoker, 15.
18. Stoker, 11.
19. Jonathan's language is his power: using Foucault's notions of discourse as power and the potential of rhetoric not only to instigate but actually commit acts of extreme violence, one can easily see Brantlinger's point that "Victorian imperialism both created and was in part created by a growing monopoly on discourse" (217).
20. Brantlinger, 195.
21. Stoker, 62. Auerbach and Skal call Korea "[a]n imperialist hot spot" (62, fn6).
22. Stoker, 266; Auerbach and Skal, 266, fn4.
23. Stoker, 215.
24. Even *within* in England, Dracula is seen moving ever westward; Seward sees a bat "flapping…to the west" (103) and Quincey also observes a westward-flying bat (250).
25. Talia Schaffer, "'A Wild Desire Took Me': The Homoerotic History of Dracula." In Bram Stoker's *Dracula: A Norton Critical Edition*, eds. Nina Auerbach and David J. Skal (New York: Norton, 1997), 480.
26. Stoker, 54.
27. Stoker, 26.
28. Arata, 465. Stephen D. Arata, "The Occidental Tourist: *Dracula* and the Anxiety of Reverse Colonization," *Victorian Studies* (Summer 1990). Reprinted in *Dracula: A Norton Critical Edition*. Eds. Nina Auerbach and David J. Skal (New York: W.W. Norton & Co., 1997): 462–70.
29. Stoker, 86–87.
30. Stoker, 187.
31. Auerbach claims that Stoker "gentrified female vampires," rendering them "monogamously heterosexual" for the first time. She demonstrates how much of the explicit eroticism of earlier vampire novels dissipated in Stoker's text, while the erotic anxiety grew. Nina Auerbach, "*Dracula:* A Vampire of Our Own." *Bloom's Modern Critical Interpretations: Bram Stoker's* Dracula. Ed. Harold Bloom (Philadelphia, PA: Chelsea House Publishers, 2003), 204.
32. Stoker, 192.
33. Marjorie Howes discusses the fear of women's sexuality, especially nonheteronormative expressions; Phyllis Roth argues that "for both the Victorians and twentieth century readers, much of the novel's great appeal derives from its hostility toward female sexuality" (411); Carol Senf and Margot Backus see Lucy's staking as a symbolic group rape; Christopher Craft asserts that monstrous women in the novel serve both to deflect anxiety regarding same-sex desire and to justify "a violent explusion of this deformed femininity" that dares to usurp the sexual power seen as the prerogative of men (448). Marjorie Howes, "The Mediation of the Feminine: Bisexuality, Homoerotic Desire, and Self-Expression in Bram Stoker's *Dracula,*" *Texas Literary Studies in Literature and Language* 30, no. 2 (Spring 1988): 104–20. Phyllis A. Roth, "Suddenly Sexual Women in Bram Stoker's *Dracula*" (1977), in Bram Stoker's *Dracula: A Norton Critical Edition*, eds. Nina Auerbach and David J. Skal (New York: Norton, 1997): 411–21. Carol A. Senf, "Dracula: The Unseen Face in the Mirror" (1979), in Bram Stoker's *Dracula*, eds. Auerbach and Skal, 421–31. Margot Gayle Backus, *The Gothic Family Romance: Heterosexuality, Child Sacrifice, and the Anglo-Irish Colonial Order* (Durham: Duke University Press, 1999). Christopher Craft, "'Kiss Me with Those Red Lips': Gender and Inversion in Bram Stoker's *Dracula*" (1984), in Bram Stoker's *Dracula*, eds. Auerbach and Skal, 444–59.
34. Stoker, 59.

35. Stephenie Meyer, *New Moon* (New York: Little, Brown, & Co., 2006), 76.

36. Mary Rowlandson, *The Sovereignty & Goodness of God, Together, with the Faithfulness of His Promises Displayed; Being a Narrative of the Captivity and Restoration of Mrs. Mary Rowlandson. Commended by the Second Addition Corrected and amended.* (1682).

37. Kate McCafferty, "Palimpsest of Desire: The Re-Emergence of the American Captivity Narrative as Pulp Romance," *Journal of Popular Culture* 27 (1994): 43–56.

38. Stephenie Meyer, *Eclipse* (New York: Little, Brown, & Co., 2007), 240, 241, and 243.

39. Ward Churchill, *Fantasies of the Master Race: Literature, Cinema and the Colonization of American Indians.* Ed. M. Annette Jaimes (Monroe, Maine: Common Courage Press, 1992. Print), 19.

40. Meyer, *Eclipse,* 106.

41. Similarly, when, during the bonfire, Billy notes that the Quileutes have survived over the centuries because of the "magic" in their blood (244), no mention is made of conflicts with European explorers or settlers. A vague reference to "others who coveted our land" is followed by the report of how "a larger tribe moved against us" (244–245), suggesting that it was other American Indian nations, not European Americans, who were the true antagonists. And when Jasper's backstory is introduced, set against the history of the U.S. Civil War, no mention is made is slavery or African Americans.

42. Churchill, 22.

43. Ibid., 37.

44. One documented incident of racist and homophobic slurs by Tea Party members: "A staffer for Rep. James Clyburn (D-S.C.) told reporters that Rep. Emanuel Cleaver (D-Mo.) had been spat on by a protestor. Rep. John Lewis (D-Ga.), a hero of the civil rights movement, was called a "ni--er." And Rep. Barney Frank (D-Mass.) was called a "faggot," as protestors shouted at him with deliberately lisp-y screams." Sam Stein, "Tea Party Protests: 'Ni**er,' 'Fa**ot' Shouted at Members of Congress." Huffingtonpost. com (March 20, 2010), Web. Accessed August 27, 2010. np. Arizona's SB 1070's use of "reasonable suspicion" to determine whether a person is undocumented encourages racial profiling as the method to ascertaining immigration status.

45. Stephenie Meyer, *Twilight* (New York: Little, Brown, & Co, 2005), 123. McCafferty notes in her work on captivity narrative romance novels that "[s]exuality is universally hetero, taking place between an experienced, proficient male and an eager but virginal female. Mutually ecstatic from the first, it leads to the Native man's monogamous bonding with the 'rare' and 'unique' female hero" (Macafferty, 47). Bella is repeatedly described as exceptional and "unique" throughout the series, which again resonates with the protagonists of historical romance novels.

46. Meyer, *Twilight,* 126.

47. Ibid., 156.

48. Ibid. Notably, however, the *Twilight* series has created a fascination with new trendy occult—one whose buyers often visit these selfsame New Age stores for their accoutrements. The saga thus has vast market appeal to a broad base of consumers.

49. Stoker, 5.

50. Stoker, 30.

51. Stoker, 35.

52. Stephenie Meyer, *Breaking Dawn* (New York: Little, Brown, & Co., 2008), 704.

53. Ibid., 264.

54. Meyer, *Moon,* 323.

55. Meyer exoticizes the darker complexioned members of the vampire world in disturbing ways as well. The Egyptians carry themselves with an air of mystery and "all looked so alike, with their midnight hair and olive-toned pallor, that they easily could

have passed for a biological family" (*Dawn* 609). Dark skinned, interchangeable, and inscrutable, they seem to have more in common with the Quileute shapeshifters than the Cullens. Comparatively, the vampire sisters from the Amazon are described as frighteningly wild and animalistic: the "ferine" trio (612) wears only animal pelts, and the repeated reference to their elongated bodies makes them seem more alien than the Cullen clan and their other vampire guests: Zafrina, Kachiri, and Senna possess "long arms and legs, long fingers, long black braids, and long faces with long noses" (612).

56. Meyer, *Eclipse*, 17.
57. Meyer, *Dawn*, 25.
58. Meyer, *Eclipse*, 17 and 224; *Dawn*, 438 and 529.
59. Meyer, *Dawn*, 29 and 42.
60. Meyer, *Eclipse*, 17 and 33; *Dawn*, 48; *Eclipse*, 232; *Dawn*, 33.
61. Meyer, *Dawn*, 283 and 349.
62. Meyer, *Eclipse*, 115.

CHAPTER 15

THE GREAT AMERICAN LOVE AFFAIR: INDIANS IN THE *TWILIGHT* SAGA

BRIANNA BURKE

> For most whites throughout the past five centuries, the Indian of imagination and ideology has been as real, perhaps more real, than the Native Americans of actual existence and contact.
>
> —Robert Berkhofer, *The White Man's Indian*

NOW A POP CULTURE SENSATION, Stephenie Meyer's *Twilight* saga has been praised as an innovative reimagining of the vampire genre, albeit one that panders to teenage girl fantasy. However, Meyer's portrayal of Indians is anything but inventive and relies on tired and well-worn stereotypes created about Native peoples since the landing of Columbus. Although Bella Swan is an atypical heroine, her two love interests—the Euro-American vampire Edward Cullen and the Indian/werewolf Jacob Black—are contrasting racial hypermasculine stereotypes. As millions of girls worldwide sigh over the impossibly gorgeous and endlessly sensitive Edward Cullen, Jacob Black presents an alternative to the artfully rich and carefully mannered vampire, embodying the space of the exoticized Other complete with warrior prowess, a bronze hard body, and glistening long black hair. Surrounded by teenage girls in a theater watching the newest movie installment of the *Twilight* series, *New Moon*, I heard both sighs and nervous giggles when Jacob Black (played by Taylor Lautner), in a moment of uncontrollable masculine concern for the wounded and conveniently accident-prone damsel-in-distress Bella, ripped off his shirt to tend to her bleeding head, leaving his ridiculously chiseled chest bare for full admiration. He and his Indian friends remain that way for much of the movie—chests bared—often dripping with rain, glistening and hot, tall, dark, and handsome temptations.

Gazing on the half-naked body of the exoticized Indian male is nothing new in American film or literature and Stephenie Meyer's novels are not unique in this regard. America has always been in love with the figure of the Indian who is both noble and savage, sensitive and a warrior, naturally beautiful and close to the earth in a way Euro-Americans long to be. In this chapter, I examine how Jacob conforms to American stereotypes of Indian men and then show how Meyer's characterization deviates from and embellishes this standard image. Although Meyer's depiction of Jacob may differ slightly from entrenched images of Indians, the new elements she includes serve the dominant ideology working to undermine Native sovereignty and cultural survival and reinforce preexisting stereotypes. Her reiterations irreparably damage the work Native peoples have done for centuries to overturn these harmful images, now entrenched for a whole new generation as "cool" and sexier than ever.

My use of the term "Indian," rather than "Native American" (or a tribal name, which is even more preferable) is purposeful, because although Stephenie Meyer uses an existing tribe in her novels—the Quileutes—her portrayal of them relies heavily on the longstanding American construction of Indianness, which lumps all Indigenous peoples into one category and erases cultural difference between nations.[1] "Indian" refers to the "profoundly contested space" of "'the white man's Indian,' which for the critical mass is *the* authentic representation" argue Clark and Powell.[2] Forged through the endless repetition of images and stereotypes, simulated Indianness becomes authentic, "more real than real" as if it "presupposes and precedes the real."[3] Packed into a tightly woven knit of interdependent symbols, such as buckskin and war paint, Indianness becomes a product that can be consumed and known, available for cooptation and inhabitation like a costume.

The construction of Indianness began with Columbus, persisted through the Boston Tea Party, and was used to create a distinctly *American* identity separate from Europe: Indians were what made America unique and they symbolized natural freedom and rights. However, after the American Revolution, Indians were used to define American identity through opposition and their image was codified as an uncivilized people whose condition justified conquest, removal, and assimilation policy. Although there are two versions of this stereotype, the Noble Savage and the Indian Princess, Meyer reiterates only the male version. This construction of the Indian is so ubiquitous in American culture that he is easily recognizable: he often rides a horse with a feather bonnet, understands nature, is anachronistic and culturally frozen in time, lives in a tipi and roams the plains looking for buffalo to hunt or white settlers to scalp. The Noble Savage has always contained a contradiction, thanks to the writings of Columbus, who portrayed the Native peoples he met as both kind and generous *and* savage and brutal,[4] and the figure became a fixture in the American collective imagination, reinforced time and again with each new generation. In the early 1900s, however, the iconographic Indian was renovated as the American public began to feel a little sympathy toward indigenous peoples now settled onto reservations and a new stereotype emerged—the Romantic Savage—that coincided with portrayals of the Noble Savage and persists today.

The Romantic Savage is a lost soul, caught between the pressures of civilization and tradition. He is passionate, *always* attractive, elegiac about his doomed people, and yet, still exotic, still at one with nature, and still—if threatened—capable of savage violence. This particular image of the Indian regained unprecedented popularity with late twentieth-century films like Kevin Costner's 1990 *Dances with Wolves* and Michael Mann's 1992 *The Last of the Mohicans,* and is now reinforced by the *Twilight* series.

Academics such as Leslie Fiedler, Roy Harvey Pierce, Fergus M. Bordewich, and Robert Berkhofer wrote the first wave of scholarship arguing that the Romantic Savage was created to serve national interests and persists because he remains a mirror of dominant society's anxieties and desires. Most importantly, this image eclipses the identities of real living Native peoples in the United States today; it is repeated so often that it is taken as the truth, as Robert Berkhofer notes in the epigraph at the beginning of this piece. This is the danger of Meyer's use of Indian characters in her novels: if this version of the Indian is "real," actual Native people become poor imitations and their continual domination justified. Their cultures (as they "once were," because they no longer exist in their "pure" forms) become singular—Indian *culture*—because all Native peoples are believed to be the same, and since they no longer practice their own culture, it is now the property of mainstream society. Indigenous people simply cease to exist, replaced by simulacra. In either case, the endless reiteration of the stereotype makes political exploitation possible and impedes the fight for rights and sovereignty.

Jacob's identity conforms to the stereotype of the Romantic Savage, shaped by the Enlightenment and the American Romance writers of the late eighteenth century. As Enlightenment thinkers chafed under what they considered the tyranny and oppression of baroque civilization, the life of Indian people—in supposed harmony with nature and theorized as living in a "pre-industrial state"—began to look more appealing. The stereotypes of Indians in this era were popularized and embellished in the novels of American writers such as Herman Melville, Nathaniel Hawthorne, and James Fenimore Cooper. In this figuration, the "primary task of the artists" of the era was to "evoke feelings of compassion, sentimentalism and romantic love as well as the lessons of nature, all enhanced through symbolism."[5] The Romantic Savage became the perfect symbol to evoke these emotions, because he "depended upon passion and impulse alone."[6] Jacob conforms exactly to this stereotype throughout the *Twilight* series. In *New Moon*, he relentlessly declares his affection for Bella and continues to pursue her well into *Breaking Dawn*, frequently claiming that she loves him, she just does not know it yet. Compared to Edward's inhuman emotional control, Jacob is more than just a hotheaded impulsive teenager, letting his emotions (or hormones) guide him: his passion literally changes him into an *animal*.

Jacob's ability to turn into a wolf contributes to the romantic stereotype in two ways. First, it reinforces the ideology that Indians live in harmony with nature and have a "natural" existence, as Berkhofer argues above. One only has to read the novels of James Fenimore Cooper to understand that Indians can see in the dark, walk through the forest without making a sound or disturbing a leaf (as Jacob frequently does in *New Moon, Eclipse*, and *Breaking Dawn*), and have an uncanny ability to understand natural world. In fact, Jacob and his Indian brethren are so close to nature that they can *transform into it*. As (were)wolves, they become part of nature itself, conforming to the laws of wolf behavior and pack mentality. Jacob, in particular, is closer to nature than the rest of his pack, since he leaves them for a while and literally lives in his wolf form, eventually becoming the Alpha male (although he is always the *Beta* in Bella's affections). In *Breaking Dawn*, Jacob acts like a fully feral animal when he hunts deer with Leah and rips the animal apart with his teeth. Meyer's version takes the stereotype of the "nature-loving Indian" to a whole new level, portraying Jacob as a part of nature itself and controlled by the natural laws of the animal kingdom.

Because Jacob often "phases" (like the moon, yet another nature metaphor to describe his behavior and a convenient reference to the titles of the novels), he is frequently half-naked throughout the series, again reinforcing the romantic stereotype while simultaneously updating it to conform more closely with the twentieth-century popular romance genre, which continues to endlessly fetishize Indian men on book covers and in Harlequin Romances.[7] Meyer, in *Eclipse* and *Breaking Dawn*, is careful to note that Jacob and his pack-mates often tie their shorts to their legs when changing forms so that they won't be incessantly naked, conforming their behavior to the strict religious sexual morality which dominates the series. At the same time, she also notes in *Breaking Dawn* that before Leah Clearwater joined the pack, the boys were frequently nude together, giving her teenage girl readers permission to imagine this very scenario. The films add to Meyer's fetishization of Indian men with visual reinforcement that equates Indians with nudity and prelapsarian fantasy. This is especially egregious in *New Moon*, where the male Native actors are seldom seen wearing anything other than tight shorts riding low on their hips. All of them are equally gorgeous, and all of them have perfectly sculpted forms, usually shot so that the viewer can see their bare chests and the very top of their jean shorts. None of them, however, are heartthrob candidates for the young viewers since none of them are fully realized characters. Taylor Lautner (Jacob Black) is portrayed similarly, but the camera pays special attention to his body and thus so do viewers, signaling that he is one of the two main love interests in the series. Jacob, too, is almost always half-naked, and usually dripping wet with rain, heightening his steamy portrayal.

In Peter van Lent's article on how popular culture romance novels portray Indian men, he writes:

> Most Native male characters are placed in a traditional setting, often close to nature. Nearly all of them are decent, good men. They are all shown as gentle and loving in one way or another, but they are all warriors at heart. To some degree each one of them is vulnerable...and finally, let us not forget the physical...the most immediately appealing quality that all these young men have is that they are very, very handsome.[8]

Jacob conforms to each portion of this stereotype. He is morally good, always taking Bella into consideration first, and then his fellow pack members, before himself. He is endlessly vulnerable because he loves too much, which forces him to return to Bella time and again even though she continually turns him away and thus makes him the object of desire—as well as pity—for viewers and readers. Despite his sensitive side, Jacob remains a virile fighter, taking center stage in the battle with Victoria and the "newborn" vampires at the end of *Eclipse* and becoming the ultimate Indian warrior of his tribe as he takes the position of Alpha wolf in *Breaking Dawn*. Finally, like all Indian warriors, he is not afraid to fight savagely and to the death to protect his love. All of this makes him endlessly romantic, but his heartthrob status is secured by Taylor Lautner's physical appearance, shot so that he appears much larger and more "masculine" than the Native actors in the film. There was a great deal of gossip about Taylor Lautner's new body prior to the film, since he was almost dropped from the cast of

New Moon for being too "slight" and had to "bulk up" into his current sculpted form in order to fit the image Meyer relies on of the virile Indian warrior and that readers, in turn, expect of a masculine hero.[9] Lautner's impressive physique is on continual display in the film and changed so drastically between the first and second installments that the characters are forced to remark upon the difference or it would seem absurd. When Bella sees Jacob for the first time in the beginning of *New Moon* she exclaims, "*Hello biceps.* You know, anabolic steroids are really bad for you."[10] Later, when Jacob lifts the motorcycle out of the back of her truck on his own, Bella again calls attention to Lautner's body with a statement of the obvious: "Jake, you're, like, *buff.*"[11]

Further, Jacob/Taylor Lautner has all the recognizable signifiers that mark him as the distinctly *Indian* warrior/hero seen both in Western films and in popular romance novels. Peter van Lent writes, "Native heroes all have glistening, coppery skin and long, raven-black hair . . . and they usually wear little more than a breechclout."[12] To give Meyer *some* credit, in both the film and in the book, Jacob wears more than a breech-cloth: he wears sweatpants and cut-off jeans, and his "tribal" tattoo (i.e., war paint). Yet Meyer never seems to miss an opportunity to remark on Jacob's hand-some, distinctly Indian qualities, usually in the form of commentary from Bella, who continuously notices Jacob's skin color and hair in *New Moon*, describing him as "russet-colored," having "red-brown skin" and long black hair like "satin curtains."[13] Bella thinks, "His skin was such a pretty color, it made me jealous," and remarks aloud, "Did you know, you're sort of beautiful?"[14] Repeatedly remarking on a person's skin color and how it marks them as "different" (even if that difference equates to attrac-tiveness) is usually considered racist, not exotic and sexy, and certainly not accept-able. Even as a *wolf* Jacob is "reddish brown."[15] Readers might excuse this behavior because, after all, Bella *is* a teenager and the predominant narrator of the books; but continually finding synonyms for "red" does not make mentioning his skin color any less racist than calling Jacob a "redskin," and it is important that the intended audi-ence of the novels is the same demographic as the narrator. These teenage readers will not see the subtlety of their narrator's racism and instead identify with her.

The novels and films reinforce this racism by allowing Jacob's *red* skin and half-naked body to be fully objectified and bear the burden of the desirous gaze, a long tradition in American culture that began with Columbus's study of the bodies of the half-clothed Indians on Hispaniola.[16] Even more appalling, with the release of the new Jacob Black Ken Doll from Mattel,® complete with sculpted "six-pack" abs, "tribal" tattoo, and cutoff jean shorts, the naked male Indian body is not just meant for consumption by teenage girls and adult women but now is consumed by little girls as well, indoctrinating them into this racist ideology while young (see Figure 15.1).

Jacob's skin color is important not only because it marks him as the exotic sexual Other, but also because it stands in contradistinction to *whiteness*, which is really what these books endorse. In *New Moon*, Bella has a vision where Jacob turns into Edward, which allows Meyer to pointedly compare their races: "The russet color of his skin leached away, leaving his face pale white like bone."[17] It is no mistake that Bella repeatedly chooses Edward, or *consuming* whiteness, since it is accompanied by palatial estates and luxury cars that distinguish the buying power of only the wealthi-est white elite. Further, the films enact the ideology about race and skin color that

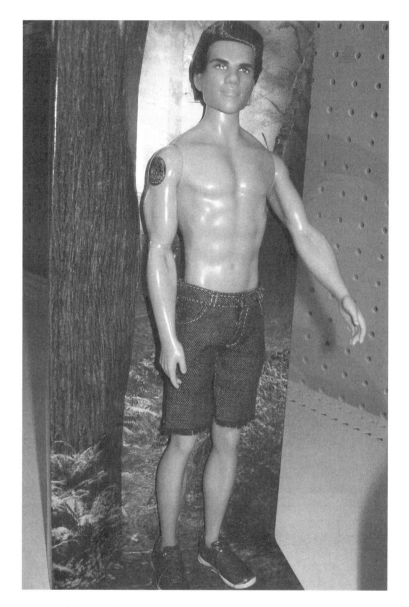

Figure 15.1   Jacob Black Barbie Doll. Copyright 2009 Mattel.

Meyer's books espouse by casting Taylor Lautner to play Jacob Black, the only Indian character not played by a Native actor. Chaske Spencer (Sam) is of mixed descent with Sioux, Nez Perce, Creek, and Cherokee heritage. Kiowa Gordon (Embry) is Hualapai; Tyson Houseman (Quil), and Bronson Pelletier (Jared) are Cree; Alex Meraz (Paul) is Purepecha. The Indian adults in the film are also Native, the most famous of whom is Graham Greene, who plays Billy Clearwater and who is Oneida. Lautner has claimed in interviews that he does have some Native American blood in his ancestry, remarking, "actually, I am part Native American...on my mother's side, she has some Potawatomi and Ottawa Indian in her."[18] Having Native blood in one's ancestry and being culturally Native American are not synonymous, and claiming ancestry is a learned, distinctly *American* response that displaces white guilt for domination and genocide and works to reshape our historical narrative.[19] Taylor Lautner may not have known it, but in accepting the role of Jacob Black he joined a long line of those who have "played Indian" for commercial success.[20] Rayna Green argues in "A Tribe Called Wannabee: Playing Indian in America and Europe" that "the living performance of 'playing Indian' by non-Indian peoples depends upon the physical and psychological removal, even death, of real Indians," which allows Americans, throughout history, to play with Indian identities.[21] The casting of Lautner may have been dictated by other factors, but it is remarkable that the movie production team was unable to find a Native actor to play the main love interest, particularly since they *did* manage to find quite a few handsome Native actors.

Peter van Lent's article helps explain this apparent discrepancy, noting that in popular romance novels, the Indian hero is described as both visibly Native in terms of skin color and hair, but also has Caucasian facial features, which maintain his candidacy as a heartthrob by preventing him from being "too alien" while simultaneously avoiding "squeamishness about miscegenation."[22] Indeed, miscegenation is a possibility these novels repeatedly reject through the Edward–Bella–Jacob love triangle but also with the pairings of the Quileute tribe members who always fall in love or "imprint" with other Indian characters. This remains true throughout the series until *Breaking Dawn*, when Jacob "imprints" with Renesme, who is herself a product of vampire and human mixing and thus a fitting companion.

Although the stereotypes Meyer relies on are at heart romantic, it is important to understand that the preexisting stereotype—that of the Savage, though Noble, Indian—never fully dissipates and is the foundation for the more "admirable" version, the Romantic Indian. The reason that the Indian of American imagination can be portrayed as romantic at all is due to what Renato Rosaldo calls "imperialist nostalgia"—once Native peoples are no longer a threat, as a nation we look upon them fondly and with nostalgia for the loss of a more innocent time and people. However, before that—before indigenous people were slaughtered and the survivors marched across the country, subdued, and trapped on reservations—they were *always* savage, always a threat. Jacob and the other Indian characters in the *Twilight* series, as romantic and handsome as they may be, are also capable of tremendous violence as wolves and warriors of their tribe. Although Stephenie Meyer does not actually show the reader how the wolves/Indians rip apart vampire bodies using their teeth, she does imply it and leave it to the imagination, in the same way she suggests their collective nudity.

In addition, in *New Moon*, Jacob's ability to transform contains the threat of potential violence, since anger can cause him to "phase" at any moment, putting those around him in physical danger. This means Bella lives under the constant threat of domestic violence throughout the series from both love interests who can lose control at any moment and "accidentally" kill her. Like abused women everywhere, Bella is continually warned to mind her behavior and not to provoke either boy, or he might "lose his temper." Emily, Sam's fiancée in *New Moon*, is physical proof of this possibility: a long scar runs down one side of her face and body, leaving her permanently disfigured because she was once too close to Sam when he "lost" his temper. "Hanging out with werewolves" (read: Indians) "truly did have its risks," Bella thinks to herself upon meeting Emily.[23] Yet, in all cases—Emily with Sam or Bella with either Jacob or Edward—this threat of domestic violence is excused because of "true love."[24] Meyer's elision of the reality of Emily's daily life as a battered woman is justified by "true love" because of the inevitability of "imprinting." Quickly excusing the abuse that both Bella and Emily experience eclipses the real tragedy of Native women who experience violence and physical assault at rates higher than any other ethnic group in the world.[25] Although Edward *might* lose control at any moment, he never does, and so it is even more poignant that Jacob *does* lose control several times, once even starting a fight and hurting one of his own pack-mates, Paul. This anger is a *genetic* trait, Meyer's books assert, evolutionarily bred into Indian men who have a natural inherent savagery, and Emily is literally scarred by being an Indian woman who chooses to remain a part of her own culture.

These stereotypical depictions of Indian people are emphasized by Meyer's portrayal of reservation life as prosaic and banal. She ignores the poverty and health problems that plague Native people across the United States at alarmingly higher rates than the rest of the population. In *New Moon*, Bella spends a remarkable amount of time at La Push—truly one of the more beautiful reservations in the United States and now the victim of endless tourism because of the novels, yet no less immune to the health and economic problems suffered by Native peoples across this country.[26] Although Bella remarks several times that the Black house is small and Jacob's room is tiny, there is never any acknowledgment of the political realities of *why* this might be. In fact, although Indians in this novel are useful as romantic love interests, Meyer is completely dismissive of the lived realities of Native peoples, perhaps because "admitting genocide would not be good box office."[27] Ignoring poverty and domestic violence is a purposeful omission, particularly when compared to the lavish existence of the Cullens.

In addition, Meyer's language when discussing legitimate Native beliefs about history, origins, and storytelling is offensive. In the beginning of *Twilight*, Jacob tells Bella the story about the "cold ones" and continues throughout *New Moon* and *Eclipse* to call his own Indian stories "superstitions" about the belief in "magic": "just like they had their legends of the great flood and wolf-men ancestors. Just stories, folklore . . . ."[28] While it is true that Meyer invents these stories, one of the problems with her writing style is that she varies her language very little, and in this case her repeated use of the terms "superstitious" and "magic" is insulting because the stories are "real" in the context of the novels. Regulating these tribal beliefs to "superstition" and "folklore" implies that all Native oral histories are invented fictional stories for amusement, like the fairytales of the Brothers Grimm. Meyer also equates Native religious ideology in these instances with the belief in "magic," inexplicable bits of trickery or sleights-of-hand that only children believe are real. The term "magic" is damaging as well because much of Native American art is mislabeled "magical realism," a term that arrogantly dismisses any way of knowing or understanding the world outside of western scientific philosophical thought.

Meyer's choice to connect these stories to a real, existing tribe instead of an invented one implies that they are culturally "authentic" indigenous tales; she thus doubly profits from stereotypes about mystical Indian healing and spiritual beliefs, along with other famous and equally exploitative writers like Lynn Andrews and Carlos Casteneda. Like invoking the Romantic Savage or playing Indian, the cooptation of Native spiritual beliefs for commercial success is a custom of longstanding tradition in mainstream American culture and is ultimately damaging to Native peoples as they struggle to keep their religious practices alive and protected from misuse. Laurie Anne Whitt argues, "When the spiritual knowledge, rituals, and objects of historically subordinated cultures are transformed into commodities, economic and political power merge to produce cultural imperialism."[29] Often stolen under the guise of "religious freedom" or First Amendment rights of free speech, or simply invented as Meyer does in the *Twilight* series, these imagined beliefs contribute to the overall stereotype of Indians as close to nature and the progenitors of some kind of ancient mystical knowledge, and in turn prevent Native peoples from educating American society on their real religious values without fear of misrepresentation and commercial exploitation. The reconfiguration of Native American religious beliefs has disastrous consequences, both for white Americans who buy into this New Age spirituality in the hope of finding healing,[30] and even more so for Indigenous peoples who are fighting to maintain cultural practices and undo the damage of the boarding school era when they were made to feel ashamed for their beliefs.

Thus far I have discussed the ways in which Meyer's Indians conform to the traditional stereotypes in the dominant American cultural imagination, but she also manipulates the images by projecting Mormon religious beliefs onto her Quileute characters. This may seem incongruous: why, if Meyer relies so heavily on repeated iterations of Indian people that portray them as savage and uncivilized would she also attribute Mormon religious values to these figures? Precisely because this portrayal mirrors the historical relationships and views that Mormons have held of Native peoples, and, in turn, reinforces the Savage Indian stereotype she draws upon for her warrior wolves; it also allows her to simultaneously distance herself from the fundamentalist Mormon values that she disavows.

In *The Book of Mormon*, a Hebrew man named Lehi journeys to the so-called New World in a boat, bringing his followers with him. Lehi had two sons: Nephi, whom he favored and who inherited the leadership of the tribe upon his death, and Laman, whose jealousy caused a split in the tribe between the righteous and those who believed in "unbelief and idolatry."[31] The Lamanites were so degenerate that God cursed them with dark skin, a visible signal of their immorality. Tensions rose, and the Lamanites slaughtered their fair-skinned Nephite relatives to become, according to *The Book of Mormon*, the ancestors of the modern Native Americans. This explains "why Columbus encountered no Caucasians when he landed in the New World in 1492" and also the condition of Indians as he described them—as savage peoples reduced to a vagabond existence, mired in superstitious pagan worship.[32]

While this account conforms to Meyer's Mormon faith, she also projects practices onto her Indian characters that contribute to their exotic racialization, such as the practice of polygamy through the story of the "third wife" in *Eclipse*. For many contemporary Americans, Mormonism is synonymous with polygamy, but this is a simplistic reduction of the religion. In reality, this principle caused the faith to split into sects: those who believe in polygamy are called Fundamentalist Latter-Day Saints and the modern Mormon Church has continually distanced itself from these believers in order to protect the reputation of their faith. It is not a coincidence that Meyer attributes this belief to the Quileute wolves, the allegedly degenerated descendants of the Lamanites, because it reinforces the stereotype of the Noble Savage by comparing Native peoples to the historical representation of polygamist Mormons in American history. The practice was said to "distinguish them [Mormons] at a glance"[33] and uprisings against polygamist Mormons were incited with the same phrases used to provoke violence against Native peoples, including the phrase "nits make lice," used before the Haun's Hill Massacre on October 30, 1838, where eighteen Mormons were killed; it was also used against the Cheyenne before the Sand Creek Massacre on November 29, 1864. Although this seems to suggest some sympathy on Meyer's part with her Indian characters—a solidarity between what Native peoples went through and what Mormons have historically faced in this nation—by attributing polygamy to her Indian characters, Meyer actually *distances* herself as a modern Mormon from this ideology, which now belongs to a raced savage people who believe in superstitious folklore and magic.

Incredibly, the most damaging element of Meyer's portrayal of Indianness in her novel is not that she reentrenches old racist stereotypes, fetishizes the exotic male, or even that she dismisses Native American religious values while supplanting them with Mormon ideology. The most dangerous element of her depiction is that she renders Native peoples mythical. By imagining her cosmic epic battle between good and evil, between vampires and werewolves/Indians, she creates a binary that implies that Native peoples are as equally fantastic, as equally fictional, as vampires. This is particularly true in *Breaking Dawn*, by far her most fantasy-driven novel in terms of genre. As the vampire friends who surround the Cullens exhibit an impressive array of superpowers rivaled only by the X-Men, the werewolves/Indians are relegated even further into the background of the series. Any visible mark of Indianness disappears, and the werewolves/Indians spend most of the book as glorified, albeit annoying, house pets and rather oversized guard dogs.

Meyer has been repeatedly criticized for her lack of artistic skills, linguistic repetition, and reliance on traditional genre formulations. While I agree with this assessment, I also think it is dangerous to dismiss these novels simply because they are poorly written. Indeed, there are remarkable moments in each novel that shine with creative ingenuity. Meyer has clearly tapped into a cultural vein that betrays a collective desire for fantastic tragic romance. Because of their immense popularity, these books/films have the potential to irreparably damage the feminist movement and harm teenage boys everywhere who will never be able to live up to the impossible standard set by Edward Cullen. Most importantly, they harm Native peoples struggling for livelihood and recognition, and undermine their very *existence* by supplanting them with stereotypes and mythic status. Because of this alone, they need to be taken seriously. Each time another teenage girl loses herself in this narrative, she is inculcated into a dangerous ideology that, while creating a fantasy world and make-believe races of vampires and werewolves, elides actual Native peoples and repeats the violence of genocide and colonial domination.

NOTES

1. A visual example of this occurs in the film *New Moon* when Jacob gives Bella a dream catcher, a traditional Anishinaabe object. It is a common American impulse to lump all Native peoples into one generic figure although there is enormous variety in the indigenous world, which in the United States alone consists of 562 federally recognized tribes that speak over 200 distinct languages. (This does not include those fighting for recognition as I write.)

2. Anthony Tyeemee D. Clark and Malea Powell, "Resisting Exile in the 'Land of the Free,'" *American Indian Quarterly* 32, no. 1 (Winter 2008): 15.

3. Ibid., 14.

4. In the digest written by Bartolomé de Las Casas from Columbus' log book on his first voyage, Columbus noted that the Native peoples were "marvelously friendly to us....In fact, they very willingly traded everything they had" (55). Later, however, after Columbus and his soldiers took many of the indigenous peoples home as slaves and they began to understand that the "occupation and conquest of the country" (as Columbus asserts in his journal) was the purpose of the visit, relations between the two groups naturally soured. Columbus left men behind on his first voyage who began to rape and pillage Native villages and were subsequently wiped out by the indigenous population. Columbus's descriptions of them changed after this, and in his second voyage he wrote: "...as for the men they [the Caribs] are able to capture, they bring those who are alive home to be slaughtered and eat those who are dead on the spot. They say that human flesh is so good that there is nothing like it in the world.... They castrate the boys that they capture and use them as servants until they are men. Then, when they want to make a feast, they kill and eat them, for they say the flesh of boys and women is not good to eat" (136). Within the diaries of Columbus, the Noble Savage was created and has persisted through the centuries. J. M. Cohen, ed, *The Four Voyages of Christopher Columbus* (New York: Penguin Books, 1969).

5. Robert Berkhofer, *The White Man's Indian* (New York: Vintage Books, 1978), 79.

6. Ibid.

7. These titles are easy to find by visiting any bookstore and wandering through the Romance section, but to view some of the more egregious examples, see any of Karen Kay's books online.

8. Peter van Lent, "'Her Beautiful Savage': The Current Sexual Image of the Native American Male," in *Dressing in Feathers: The Construction of the Indian in American Popular Culture*, edited by S. Elizabeth Bird (Boulder, CO: Westview Press, 1996), 214.

9. Samantha Chang, "Taylor Lautner: I Worked Out Nonstop for *New Moon*," *Examiner*, July 16, 2009. http://www.examiner.com/examiner/x-14380-NY-Celebrity-Fitness-and-Health-Examiner~y2009m7d16-Taylor-Lautner-I-worked-out-nonstop-for-New-Moon

10. *New Moon*, directed by Chris Weitz (Imprint Entertainment, 2009, DVD).

11. Ibid.

12. Peter van Lent, "Her Beautiful Savage," 214.

13. Stephenie Meyer, *New Moon* (New York: Little, Brown and Company, 2006), 131.

14. Ibid., 131. This line is also repeated word-for-word in the film version.

15. Ibid., 244.

16. Again, on the first voyage, Columbus noted, "They were very well built with fine bodies and handsome faces. Their hair is coarse, almost like that of a horse's tail and short; they wear it down over their eyebrows.... They are the color of Canary Islanders

(neither black nor white)" (55). Like many explorers who follow him, Columbus meticulously described Indigenous bodies repeatedly, betraying both European desire and disgust of the Other. J. M. Cohen, ed., *The Four Voyages of Christopher Columbus* (New York: Penguin Books, 1969.)

17. Ibid., 276.

18. Larry Carrol, "'Twilight' Actor Taylor Lautner Is Eager To Deliver 'Naked' Line, Master Driving Teen star also discusses his research on the Quileute tribe to play Native American character Jacob Black," *MTV*, May 20, 2008. http://www.mtv.com/news/articles/1587744/20080520/story.jhtml

19. For more on this concept, see Vine Delora Jr., *Custer Died for Your Sins*.

20. There is a long history of coopting, stealing, and inhabiting Native American identity for profit in this country—what critic Philip Deloria calls "Playing Indian"—and the farce can be incredibly lucrative, as it currently is for Taylor Lautner. One of the most famous perpetrators of this was Forest Carter (a.k.a. Asa Carter), the author of *The Education of Little Tree* and famous white supremacist who wrote speeches for George Wallace in the 1960s. There have been many others: writers, "spiritual leaders," actors, and politicians. Most recently, another writer, Nasdijj (Timothy Barrus), award-winning writer of several "memoirs" about his life as an Indian on the reservation—*The Blood Runs Like a River Through My Dreams*, *The Boy and the Dog Are Sleeping*, and *Geronimo's Bones: A Memoir of My Brother and Me*—was revealed as a fake by investigative reporting. In Hollywood, playing Indian for profit has a long history, particularly since Native actors were not hired to play leading roles in cinematic productions, a tradition the *Twilight* films continue. While this might seem insignificant—these are *actors*, after all, filling a *role*—the tradition of inhabiting Indian identities reinforces the national narrative that this country was "inherited" from Native people via Manifest Destiny and divine right, which in turn justifies removal and genocide, or ignores it all together. After removal and into the modern age, drawing on the imperialist nostalgia I discuss earlier in this chapter, Americans now claim ancestral descent from Native peoples, easing guilt for colonization and denying Indigenous peoples rights, since they are just "one of us" now.

21. Rayna Green, "A Tribe Called Wannabee: Playing Indian in America and Europe," *Folklore* 99, no. 1 (1988): 31.

22. Peter van Lent, "Her Beautiful Savage," 217.

23. Stephenie Meyer, *New Moon*, 333.

24. Ibid.

25. The National Violence Against Women Survey conducted in 2006 found that Native women experienced rape at rates 34.1 percent higher than any other ethnic group, stalking at rates 17 percent higher and assault at rates 61.4 percent higher. Meyer's books attribute this violence and the threat of domestic assault to her Indian male characters, but a study released by the Bureau of Justice Statistics, *American Indians and Crime*, shows that "9 out of 10 American Indian victims of rape or sexual assault were estimated to have had assailants" of a different race and that most crimes perpetrated against Native people are not committed by other Native Americans. Lawrence A. Greenfield and Steven K. Smith, "Bureau of Justice Statistics: American Indians and Crime," *U.S. Department of Justice*, February 1999. http://bjs.ojp.usdoj.gov/index.cfm?ty=pbdetail&iid=387. Patricia Tjaden and Nancy Thoennes, "Prevalence, Incidence, and Consequences of Violence Against Women: Findings From the National Violence Against Women Survey," *National Institute of Justice*, November 1998. http://www.ojp.usdoj.gov/nij/pubs-sum/172837.htm

26. Angela R. Riley, "Sucking the Quileute Dry," *New York Times*, February 8, 2010. Riley writes, "a tour company hauls busloads of fans onto the Quileute reservation daily. Yet the tribe has received no payment for this commercial activity. Meanwhile, half of the Quileute families still live in poverty." A21.

27. Mary Alice Money, "Broken Arrows: Images of Native Americans in the Popular Western," *American Indian Studies: An Interdisciplinary Approach to Contemporary Issues*, edited by Dane Morrison (New York: Peter Lang, 1997), 371.

28. Stephenie Meyer, *New Moon*, 81.

29. Laurie Anne Whitt, "Cultural Imperialism and the Marketing of Native America," *Natives and Academics: Researching and Writing About American Indians*, edited by Devon Mihesuah (Lincoln: University of Nebraska Press, 1998), 171.

30. Two people died and many were injured in a sweatlodge run by an illegitimate practitioner in an upscale New Age resort in Sedona, Arizona, one of many resorts and faux-healing establishments currently profiting from peddling false Native American religion. For more information, see the Associated Press articles by Felicia Fonesca: "Authorities seek cause of Ariz. sweat lodge deaths" (October 10, 2009) and "2 die, 19 overcome at Arizona retreat sweat lodge" (October 9, 2009).

31. Jon Krakauer, *Under the Banner of Heaven: A Story of Violent Faith* (New York: Doubleday, 2003), 67.

32. Ibid.

33. Dr. Barthow quoted in Jon Krakauer, 205.

CHAPTER 16

GREEN IS THE NEW BLACK: ECOPHOBIA AND THE GOTHIC LANDSCAPE IN THE *TWILIGHT* SERIES

TARA K. PARMITER

> …one day the demons of America must be placated, the ghosts must be appeased, the Spirit of Place atoned for. Then the true passionate love for American Soil will appear. As yet, there is too much menace in the landscape…
> —D. H. Lawrence, *Studies in Classic American Literature*

DISPLACED FROM HER BELOVED HOME IN ARID ARIZONA, Bella Swan of Stephenie Meyer's *Twilight* saga finds herself overwhelmed by greenery. Her new home on the Olympic Peninsula is surrounded by temperate rain forests lush with ferns, sitka spruces, and dripping mosses; even the tidal pools of the nearby beach are "teeming with life."[1] This profusion of green initially marks the landscape as a surprising setting for a gothic novel; as vampire heartthrob Edward Cullen quips, "No coffins, no piled skulls in the corner; I don't even think we have cobwebs…what a disappointment this must be for you."[2] Edward's comic reference to the crypts, dungeons, and graveyards of the traditional gothic acknowledges how firmly we associate vampires with scenes of death; after all, these monsters are the undead, animated corpses lurking in dark corners and ancient castles, lying in wait to drain the life from their unwitting victims. The landscapes they inhabit are landscapes of terror, where our most irrational and unnatural fears come horribly true.

By choosing to set her novels in the Pacific Northwest, then, Meyer complicates our initial reading of her gothic tale. Anyone who has seen the dense green of those old growth groves—whether in person or in the film adaptations—recognizes that although death and decay are essential to this landscape, they are part of the natural cycle, sustaining the life of the forest. Fallen trees become nurse logs supporting small ecosystems of ferns, mosses, and seedlings, and the heavy branches hang with epiphytes, clinging plants that draw their moisture from the perpetual rain and mist. As Meyer describes on her website, she had never seen this lush landscape before choosing it as the site of her story, but it fulfilled her particular requirements for her vampire and werewolf mythologies. "For my setting," she explains, "I knew I needed someplace ridiculously rainy. I turned to Google, as I do for all my research needs, and looked for the place with the most rainfall in the United States. This turned out to be the Olympic Peninsula in Washington State. I pulled up maps of the area and studied them, looking for something small, out of the way, surrounded by for- est…And there, right where I wanted it to be, was a tiny town called 'Forks.'"[3] As her description suggests, from the start Meyer envisioned her monsters in a wild land- scape, one "surrounded by forests" and exposed to the elements rather than confined to dark crypts and castles. But while Meyer may have selected this green landscape to debunk the tired clichés of vampire lore, her choice of gothic settings also illuminates a greater twenty-first-century uneasiness with nonhuman nature.

The fear of wild nature is commonly referred to as "ecophobia" (from the Greek *oikos*, "house," and *-phobia*, "fear"), and psychologists, educators, and literary critics see this fear as an increasing concern in our modern, urbanized world. David Sobel, a specialist in childhood education, defines ecophobia specifically as "a fear of ecological problems and the natural world."[4] In *Beyond Ecophobia*, Sobel expresses his concern that our well-meaning school curricula focusing on endangered animals and depleted Amazonian rainforests are having an unintended effect on students: rather than inspir- ing environmental activism, these classes are leading children to withdraw, distancing themselves from the numbing sense that the Earth is doomed and they can do nothing to stop it. Ecocritic Simon C. Estok depicts ecophobia more intensely as "an irratio- nal and groundless hatred of the natural world."[5] In contrast to "biophilia," biologist Edward O. Wilson's theory about the "innately emotional affiliation of human beings to other living organisms," Estok's concept of ecophobia emphasizes the lack of affili- ation between humans and the nonhuman world.[6] As he notes, "To a global audience glued before flat screens of CNN, an audience very familiar with polar ice sheets break- ing off, global warming, and Katrina, we may easily see how our media daily writes nature as a hostile opponent who is responding angrily to our incursions and actions, an opponent to be feared and, with any luck, controlled."[7] Tom J. Hilliard, in responding to Estok, acknowledges this "nearly ubiquitous cultural fascination with the hostile and deadly aspects of the otherwise nurturing image of 'Mother Nature,'" and he calls on ecocritics to examine gothic literature to help illuminate these concerns.[8] In looking at the role of ecophobia in the *Twilight* saga, then, I will show not only how these novels reflect this pervasive fear of nonhuman nature but how they simultaneously model an increased engagement and appreciation—a more biophilic response—to the natural world. In revealing how Bella learns to overcome her disdain for her green environ- ment, Meyer reimagines the outdoors not merely as a place of gothic fear but as a place to forge an intense emotional and physical connection with wild nature.

Gothic narratives have always depended on the terror inspired by their settings. Even the adjective "gothic" relates these narratives to the excesses of medieval architec- ture, with its dark gargoyles, forbidding shadows, and extravagant flourishes. In such eighteenth-century British novels as Horace Walpole's *The Castle of Otranto* (1764) or Anne Radcliffe's *The Mysteries of Udolpho* (1794), our heroines find themselves wandering the labyrinthine passages of spooky old castles, haunted by strange noises and threatening captors in the night. These confining, secluded settings titillated readers of the day, who delighted in the dangers of the domestic sphere turned upside down. But as Hilliard notes, these novels were intentionally set in far-off lands and eras to distance the readers from the frightening landscapes and excessive actions of the characters. Hilliard claims that this distancing enabled readers to "indulge their most sensational fancies about sin and wrongdoing, their most widespread social fears and anxieties, but then later safely put down the book and find a sense of superiority in knowing that those things don't happen anymore."[9] In other words, these original gothic landscapes thrilled readers with their otherness, but that same otherness of a world removed from eighteenth-century England made them safe.

The landscape of *Twilight*, however, holds more in common with late nineteenth-century British gothic novels such as Robert Louis Stevenson's *Strange Case of Dr. Jekyll and Mr. Hyde* (1886), H. G. Wells's *The Invisible Man* (1897), and most notably Bram Stoker's *Dracula* (1897)—tales that gain their eeriness from the contrast between uncanny monsters and the modern streets of turn-of-the-twentieth-century England. As the young Doctor Seward exclaims in *Dracula* when told about the ancient vampire, "Good God, Professor! Do you mean to tell me…that such a thing is here in London in the nineteenth century?"[10] The doctor's shock derives from the intrusion of something as irrational as an undead monster into the scientific world of post-Darwinian England. Part of the thrill of this mode of gothic is the subversion of the familiar, or, as Kathleen Spencer puts it in her study of the urban gothic, the "fear and revulsion at encountering what is not only unexpected, but *unnatural* according to the laws of the world [the characters] inhabit."[11] This surprise at confronting the mythical vampire in an otherwise rational setting has become a standard of late-twentieth and early twenty-first-century vampire narratives, a standard Meyer upholds by setting her novel in small-town America.

But more than the uncanny appearance of monsters in an otherwise peaceful setting, the *Twilight* saga draws its fear of the wilderness from the American gothic tradition. From the earliest Euro-American accounts, the American landscape has been seen as both bountiful and threatening, as in Columbus's land of "marvelous pine groves," "large tracts of cultivatable lands," and "fruits in great diversity" and Puritan William Bradford's "hideous and desolate wilderness, full of wild beasts and wild men."[12] Because of the harsh realities of everyday life in colonial America, the gothic image of the "howling wilderness" often trumped the more idyllic image of the New World Garden of Eden. As Roderick Nash puts it in *Wilderness and the American Mind*,

> Safety and comfort, even necessities like food and shelter, depended on overcoming the wild environment. For the first Americans, as for mediaeval Europeans, the forest's darkness hid savage men, wild beasts, and still stranger creatures of the imagination. In addition civilized man faced the danger of succumbing to the wildness of his surroundings and reverting to savagery himself. The pioneer, in short, lived too close to wilderness for appreciation.[13]

The howling wilderness of both Puritan New England and modern day Forks is a place of uncertainty and hidden dangers. As Bella muses, it is easier to believe in

Nash's "strange creatures of the imagination" while in the "green haze" of the forest than in her "clear-cut bedroom," the word "clear-cut" even suggesting that her home is like a logged forest, a space whose capacity for wonder and mystery has been mowed down.[14] Nash notes that it was not until the eastern United States had displaced the Native American populations, clear cut the countryside, and established centers of business and industry that wild nature could be looked at with nostalgia and reverence, most often from the safety of urban centers where it was easy to imagine the abstract beauty of the wilderness without having to contend with its day-to-day challenges.

The writers of the American Romantic era contributed greatly to this newfound appreciation for the wilderness. Emerson, Thoreau, Whitman, Hawthorne, Melville, and Poe sang of the wilderness as a place of beauty, but that beauty was always tinged with sublime terror. Indeed, in the American gothic, the locus of fear shifts from the dungeons and ruins of the European tradition to the darkness of the forest. In *Love and Death in the American Novel*, Leslie A. Fiedler observes that "In the American gothic…the heathen, unredeemed wilderness and not the decaying monuments of a dying class, nature and not society becomes the symbol of evil."[15] The forest where Hawthorne's Young Goodman Brown envisions the Satanic ritual of his townsfolk, the ghastly whiteness of Melville's Moby Dick, any landscape traversed by a Poe character, and Thoreau's epiphanic frenzy on the peak of Mount Ktaadin remind us that wild nature loomed with spiritual and physical force over nineteenth-century Americans.

Indeed, that simultaneous love and fear of the wilderness became a defining feature of how Americans defined themselves as *American*. So important did the wilderness become to American identity that its disappearance through the march of civilization and Manifest Destiny was perceived as a national crisis. For some, this impending loss signaled a threat to American character: Frederick Jackson Turner's classic address, "The Significance of the Frontier in American History," presented at the Chicago World's Fair in 1893, argued that Americans' love of freedom, individualism, and Yankee inventiveness came from the unique experience of confronting an ever-moving frontier. His deepest worry was that the closing of this frontier would prompt a devolution into weakness and overly civilized effeminacy.[16] For others, this threat to the wilderness served as a rallying cry to action: with the designation of Yosemite as a California state park in 1864 and of Yellowstone as the first national park in 1872, preservationists such as John Muir fought to preserve wilderness spaces for future generations, an impulse PBS documentarian Ken Burns has recently dubbed "America's Best Idea."[17]

Our early twenty-first-century fervor for all things "green" derives from these nineteenth-century ideals about sublime nature and environmental protection. And yet, just as the readers of the eighteenth century could enjoy the excesses of gothic literature from the safety of their homes, our cherished ideas about green spaces and wild nature often mask our lack of contact with what Thoreau ecstatically called "the *solid* earth! the *actual* world!"[18] Whereas the early pioneers were too close to the wilderness to appreciate it, our appreciation of wilderness suggests that we may be too far away. In "The Trouble with Wilderness," historian William Cronon argues that our passion for wilderness spaces—while essential to the preservation of these lands—relies on a separation that privileges the nonhuman world apart over the human world at home. In other words, when we focus our attention on saving the distant wilderness, we neglect the wildness "in the seemingly tame fields and woodlots of Massachusetts, in the cracks of a Manhattan sidewalk, even in the cells of our own bodies."[19] Cronon assures us that he does not reject the actual wilderness—as an environmentalist, he will fight heartily to protect green spaces—but he rejects the *idea* of wilderness that frames it as separate from humans, a paradox that requires our absence from wild nature to keep it sacred. While Cronon asserts that one of the most obvious dangers of this separation is that we will not protect the environment if we do not feel a direct connection with it, equally troubling is the threat that this separation makes wild spaces seem more foreign and more frightening, as they have increasingly become in our urban, technologically advanced society.

In 2005, the same year that *Twilight* first appeared on bookshelves, educational activist Richard Louv took on this dilemma, confronting what he saw as an unhealthy separation between humans and wild nature. In *Last Child in the Woods: Saving Our Children from Nature Deficit*, Louv examines the disconnection between twenty-first-century American children and the natural world, arguing that this separation threatens their physical, emotional, mental, and spiritual well-being. Louv refers to "nature deficit" as the emotional and psychological effects of a loss of nonstructured outdoor play and engagement, and worries that this deficit endangers not only humans but our stewardship of the environment. Seeking to explain what has distanced us from wild nature in recent years, Louv argues that our relationship to the wilderness has reverted to that of Puritanical fear. Popular culture abounds with images of threatening nature, growling just outside our doors. Mountain lion attacks in western communities and the rising population of black bears in suburban New Jersey make headlines,[20] reminding us that animal predators wait in the shadows, joining the fictional Leatherfaces, Jasons, and Blair Witches of our slasher films.[21] Less visible threats, such as the deer ticks that spread Lyme disease or the acid rain that kills our lakes and streams, have a haunting presence, the unseen unknown that makes the gothic so frightening. Because of these heightened fears, Louv contends, "Our society is teaching young people to avoid direct experience in nature," a loss that could have lasting effects on future generations and on the environment that sustains them.[22]

It is fair to say that Bella Swan suffers from nature deficit in the opening of *Twilight*. When she arrives in Forks, the intense greenness serves as a frustration, a reminder of how far she had traveled from the warmth of the desert and her mother's home. In the first pages of the novel, she sets up the opposition between her beloved Phoenix and the dreaded Olympic Peninsula by focusing on her clothing and the weather: whereas she left Arizona wearing a "sleeveless, white eyelet lace" shirt, an article of clothing that suggests lightness and openness to the elements, her "carry-on item was a parka," a hefty protective layer meant to form a barrier, shutting out the outside world.[23] The sunlight and "blistering heat" she had so adored are replaced by a "gloomy, omnipresent shade" that she observes sullenly from within her father's car.[24] Although she can acknowledge the beauty of the lush landscape, she still finds its pervasive greenness uncanny: "Everything was green: the trees, their trunks covered with moss, their branches hanging with a canopy of it, the ground covered with ferns. Even the air filtered down greenly through the leaves. / It was too green—an alien planet."[25] Whereas heroines of the eighteenth-century gothic were oppressed by dark, confining architecture, Bella here feels equally oppressed by a landscape "covered" in moss and ferns. Bella's concern that the scene is *too* green reflects not merely the change from desert to rainforest locales but an ecophobic reaction to the natural world. Bella feels at home in the city but alienated by the forest where "everything" down to the air is green. In Bella's earliest observations of wild nature, then, she positions humans as separate from their environments, shut out by parkas and car windows from the world environing them.

This separation intensifies when Bella learns of the Cullens, the vampire clan that lives secluded in the woods outside of town. The Cullens are literally described as outsiders: as the students of Forks understand it, the family is very outdoorsy, and whenever the sun shines, they head to the mountains to hike and camp. Readers come to understand that "camping" and "hiking" are euphemisms for the Cullens's vampiric hunting trips and that they avoid the sun because it makes their skin glitter like diamonds, a decidedly nonhuman trait. It is notable, though, that whatever the reason, the choice to spend time in the wilderness is perceived as another sign of the family's freakishness: not only are they uncommonly beautiful but they regularly spend time communing with nature—how strange! For even though Bella's friends live surrounded by a glorious wilderness, they enter it infrequently. Mike Newton's family may own the outdoors store where Bella eventually works, but Mike is more interested in selling goods to enable others to enter the woods than going hiking himself. And while the gang blithely hangs out at the LaPush Beach for a driftwood bonfire in *Twilight*, Bella emphasizes how out of place they seem in the surrounding forests. Listening to her friends as they hike a path through the trees, Bella reflects that "the green light of the forest was strangely at odds with the adolescent laughter, too murky and ominous to be in harmony with the light banter around me."[26] Bella cannot help thinking she and her friends are out of place under that "green light": rather than being in harmony with the natural surroundings, their adolescent banter strikes a dissonant chord.

The Cullens's connection to the outdoors marks them as freakish in another way: they regularly hunt bears, mountain lions, elk, and deer because unlike other vampires they have chosen to abstain from feeding on humans. Edward jokes that they call themselves "vegetarians," a term that frames them as marginalized eaters, but also eaters who make ethical decisions about how their food choices affect their environments.[27] When Bella quizzes him on this practice, he reveals that he is not only concerned about human life but animal life: "we have to be careful not to impact the environment with injudicious hunting. We try to focus on areas with an overpopulation of predators."[28] Though Edward speaks these words with a smile, striking a tone of playful banter, he reveals a thoughtfulness and respect for wild nature that comes from close contact; as a powerful hunter himself, Edward understands the need for predators in a well-balanced ecosystem.[29]

Through Edward, Bella begins to appreciate the beauty of the wilderness, but she also draws closer to its dangers. Although he takes her hiking up to a glorious alpine meadow of wildflowers, that same meadow later becomes the site where the tracker James first picks up her scent (*Twilight*), where the vampire Laurent nearly murders her (*New Moon*), where Victoria's army of newborns attempts to destroy her (*Eclipse*), and where the Volturi stage their final attack (*Breaking Dawn*). The meadow is an Edenic refuge by day, but in the dark it is a gothic battlefield, suggesting that we can take nothing for granted when we venture out of doors. Similarly, when Edward leaves Bella in *New Moon*, she stumbles blindly through the woods in her despair and gets inextricably lost in the trees; later, her reckless longing for Edward prompts her to take risks outside, from riding motorcycles on the LaPush reservation to jumping off sea cliffs into the surging waves of the ocean. In these reckless actions, Bella attempts to reconnect with life, to reaffirm her own vitality, and it is telling that the most dangerous activities she can imagine take place in wild spaces.

Of the novels, *New Moon* most consistently links the outdoors with danger, thrill, and pain. This novel chronicles Bella's darkest nights, the "new moon" phase of her life, when all the light has drained from her world. Besides her feats of endurance, Bella also suffers from repeated nightmares after Edward abandons her. While these dreams in some ways replay her panic from the night Edward left, they also conflate her longing for Edward with a fear of the outdoors. In her recurrent nightmare, she finds herself in the gloomy darkness of the forest, not afraid of the usual "zombies," "ghosts," or "psychopaths" that populate the woods in teenage horror films,[30] but rather of the emptiness, the silence, the nothingness of heartbreak:

> I hurried through the gloom without a path, always searching, searching, searching, getting more frantic as the time stretched on, trying to move faster, though the speed made me clumsy.... Then there would come the point in the dream—and I could feel it coming now, but could never seem to wake myself up before it hit—when I couldn't remember what it was I was searching for. When I realized that there was nothing to search for, and nothing to find. That there had never been anything more than just this empty, dreary wood, and there never would be anything more for me...nothing but nothing...[31]

Bella's metaphorical search obviously refers to her longing for Edward and her fear that he does not love her, but her fear and despair manifest themselves in images of the pathless forest. Although the lush rainforests of Forks pulse with life and growth, in her dreams Bella finds them only "empty" and "dreary," deplenished of their natural richness. The dreams present the forest as an undesirable landscape, a place of nothingness where she might search for answers, but "without a path" she can never find them. Unlike a howling wilderness, which would at least have *something* lurking in the shadows, the forest of her dreams leaves her entirely alone and disconnected, neither in contact with the vampire she loves nor the landscape around her. She is shut out of the natural world, and that horrific image has her waking up screaming every night.

Bella's dream of the empty forest, devoid of life, reminds us that the *Twilight* saga is deeply engaged with questions about what is natural and what is unnatural. Both Edward and Jacob Black, Bella's werewolf friend, struggle with what they perceive as a loss of humanity in their states. They repeatedly berate themselves as "monsters" and desperately try to shield Bella from the same indeterminate fate. In a telling exchange at the LaPush beach, Jacob offers Bella a short "nature lecture" on why she should not mingle with monsters.[32] Drawing her attention to an eagle catching a fish in its talons, Jacob muses on the harsher side of the natural world, what Tennyson famously describes as "Nature, red in tooth and claw": "Nature taking its course—hunter and prey, the endless cycle of life and death…And yet, you don't see the fish trying to plant a kiss on the eagle."[33] Jacob's jealous jibe here signals a confusion about what *is* natural: If it is natural for the hunter to attack the prey, what does it mean that Edward, a vampire and thus predator of humans, loves Bella and strives to protect her from harm, or that Bella, as vulnerable and apparently as tasty as a young lamb, has fallen in love with a predator capable of taking down lions? Jacob sees Bella and Edward's love as unnatural, and yet what the novels suggest on the whole is that nature is more complicated than we give it credit for being. In Meyer's gothic landscapes, figures we usually consider evil emerge as heroes and protectors, both of the people and of the land; her monsters may exist on the margins of the human world, but they are closely entwined with nonhuman nature. Whereas we once feared vampires, werewolves, and other monsters because they seemed unnatural, Meyer's monsters seem *more* natural than their human neighbors, in closer contact and balance with the green world.[34]

It may not be surprising, then, that Bella longs so fervently to forfeit her life to become a vampire, joining the Cullens in their marginal existence on the edge of the human world. In the first three books of the series, Bella reveals a passionate yearning for vampire immortality, despite Edward's desperate desire to keep her alive. Numerous critics have expressed their concern that Bella willingly dies to stay forever young with her vampire lover. Feminists have found Bella's choice particularly fraught, worrying that she is presented as a tough twenty-first-century heroine but really conforms to subservient notions of 1950s femininity.[35] Bella's attitude may initially appear like a rejection of life, but in becoming a vampire she instead gains greater access to and appreciation for everything living, again complicating our understanding of what is natural or unnatural. Edward's venomous bite stirs heightened senses in her; like a Sleeping Beauty or Snow White awakened with a kiss, Bella rises from her transformation with all five senses blazing. Meyer devotes long paragraphs to describing the tastes and smells in the air, the remarkable clarity of Bella's new vision, the colors and sounds that her human senses never perceived.[36] In the moment her transformation is complete, Bella exclaims, "I opened my eyes and gazed above me in wonder," echoing naturalists such as John Burroughs, Rachel Carson, and Annie Dillard who encourage us to pay closer attention to the details of our environments and keep our eyes open to the marvels around us.[37]

Bella takes this sense of wonder with her on her first foray into the forest as a vampire, marveling at how "while I rocketed over, under, and through the thick jade maze at a rate that should have reduced everything around me to a streaky green blur, I could plainly see each tiny leaf on all the small branches of every insignificant shrub that I passed."[38] Her attentiveness heightens her concern for the wilderness, for when she notices that "the forest was much more alive than I'd ever known—small creatures whose existence I'd never guessed at teemed in the leaves around me," she also grows more protective, "worried about the forest getting hurt."[39] Unlike the Bella from the opening pages of *Twilight*, who found the "green blur" around her oppressive and "alien," the vampire Bella of *Breaking Dawn* celebrates each wild detail around her, from the dust motes in the air to her daughter's beating heart to the vibrant green of her shady refuge.

From an urban teenager, reluctant to come into contact with the wet, green forests of Washington state, to a powerful newborn vampire, dead yet alive to the pulse of the natural world, Bella not only transforms physically but mentally and emotionally. Her love for Edward and friendship with Jacob draw her outside of her previously sheltered life and expose her to the dangers and wonders of nonhuman nature. The resolution of the final novel—"The Happily Ever After," as the last chapter title promises—leaves her living in loving harmony with Edward in a fairy tale cottage, a home that "belonged [in the forest clearing] so absolutely that it seemed as if it must have grown from the rock, a natural formation."[40] Though Bella resented then feared the forest early in the series, her depiction of the cottage in the clearing shows that the landscape is not the empty space of nothingness that had haunted her dreams. Instead, it is a home, a place of profound connections to loved ones and the environment. This home in the forest reminds us that the gothic has traditionally been a conservative genre under its excessive surface: while the protagonists are subjected to horrors and transgressions, the endings usually return the deserving characters to the safety of the domestic sphere and marriage. Though this pattern is true of the *Twilight* series, in this case the domestic sphere has merged with the wilderness, fulfilling both the Puritan's anxiety over "succumbing to the wildness of his surroundings"[41] and Cronon's dream of a renewed relationship with nonhuman nature. "If wildness can stop being (just) out there and start being (also) in here," Cronon muses, "if it can start being as humane as it is natural, then perhaps we can get on with the unending task of struggling to live rightly in the world—not just in the garden, not just in the wilderness, but in the home that encompasses them both."[42] If we remember that etymologically the word "ecophobia" means fear of the "house," we can see that in learning to love her natural surroundings Bella also finds a home for herself in the wilderness. Bella's ecophobia has been replaced with biophilia because she has learned to break down that separation between human and nonhuman, out there and in here, wilderness and home.

The difficulty in celebrating Bella's transformation, however, is that none of us can follow her lead; though Bella can get closer to the natural world by joining the ranks of the undead, she hardly presents a model for her readers to emulate. And yet, the popularity of the *Twilight* novels has had an interesting influence, inspiring thousands of readers to make the trek to the actual Forks, Washington, to retrace the footsteps of their favorite supernatural teen lovers.[43] The city of Forks has responded enthusiastically to the tourist interest in their small town: local homes have volunteered to be designated as the Swan house and the Cullen house, the hospital parking lot has reserved a space for Dr. Carlisle Cullen, and the town outfitters, where Bella worked in the novels, occasionally pages Bella over the intercom. These Disney-esque "landmarks" undoubtedly delight many fans, despite the obvious problem that the characters in the book never actually lived in Forks.[44]

But the fascination with the fake details of the landscape calls into question what the tourists truly see on their pilgrimages to Bella and Edward's hometown. As George Beahm acknowledges in *Twilight Tours: An Illustrated Guide to the REAL Forks*, "it's not the scenery, though it is breathtakingly beautiful" that draws thousands of tourists to the town each year: it's their love of vampires.[45] But despite his assertions to the contrary, Beahm's beautifully illustrated guide prominently features sweeping panoramic shots of sea stacks off the Olympic coast, mossy green rain-forests, and snowcapped Olympic mountains, highlighting the importance of the natural landscape to our understanding of the "real Forks" and the *Twilight* novels. The simple fact is that any traveler to these vampire attractions will be exposed to the natural wonders of the Pacific Northwest. As Alicia McDonald reminds us in her study of literary tourism in Forks, part of the power of a trip to these lush landscapes is "to extend the reader's involvement in the books while taking advantage of incred-ible natural settings."[46] Thus, even though the Twilight Tours around town stop at all the fabricated landmarks based on the books, they also point the way to the real First and Second Beach, blurring fact and fiction by directing tourists "through the forest where the wolves have their meetings" and to "the driftwood logs where Jacob first told Bella what Edward was!"[47] Writer and critic John Granger suggests that fans "come [to Forks] because of the books [but] their delight when they get here is because of the natural beauty of the place, an echo of that resonance they got in the story."[48] Perhaps in the process of visiting this real landscape, of seeing the col-ored pebbles and bleached driftwood of the Olympic coast, of feeling the mist and damp of the rainforests, of confronting both the glorious greenery and the devastat-ing clear cuts left by the logging industry, these readers will find a connection to the Pacific Northwest that transcends the pages of their favorite novels. And perhaps that engagement will carry over into their lives at home, encouraging them, like Bella, to open their new eyes and gaze about them "in wonder."

Meyer's vampire novels will obviously not solve the eco-crises facing us today. But by situating her vampire narrative within a green gothic landscape, Meyer invites readers to examine their fears of the howling wilderness, prompting us to question our ecophobia and open our eyes to the wonders of the natural world. As she shows us, wild nature *is* a transformative space, whether fueling our sense of wonder for the world around us or forcing us to face the monsters in the shadows. What is most important is that these young adult novels with such a large fan base promote direct contact with the natural world; instead of teaching us to fear nonhuman nature, they encourage us to embrace it. By the saga's end, Bella and her readers can better appreci-ate the power and the beauty of the world around them, no longer seeing "too much menace in the landscape."[49]

NOTES

1. Stephenie Meyer, *Twilight* (New York: Little, Brown and Company, 2005. Print), 117.
2. *Twilight* 329.
3. Stephenie Meyer, "The Story Behind *Twilight*." *The Official Website of Stephenie Meyer.* Web. Accessed January 15, 2010.
4. David Sobel, *Beyond Ecophobia: Reclaiming the Heart in Nature Education* (Great Barrington, MA: The Orion Society and the Myrin Insistute, 2004. Print).
5. Simon C. Estok, "Theorizing in a Space of Ambivalent Openness: Ecocriticism and Ecophobia," *ISLE* 16.2 (2009: 203–225. Print), 205. Ecocritics study the "relationship between literature and the physical environment," taking "an earth-centered approach to literary studies" (Glotfelty xviii). For a good introduction to their work, see Cheryll Glotfelty and Harold Fromm, eds., *The Ecocriticism Reader: Landmarks in Literary*

Ecology (Athens: Univeristy of Georgia Press, 1996. Print) or consult the articles in *ISLE*, the journal produced by the Association for the Study of Literature and the Environment.

6. Edward O. Wilson and Stephen R. Kellert, eds. *The Biophilia Hypothesis* (Washington, DC: Island Press, 1993. Print), 31.

7. Estok 209–10.

8. Hilliard 688. Tom J. Hilliard. "'Deep Into That Darkness Peering': An Essay on Gothic Nature." *ISLE*. 16.4 (2009): 685–695. Print.

9. Hilliard 690.

10. Bram Stoker. *Dracula*. Ed. Nina Auerbach and David J. Skal (New York: Norton, 1997. Print.), 172.

11. Spencer 199, emphasis in original. Kathleen Spencer. "Purity and Danger: *Dracula*, the Urban Gothic, and the Late Victorian Degeneracy Crisis." *ELH* 59:1 (1992). Print.

12. Columbus 36; Bradford 168. Christopher Columbus. "Letter to Luis de Santangel Regarding the First Voyage," pp. 34–36, and William Bradford. "Of Plymouth Plantation," pages 157–96. *The Norton Anthology of American Literature*. 6th Ed. Volume 1. Ed. Nina Baym et al. New York: W. W. Norton & Company, 2003. Print.

13. Roderick Nash, *Wilderness and the American Mind*. 3rd ed. (New Haven: Yale University Press, 1982. Print), 24.

14. *Twilight* 137.

15. Leslie A. Fiedler, *Love and Death in the American Novel*. 1960. Normal, IL: Dalkey Archive Press, 1997. Print), 160.

16. The humans in Disney-Pixar's *WALL-E* (2008)—amorphous blobs pampered and petted by the technology of their spacecraft—offer a compelling contemporary depiction of Turner's fear.

17. *The National Parks: America's Best Idea*. Dir. Ken Burns. 2009. PBS Video, 2009. DVD.

18. Henry David Thoreau. *The Maine Woods*. Ed. Joseph J. Moldenhauer (Princeton: Princeton University Press, 2004. Print), 71.

19. William Cronon, "The Trouble with Wilderness; Or, Getting Back to the Wrong Nature." *Uncommon Ground: Toward Reinventing Nature*. Ed. William Cronon (New York: W.W. Norton & Company, 1995. 69-90. Print), 89.

20. The highly publicized death of Iris Kenna from a mountain lion attack in 1994 prompted a fury of debates in California over wildlife management and suburban encroachment into the animals' territory; see, for example, Marc Peyser's discussion in "Predators on the Prowl," *Newsweek*, January 8, 1996, and Joe Deegan's "Mountain Lion Hype," *The San Diego Reader*, September 9, 2004. Issues of wildlife management and suburban encroachment have also been hot topics in New Jersey, where a perceived overpopulation of bears led the state in 2003 to institute its first bear hunt in 33 years; see, for example, Tina Susman, "Not Grinning, Nor Bearing It: Humans Threatened by Growing Presence," *Newsday*, September 28, 2003: A 16.

21. Leatherface is the crazed killer with a chainsaw in *Texas Chainsaw Massacre* (1974) and its sequels and remakes; Jason is the murderer in a hockey mask in the *Friday the Thirteenth* franchise (original release 1980); the Blair Witch is an eighteenth-century witch haunting the woods in *The Blair Witch Project* (1999). All these films capitalize on the terror of young people being cut off from civilization—*Texas Chainsaw Massacre* is set in the rural countryside of Texas, *Friday the Thirteenth* at an abandoned summer camp, and *The Blair Witch Project* in the Black Hills of Maryland—and suggest that we're likely to meet a violent end when we wander into the wilderness.

22. Richard Louv. *Last Child in the Woods: Saving Our Children from Nature-Deficit Disorder*. Updated and Expanded Edition. (New York: Algonquin Books of Chapel Hill, 2008. Print), 2.
23. *Twilight* 3.
24. *Twilight* 4 and 3.
25. *Twilight* 8.
26. *Twilight* 116.
27. *Twilight* 188. Several philosophers have considered the complexity of this metaphor; see, for example, Jean Kazez, "Dying to Eat: The Vegetarian Ethics of *Twilight*," and Nicholas Michaud, "Can a Vampire Be a Person?" in *Twilight and Philosophy: Vampires, Vegetarianism, and the Pursuit of Immortality* (Hoboken, NJ: John Wiley & Sons, 2009). I want to emphasize here that the Cullens use the term "vegetarian" as a joke, recognizing full well the animal source of their blood diet; when they talk about sustainable hunting practices, however, they reveal a serious awareness of their impact on the environment that is worth noting.
28. *Twilight* 215.
29. See William Stolzenburg's *Where the Wild Things Were: Life, Death, and Ecological Wreckage in a Land of Vanishing Predators* (New York: Bloomsbury, 2009) for an account of the role of top predators in biological diversity, and Aldo Leopold's classic "Thinking Like a Mountain," *A Sand County Almanac* (New York: Ballantine Books, 1984), for his succinct observations on how predators support the environment by checking the population of foraging animals such as deer.
30. Stephenie Meyer. *New Moon*. New York: Little, Brown and Company, 2006. Print. 122.
31. *New Moon* 122–23, ellipses in the original.
32. Stephenie Meyer. *Eclipse*. New York: Little, Brown and Company, 2005. Print. 109.
33. *Eclipse* 109.
34. Meyer takes a noticeably different approach to her monsters in *The Short Second Life of Bree Tanner* (New York: Little, Brown and Company, 2010. Print), which focuses on a girl conscripted into the vampire army designed to eradicate the Cullen clan. Since Bree lives in the thrall of Victoria, one of the more formidable villain vampires of the saga, her relation to the natural world differs vastly from Bella's and Edward's. Not only does Victoria exploit the trappings of the traditional gothic narrative—locking her charges in a dark basement during the day and convincing them that old vampire myths about the dangers of the sun are true—but she also disrupts the ecological balance by producing an unsustainable overpopulation of newborn vampires. We learn that because Bree was initially afraid to remain outside during the day, she had only ever seen the trees around her as black rather than green. Bree's experience reminds us that Meyer's monsters must choose to live in balance with the natural world, a choice we also must make for ourselves.
35. See, for example, Naomi Zack's "Bella Swan and Sarah Palin: All the Old Myths are *NOT* True" and Bonnie Mann's "Vampire Love: The Second Sex Negotiates the Twenty-First Century" in *Twilight and Philosophy: Vampires, Vegetarianism, and the Pursuit of Immortality* (Hoboken, NJ: John Wiley & Sons, 2009).
36. As Louis recounts in Anne Rice's 1976 *Interview with the Vampire* (New York: Knopf, 1990), he too awoke from his vampire transformation with new eyes: "I saw as a vampire . . . It was as if I had only just been able to see colors and shapes for the first time" (18). Anne Rice's vampires have been highly influential, and it is very likely that Meyer's description of Bella's awakening is indebted to Rice.

37. Stephenie Meyer, *Breaking Dawn* (New York: Little, Brown and Company, 2008. Print), 386. For examples of the work of the cited writers, see *The Art of Seeing Things: Essay by John Burroughs*, ed. Charlotte Zoë Walker (Syracuse: Syracuse University Press, 2001); Rachel Carson, *The Sense of Wonder* (New York: HarperCollins, 1998); and Annie Dillard, *Pilgrim at Tinker Creek* (New York: HarperCollins, 1988), particularly chapter 2, "Seeing."

38. *Breaking Dawn* 413.

39. *Breaking Dawn* 413 and 410.

40. *Breaking Dawn* 475.

41. Nash 24.

42. Cronon 90.

43. Alicia McDonald notes that tourism in Forks has risen rapidly since the publication of *Twilight*, from 6000 visitors a year in 2006 to 23,700 in the first six months of 2009 alone. See "Literary Tourism—*Anne of Green Gables* and *Twilight* as Tourist Attractions." L. M. Montgomery Institute's Ninth Biennial International Conference: L. M. Montgomery and the Matter of Nature. University of Prince Edward Island. June 26, 2010.

44. Architectural critic Ada Louise Huxtable discusses this problem of the "themed environment," where "distinctions are no longer made between the real and the false," in *The Unreal America: Architecture and Illusion* (New York: The New Press, 1997), 2. Forks tourism necessarily embraces the fake environment of the fictional stories, but I believe tourists can still benefit from sheer exposure to the "real" natural environment surrounding the theme-park-like attractions of the town.

45. George Beahm, with the Forks Chamber of Commerce. *Twilight Tours: An Illustrated Guide to the REAL Forks* (Nevada City, CA: Underwood Books, 2009. Print), 19.

46. McDonald 13.

47. "Twilight Locations in Forks." *Twilight in Forks: A Twilight Travel Guide to Forks, Washington*. Web. September 16, 2010. http://twilight.inforks.com/twilight-locations.

48. Quoted in McDonald, 8–9.

49. D. H. Lawrence, *Studies in Classic American Literature* (New York: Viking Press, 1969. Print), 51.

Selected Bibliography

5by5creations. *Soul Searching*. April 12, 2009. http://www.twilighted.net.
———. *Vanquish*. May 17, 2009. http://www.twilighted.net.
Acocella, Joan. "In the Blood: A Critic at Large." *The New Yorker* (March 16, 2009): 103. http://www.new-yorker.com/arts/critics/atlarge/2009/03/16/090316crat_atlarge_acocella?currentPage=2.
Auerbach, Nina. "*Dracula*: A Vampire of Our Own." *Bloom's Modern Critical Interpretations: Bram Stoker's* Dracula. Ed. Harold Bloom. Philadelphia, PA: Chelsea House Publishers, 2003. 191–228.
———. *Our Vampires, Ourselves*. Chicago, IL: University of Chicago Press, 1995.
Auerbach, Nina, and David J. Skal, eds. *Dracula*, by Bram Stoker. Norton Critical Edition. New York: W.W. Norton, 1997.
Austen, Jane. *Emma*. London: J.M. Dent & Company, 1892.
———. *Pride and Prejudice*. New York: Dover Publications, 1995.
Barnes, Brooks. "Media Vampires Beware," *The New York Times*, November 13, 2009, AR1.
Beahm, George, with the Forks Chamber of Commerce. *Twilight Tours: An Illustrated Guide to the REAL Forks*. Nevada City, CA: Underwood Books, 2009.
Bell, Amanda. "Jacob Black 'Twilight' Barbie just released." *Examiner*. November 13, 2009. http://www.examiner.com/x-4908-Twilight-Examiner-y2009m11d13-Jacob-Black-Twilight-Barbie-now-available
Bentley, C. F. "The Monster in the Bedroom: Sexual Symbolism in Bram Stoker's *Dracula*." *Literature and Psychology* 22 (1972): 27–34.
Bierly, Mandi. "'New Moon' costume designer Tish Monaghan on Edward's suit and Jacob's cut-offs," *Entertainment Weekly*, November 28, 2009. n.p.
Blackbook.com. "*Twilight* Fans Sell Out Alaskan Vampire Cruise," *Blackbook Magazine*. http://www.blackbookmag.com/article/twilight-fans-sell-out-cruise/8069.
Botting, Fred. *Gothic*. London: Routledge, 2005.
———. *Gothic Romanced: Consumption, Gender, and Technology in Contemporary Fictions*. London: Routledge, 2008.
Brontë, Charlotte. *Jane Eyre*. Norton Critical Edition, 3rd edition. New York: W.W. Norton & Company, 2001.
Brown, Caitlin. "Feminism and the Vampire Novel." *Thefword.org*. September 8, 2009.
Brown, Jennnifer M. "*Twilight* in Translation." *Publishers Weekly*. October 31, 2005. http://www.publishersweekly.com/article/CA6278874.html.
Brown, Laura. "Robert Pattinson and Kristen Stewart's Wild Ride," *Harper's Bazaar*, November 2009, n.p.
Bruner, Kurt D. and Olivia. *The Twilight Phenomenon: Forbidden Fruit or Thirst-Quenching Fantasy?* Shippensburg, PA: Destiny Image, 2009.

Byron, Glennis. "'As one dead': *Romeo and Juliet* in the 'Twilight' Zone." In *Gothic Shakespeares*, eds. John Drakakis and Dale Townshend. New York: Routledge, 2008. 167–85.

Carrol, Larry. "'Twilight' Actor Taylor Lautner Is Eager To Deliver 'Naked' Line, Master Driving Teen star also discusses his research on the Quileute tribe to play Native American character Jacob Black." *MTV*. May 20, 2008. http://www.mtv.com/news/articles/1587744/20080520/story.jhtml

Carter, Margaret. "Vampire–Human Symbiosis in *Fever Dream* and *The Empire of Fear*." In *The Blood is the Life*, eds. Heldreth and Pharr. 165–76.

Case, Sue-Ellen. "Tracking the Vampire." *Differences: A Journal of Feminist Cultural Studies* 3 (Summer 1991): 1–20.

Chang, Samantha. "Taylor Lautner: I Worked Out Nonstop for *New Moon*." *Examiner*. July 16, 2009. http://www.examiner.com/examiner/x-14380-NY-Celebrity-Fitness-and-Health-Examiner~y2009m7d16-Taylor-Lautner-I-worked-out-nonstop-for-New-Moon

Chen, Sophie. "Bloodlust: Why women are suckers for bloodsuckers." *Psychology Today* 42 (Nov-Dec 2009).

Click, Melissa, Jennifer Stevens Aubrey, and Elizabeth Behm-Morawitz, eds. *Bitten by Twilight: Youth Culture, Media, and the Vampire Franchise*. New York: Peter Lang, 2010.

Cohen, Jeffery. *Monster Theory*. Minneapolis: University of Minnesota Press, 1996.

Dawtry, Adam. "*Twilight* gives new Brontë films wings." *Guardian.co.UK*, December 2, 2009. http://www.guardian.co.uk/film/2009/dec/02/twilight-new-bronte-films.

Denby, David. "Twilight," *New Yorker*, December 8, 2008. http://www.newyorker.com/arts/reviews/film/twilight_hardwicke .

Doane, Janice and Devon Hodges, "Undoing Feminism: From the Preoedipal to Postfeminism in Anne Rice's Vampire Chronicles," *American Literary History*, 1990, 2 (3), 422–42.

Doyle, Sady. "Girls Just Wanna Have Fangs." Prospect.org. November 19, 2009.

Ellwood, Mark. "Vampire chic: Gothic glamour rules, from fashion to makeup," *New York Daily News*, November 22, 2008, n.p. "Five Scenes That MUST Be in *Breaking Dawn*," *Eclipse* movie website. http://www.eclipsemovie.org/five-scenes-that-must-be-in-breaking-dawn/

Flanagan, Caitlin. "What Girls Want." *The Atlantic Monthly* (December 2008): 108–120. http://www.theatlantic.com/magazine/archive/2008/12/what-girls-want/7161/.

Fudge, Rachel. "The Buffy Effect." *Bitch: Feminist Response to Pop Culture*, no. 10 (Summer 1999). http://bitchmagazine.org/article/buffy-effect.

Goldstein, Patrick. "'The Twilight Saga' puts Summit in the mega-franchise business." *The Los Angeles Times* "The Big Picture" Blog, November 24, 2009. n.p.

Gomez, Jewelle. "Recasting the Mythology: Writing Vampire Fiction." In *Blood Read: The Vampire as Metaphor*, eds. Gordon and Hollinger. 85–94.

Gordon, Joan and Veronica Hollinger, eds. *Blood Read: The Vampire as Metaphor in Contemporary Culture*. Philadelphia: University of Pennsylvania Press, 1997.

Grossman, Lev. "Stephenie Meyer: A New J.K. Rowling?" Time.com. April 24, 2008. http://www.time.com/time/magazine/article/0,9171,1734838,00.html.

Halberstam, Judith. *Skin Shows: Gothic Horror and the Technology of Monsters*. Durham: Duke University Press, 1995.

Hamilton, Laurell K. *Guilty Pleasures. Anita Blake, Vampire Hunter*. New York: Berkley Books, 1993.

———. *Obsidian Butterfly*. New York: Ace Books, 2000.

———. *Blood Noir: An Anita Blake, Vampire Hunter, Novel*. London: Orbit. 2008

———. *Skin Trade: An Anita Blake, Vampire Hunter, Novel*. London: Headline Publishing, 2009.

———. *Flirt: An Anita Blake, Vampire Hunter, Novel*. London: Headline Publishing, 2010.

Handley, Cassandra. "Q&A: *Twilight's* Robert Pattinson," *Vanity Fair*, November 5, 2008. n.p.

Harding, Kate. "Could 'New Moon' be a feminist triumph?" Salon.com. December 9, 2009.

———. "Why not Team Bella?" Salon.com. December 2, 2009.

Hardwicke, Catherine, dir. *Twilight*. DVD. 2008. Santa Monica: Summit Entertainment, 2009.

Harris, Charlaine. *Dead Until Dark*. London: Gollancz, 2009.

———. *Definitely Dead*. New York: Ace Books, 2006.

Heldreth, Leonard and Mary Pharr, eds. *The Blood is the Life*, Bowling Green, OH: Bowling Green State University Popular Press, 1999.

Holmes, Trevor. "Coming Out of the Coffin: Gay Males and Queer Goths in Contemporary Fiction," in *Blood Read: The Vampire as Metaphor*. Eds. Gordon and Hollinger. 169–88.

Holte, James Craig, ed. *The Fantastic Vampire: Studies in the Children of the Night. Selected Essays from the Eighteenth International Conference on the Fantastic in the Arts*. Westport, CT: Greenwood Press, 2002.

Honeyman, Susan. *Elusive Childhood: Impossible Representations in Modern Fiction*. Chicago, IL: Ohio State Press, 2005.

Housel, Rebecca. "The 'Real Danger': Fact Vs. Fiction for the Girl Audience." In *Twilight and Philosophy*, eds. Housel and Wisnewski. 177–90.

Housel, Rebecca and J. Jeremy Wisnewski, eds. *Twilight and Philosophy: Vampires, Vegetarians, and the Pursuit of Immortality*. Hoboken, NJ: John Wiley & Sons, 2009.

"Interview with Stephenie Meyer." *Journal of Adolescent & Adult Literacy* 49 (2006): 630–632. http://www.jstor.org/stable/40017638.

Jacks, Brian. " 'Breaking Dawn' Sells 1.3 Million Copies in One Day." *MTV.com*. August 4, 2008. http://moviesblog.mtv.com/2008/08/04/breaking-dawn-sells-13-million-copies-in-one-day.

Jones, Beth Felker. *Touched by a Vampire: Discovering the Hidden Messages in the Twilight Saga*. Colorado Springs: Multnomah Books, 2009.

Karras, Irene. "The Third Wave's Final Girl: Buffy the Vampire Slayer." *Thirdspace* 1.2 (2002), http://www.thirdspace.ca/articles/karras.htm.

Kaveney, Roz, ed. *Reading the Vampire Slayer: the New Updated, Unofficial Guide to* Buffy *and* Angel. London: Tauris Parke, 2004.

Kirschling, Gregory. "Stephenie Meyer's 'Twilight' Zone" http://www.ew.com/ew/article/0,,20049578,00.html.

Knowles, Claire. "Sensibility Gone Mad: Or, Drusilla, Buffy and the (D)evolution of the Heroine of Sensibility." In *Postfeminist Gothic: Critical Interventions in Contemporary Culture*, eds. Benjamin A. Brabon and Stéphanie Genz. Basingstoke: Palgrave Macmillan, 2007. 140-153.

"Kristen Stewart Steals Bella's Style," *InStyle*, June 1, 2009. n.p.

La Ferla, Ruth. "A Trend With Teeth," *The New York Times*, July 1, 2009, E1.

Latham, Rob. *Consuming Youth: Vampires, Cyborgs, and the Culture of Consumption*. Chicago, IL: Chicago University Press, 2002.

Lorrah, Jean. "Dracula meets the New Woman." In *The Blood is the Life*, eds. Heldreth and Pharr. 31–42.

Lutz, Deborah. *The Dangerous Lover: Gothic Villains, Byronism, and the Nineteenth-Century Seduction Narrative*. Columbus, OH: Ohio State University Press, 2006.

Magsaysay, Melissa. "Oh, that seductive 'Twilight' merchandise," *Los Angeles Times*, November 15, 2009, A4.

Mangan, Lucy. "Dangerous Liaisons," *The Guardian*, December 4, 2008. http://www.guardian.co.uk/film/ 2008/dec/04/twilight-film-vampire.

Mann, Bonnie. "Vampire Love: The Second Sex Negotiates the Twenty-First Century." In *Twilight and Philosophy*, eds. Housel and Wisnewski. 121–9.

Marche, Stephen. "What's *Really* Going on With All These Vampires," *Esquire Online*, October 13, 2009. http://www.esquire.com/features/thousand-words-on-culture/vampires-gay-men-1109.

Martens, Todd. "'Twilight Saga: New Moon' and its vampy sounds," *The Los Angeles Times.* "Hero Complex" Blog, October 26, 2009, n.p.

Masters, Anthony. *The Natural History of the Vampire.* New York: G.P. Putnam's Sons, 1972.

McClimans, Leah and J. Jeremy Wisnewski. "Undead Patriarchy and the Possibility of Love." In *Twilight and Philosophy*, eds. Housel and Wisnewski, 163–75.

McDonald, Alicia. "Literary Tourism—*Anne of Green Gables* and *Twilight* as Tourist Attractions." *L.M. Montgomery Institute's Ninth Biennial International Conference: L. M. Montgomery and the Matter of Nature.* University of Prince Edward Island. June 26, 2010. Address.

McDonald, Beth E. *The Vampire as Numinous Experience: Spiritual Journeys with the Undead in British and American Literature.* Jefferson, NC: McFarland & Co., 2004.

McIntosh, Jonathan. "What Would Buffy Do?: Notes on Dusting Edward Cullen," *Bitch: Feminist Response to Pop Culture*, August 12, 2009. http://bitchmagazine.org/post/what-would-buffy-do-notes-on-dusting-edward-cullen.

Melton, J. Gordon. *The Vampire Book: The Encyclopedia of the Undead.* Detroit: Gale Research, 1994.

Meyer, Stephenie. Author homepage. No date. http://www.stepheniemeyer.com/

———. *Breaking Dawn.* New York: Little Brown and Company, 2008.

———. "Breaking Dawn: Frequently Asked Questions," *Stephenie Meyer's Official Website.* http://www.stepheniemeyer.com/bd_faq.html.

———. *Eclipse.* New York: Little Brown and Company, 2007.

———. *Fascination.* Trans. Luc Rigoureau. Paris: Hachette, 2005.

———. *Midnight Sun.* No date. http://www.stepheniemeyer.com/

———. *New Moon.* New York: Little Brown and Company, 2006.

———. "The Story Behind *Twilight*." *The Official Website of Stephenie Meyer.* Web.

———. *The Short Second Life of Bree Tanner.* Little, Brown and Company, 2010.

———. *Twilight.* New York: Little Brown and Company, 2005.

Miller, Laura. "Buffy Fans: Read This." Salon.com, June 23, 2009 http://www.salon.com/books/feature/2009/06/23/vampire_fiction/index.html.

———. "The spirit of the vampire slayer lives on in the kickass young heroines of urban fantasy fiction." *Salon.com.* June 23, 2009. http://www.salon.com/books/feature/2009/06/23/vampire_fiction/print.html.

———. "Touched by a Vampire Preteen girls—and their grown-up moms—are sinking their teeth into Stephenie Meyer's gothic. 'Twilight' books by the millions. Move over, J.K. Rowling." http://www.salon.com/books/review/2008/07/30/Twilight/index.html.

Minzesheimer, Bob and Anthony DeBarros. "Sellers basked in Stephenie Meyer's 'Twilight' in 2008." *USA Today.* January 15, 2009. http://www.usatoday.com/life/books/news/2009-0 -14-top-sellers-main_N.htm.

Myers, Abigail E. "Edward Cullen and Bella Swan: Byronic and Feminist Heroes…Or Not." In *Twilight and Philosophy*, eds. Housel and Wisnewski, 147–62.

Norris, Shambrala. "Twilight by Stephenie Meyer—Book Review" (July 14, 2010): http://romancefiction.suite101.com/article.cfm/twilight-by-stephenie-meyer-book.

Nuzum, K.A. "The Monster's Sacrifice—Historic Time: The Uses of Mythic and Liminal Time in Monster Literature." *Children's Literature Association Quarterly* 29, No. 3 (2004): 217–27.

Pender, Patricia. "I'm Buffy and You're…History." In *Fighting the Forces: What's at Stake in Buffy the Vampire Slayer*, eds. Rhonda V. Wilcox and David Lavery. Lanham, MD: Rowman & Littlefield, 2002.

———. " 'Kicking Ass is Comfort Food' Buffy as Third Wave Feminist Icon." In *Third Wave Feminism: A Critical Exploration*, eds. Stacy Gillis, Gillian Howie and Rebecca Munford. New York: Palgrave MacMillan, 2007. 224–236.

Penzler, Otto, ed. *The Vampire Archives: The Most Complete Volume of Vampire Tales Ever Published.* New York: Vintage Crime/Black Lizard, 2009.

Peretz, Evgenia. "*Twilight*'s Hot Gleaming," *Vanity Fair*, December 2009, n.p.

Radish, Christina. "Twilight's Author and Director Talk About Bringing The Film To Life." *MEDIA BLVD Magazine.* September 17, 2008. http://www.mediablvd.com/magazine/ the_news/celebrity/twilight%27s_author_and_director_talk_about_bringing_the_film_ to_life_200809171287.html.

Reagin, Nancy. *Twilight and History.* Hoboken, NJ: John Wiley & Sons, 2010.

Rice, Anne. *Interview with a Vampire.* New York: Ballantine Books, 1997.

———. *The Vampire Lestat.* London: Sphere, 2009.

Richardson, Maurice. "The Psychoanalysis of Count Dracula" in *Vampyres,* ed. Christopher Frayling. London: Faber & Faber, 1991.

Rickels, Laurence A. *The Vampire Lectures.* Minneapolis: University of Minnesota Press, 1999.

Riley, Angela R. "Sucking the Quileute Dry." *New York Times.* February 8, 2010.

Roth, Phyllis. "Suddenly Sexual Women in Bram Stoker's *Dracula.*" *Literature and Psychology* 27 (1977): 113–21.

Ryan, Alan, ed. *The Penguin Book of Vampire Stories.* New York: Penguin, 1989.

Sage, Victor, and Allan Lloyd Smith. *Modern Gothic: A Reader.* Manchester: Manchester University Press, 1997.

Saxey, Esther. "Staking a Claim: the Series and its Slash Fan Fiction." *Reading the Vampire Slayer: the New Updated, Unofficial Guide to Buffy and Angel.* 187–210.

Seifert, Christine. "Bite me! (Or Don't)." *Bitch Magazine. Feminist Response to Pop Culture.* Winter 2009, no. 42, 23. http://bitchmagazine.org/.

Seltzer, Sarah. "*Twilight*: Sexual Longing in an Abstinence-Only World," *The Huffington Post*, August 9, 2008, http://www.huffingtonpost.com/sarah-seltzer/twilight-sexual-longing-i_b_117927.html.

shoefreak37. *The Strange Design of Comfort.* October 28, 2009. http//www.twilighted. net.

Siegel, Carol. "Female Heterosexual Sadism: The Final Feminist Taboo in Buffy, The Vampire Slayer and the Anita Blake Vampire Hunter Series." In *Third Wave Feminism and Television Jane Puts it in a Box*, Eds. Merri Lisa Johnson. London: I.B. Tauris & Co, 2007. 56–90.

Silver, Alain and James Ursini. *The Vampire Film: from* Nosferatu *to* Bram Stoker's Dracula. New York: Limelight Editions, 1994.

Simmons, Rachel. "You Asked for It: How to Talk to Girls About the Messages of *New Moon*." Rachelsimmons.com. December 2, 2009.

Singh, Anita. "Harry Potter Under Threat from Bella Swan in New Vampire Film Twilight." *The Daily Telegraph.* August 22, 2008. http://www.telegraph.co.uk/news/newstopics/ celebritynews/2602938/Harry-Potter-under-threat-from-Bella-Swan-in-new-vampire-film-Twilight.html

SnowWhiteHeart. *Dear God.* November 29, 2009. http://www.twilighted.net.

Spencer, Kathleen. "Purity and Danger: *Dracula*, the Urban Gothic, and the Late Victorian Degeneracy Crisis." *ELH* 59:1 (1992).

starshinedown and pogurl. *Love Man.* January 19, 2009. http://www.twilighted.net

Stein, Sadie. "What Women Want: Gay Vampires." *Jezebel*, October 13, 2009. http://jezebel. com/5380824/what-women-want-gay-vampires

Stevens, Dana. Review of *Twilight*, directed by Catherine Hardwicke. *Slate*, November 20, 2008. http://www.slate.com/id/2205013/.

Stevenson, John Allen. "A Vampire in the Mirror: The Sexuality of Dracula." *PMLA: Publications of the Modern Language Association of America* 103 (March 1988): 139–49.

Stoker, Bram. *Dracula*. Eds. Nina Auerbach and David J. Skal. New York: Norton, 1997.

Teran, Andi. "A Spotlight on Twilight at the Apple Store," *Vanity Fair*, November 4, 2008, n.p.

"The Top 100 Titles of 2008." *USA Today*. January 14, 2009. http://www.usatoday.com/life/books/news/2009-01-14-top-100-titles_N.htm. del Toro, Guillermo and Chuck Hogan. "Why Vampires Never Die." *The New York Times, Op-Ed Column*. July 31, 2009. http://www.nytimes.com/2009/07/31/opinion/31deltoro.html [Accessed August 13, 2009]

Trites, Roberta Seelinger. *Disturbing the Universe: Power and Repression in Adolescent Literature*. Iowa City: University of Iowa Press, 2000.

Turan, Kenneth. "Movie Review: You Wanna Neck? 'Twilight.'" *The Los Angeles Times*. November 21, 2002. http://articles.latimes.com/2008/nov/21/entertainment/et-twilight21. "*Twilight* Fashion," *InStyle*, n.p. http://www.instyle.com/instyle/package/general/photos/0,,20241149_20231628_20536039,00.html and http://www.instyle.com/instyle/package/general/photos/0,,20241149_20231628_20523541,00.html.

"Twilight Influences Most Popular Baby Names of 2009," *USA Today*. usatoday.com. http://content.usatoday.com/communities/entertainment/post/2010/05/twilight-influences-most-popular- baby-names-of-2009/1.

Twitchell, James B. *The Living Dead: A Study of the Vampire in Romantic Literature*. Durham: Duke University Press, 1981.

Valby, Karen. "Stephenie Meyer: 12 of My 'Twilight' Inspirations." *EW.com: Entertainment Weekly*, September 29, 2009. http://www.ew.com/ew/gallery/0,,20308569_20308554,00.html.

Valenti, Jessica. *The Purity Myth: How America's Obsession with Virginity is Hurting Young Women*. Berkeley: Seal Press, 2010.

Waller, Gregory A. *The Living and the Undead: From Stoker's Dracula to Romero's Dawn of the Dead*. Urbana: University of Illinois Press, 1986.

Waltje, Jörg. *Blood Obsession: Vampires, Serial Murder, and the Popular Imagination*. New York: Peter Lang, 2005.

Weitz, Chris, director. *New Moon*. DVD. 2009. Santa Monica, CA: Summit Entertainment, 2010.

Whedon, Joss. *Angel* (television series). Perf. David Boreanaz, Alex Denisof, Charisma Carpenter. Kuzui Enterprises, 1999–2004.

———. *Buffy the Vampire Slayer* (television series). Perf. Sarah Michelle Gellar, Nicholas Brendon, Alyson Hannigan. Mutant Enemy, 1997–2003. Television.

White, Luise. *Speaking with Vampires: Rumor and History in Colonial Africa*. Berkley: University of California Press, 2000.

Wilcox, Rhonda. *Why Buffy Matters: The Art of Buffy the Vampire Slayer*. London: I.B. Tauris & Co., 2005.

Williamson, Milly. *The Lure of the Vampire: Gender, Fiction and Fandom from Bram Stoker to Buffy*. London: Wallflower Press, 2005.

Wood, Martin. "New Life for an Old Tradition: Anne Rice and Vampire Literature." In *The Blood is the Life*. eds. Heldreth and Pharr, 59–78.

Wright, Dudley. *The Book of Vampires*. New York: Causeway Books, 1973.

Zack, Naomi. "Bella Swan and Sarah Palin: All the Old Myths are *Not* True." In *Twilight and Philosophy*, eds. Housel and Wisnewski, 121–29.

Zanger, Jules. "Metaphor into Metonymy: The Vampire Next Door." In *Blood Read: The Vampire as Metaphor*, eds. Gordon and Hollinger, 17–26.

Contributors

Giselle Liza Anatol is an associate professor of English at the University of Kansas in Lawrence, Kansas. She has previously edited two other popular culture collections: *Reading Harry Potter: Critical Essays* (Praeger, 2003) and *Reading Harry Potter Again: New Critical Essays* (Praeger, 2009). Besides teaching and researching in the field of children's literature, Anatol also teaches courses in Caribbean literature, African American literature, and multicultural US literature. She has published on the works of Nalo Hopkinson, Jamaica Kincaid, and Langston Hughes, among others, and is currently at work on a monograph about images of black female vampires.

Tracy L. Bealer is an independent scholar working out of Charleston, South Carolina. She received her PhD at the University of South Carolina, where she specialized in twentieth-century American fiction and gender studies. Her research interests include pop culture, speculative fiction, and film. She has published on Alice Walker, J.K. Rowling, and Quentin Tarantino, and is currently coediting a collection of essays on Neil Gaiman.

Brianna Burke is currently the Ann Plato Fellow in English and American Studies at Trinity College and will complete her PhD at Tufts University in the spring of 2011. She specializes in Native American literature, environmental and social justice, and multicultural literature in the United States.

Angie Chau is a PhD candidate in comparative literature at University of California, San Diego. Her areas of interest are early twentieth-century Chinese, French, and English literature, popular culture, and visuality, especially the work of Chinese expatriate writers, poets, and painters in Paris during the 1920s and 30s.

Kristina Deffenbacher is an associate professor of English at Hamline University in Saint Paul, Minnesota. She teaches and has published articles on Victorian British literature and culture. Since her reanimating collaboration with scholar Mikayla Zagoria-Moffet, Kristina has undertaken a project on gender and sexuality in urban fantasy fiction.

Tammy Dietz is an instructional designer and liberal arts professor who has designed and managed training and educational programs for numerous companies including AT&T, DeVry University, Netflix, Microsoft, and more. She earned an MFA in creative nonfiction from Pacific University and lives near Seattle with her husband and three children.

Kim Allen Gleed is associate professor of English at Harrisburg Area Community College. She has a PhD in comparative literature with a concentration in Irish and French literature and translation studies from Binghamton University, State University of New York. She is also a freelance translator with over a dozen book-length publications. Kim resides in Carlisle, Pennsylvania (how fun is *that* for a *Twilight* fan!) with her husband and two children.

Michael J. Goebel holds degrees in literature and American studies and is currently working on his PhD in cultural studies at George Mason University. His primary fields of study are American popular culture, masculinities, and consumer culture.

Amy L. Hume is a doctoral candidate at the University of Kansas who specializes in twentieth-century authorship, autobiography, trans-Atlantic modernism, and trauma studies. She has published on the work of T.S. Eliot. Her future projects consider human rights, ethics, and activist figures in literature, such as the queer vampire.

Joo Ok Kim is a doctoral candidate in literature at the University of California, San Diego. Her research interests include multiethnic and multicultural literature in the United States, literatures of the Korean Diaspora, and late nineteenth-century narratives on empire.

Margaret Kramar is a doctoral candidate in literature at the University of Kansas in Lawrence. As a recent winner of the first Helen Keller Foundation memoir competition, her essay about a disabled child is anthologized in *Reading Lips and Other Ways to Overcome a Disability* (Apprentice House, 2008). She has also been published in *Contemporary American Women: Our Defining Passages* (All Things That Matter, 2009). Kramar is currently writing a memoir titled *My Son the Actor*. She and her family live in Big Springs, Kansas, where they grow organic vegetables and raise free range chickens.

Maria Lindgren Leavenworth is an assistant professor at the Department of Language Studies, Umeå University, Sweden. Her previous research focused on travelogues, the north, and concepts connected to the cold. Publications include "'The Art of Bookmaking': Selina Bunbury's Northern Journeys" (2008) and "Hatred was also left outside": Journeys into the Cold in Le Guin's *The Left Hand of Darkness*" (2009). She has also analyzed remediation in the article "'A Life as Potent and Dangerous as Literature Itself': Intermediated Moves from *Mrs Dalloway* to *The Hours*." Lindgren Leavenworth's current research focuses on fan fiction, which in different ways employs the vampire trope and her article "Lover Revamped: Sexualities and Romance in the Black Dagger Brotherhood and Slash Fan Fiction" is published in *Extrapolation* 50 (2009).

Dr. Rhonda Nicol is an instructional assistant professor of English at Illinois State University. Her presentations and publications address issues of gender, power, and identity in popular cultural texts. Recent works include "'Something That Looks So Fragile': Holly Black's and Melissa Marr's Feminist Faerie Tales" (Sirens, 2009), and "Harry Potter and the Reluctant Reader: Teaching Harry Potter in the College Classroom" (*Terminus: Collected Papers on Harry Potter*, 2010).

Tara K. Parmiter received her PhD in English from New York University, where she teaches in the Expository Writing Program. Her areas of interest include literature and the environment, children's literature, turn-of-the-twentieth century women's literature, and popular culture. She has published articles on summer vacationing in Kate Chopin's *The Awakening*, the imagined landscapes in L. M. Montgomery's *Anne of Green Gables* novels, journey narratives in the Muppet movies, and the quirky dialogue of TV's *Pushing Daisies*.

Joseph Michael Sommers is an assistant professor of English at Central Michigan University where he teaches children's and young adult literature as well as courses in modern and contemporary Anglophone literature, visual narratives, and critical theory. He has published essays on figures such as Gary Paulsen, Hunter Thompson, Denise Levertov, and Judy Blume. He is currently working on articles on the culture of children in nineteenth-century lady's journalism, the maturation of Marvel Comics' characters in the Post-9/11 Moment, and Hellboy. His future projects include a book-length collection of essays on postapocalyptic literature. He is an editor at *The Read Feather Journal* and, most importantly, the luckiest husband and father he knows.

Carole Veldman-Genz is head of the Scientific English Department in the Language Center at RWTH Aachen University, Germany. She specializes in contemporary gender and cultural theory, popular culture, and genre theory. She has published articles on popular culture, the Gothic, and the romance.

Meredith Wallis is a practicing lawyer who represents political dissenters. She is working on a PhD at Stanford University in modern thought and literature.

Merinne Whitton has a master's in women's studies from the University of Oxford in England; her dissertation was an analysis of the interactions of feminist theory with the transsexual phenomenon. She has been fascinated by manifestations of the vampire myth for many years, particularly more recent constructions in film and fiction. She is particularly interested in how myths of the supernatural relate to issues of sexuality and gender, and how those myths adapt to cater to the prevailing anxieties of the cultural moment. She currently lives and works in London.

Mikayla Zagoria-Moffet is a student at Hamline University, in Saint Paul, Minnesota. She has presented at both undergraduate and professional conferences, including a presentation titled "Biting Back: *Twilight* in Feminist and Literary Contexts" at the 2010 Southwest/Texas Popular Culture Association/American Popular Culture conference in Albuquerque, New Mexico. Her ongoing research on gender roles and representations of girlhood in teen fantasy novels has also informed an honors research project and her own fiction writing.

INDEX